HIGH PRAISE FOR EDWARD LEE!

"The living legend of literary mayhem.
Read him if you dare!"
—Richard Laymon, Author of *Flesh*

"Edward Lee's writing is fast and mean as a chain saw
revved to full-tilt boogie."
—Jack Ketchum, Author of *Cover*

"He demonstrates a perverse genius for showing us a Hell
the likes of which few readers have ever seen."
—*Horror Reader*

"Edward Lee continues to push the boundaries of sex,
violence and depravity in modern genre lit."
—*Rue Morgue*

"One of the genre's true originals."
—The Horror Fiction Review

"The hardest of the hardcore horror writers."
—*Cemetery Dance*

"Lee excels with his creativity and almost trademark
depictions of violence and gruesomeness."
—*Horror World*

"A master of h...
reac...

GU00750224

THE HOUSE OF EVIL

"Cricket was fourteen when she died, while Mary was chubby—more squat-bodied—and blonde. Four years older than Cricket. They both died on the same day, incidentally. April 30, 1862. And, yes, they were murdered by Harwood Gast. Their bodies were discovered on May third by the town marshal." Sute's eyes thinned. "Where did you see the girls? In the hotel?"

Collier could only peer at the man. "You're talking about ghosts as though you personally believe in them."

"Oh, I do. Very much so. And though I may not have been totally honest with you during our lunch, I very much believe that Mrs. Butler's inn—the Gast House—is full to bursting with ghosts. I believe that it is *permeated* with the horrors of its original owner . . ."

Other *Leisure* books by Edward Lee:

THE GOLEM
BRIDES OF THE IMPALER
HOUSE INFERNAL
SLITHER
THE BACKWOODS
FLESH GOTHIC
MESSENGER
INFERNAL ANGEL
CITY INFERNAL

THE BLACK TRAIN

EDWARD LEE

LEISURE BOOKS NEW YORK CITY

For Paul Legerski

A LEISURE BOOK®

November 2009

Published by

Dorchester Publishing Co., Inc.
200 Madison Avenue
New York, NY 10016

ISBN 10: 0-8439-6227-5
ISBN 13: 978-0-8439-6227-7
E-ISBN: 978-1-4285-0760-9

The name "Leisure Books" and the stylized "L" with design are trademarks of Dorchester Publishing Co., Inc.

Printed in the United States of America.

10 9 8 7 6 5 4 3 2 1

Visit us online at www.dorchesterpub.com.

ACKNOWLEDGMENTS

This is a revised edition of *Gast*, originally published as a limited-edition hardback by Camelot Books, and for that original edition, I'd like to especially thank Tony and Kim Duarte, and artist *extra ordinaire* Glenn Chadbourne. I also need to thank, among others, Wendy Brewer, Don D'Auria, Bob Strauss, Tim M., Liz, Karyn, Bill, Christy, Alicia (who is a YANKEES fan first and foremost), Tim and Anda, Charlie, Tim Fogarty, Ken Arneson; Nick and Rhonda from Wild Willy's Bar in Largo; Tom Moran, Judy Comeau and Count Gore; Amy, Paul and Kirk at Ricky T's; Art at Sweet Bay; Geisenhuth, Travis Deputy Theinsatiablebookreader, Nanci Kalanta, Mark Justice; Scott Bradley, Del Howison and Amy Wallace of Book of Lists; Ian Fischer, Miranu Lepus, Lefteris Stavrianos, Nick Nick Roussos, Kathy Rosamilia; dutiful fans Linda Reed and Caroline Vincent of States Saving Bank; Josh Boone, Thomas Deja, Jeff Funk, Ryan Harding, Pam Herbster, Monica Kuebler, Michael Ling, Michael Pearce, Shay Prentiss, Terry Tidwell, Tom Weisser, Aaron Williams at Wheels of Terror; Christine Morgan and Nick Yak from HFR; lthrby1, Chris aka flahorrorwriter, bateman, jpoleka, jonah, Trever Palmer, onemorejustincase, godawful, harleymack, serra, GE65, babaganoosh, horrorfan, Andrew Myers of the 1st Armored Division, Bobby "Smitty" Smith, Brandon Lee Spitler, darkthrone, xrascalxkingx, mrliteral, psychomule, VT Horror Fan, Dathar, Aaron2010, Boota, Harvester, Lazy, madtrav, RabidDecay, sjmsy, Jimbo1168, Jack Staynes, Mille Umbra, Smokey-101, vredebyrd and Wetbones.

THE BLACK TRAIN

PROLOGUE

Gast, Tennessee
1857

thunk!

Morris chopped off the girl's hand with a hatchet, then guttered laughter. The poor mulatto wailed, her stump pumping.

"What'choo do that for!" Cutton bellowed. He hadn't even gotten his trousers off before Morris had pulled this move.

Morris had giggled some spittle onto his shabby beard. "She's mixed, Cutton, a mixed *whore*. And I paid her a dollar." He was rubbing his crotch with the girl's severed hand. "Mixed don't charge but twenty cents nohow."

Cutton could barely speak as he refastened his belt. "You're crazy, Morris! The whore-mother in the other room's gonna fetch Marshal Braden!"

The girl was shuddering beneath Morris's spread thighs, entering shock. "Awwwwww, shee-it. Gast owns the marshal, and we work for Gast. We was just havin' some fun in a whorehouse is all."

Fun? Choppin' off a girl's hand is fun? Cutton tugged a leather string from one of his Jefferson shoes and tied off the girl's stump. "You're about as smart as dog puke. This girl could die."

Morris dropped the hand on the girl's quivering stomach. "She ain't gonna die, Cutton. Look, see, I'll make it right." He dropped a five-dollar silver piece on the floor.

"You're one crazy son of a bitch. That's the last time I go drinkin' with you," Cutton raged and walked for the door.

Morris couldn't believe it. "Ain't you even gonna take your turn?"

Cutton stalked out of the brothel into dusty darkness. *Shit.* He'd known Morris a while now; they'd worked the Delaware track together. But it just seemed like that man had turned crazy since they'd signed on with Gast and his rail crew.

Crazy . . . or evil? he wondered.

Number 3 Street stood dark. On the next block, he could hear they were still drinking at Cusher's Tavern. But Cutton didn't want to go back there. They'd ask him how it went.

The door flapped open behind him. Morris, with his kersey work pants back on, implored, "Aw, come on, Cutton. What's your dander up for? She's mixed, for God's sake!"

Cutton walked off. He didn't care that she was half Negro; it wouldn't even matter if she were full. *Lynchin' a slave for stealin' or rape's one thing, but what he done is just plain ungodly.* Cutton loped into more darkness. There was nothing left to do now but head back to the bunkhouse and get some sleep. He'd spent most of the day on his horse, inspecting track and making sure Gast's slaves were up to speed. *Dog tired, I am.* All he'd wanted was a quick one with a whore.

Not . . . this.

"You done with your carryin'-on?" a soft voice stopped him.

Cutton turned at the crossroad. It couldn't be someone from the whorehouse; that was the opposite direction. He squinted.

More feminine words: "You done or lookin' for more?"

Cutton's eyes fixed on the ghostly image: a curvaceous white blur. The shadow of a branch obscured her face.

"Lady, I just walked out of some carryin'-on that I didn't care for at all," he said. "Who're you?"

"Come on!" And then a warm hand grabbed his and pulled.

She led him up the hill, brambles crackling. Nets of moonlight through the trees never quite allowed any detail, but as Cutton hustled behind her, he eventually could tell she was naked beneath the sheer gown.

"You ain't from the whorehouse, are ya?"

A soft chuckle fluttered. "Just come on."

Cutton grew half aroused just from the feel of her hand, that soft warmth over his calluses—that, and something more abstract, like anticipation. She seemed desperate as she led on.

"Where are you taking m—"

"Don't talk! We'll be at the house in a second . . ."

House. Something heavy slipped into Cutton's heart. *There ain't but one house up this hill,* he knew. A servant girl? But he'd heard that all of Gast's house staff were Negroes. "You work for Mr. Gast?" he asked.

"No," she giggled, "but I'm married to him."

Cutton stopped like a grapeshot blast to the chest. He turned her around and looked her right in the face, a face like a beautiful blur, curly hair glowing the same color as the moon. "Shit! You ain't lyin'!"

"Are you coming or not?"

Cutton froze. "You're—you're my boss's wife . . ."

"Say it louder so the slaves'll hear you all the way over at the Sibley compound." Now the moonlight fixed on her; she seemed to glow. "My husband's in Tredegar, at the iron works. He's buying more track from a federal broker. He won't be back until *tomorrow.*" Her voice was sweet as syrup. Next, she lifted one breast out of the gown's top and simultaneously cupped Cutton's crotch. "Come inside now . . ."

The great angular house stood like a shadowed mesa. He'd only seen it from afar, and didn't care about it now. The door clattered; then they were in and she was guiding him up the stairs. Cutton ignored the sumptuous details of the interior, focusing instead on the sheer gown sliding around her rump, and the sides of her breasts swaying. Down a carpeted hall lined with framed pictures, then—*click*—into a room.

Woo . . .

The room smelled bad right off, and usually when the room smelled bad, so did the woman. But Cutton stood corrected—or it should be said that he *knelt* corrected—when she immediately pushed him to his knees and raised her nightgown. It was that abrupt—no need for courting or sweet talk. Cutton had time to think, *What I get myself into? This is my boss's wife!* when the next realization slapped him like a hand. He expected a downy patch of hair that matched the blonde tresses on her head but found a hairless pubis in his face instead.

Cutton had heard of women doing this—upper-crust women—but he'd never seen it himself. He stared in awe, frozen. *Shaved bald . . . ain't that somethin' . . .* His fingers traced over the fresh white triangle. *A clean shave, too, hardly any stubble . . .*

The bare stomach quivered before his eyes; then, something less than the Southern belle, she ordered, "Lick it."

The soft buttocks was hot in his hands. She tasted like rosewater.

He couldn't concentrate, however, and she seemed to sense this, her nails digging into the back of his neck when he faltered. Cutton's mind swam as his tongue roved. Once he stopped, looked up at her face: "But, uh, Mrs. Gast, if your husband comes home early, I will be in a bad way." She skimmed the nightgown off entirely. "I told you, he's buying more track!" And then she urged him all the way to the floor and sat on his face.

"Now *lick it!*"

Her sex pressed down over his mouth. *Gast would have me killed,* Cutton suspected. Other men had whispered of this woman's delights but was it worth it? Cutton gave her succor until she spasmed. Her white thighs quivered against his cheeks . . .

"That was lovely," she sighed and rolled over. "The perfect way to begin."

At least Cutton liked the sound of that.

"The bed, now," she said.

The bed stank, but Cutton wasn't a delicate man. She lay beside him, running her hands up and down the white body, fingertips twisting dark nipples. "I apologize about the odor. I'll have to get Jessa to replace the mattress again."

Again. Cutton guessed she'd had many men on this bed, most of them dirty from the field, and some of the slaves, too—he'd heard—right off the line. But what else did she say? A name.

Jessa?

The maid! Cutton realized. "What, uh, what about the maid? What if she hears us? What if she comes in?"

"The maid does what I say."

"And your children. You didn't even lock the door. They could walk in any sec—"

"They're *asleep,* like all decent people at this hour." She smiled at the implication.

Cutton was generally a man of good judgment; this was his employer's wife, he should *not* be here, he should've walked away when he'd met her on the street. And if word got out? *Gast'd have me buried alive,* he felt sure. Couple men who worked for Gast had disappeared shortly after rumors, and several of the slaves had been executed in the field, for the same allegations . . .

Her gentle accent lifted. "Now, are you going to fuck me, or will I be forced to find someone else?"

Those words were all it took to erase Cutton's good judgment as if it had never existed . . .

Two hours later, he lay exhausted. She kept her arms and legs wrapped around him, his member limp now but still in her.

Her horniness didn't abate even after all Cutton had given her; she'd broken out in a prickly heat, her cheeks blushed along with her belly and the soft skin below her throat.

In a parched mewl, she giggled, "You're quite the man, sir."

Quite the DEAD man if'n I don't get out'a here, he thought. But his lust had been sated—his reason returned. "I gotta get my ass out'a here, Mrs. Gast." He began to push off but her arms and legs tightened back around him. She wasn't letting him go, wasn't letting him pull out.

"Not just yet," she whispered. One more thing remained for him to do.

Next morning, Cutton watched two strong-armers decapitate one of the nigrahs in the field. That was the first thing he saw when he dismounted his horse.

They're killin' another one . . .

Cutton hadn't heard anything about it.

Bean and cotton fields lined either side of the several miles of track they'd already lain; Cutton understood that the beans were that newfangled one from the Orient, something called soya. The female slaves worked the field, while the men drove the spikes. It was a strange sight now . . .

Total silence stretched out over the sunlit morn. The hundred or so slaves who lined the trackway seemed to stand at attention, akin to a military formation, along with Gast's white foremen and other hires.

"That's a good clean cut," Morris said from the field. The strong-armer who'd done the work had used an adze, a chopping tool like an ax but perpendicular-bladed. Standing beside Morris, he held the Negro's severed head for all—especially the slaves—to see.

Morris shouted out, "As yawl know, 'round here this is what happens to nigrahs who commit crimes. Yawl have been guaranteed your freedom once this railroad's finished, so's ya need to think real hard before you do somethin' stupid. This slave here molested a white woman who shall remain nameless"—Morris grabbed the head and looked at it—"and this is the price he pays. Mr. Gast is a fair and generous man, but we don't tolerate insubordination or crime. This poor, stupid slave will never be a free man, but you all most certainly will if ya work hard, stay in line, and keep your hands off what they ought not be touchin'."

Wide white eyes blazed in fear from the long row of black faces along the track line. Other strong-armers stood back, holding repeater pistols and blunderbuss shotguns that could drop a row of men with one squeeze of the trigger.

Shit, Cutton thought. The slave they'd executed was one he knew—called Meti. Gast let all the slaves take African names. They were well clothed, well fed, and well housed, and with the promise of freedom when the final rail was spiked in Maxon, they all listened well. Meti had been one of the strongest spike-drivers of them all. It was bad to lose a good worker. He'd been stripped of his valuable working clothes and boots. Now he'd been reduced to a headless, naked body.

Poor bastard should'a kept it in his pants. Probably raped one'a the town girls.

But when Cutton peered farther down the line, he thought *Shit!* again. Perched atop the familiar white steed was Mr. Gast, spectating. Gast nodded to Morris when eye contact was made.

"Bring up the sledges!" he ordered. "Yawl know the drill."

Four assigned slaves stepped forward with twenty-pound sledgehammers.

"I'm sorry you fellas have to do this to one of your own—that's the way it is. But it ain't just a lesson to yawl, it's a lesson to white men, too. We'se doin' serious work for our country buildin' this railroad. The Yankees got close to thirty thousand miles of train track but the South ain't got but nine. Mr. Gast's railroad is important for the future. We all have to keep our minds on the task." Morris paused, perhaps only for effect. "Pound him."

The sledgehammers rose and fell, landing great sickening thuds. The headless body was pummeled, and in a minute it was crushed, every bone in the dead man's body fractured.

"Axes!" Morris ordered.

Four more slaves stepped up, just as grim-faced as the first. In unison their axes blurred down in scarlet arcs, like a diabolical camshaft. In moments the pulverized body was chopped up into pulp.

"Shovels and hoes!"

The finality now. The slaves hoed the pulp into the soil.

Morris bellowed, "We're stronger by losin' this one, and now his useless criminal body will finally do some good, by fertilizin' this good land which puts food in our bellies! Mr. Gast just done got back from a long trip to Virginia to bring us more rail and ties, so let's make him proud, and lay a quarter mile plus! Right, men?"

The hundred slaves snapped out of their gloom and cheered.

"Remember, your freedom's at the end of this track! Right?"

More cheers, more rallying.

"Now take twenty! Then we're back to work!"

Cutton remained speechless as the ritual ended: the two strong-armers in the field placed Meti's severed head on a high stake and sunk it in the ground.

Good Jesus . . .

Morris came down to the track line. "Hey, Cutton. Sorry, I didn't know you were the squeamish type." He pronounced the word "type" as "tap." "But you shouldn't've bailed last night. I dropped five in the whore-mother's hand'n she forgot *all about* what I done to that little mulatto girl. And she got me two more girls! I had me plenty of fun."

Cutton tried to banish the image. "Meti was a fine worker, Morris. What exactly he do? Force himself on a town girl?"

Morris bit off some tobacco. "Between you'n me?"

"Sure."

"Gave Mrs. Gast's ass a squeeze, he did."

Cutton's gut shimmied. *If they cut off his head and tilled his corpse into the field for grabbin' her ass . . . what would they do to me?*

"Wouldn't be surprised if she asked for it, though. And *that's* between you'n me, too."

Cutton yearned to change subjects. His eyes flicked to the prominent, long-coated man on the white horse. "I thought Mr. Gast wasn't comin' back till tonight."

Morris shrugged. He glanced up at the severed head on the stake but seemed unaffected. "Got back this mornin'. And he brought four flat cars stacked high with track segments."

"Iron from Tredegar, I heard."

"That's right."

"A damn sight better than Yankee iron. Costs more, too."

"Well, Mr. Gast wants only the best for his railroad." Another glance to the field showed normality returning, even with the staked head looking down at them. Female slaves in cool cotton dresses began to walk back to the soybean rows with their wicker baskets. Morris looked one more time at the head.

Did he smile?

Cutton shuddered.

A sudden shadow crossed them. Cutton looked up . . . and nearly froze.

"Mornin', Mr. Gast," Morris greeted.

The stern-faced man nodded. Salt-and-pepper muttonchops bristled his face. "Morris. It's a shame about the slave, but you talked it up just right, as always."

"Thank you, sir. Like you taught me, don't put 'em down, even when we gotta discipline 'em."

"Mornin', Mr. Gast," Cutton said over his unease. *Holy shit, why do I got a feelin' he knows I fucked his wife?*

"Mornin', Mr. Cutton. How have the track inspections looked in my absence?"

"'Bout as perfect as I ever seen, Mr. Gast." His struggled to talk through the dryness of his throat. His heart was pounding. "Gauge is dead-on. We've done close to five miles already, and we ain't even been goin' two weeks. And the coupling work is perfect."

"Good, good." Gast turned his darkened face up to the sun. "My wife mentioned that she spoke with you yesterday."

Cutton's heart felt like a rock that had just slid down into his stomach. "I—Why, yes, sir, I did tip my hat to her, yes, sir."

"She tells me you're a courteous gentlemen—"

"That's, uh, right kind of her—"

"—even though you're from Delaware."

The moment turned rigid. Then Gast and Morris broke out in laughter.

Cutton almost pissed his canvas trousers, but eventually he got it and laughed, too, however nervously.

"I'm just havin' some fun with ya, Mr. Cutton," Gast assured. He looked down at them both. "You men are doin' damn fine work. Keep it up."

"Yes, sir," Morris said.

Cutton added, "We surely will."

Gast took his horse off, back down the track line where the flat cars laden with rail and ties sat.

But Cutton couldn't help but notice . . . *Gast's eyes.* Just before he'd ridden away, when he'd looked down—the whites of the man's eyes seemed stained, off-yellow, like maybe jaundice.

"Is Mr. Gast under the weather?" Cutton mentioned.

"Not that I know of. Why?"

Cutton chewed his lips. "Thought his eyes looked a little funny."

"Looked fine to me, Cutton, and I got a burr in my ass now."

"Why's that?"

"He calls me Morris but he calls you *Mr. Cutton.* Shee-it." *Does he?*

"Bet'choo suck his willy ever nat, huh?" Morris bellowed a laugh and slapped Cutton hard on the back. "Let's go to the whorehouse again tonight. Have us some fun."

Cutton easily remembered Morris's idea of fun. He was drenched in nervous sweat. "Maybe. I'll see how I feel after we're done with work."

Cutton looked one more time at the staked head. No one noticed, no one cared in the least. Just another killing of a rowdy slave. He shook his head when Morris offered him a chew.

And noticed something.

Ain't that the damnedest . . .

The whites of Morris's eyes looked a bit sickly. Tinged a pale yellow.

Just like Gast.

He shook his head. *Must be the light or somethin',* he dismissed.

"You two!" Morris shouted to the two strong-arms in the field. "Get these slaves back on the line. Time to get back to work." He slapped Cutton hard on the back again, billowing dust. "See ya tonight, buddy."

Morris got back to his business. The slaves began to branch off into their assigned groups, and soon tools could be heard clanging.

Cutton mounted his horse but held up a moment. His gaze still hung on the severed head and its yawning dead face. *Is this really justice?* he wondered. Then the most unbidden inclination told him it was more than that.

CHAPTER ONE

I

"So you just leave, just like that?" the voice whined. "That's so *you,* Justin. When there's a problem, all you do is get on a plane and fly away."

Collier felt cramped in the rental car, and annoyed that the squawking phone call was diverting him from the scenery. "Evelyn, dear, I wouldn't define a divorce as a *problem.* It's merely an event. The problem is the notion that you and I ever thought we could be compatible marital partners . . . but that's a moot point by now."

The tiny cell phone seemed to vibrate when she objected, "What's that supposed to mean!"

"Look, Evelyn, I have to finish this book. The deadline is next week. If I miss my deadline, then there's the theoretical possibility that my publisher would cancel the contract in which case I'd have to *pay back* the fifty-thousand-dollar advance. Now, put your little thinking cap on and consider *those* ramifications, since you'll likely get *half* of that advance in the divorce settlement."

Silence. Then, "Oh."

"Yes, my love. Oh. Along with *half*—and I repeat: HALF. Of everything else I've earned."

Another rail: "Hey, I work, too!"

"Honey. Caterers in L.A. are like old people in Florida, i.e. *too many.*"

Collier knew he shouldn't have referred to her failed business endeavor. He knew what she would say even before she said it:

"I'm glad your stupid show's getting kicked off the air, you pompous asshole!"

Ahh, the good life, Collier thought. *True love and domestic bliss.* "Evelyn, let's not fight. I'll be back in a week to sign the papers, okay? I'm not *evading* the issue, if that's what you think. But I have to do this."

"What do you have to go to *Tennessee* for? You write books about beer."

"I only have one more entry before the book's done, and I think I may have found it here. I need it to be unique. I can't just throw in some run-of-the-mill microbrew."

"Well . . . fine." She simmered down.

"I've got to go now. I left the airport four hours ago, and I'm still lost. Tell you what, I'll call you midweek to see how you're doing."

"Okay. 'Bye."

click

Collier felt as though a large animal had just climbed off his back. He banged his elbow when he put the cell phone away. *Why'd I ever get married? All my married friends told me not to. When married people tell you to NEVER get married? That's like the chef coming out of the kitchen and telling you the food sucks. Pretty qualified advice.* Evelyn was beautiful, of course, but quite a few other men in L.A. seemed to think so, too. *It's the way of the modern world. You have great sex; then you get married; then you get divorced. And the man gives the woman HALF.*

Great sex wasn't worth it. By now, in fact, he'd forgotten what great sex was.

Deliriously green pastures and farmland swept by on

either side. Collier loved the view, especially after four years in L.A. It wasn't a city, it was a city-*state*. Hollywood! Spago! Venice Beach! Rodeo Drive! *They can have it,* he thought. Had the town lost its charm, or was it something else? He found that the older he got, the less interested he was in *things.* His Food Network TV show, *Justin Collier: Prince of Beer,* paid enormous money for the first three seasons but now they were giving his slot to some hotshot chef from San Francisco. *Seafood Psycho,* they were calling it. Just as well. Collier hated L.A., and the show—though it had turned him into a semi-celebrity—was wearing him down. At forty-four, most of his hair was gray now, and he felt like a ninny having some makeup girl at the studio dye it for him. His books on craft-made beer always did well enough to make him a solid living, and that's what he yearned to go back to.

Maybe I'm just getting old, he considered. But forty-four wasn't *old,* was it?

Damn . . .

The only thing Hertz had to rent at the airport was this awkward VW Bug. *It looks like a kiddie car,* was the first simile that came to mind when the clerk gave him the keys. Worse was the color: sherbet green. *Yeah, I can see me driving THIS on the 405.* The inside was aggravatingly cramped, but he could still see Lookout Mountain, site of a famous Civil War battle that had put the final nail in Confederate pomp. The image soothed him, not that the mountain signified a wartime slaughter, but the assurance it brought that he was nowhere near L.A.

More miles passed behind him. When he'd run a Map-Quest for Gast, Tennessee, he kept getting that PAGE EX-PIRED message. He'd found it on a 7-Eleven map but the convolution of minor roads had turned into a maddening webwork. How hard could it be to find a town with such an unlikely name? It took another hour before he came upon a sign: GAST, TENNESSEE—TOWN LINE. A CIVIL WAR HISTORICAL SITE.

Finally!

The town stood bright in its reincarnated anachronism: fine clapboard buildings lining a cobblestone main drag called NUMBER 1 STREET. Normal-looking middle-classers walked to and fro on immaculate sidewalks, past the expected antique shops, bistros, and collector's warrens. MINIE BULLETS! one sign boasted. BATTLEFIELD MAPS!

At the corner, two elderly ladies strolled by and smiled. Collier smiled back—"Good afternoon, ladies"—but then it appeared they were chuckling. *It's this eyesore on wheels!* he realized. The oddball car stuck out here like a sore thumb. *Hurry up and turn green!* he thought of the traffic light. More pedestrians, now, stopped to eye the car with furtive smiles. *That's definitely making an entrance . . .* He turned aimlessly, just to get away from the passersby but immediately spotted the sign and arrow: LODGING.

Collier bisected roads similarly marked—NUMBER 2 STREET, NUMBER 3 STREET, etc.—but noted the road he was on: PENELOPE STREET. Collier peered ahead. The road sidewound up plush green hills, atop which sat a splendid antebellum house. Could it be a hotel?

Some joint. Collier wasn't much into architecture but when he pulled round the center court, he couldn't help but be impressed. An elaborate two-story veranda formed the main structure's face, propped by Doric columns chiseled with intricate fluting. The center edifice was octagonal and walled by handmade red bricks, while four more one-story wings flanked outward. White clapboard comprised these wings, and each possessed a deep wraparound porch. Out front a granite boy in Confederate dress blew water from a flute into a mortar-and-stone pond beside which grew a gnarled oak tree more massive than any Collier could remember. He parked and got out. The shadow of the central building cooled him.

Lush weeping willows, fifty feet high, fronted the estate, while some even older oak trees seemed to circle the immediate property.

Collier approached. Streams of ivy crawled up the octagon's eroded brick walls. He noticed several cars parked in a side lot, and hoped they belonged to guests, not just staff; in spite of the building's old splendor, Collier didn't want to be the lone lodger. Though he couldn't be sure, he believed he might've seen a face peering at him from a narrow window on the closest addition. The face looked inquisitive, or warped by old glass.

WELCOME TO THE BRANCH LANDING INN, the high stone entablature read. A low brick next to the door had been crudely engraved: MAIN HOUSE, 1850.

White granite blocks framed a massive front door. Since this was obviously a rooming house, he didn't feel the need to knock in spite of the presence of a peculiar knocker: a face of brass bearing wide, empty eyes but no nose or mouth. For some reason, the knocker caused an odd sensation; then he reached for the brass doorknob and noticed that it, too, had been imprinted with the featureless face.

Collier almost shouted—

An unseen hand opened flat on the small of his back, while another hand opened the door for him.

"Jesus!"

A short woman in her early thirties had come up behind him without making a sound. Collier looked at her after the start she'd given him: short, petite, and shapely. She was barefoot and dressed in a shoddy denim frock. *Couldn't be a guest,* he thought, but then he spotted a name tag: HELLO! MY NAME IS LOTTIE.

Collier brought a hand to his chest. "Wow, you really scared me. I didn't see you."

She smiled and remained holding the door for him.

"So you work here?"

She nodded.

Now that the scare had receded he noticed that her body was exceptional but her face was less than comely, and her eyes seemed dull, even crooked. She smiled again. A shag of unkempt muddy brown hair had been cropped at the middle of her neck.

The moment seemed disarrayed. She simply stood there without saying a word, holding the door.

"Thank you."

He entered a small but ornate vestibule which fronted another set of doors, only these were angled plate glass. The thick oval throw rug beneath their feet appeared handwoven.

"So, Lottie. Do you have any rooms available?"

She nodded again.

Not exactly a chatterbox.

A pleasant chime pealed when the next door came fully open. They stepped into an enormous entrance salon, whose thirty-foot-high ceiling dragged Collier's gaze upward. Very large oil paintings hung high behind the service counter, and higher than those stretched a long stair hall. More patterned throw rugs covered the hardwood floor, these much more refined than the thick vestibule rug. Antique sitting tables surrounded by high-back chairs were arranged about the great open space, and glass-faced book and display cases lined the walls.

Impressive, Collier thought.

Semicircular stairwells swept up on either side of the long mahogany service counter, and behind the counter a wall of stained oak pilasters touted hand-carved flower designs.

"This really is a beautiful place," Collier mentioned to the girl.

She nodded.

It was twenty feet to the check-in counter; behind it, an old woman's face looked up and smiled through wrinkles. Midsixties, probably. A storm cloud–gray perm of curls, very short, crawled around her head—the kind of hairstyle that only women close to nursing-home age thought looked good. Even at a distance, Collier could detect the deepness of the wrinkles, and bags under her eyes, and the face seemed almost masculine with its slab cheeks and heavy jaw. Collier immediately thought, *If Jack Palance had a twin sister . . . I'm looking at her.*

"We'll I'll be!" her peppy twang rang out. "I say it must be celebrity month!"

"Pardon me?"

"I *swear* I seen you on the TV!"

Collier hated to be "recognized."

The elderly eyes glittered between puffy lids. "Couple weeks ago we had some fella from the New York Yankees check in, and now we got the Prince of Beer!"

"Hi," Collier said, depressed already. Now he had to put up the front. "Justin Collier," he said and extended his hand.

"I'm Mrs. Helen Butler, and welcome to the Branch Landing Inn. That short little thing standin' next to you's my daughter, Lottie. I run the place, she keeps it spick-and-span."

Collier nodded to Lottie, who nodded eagerly back.

"Lottie don't talk," Mrs. Butler explained. "Never could for some reason. She tried when she was a tot but could just never get it, so one day she quit tryin'."

Lottie splayed her hands and shrugged.

Mrs. Butler jabbered on. "Why, I saw ya on the TV just last night."

"Oh, so you're a beer connoisseur, Mrs. Butler?"

"Actually, no—I won't lie to ya. I'se always watch the show comes on after yours, *Savannah Sammy's Sassy Smokehouse.*" She added rather dreamily, "I just adore that man, Savannah Sammy."

That dick! Collier's pride rebelled. The comment challenged him. *First of all, he's not even from Savannah, he's from fucking Jersey, and he doesn't even write his own shows!* Collier felt wounded, but what could he say? "Yes, ma'am, Sammy's a great guy."

"But don't get me wrong, your show's terrific, too. In fact, my son watches it all the time, raves about it." She leaned forward, lowered her voice. "Say . . . do you know Emeril?"

"Oh, sure. Great guy, too." Actually, Collier had never met the man.

"Oh, please, Mr. Collier," she gushed next. "Please tell me that you'll be stayin' with us a spell."

"Yes, I'd like to stay for at least a few days."

"That's *wonderful!* And it just so happens that the room with the best view is available."

Collier was about to thank her but instantly fell to speechlessness when the old lady stood up and rushed to the key cabinet.

I don't believe this . . .

Mrs. Butler wore a simple orchid-hued button-front blouse and matching knee skirt. But it wasn't the attire that stunned Collier, it was the body.

Brick shit-house, he had to think.

Her plain clothes clung to a proverbial hourglass physique. Wide-hipped but tiny-waisted; strong, toned legs like a female swimmer, and a burgeoning bust, heavy but high—and Collier didn't detect a bra line. *This broad's got the wrong head on her shoulders,* he thought.

The bosom rode with each vigorous step back to the counter. She handed him a brass key, like the old-style keys that fed into a large circle-atop-a-flange keyhole. But the woman's physique continued to waylay him. *How could a woman with a face that old and haggard have a body like THAT?*

"Room three, it's our best, Mr. Collier," her drawl assured. "Best view, I'm tellin' ya—the *best.*"

"I appreciate that." But he thought, *The view of your rack is pretty damn good, too.* His sexism made him feel unrefined and juvenile but the bizarre sexuality seemed to reflect off her like sunlight off a mirror. "Let me go grab my bags and I'll be right b—"

"Just keep your feet right where they are," she ordered. "Lottie's gettin' 'em."

Collier noticed now the girl was gone. "Oh, no, Mrs. Butler. Lottie's a small frame to be hauling luggage."

"Don't'cha bet on it . . ." Mrs. Butler came around the counter. The bosom tremored with each step. "Lottie don't weigh a hundred pounds but she can sure as heck tote twice that. Strong gal, hard-workin' as they come. Poor thing's thirty now, and can't get a man. Lotta folks think she's slow 'cos she can't talk, but she's really smart as a whip."

"I'm sure she is," Collier said. He stared at the back of her toned legs as she led him to the center of the salon.

"Anyways, once you're settled in your room, come back'n see me. I'll'se show ya the whole place. See, we're more than just another Southern inn, we're a bona fide historical landmark. What we got here's better than the museum in town."

Collier dragged his eyes off the wide, tight rump. "Yes," he uttered, an afterthought. "All the display cases. I noticed when I came in."

"And lots more. I'll show ya."

He tried to snap out of his warped sex-daze and say something. "I look forward to it . . ."

"Most folks don't know a lot of things 'bout how people lived back then." Speaking of this clearly enlivened her, her eyes even brighter now in the bagged lids.

But Collier's brain continued to ooze the dirtiest thoughts. He imagined closing his hands over the plump breasts, which were surely as firm as grapefruits.

Then he winced at himself and ordered his mind off the subject. He turned quickly . . .

A large oil painting hung on the sidewall: a stern-faced

man in coattails and muttonchops. His expression looked preoccupied and unpleasant. "Who's that?"

Mrs. Butler's craggy face seemed to grow more craggy when he asked. "That's the man who built the house your two feet are standin' in right now. Mr. Harwood Gast. The most famous man to ever live in this town."

"The town's founder, I presume."

Why did she seem perturbed now? "No, sir. The town was originally called Branch Landing."

"Same as your bed-and-breakfast. But . . . I don't understand." Without conscious forethought, his eyes were back to roving the richly curved body tight in the cotton garments. *Jesus* . . .

"The town was called Branch Landing 'cos three main roads branched out from it, to three major rail cities. But when Harwood Gast arrived with all his cotton money—and his damn railroad—the townsfolk were all too happy to rename the place in his honor. This house, in fact, was called the Gast House until the day I bought it from my uncle. See, he was related to the folks who bought the place in 1867. But the minute I took over here, I changed the name of the inn."

The words floated. Collier, ignoring the woman's old face, was rapt again on the filled bosom, and obsessed with the idea of what they must look like nude. But as the image percolated, he finally became aware of this strange taint of his character.

What the hell is wrong with me! he yelled at himself. At once he felt ashamed. *I'm lusting after an OLD LADY, for God's sake! Get your head on straight, you pervert!* Then he shoved his attentions back to her discourse.

She changed the name, he thought. *Why?* "I'm still a bit confused. This entire town is a Civil War attraction. Why not call your bed-and-breakfast the Gast Inn? It seems to make the most commercial sense to *keep* the name of the town's most famous figure, doesn't it?"

Sullenness fell over the old woman like a cloud's shadow. "No, Mr. Collier, and I'll tell ya why. Harwood Gast weren't just the town's most famous figure. He was also the town's most evil figure."

II

Another day, another hustle, the young man thought but then he said, "That's it, bitch. You're learnin'."

The fat man, on his knees, moaned in anguish, his head going back and forth at the young man's bare crotch. Tears flowed from squeezed-shut eyes—tears of joy.

The sun glowed on the younger man's bare back; he always took his shirt off for this one. Sweat made the muscled lines gleam. He wasn't attracted to the fat man at all, of course, which is why he filled his head with images of Hollywood's most preeminent men: Cruise, Pitt, Crowe. It was always necessary when his "job" required him to perform in this rather opposite fashion. But no amount of fantasy could shut down the reality. The man so urgently fellating him was nothing to look at—and close to sixty—and whenever he opened his eyes, Pitt's chiseled visage turned into the fat man's bald head. *Gotta get this over with.* He grabbed the man's fat jowls and pushed his mouth off, then began to masturbate . . .

"Yeah, that's right, honey, you like that, don't'cha? Yeah, you got some BIG fat tits on ya. Next time I just might have me a tittie-fuck as much fat as you got."

"Oh, God, yes!" The fat man paused and sobbed.

A minute later, the deed was done, and the fat man—his face splattered—fell back into the grass, moaning.

"How'd ya like *that,* ya big fat bitch?"

"I-I simply adore you . . ."

The younger man stepped back in the sun. *Poor fucked-up bastard,* he thought. He'd made a mess of the fat man's mustache and Vandyke.

"Game's over," the younger man said, hitching up his jeans.

"I-I adore you . . ."

"Aw, come on now. You know the rules. I gotta go."

"But—please. Just—"

The gleaming washboard abdomen flexed when the younger man pulled his tight T-shirt back on. "Huh?"

Sheepish, embarrassed. "You know."

The younger man frowned. "Oh, yeah." He stepped forward and—

cccccccur-HOCK!

—spat in the fat man's face.

"Oh, God! Thuh—thank you!"

I HATE turning tricks like this, the younger man thought. Now that he was done, he gazed across the sweeping field. Trace breezes shifted the miles of belt-high rye grass. He'd heard that during the Civil War, Gast's plantation tracts took up thousands of acres: cotton, soybeans, and corn, mostly. Now it was just green wasteland, and he knew why. But he was not quite complex enough to realize how securely he was standing on a plot of significant American history.

The fat man was still on his knees, crying.

Aw, Jesus! "Why don't'cha git up now? I need to be gettin' back."

Chopped sobs hacked out the words, "But you're so important to me! I couldn't live without you!"

Pain in the ass. The younger man only understood a little of this. *Usually they pay me to do the sucking, not to GET sucked.* Had he been more learned, he'd know that the sexual psychology of some folks was quite skewed. Debasement, like masochism, for instance, served a strange toggle in the mind that had been conditioned for years (since childhood, often) such that what tended to turn most people off—ugliness, abuse, exploitive behavior—lit the fuse of arousal. *Oh, well.* He didn't particularly like the overweight bald man, but he similarly didn't enjoy treating him like sexual garbage. He'd heard somebody talking once about this guy a long time ago named Hitler, who was, like, the king of Germany, and this guy couldn't even get aroused unless a gal shat on him. The younger man guessed something similar was going on here. *Weird,* he thought. "Come on now, let's git. Oh, and where's my money?"

The quivering, plump hand held it out, a personal check for thirty dollars.

"Thanks," the younger man said.

"Let's go to lunch," came more hacked sobs. "Anywhere you want."

"Naw. Got business."

Wet eyes implored him. "At least, at least tell me I do it better than your lover . . ."

A futile exhalation. "You do fine, that's for sure," came the overly generous charity. Actually, it was mediocre work. "But I told you, I ain't got no lover, and I don't *never* get attached in somethin' like this. You know that. This deal's gotta be like what we agreed. One thing in exchange for another. Right?"

Dismally, the fat man nodded.

"Here, lemme help ya up," the younger man offered. He grabbed a fat hand. *Ooof! Ya damn near weigh more than a fuckin' washer'n dryer!* Once up, the guy wouldn't let go of his hand. *Ain't nothin' worse than a mushy fag.* He pulled away.

The fat man stared, tears still streaming. "I'd do anything for you . . ."

Oh, man! The younger man knew he needed to be careful. After all, this was good money for fast work. "Look, I can tell you're out'a sorts right now, so I'm gonna take off. I'll walk back. But just you stay here a while and calm down, git yourself together. You don't wanna be going back to town all cryin' like ya are. And wipe that mess off your face."

A jowly nod, a handkerchief across the eyes, lips, and Vandyke.

"That's better." The younger man held up the check. "You call me when ya wanna go again." And then he turned and walked off.

He strode right out of the clearing into a path between the high grass not even shoulder-wide. Dissolving words faded behind him:

"I love you . . ."

Shee-it . . .

He strode faster, to get away. Walking was fine. He liked the fat man's car—a new Caddy, with some fine a/c—but when he got in these mushy moods, shit—

I'll walk.

Another step and—

Damn it to hell!

—he stumbled and fell. His knees thunked, and when he arched around to see what he'd tripped on . . .

His mind quieted.

A brown skull, half buried, looked back at him.

He wasn't squeamish but then he did believe some of it. He'd seen some things, for sure—out here, and at the house . . .

A quick chill rippled up his sunbaked back. He knew the skull was very old. He also knew it was likely the skull of a slave, not a soldier killed in the field.

The skulls were actually all over the place.

CHAPTER TWO

I

"You're right," Collier said to the old woman. He marveled over one of many glass display cases. "Your inn is like a mini-museum." Below his gaze lay an array of Civil War–era implements. Each one was labeled. MESS PAN—1861, MORTISE TWIVEL—1859, .36-CALIBER SELF-COCKING STARR REVOLVER—1863.

"Just you take a look at the Gast Museum downtown and tell me what we got here ain't a lot finer'n more interesting," Mrs. Butler bragged.

The next case sported gloves, belts, and footgear. "Brogen?" he asked of the clunky black shoe.

"That was the standard combat boot back then. They were as important to a fella's survival on the battlefield as his rifle." She leaned, pointed to a different styled shoe. The gesture caused Collier to run his gaze across the sweep of her bosom, after which he blinked hard to sideswipe the distraction.

"But this 'un here," she continued, "was the cream'a the shoe crop. The Jefferson shoe, or bootee as it was called. Mr. Collier, you could put that shoe on right now and it'd fit better than any fancified Gucci you might buy today."

Collier looked at the high-top leather shoe. Save for a few scuffs, it looked in excellent condition. The label read: FEDERAL PATTERN JEFFERSON BOOTEE—1851—WORN BY MR.

TAYLOR CUTTON, RAIL INSPECTOR FOR THE EAST TENNESSEE AND GEORGIA RAILROAD.

"Everything here was found on this premise at one time or another," Mrs. Butler said. Now she stood back proudly, crossing her arms under her breasts, which made them appear even larger. "I get a tax break through the state historical commission by displayin' it all . . . and by keepin' that blasted portrait of Gast hangin' up there."

The most evil man to ever live here? Collier was amused. It was likely just promotion. "If this man was so evil," he baited, "I suppose the house is haunted, huh?"

"Only by the memory of that low-down bastard," came the strange response.

Collier changed the subject, back to the Jefferson shoe and its long-dead owner. "But I've never heard of this railroad. Was this prewar?"

"They started in 1857 and finished in 1862," she said. "It was Gast's railroad. He put down track from here to the middle'a Georgia, the perfect junction from the main roads that branched into town. He built it with a hundred slaves and fifty white men—not a bad feat for back then. That's a lotta rail to lay."

The notion impressed Collier. They had no machines to do it back then, just hard-muscled humans lugging iron rails and driving spikes with hammers. *Five years . . .* Collier suspected that the hardest labor he ever did was carrying groceries from the car to the house.

"And this?" he asked.

ASH CAKE—1858

"Ash cake is what they used for soap back then," Mrs. Collier went on. "Weren't no Ivory or Irish Spring, you can be sure."

The grayish cake was the size of a hockey puck. "How was it made?"

"They threw a bunch of animal fat in a barrel of boiling water. Horse fat, mostly. Never pork or beef 'cos them was good for eatin'. So they boil the fat and slowly add ashes—any kind: leaves, grass, plants. Boil some more, then add more ashes, boil some more, then add more ashes, like that all day long. By the time the water's all cooked off, the fat's broken down and mixed with the ashes. That's when you cut your cakes and set 'em out to dry." Her old finger tapped the glass. "Works as good as anything they make today in fancy factories. It's rough but gets you cleaner than a whistle. See, people didn't wash much back then, only every Saturday before the Sabbath, and not much at all during the winter—back then a bath could give you pneumonia. Ladies would clean themselves a bit more than fellas, though, with hip baths."

"Hip baths?"

"Just a little tub with leg cutouts. You lower your privates into it. We've got one here—upstairs right next to your room's a matter of fact. I'll show it to ya."

Collier couldn't wait to see the hip bath.

"So much about the old days folks just got the wrong idea about. About the South in general."

The next objects in the case seemed bizarre: six-inch-long metal implements with coiled springs on the end. NAUGHTY GIRL CLIPS—1841. "What on earth are these? They look like clothespins."

Mrs. Butler smiled, and reached for the cabinet.

Collier's eyes widened as she leaned forward. He just couldn't keep his gaze off her bosom . . .

"Stick your finger out, Mr. Collier," she instructed.

"What?"

"Go on. Stick it out."

Collier chuckled and did so.

The tines squeezed down and began to hurt at once.

"See, when little girls were naughty, their daddies put one'a these on their finger."

Only five seconds had passed and Collier was wincing.

"How long the clip'd stay on depended on how bad the little girl was, see? Say she didn't do her mornin' chores, for example; then she'd likely get the clip on for fifteen seconds." The old lady's eyes smiled. "Hurt yet, Mr. Collier?"

"Uh, yeah," he admitted. It felt like pliers on his finger.

"Or say she stole a piece of rock candy from the general store; then she'd probably get a minute . . ."

Collier's finger was *throbbing* in pain, and he'd only done twenty seconds so far.

"And if she ever dared talk back to her momma or daddy—two minutes at least."

Collier chewed his lip a few seconds more, then insisted, "Take it off!"

Mrs. Butler complied, clearly amused. Collier's crimped finger was red above the joint. "Aw, but you barely done thirty seconds, Mr. Collier."

He wagged his hand. "That hurt like hell . . ."

"I'll bet'cha it did. That's why little girls didn't act up much in the good old days. A couple minutes with the clip was all the discipline they needed. Wasn't uncommon for a little girl to wear it five minutes for usin' profanity, or gettin' sent home from the schoolhouse."

"Five minutes?" Collier objected. "In this day and age, they'd call that child torture."

"Um-hmm. But I dare say, if our teachers used these clips in the schools today, we wouldn't be havin' all these problems we see on the news." She put the bizarre clip back in the case. "I'm sure you agree."

Collier couldn't dredge a reply. "But those clips were only used on girls?"

"That's right."

"What about the boys?"

A self-assured snicker. "When boys misbehaved, their daddy'd simply take 'em out to the woodshed for a thrashin'."

"Ah. Of course." Collier rubbed his finger. He was a bit pissed by the history lesson. *That hurt like hell!* he wished he could bark at her. But her next gesture deleted the incident.

She unfastened her top button, then vigorously fanned the V of her blouse—which only revealed more of the awesome bosom.

"I keep forgettin' to turn the a/c up higher this time of day," she said. The sun was beating in through the high front windows. "Are you hot, Mr. Collier?"

Only below the belt, he thought. The image of the flesh of her bosom and the deep cleavage stoked him. "A little, now that you mention it."

"I'll take care of that presently." She kept puffing the blouse; Collier could see a mist of sweat frosting the skin within.

Something else caught his eye in the last case: a pale gray slip of paper that looked like an old bank check. He squinted.

RECEIVED OF: *Mr. N. P. Poltrock,* AGENT OF THE EAST TENNESSEE AND GEORGIA RAILROAD COMPANY, *Fifty* DOLLARS.

"Wow," Collier remarked when he noted the check's handwritten date. *Sept. 16, 1862.* "What an old document, and it looks in perfect shape."

Mrs. Butler stopped puffing air through her cleavage. Her expression soured. "A paycheck from Gast's damned railroad. But, yes, it is quite old."

Gast again. The very mention of anything related to him corrupted her disposition.

"It's just terribly interesting, isn't it?"

"What's that, Mr. Collier?"

"A piece of paper signed by someone during the Civil War."

"We prefer to call it the War of Northern Aggression," she insisted.

"But wasn't it *Southern* aggression that actually started the war?" Collier said and immediately thought better of it. "It was the Confederacy that bombarded Fort Sumter."

"But it was the *North,* Mr. Collier, who begged for it by charging high tariffs on cotton exports," she snapped.

"I see . . ." Collier looked at the check again, imagining it being signed nearly a hundred and fifty years ago, when the solidity of the nation was dangling by a thread.

"Where is that silly child with your bags?" she asked, frowning at the door.

"I better go help her. They're pretty heavy—"

"No, no, please. Believe me, it's a thrill for the poor thing. It'll tickle her pink to carry a celebrity's bags."

Collier frowned when she wasn't looking. *I was a minor celebrity at best, and now I'm a has-been celebrity.* He didn't have the fortitude to tell her his show was being canceled. *Then the myth would be shattered, and all I got is the myth . . .*

The bell at the desk rang. Collier noticed two guests— a couple in their thirties. *Tourists,* he discerned. A camera slung around the man's neck. He was nondescript in a tasteless striped short-sleeve shirt and beige Dockers strained at the waist. He held a finger up to Mrs. Butler.

"Oh, the Wisconsin folks," she muttered. "They must want a tour brochure. I'll be right back, Mr. Collier."

"Sure."

Some unknown force commanded Collier's eyes to fix on her rump as she hurried to the desk. *If she only had a face that wasn't quite so . . . OLD!* He felt prickly sweat at his brow . . .

He pretended to survey more oddments in the case: a hand-scraped burl bowl from the early 1700s, a debarking iron from a century later. The next item looked intimidating: a brass-hilted knife that had to be a foot and a half long. GEORGIA ARMORY SABER BAYONET—CIRCA 1860— OWNED BY MR. BEAUREGARD MORRIS OF THE EAST TENNESSEE AND GEORGIA RAILROAD COMPANY. The sheer size of the blade gave Collier a twinge. The blade looked almost new and didn't show a speck of rust. *I wonder if anyone was ever killed by that thing?* the question blared into his mind.

He scanned more items as Mrs. Butler's charming

drawl engaged the new couple. She was passing them some local tour brochures . . . Now Collier was eyeing the tourist woman. A plain Jane with a little paunch but still shapely. Wide hips stretched her own beige slacks— also too tight, like the husband's—and Collier's vision focused at the bosom, and then an image barraged his mind: Collier pulling her top off and pressing his face between her breasts . . .

He winced until the dirty image was gone.

When he looked again, the woman was on her tiptoes, a great big white dental-bleached smile. She was waving at him.

"Pardon me, pardon me," she was saying.

"Yes?"

"You're Justin Collier, aren't you?"

Collier tried not to sigh. "Why, yes."

"Oh, we're big fans! Look, honey, it's the Prince of Beer!"

The husband waved, too. "Love your show, Mr. Collier."

"Thanks."

The wife: "Could we get your autograph?"

He could've groaned. "It would be my pleasure—" But then the vestibule doors opened, and in trod Lottie with his suitcase and laptop bag. *Off the hook for the moment,* Collier thought. "But let me catch you later today. I'm just now checking in."

"Of course," the giddy woman said. "Nice meeting you!"

"Last room on the stair hall, Mr. Collier," the old lady added.

A fake smile; then he rushed to Lottie.

"Here, let me take one," he said, but she just grinned and shook her head no.

The old lady's right, she's strong as a mule. She effortlessly hauled the cumbersome bags up the staircase. Lean legs took the steps two at a time. Collier wasn't sure why at first—he deliberately lagged several stairs behind her—but then . . .

More pervert instinct, he assumed.

He was trying to look up her denim skirt. For only a second he caught white panties bunched up the crack of a delectable little rump.

What is WITH me today?

Maroon carpet took them down the main stair hall; over the rail Collier could hear Mrs. Butler's jack-jawing with the Wisconsin couple. He fought the urge to look down, hoping for a cleavage view of both women but this time he gritted back the impulse. *How come I'm suddenly obsessed with sex!* he demanded of himself. When no answer came, he took to eyeing Lottie's rump and the backs of her toned legs. He felt crazed by the imagery, and could imagine no reason why. Even her Achilles tendons and her bare heels seemed enticing, and the drab shanks of hair, the backs of her arms, her fingers wrapped around his suitcase handles seemed inexplicably erotic . . .

When she stopped and set the cases down, he stalled, then remembered he'd already been given his key. *Last room on the stair hall,* he'd been told. He put the key in—

Lottie tugged his arm, shaking her head. She pointed to the door she stood beside.

"I thought your mother said last room on the—"

She seemed to lip something he didn't catch—

A strong male voice intervened, "What my mom meant is the last regular room." A tall man, thirtyish, stepped up, wearing a confident smile and jeans, work boots, and a T-shirt. "Howdy, Mr. Collier. I'm Helen's son, Jiff."

Collier shook a toughened hand. "Hi, Jeff."

"No, sir, that's Jiff—you know, like the peanut butter?" The tight T-shirt sculpted a toned upper body; he had a blond buzz cut and similar drawl. "This room here ain't yours. We don't rent it out." He pointed to the next door. "This one's yours, and it's our best."

"Well, it's nice to meet you, Jiff."

"Lemme take these bags from my little pipe cleaner of a sister, and get'cha set."

Collier unlocked what was actually the second-to-last door, but he quickly noted that the third door stood more narrowly and sported a plaque, which read ORIGINAL GAST BATH AND WATER CLOSET. "So what's this here, Jiff?"

Lottie glared as Jiff yanked the cases from her; she may have even mouthed *Fucker!*

"That room we never renovated 'cos a lot of tourist folks like to see what a real bathroom from the old days looked like. I'll be happy to show it to ya, and give ya a tour of the whole house when you're ready."

"Thanks, I'd like a tour."

Collier entered his room, and heard Jiff mutter "Out'a my way, dopey!" to his sister behind him. They seemed to be fighting over Collier's attention. "Yes, sir, I seen your show many times," Jiff assured him. "It's a real pleasure to have such a famous TV fella staying with us."

Collier couldn't have felt less genuine when he replied, "Thanks."

"You here for anything to do with your TV show?"

"No, Jiff, actually I'm here to finish a book. Besides my *Prince of Beer* show I also write books about the art and craft of beer—" And then he quickly said, "Ah, perfect," of an antique scroll-top desk, which sat before a broad window. "I can work on my laptop right there."

Jiff put the laptop case on the desk. "I hope the room's to your likin'."

"It'll do just fine." *Cozy,* Collier thought. Heavy rust-colored carpet wall to wall, and furnishings of the expected post-Colonial bent. The four-poster bed sat unusually high. Gold and maroon wallpaper covered the half-paneled walls. "Oh, and let me check out this view your mother promised." And he went through a pair of French doors out to an elaborately railed balcony. Jiff stepped out with him.

The second-story view showed him an impressive

garden bisected by flagstone trails. "Beautiful garden," Collier commented. The meld of fragrances reached him on a warm breeze.

Centered in a small cove at the end of the perimeter sat a crude chimney made of flat beige stones piled high and set with mortar. Several ducts seemed to exist in the structure's body, and then Collier noticed a chained beam hanging on the side, attached to a large version of a fireplace bellows. A separate shed sat beside it all.

"What's all that there, that chimney-looking thing?"

"Harwood Gast's personal iron forge," Jiff replied. "Any rich man had a forge and blacksmith on the property. Lotta tourists and historians come here just to see that one. It's in perfect condition; only thing new on it is the leather for the bellows."

This, like some of the artifacts downstairs, fascinated Collier. "And the shed next to it?"

"Fuel house. They used coal or charcoal; couldn't use regular wood 'cos it wouldn't get hot enough. One fella ran the whole show, pumpin' the bellows, turnin' the ore, then pullin' out the blooms to knock the iron out of 'em. Tricky process. The smith'd have to shape the iron before it got too cold." He pointed to a sawn tree stump that housed an anvil. "It was hard work but those fellas could damn near make anything, and they did it all with a hammer and molds."

The sight made Collier realize how little he knew of the world. "I'd love to see that some time."

"I'd be happy to show it to ya whenever you like," Jiff said. Then he pointed beyond. "And there's the mountain."

Collier could still see it, even at this distance, its peaks and edges ghosted by mist that looked purple. But past the garden stretched an endless scrubland that wasn't much for scenery. "How come no one farms all that land out there?"

36 Edward Lee

"Used to be one of the biggest cotton plantations in the South," Jiff said, "back before the war."

"World War Two? Or do you mean—"

"The War of Northern Aggression, sir."

Collier smiled. He struggled with more distraction when Lottie listlessly leaned over the rail and looked down, and was just able to resist overtly looking down the top of her denim frock. "So it's just wasteland now? Surely it's been farmed since then."

"No, sir. Not a square foot."

"A developer's sitting on it?"

"No, sir."

The deflection of the issue intrigued Collier. "Well then why not use all that valuable farmland?"

Lottie looked at him. She slowly shook her head.

"Folks think the land's cursed is all, Mr. Collier," Jiff informed. "Lotta old legends and ghost tales 'round here, but don't pay 'em no mind. Man who used to own that land was Harwood Gast. The cotton his slaves harvested clothed most'a the Confederate army, and the soybeans he grew out there fed it. Bet'cha didn't know they had soybeans back then, did ya?"

"Actually . . . no." But Collier delighted in ghost stories. "And why is the land supposedly cursed?"

Jiff crooked his head. "Aw, you don't wanna hear that silly talk, sir. Oh, look, there's them folks from Wisconsin."

He sure changed that subject fast. Collier's eyes darted down and, indeed, there walked the married couple he'd seen downstairs. The woman seemed to sense Collier's eyes, and jerked around to wave.

"Can't wait for that autograph, Mr. Collier!"

Jesus . . . Collier nodded and smiled. "Let's go back inside."

Lottie skipped ahead of him; he couldn't take his gaze off the toned, gymnastlike legs. But then his loins surged when the spry girl leaned over for his suitcase. *Jackpot!* Collier thought. The action afforded only a glimpse, but as the top edge of the frock dipped from gravity, Collier noted breasts the size of peaches, and probably as firm. *Good God...* This sudden thrill of voyeurism left him mystified; it simply wasn't like him. Nevertheless, the glimpse made him feel as though he'd received a wonderful surprise gift.

She hauled the suitcase atop the bed, opened it, and began to hang his clothes up in the wardrobe.

"Thanks, Lottie, but that's really not necessary . . ."

"It's our pleasure, Mr. Collier," Jiff offered.

Next, Lottie grabbed a pair of shoes from the case, then turned and bent down to place them at the bottom of the wardrobe. Collier got an adrenaline jolt from a perfect shot of her white-pantied bottom.

Jiff gave her a hard smack. "Have some respect, girl! Mr. Collier don't wanna look at your scrawny bee-hind!"

Yes I do! Yes I do! Collier objected. The girl stood straight, grinned sheepishly.

But it was just more incomprehension. Even the air seemed gorged with desire; he inhaled it like smoke. Collier had all but forgotten such sexual awareness, but all of a sudden . . .

His chest felt tight. He felt antsy.

"So what was that you was sayin', Mr. Collier?" Jiff repaired the awkward moment. "You come here to work on a beer book?"

"Uh, yes, Jiff. I'm writing a book about classic old American beers, and the reason I've come to Gast is because I heard some fellow connoisseurs speaking particularly of a beer brewed in this town, at a place called—"

But Jiff was already nodding, arms crossed. "Cusher's, ya mean. Next words out'a my mouth was gonna be how the Prince'a Beer surely *must* throw a few back at Cusher's."

"It's a restaurant and tavern, right?"

"Sure is, and a fine one. Old-time vittles like they made

in the old days, and some beers they make themselves right there in the place. I stop in myself every now and then. It's right down on the corner of Number One Street."

This was good fortune, and Collier didn't like going to new places by himself, especially in a strange town. "That's very helpful, Jiff. And if you're not doing anything later, I'd love to take you and your sister there for dinner. My treat."

Jiff and Lottie showed gushing grins. "That's a right nice'a ya, Mr. Collier. I'd be a honored to go out with a celebrity such as yourself," Jiff accepted, but then shot a scowl to his sister. "Unfortunately Lottie won't be able to join us on account she's still got all the guest linens to wash—"

"Oh, that's too bad—"

Lottie's lips pressed together, infuriated.

"Which she'd best get to doin', like *right now*. Right, Lottie? Ma done told ya already."

The girl's eyes dampened with tears; she stormed out. Collier was fairly sure she'd mouthed *Eat shit!* to her brother upon exit.

Jiff shrugged. "Lottie—God love her—is a little off, Mr. Collier. It's best she stay 'round the house. She gets all silly even after, like, one beer, and then she gets to cryin' and all on account she can't talk."

Collier felt saddened by the cruel fact but then his mind served back up the glances he'd stolen. "Oh, I see . . . Anyway, how about seven o'clock?"

"Seven o'clock it is, Mr. Collier." Jiff clapped his hands. "Ooo-eee! First time in my life I ever been out with a genuine celebrity!"

Collier sighed.

"You need anything durin' your stay," Jiff said and pointed, "just you let me know."

"Thanks, Jiff." When Collier tipped him a ten, the man's eyes beamed. "See you at seven."

Jiff left, whistling. Collier locked the door.

He set up his laptop but found himself contemplating the sudden and unlikely sexual awareness that seemed to envelop him since he'd arrived. *Christ, what's wrong with me? Since the minute I got here I've felt hornier than I've been in years.* Yet, it had been six months at least since he and Evelyn had made love and probably as long since he'd had a potent sexual fantasy.

Why all this horniness now? he wondered.

It was a good question. Now that he thought about it, he realized his sex drive had been pretty much dead since the second season of the show. The spoiling marriage only killed it more. *Job stress, stress at home, and just the stress of living in that California hellhole,* he guessed. *I NEVER think about sex anymore . . . until today. I walk into this place sweating a book deadline and suddenly I've got the sex drive of a seventeen-year-old. I'm going bonkers over an old lady with Jack Palance's face and her redneck daughter who can't talk.*

So much for self-revelation.

He pulled the laptop power cord from its case but inadvertently dropped it. When he leaned down to retrieve it, he noticed something . . .

The gap under the bedroom door . . .

Somebody's standing right outside my door—right now, he could see.

Bare toes showed in the gap. *Must be Lottie,* he guessed. She'd been barefoot, hadn't she? Collier got on his hands and knees and crawled over. The toes were still there; they hadn't budged. It occurred to him that he should stand up right now and open the door.

But he didn't.

The keyhole . . .

The lock, knob, and keyhole were likely original: old, well-crafted brass. Collier held his breath and put his eye to the hole.

You've got to be shitting me . . .

A woman's pubis was positioned directly on the other side of the keyhole. It was creamy white, freshly shaved—a beautiful, private triangle.

That's what Collier saw when he looked through the keyhole.

He leaned back, blinked, and sighed. *There's a nude woman standing on the other side of this door,* he resigned. But that was impossible, wasn't it?

It must be a trick of light.

He looked again. The shaved pubis was still there. He noticed a detail now: a single freckle an inch above the clitoral hood.

All right . . . It was no trick of light; it was really there. He let his mind tick a moment, mulling choices, but there were really only two. *I can ignore it,* he knew. *Or . . . I can open the door and see who it is.*

However . . .

Who could it be?

It was almost as though she *knew* Collier would see.

Impossible.

He stood up and opened the door.

No one faced him in the doorway, just the open atrium beyond the railing of the stair hall. Collier looked quickly left, then right, and saw no woman, nude or otherwise, hurrying away.

This is screwed up, he thought. *This is REALLY screwed up.*

He sat on the bed and he considered the day in objective terms. He'd come to Tennessee in search of an obscure lager he thought might be worthy of inclusion in his book. The conservative sedan he'd booked at the car rental company hadn't been available, so he got a preposterous lime-sherbet VW. What should've been a one-hour drive turned into a four-hour drive. After which Collier had arrived at this strange little bed-and-breakfast only to find his normally dead-in-the-water libido sent into the red zone by an old woman with a great body and her probably retarded daughter. In summation, all of the above aggregated into the most bizarre day of his life. And just when he thought it couldn't get any more bizarre . . .

A woman flashed her shaved beaver in my keyhole . . .

Collier rubbed his temples.

I either saw it, or I had a hallucination.

Was there something wrong with him? Something clinical, perhaps?

It couldn't be.

I know I'm not crazy . . . and I never took drugs so it couldn't be some sort of a flashback.

And if it *hadn't* been a hallucination, who was this discreet exhibitionist with the mystery pubis?

At first, the bare feet made him think of Lottie, but now that he thought of it, the hips seemed too wide and the flesh too plush for Lottie. Mrs. Butler, then? *No,* he thought crudely. *There's no way . . .*

The woman from Wisconsin? *There's a thought.* Collier thought of the groupie phenomenon, women who lose their inhibitions simply because a man's a musician, a pro athlete, or . . . a TV personality. Collier had heard of such things, especially with the more flamboyant men on the channel. *Like that Savannah Sammy asshole.* Women mailed him their panties, for God's sake. But as for Collier himself . . .

He'd never met a "TV groupie," and doubted that any existed for the "Prince of Beer."

He shook his head, bewildered to the point of headache.

Hallucination or not, something's come over me. I'm hornier than I can ever remember, so what's the reason?

But why think so negatively? Just that his sex drive had turned hyper didn't mean there was necessarily anything wrong with him, did it? A healthy sex drive was . . . healthy. Something was resurfacing in him: a vigorous response to sexual attraction via the genetic urge to be reproductive . . .

That must be it.

Collier felt a lot better after coming to this conclusion, but in truth it was none of these things that were making him hornier than an ape in rut.

It was the house.

CHAPTER THREE

I

1857

When N.P. Poltrock closed his eyes he saw rotten heads and blood being drunk from goblets. He saw limbs shorn by axes and hewers, and men and women thrown naked and very much alive into the belly of a red-hot coal bed. He saw children being raped in the dirt by faceless soldiers in stiff gray uniforms; others were merely masturbated on and strangled. Horses dragging old men and women by nooses around their necks galloped regularly into the hot, smoky compound; just as regularly great jail wagons rolled in from the nearby depot—wagons so stuffed with the beaten and the starving that the bar frames seemed fit to burst. One soldier skewered a little boy in the eye with his bayonet and flung him into the coal bed, while a little girl, no more than fourteen but hugely pregnant, was flung in behind him.

These were the visions that poured into the darkness behind Poltrock's closed eyes. He heard endless screams and smelled the stench of human incineration.

When he opened his eyes, another stench briefly filled his nostrils: old urine.

Sick.

Sick.

That's how Poltrock had felt since the first day he signed on with Gast.

"We will lay one hundred miles of track per year," Gast had told him that day.

Not with only a hundred workers you won't, Poltrock thought but chose not to voice.

Gast had told him this in the den of the mansion he shared with his wife and children. A beautiful house in the center of town, ringed by trees and full of flowers.

So why did Poltrock keep smelling piss?

The whites of Gast's eyes looked yellow, and Poltrock thought he'd noticed that same look in the other men who'd been hired.

Just my imagination. I'm under the weather, that's all. Too much to drink last night after the long ride out . . .

Gast himself looked like exactly what he was: a vastly wealthy Southern plantation owner. Tailcoats, linen shirt, bow tie, and pointed leather shoes that shined like oil. He stood tall and lean, and the lines in his face suggested he must be upward of fifty. Trimmed mutton-chops didn't look right in the incised, overserious face. "I have signed on fifty men already, some of the finest rail men in the state," Gast assured. He'd turned just then, looking out the bow window. "But I need an operations manager. You."

Poltrock fought off the repeated distractions. "I appreciate your offer, Mr. Gast," he said in a distinct Southern accent. "But why me?"

"Because you built the great railroads in Ohio and the Pennsylvania Commonwealth. I need a man like you to run my construction operation."

Poltrock felt dizzy. He kept looking to the splendid furnishings and draperies, the crystal vases filled with blooming flowers, but then thought the strangest thing: *It's all covering something up . . .* The house, indeed, in-

side and out, looked beautiful but it felt . . . ugly. Corrupted. A sick person in fine clothes.

For a moment—just a fraction of a moment—again, he
smelled urine. But when the moment passed, so did the
haunting stench.

A black maid ushered in a silver tray with cups of
minted tea. She said nothing, simply set the service on
the desk, glanced once at Poltrock, and left.

The glance showed Poltrock eyes full of fear. He
closed his own eyes again at a wave of nausea. He could
not dispel the image that rose: two strong white hands
clamped about the maid's throat, squeezing until the
dark face turned even darker, until veins swelled fat as
earthworms and the bones in the neck could be heard
cracking. When the hands let go, the dead woman's
mouth fell open to ooze abundant semen.

Then the image retracted to reveal whose hands they
were: Poltrock's.

God help me, he thought. *Where did that unholy vision
come from?*

Poltrock had never thought anything so vile in his life.
He was a God-fearing Christian. What had caused such a
sight to come into his head?

Gast turned back around, with his yellow eyes. He
must have some liver disorder. "Work for me," he said
and handed Poltrock a check.

It was a finely printed check on heather gray paper. It
read RECEIVED OF: *Mr. N. P. Poltrock,* AGENT OF THE EAST TENNES-
SEE AND GEORGIA RAILROAD COMPANY, *Fifty* DOLLARS.

The unease of the house hampered Poltrock's reaction. Movement caused him to look to the doorway. He
could see into the foyer, where a dowdy teenage girl in a
white dress sat on the stairs' second step. She was pet-
ting a dog—a small, wrangly thing with drab brown
fur—and scratching behind its ears. For a moment the
girl's eyes looked at Poltrock. She smiled coyly. Now the
dog had its head under her dress.

Poltrock winced and looked away. He reminded himself of the check he'd just been given. *Lord, that's good money.* "Just so I'm sure we understand each other, Mr. Gast, but you aim to lay a hundred miles of track per year with a hundred men?"

"I have a hundred slaves, plus fifty strong white foremen and rail engineers."

"I see. So . . . like I was saying, sir, a hundred miles of track per year. From where to where?"

"From Camp Roan, just outside of town, to Maxon."

"Maxon, *Georgia,* Mr. Gast?"

"That's correct."

"That's halfway to Atlanta, sir," Poltrock almost raised his voice. The notion was absurd. "That's five hundred miles."

"I'm aware of that." Gast turned back to the window, with his tea. The sunlight through the trees seemed to create a dark fog about his head. "I, like many, Mr. Poltrock, believe that a war is coming. It will be a great war that will forge our Southern brotherhood into the strongest nation on earth. I have confidantes who believe such a rail line would be imperative for the South to survive such a war."

Poltrock shook his head. He didn't believe any of this war talk. The Congress would make things right for the South. *Gast must not remember what the federal army did to Mexico not too long ago.* And who were these confidantes? *Probably just big money people, more plantation barons. Lots of money and lots of big ideas.*

When he looked again, the girl with the dog was gone from the foyer, but he could swear he heard children giggling from deeper within the house. And—

There was that smell again: the stench of urine.

It must be in his mind, for Gast clearly didn't detect it.

"The East Tennessee corridor is ideal," Gast went on. "All the way to Maxon we won't have to spend a penny excavating; we'll scarcely have to fell a single tree."

"The only thing I know of in Maxon, sir, is the old armory and barrel works."

Gast turned again, impressed. "You're a learned man, Mr. Poltrock. That's quite correct."

"But I also know the furnace there has been permanently shut down. They haven't made a gun barrel in Maxon since 1814."

The jaundiced eyes looked blurred. "Again, you're correct. But that's not my interest, nor is it in the interest of my confidantes."

Confidantes again, Poltrock thought. *Gast just ain't right in the head and that's all there is to it. It's downright crazy to lay five hundred miles of track to a dead town.*

"You just leave that to us," Gast said, "while we leave the construction of the railroad to you."

Poltrock severed his next objection when more movement caught the corner of his eye. A beautiful woman in white had just swept into the room.

"Mr. Poltrock. Allow me to introduce you to my wife, Penelope."

Poltrock stood up at once.

The sight hijacked his gaze. All he saw first was the beaming face surrounded by tousles of hair the color of sunlight. A graceful white hand daintily held a fan with embroidered roses.

"Mrs. Gast," Poltrock nearly stammered. "It is truly my honor to make your acquaintance."

"Likewise, Mr. Poltrock."

She extended her hand, which felt hot when Poltrock took it. An erection that made no sense suddenly ached in his trousers. The fragrance of flowers seemed to emanate from her. Poltrock knew he dare not stare but one stolen glance revealed the rest of her: a figure of perfect contours fitted into a pleated bustle dress white as the clouds. By the tenets of the day, it was crude to look directly at another man's wife—especially a wealthy man's—and Poltrock found it close to impossible to keep his eyes from falling to the lacy neckline and considerable cleavage exposed.

"Your fine husband and I were just discussing—"

"Business," Gast said abruptly.

"Oh, I know," the lilting accent drifted from her lips. "Your important railroad, which will help confederate our Southern states into the most powerful nation in the world."

"You can be sure, my dear," Gast said. "My railroad will be more important to the South than the depot in Chattanooga." But the look in Gast's tinted eyes said that he did not appreciate the interruption.

Penelope Gast stroked her fan a few times, which blew a few strands of golden hair upward. "Will Mr. Poltrock be joining us for lunch?"

"Of course he will," Gast answered before Poltrock could. "But we still have business to discuss, so—"

"Of course, dear," the woman said. "Have a fine day, Mr. Poltrock."

Poltrock gulped and nodded. "And you, too, ma'am."

The stunning beauty of the woman rocked Poltrock. He hoped he'd recovered well when he sat back down and said, "You have a wife of great culture and beauty, Mr. Gast. You must be very proud of her."

"I certainly am, Mr. Poltrock."

Poltrock didn't think his erection had been noticeable. *Good God, I hope not.* He closed his eyes again for a moment . . .

At once, his nostrils flared and his stomach clenched: the stench of stale urine seemed thick as fog. And then came the words:

"She's a whore of the first water. She smells of piss and reeks of weakness and gluttony. She's fucked dozens of men behind my back, sometimes even slaves. One day, and you can mark my words, I'll see her raped to the brink of death and then I will personally halve her detestable pussy with an ax."

Poltrock's eyes shot open at the devilish talk, but when he looked around the den . . .

Gast wasn't there. Poltrock was alone.

He shuddered in place. First those vile images and now this evil talk. *Crazy,* he thought. *This is a crazy house . . .*

What's happening to me?

In his hand, he noticed that he was still holding the check.

Gast's fine leather shoes snapped back into the room over the hardwood floor. "My wife is quite a busybody, as I'm sure you noticed. Forgive the interruption to our important discourse."

Poltrock tried to shake cobwebs from him head. "I'm sorry, Mr. Gast, but I must be much more fatigued from my trip than I thought. I feel so distracted. I didn't even see you leave the room."

"Your long journey from Raleigh, yes—certainly," Gast remarked. "I escorted my wife to the kitchen; she insisted on showing me the funnel cakes she'd made. Oh, I know she didn't really make them—she's terrible in the kitchen—but I let her believe that I think she did. She's quite worth the accommodation."

He wasn't even in the room when I heard the voice . . .

Poltrock was sweating. He was trying to order his thoughts. Somewhere, a dog was barking.

"Work for me, Mr. Poltrock. You'll be doing yourself and this great land of ours a proud service."

The job, the railroad, Poltrock finally remembered. *A hundred miles of track per year, from here to Maxon . . .* He looked at the impressive check still in his hand. "Mr. Gast, fifty dollars a month is indeed a handsome salary, especially with the economy so deflated from Northern taxes, but it's just that—"

"I apologize for not making myself clear in the first place," Gast interrupted with a raised finger. "Not fifty dollars per month, Mr. Poltrock. Fifty dollars per week."

Poltrock stared at the man and his overwhelming offer, and as the words left his mouth to take the job, Poltrock could've sworn he smelled urine.

CHAPTER FOUR

I

Collier couldn't remember what happened in the dream, but he remembered what it smelled like:

Urine.

He wakened from the nap aggravated and drymouthed. Yes, it was the smell of urine that permeated his slumber, and as he leaned up, he thought he recalled other details, not sights, but sounds.

A steady and nearly musical sound of metal striking metal. He thought of metal bars being clanged together, or hammers hitting steel. And something else, too . . .

A whistle?

Yeah. Like a whistle in a train yard.

He rarely dreamed at all, but when he did it was typically of things he could see: people, places. Not sounds and smells.

When he turned out of bed, he caught himself musing over, first, Lottie's body, then Mrs. Butler's.

Damn it!

A narrow night table stood by the desk, marble-topped. On it the clock told him it was 6:30 P.M. *I invited Jiff to Cusher's, didn't I? At seven.*

He roused, then showered in the small but homey bathroom.

Why smell piss in a dream?

More puzzlement, a chaser for the entire day. But a brief relief came when he thought again of the sounds. Metal striking metal. *Hammers! Sledgehammers driving spikes—of course!* This could only signify the sound of men laying railroad track, which made grateful sense since Mrs. Butler had mentioned something about Harwood Gast building a railroad in the late 1850s. Collier remembered the old paycheck in the case she'd shown him—a railroad check.

The East Tennessee and Georgia Railroad, he remembered. The whistle in the dream, too, could only have been a train whistle.

One mystery solved, however useless. Next, in the sudden daydream, he pictured himself in the shower . . . with Lottie . . .

If all this horniness is from the fresh air and great outdoors, then I'm MOVING here once Evelyn gets her divorce, he joked to himself. But he couldn't laugh, for one thing still bothered him.

That smell . . .

One of Collier's earliest childhood memories, regrettably, involved the smell of urine. He'd been about ten when his father had taken him for a long drive. "Come on, kiddo. We're going to go visit Granddad at that special apartment he lives in." Collier was too young to grasp the entire concept of nursing homes, but he got the idea. The whole place smelled bad and was very quiet save for distant shouts. "Here's his room, son. Now, remember like I told you. Granddad hasn't been feeling well for a while, and he might not recognize us. But let's just act like everything's normal." Collier guessed Granddad wasn't in very good shape. When they entered the drab room, though—Collier gagged, and so did his father. The room *reeked* of urine.

Granddad's bed lay empty and stained yellow. Another man in the next bed, who looked like a gray skeleton, jerked his face right at them and toothlessly bellowed, "That fucker don't do nothin' but jabber and piss! Turned the damn bed into a damn piss sponge—" A bony finger wagged at them. "—and these lazy fucks here don't never change the mattress 'cept when one of us dies!" Collier broke out in tears from the shocking rant, but he already had tears in his eyes from the sheer potency of the stench. Strong, saturated, and old. His father ushered him out quickly and that's when they learned that Granddad had died that morning. Collier remembered riding home in strange, choking silence, eyes still stinging long after the tears had abated. Even their clothes reeked of the smell.

The same unmistakable smell of Collier's dream, only the dream had been worse.

Collier stepped out of the shower. *Now why the hell would my mind make me dream of the smell of piss!*

He dried off, then slipped on the robe hanging on the door. Gold embroidery on scarlet terry read BRANCH LANDING INN with crossed cannons beneath the letters C.S.A. *She really takes this Civil War stuff seriously.*

He stepped back in the bedroom, and stopped.

Sniffed.

That's not urine I smell . . . is it?

It was his mind now, he was sure. Like when you were in the woods and were *certain* you felt a tick on your leg but when you looked there was nothing there . . .

He sniffed again and found the only scent to be a cinnamonlike tinge from a bowl of potpourri.

Thank God . . .

Knuckles rapidly tapped at the door.

Who the . . . Collier looked at the clock and saw he still had plenty of time before he met Jiff.

"Hi, sorry if this is a bad time!" The smiling housewifey face beamed when he opened the door. It was the Wisconsin woman.

Huh? Collier thought. "Oh, of course, your autograph. I hadn't forgotten." But he thought, *Jesus, lady! Can't you see I just got out of the shower?*

"We're going out to dinner now," she explained, "and we didn't want to miss you. Oh, but we'd love for you to come along."

"Oh, thanks, but I've already got plans . . ."

"Here, could you sign on this please? It would be a wonderful souvenir."

She handed him a napkin that had the inn's name on it. "Sure." He tried to sound enthused. A flashing glimpse revealed her more closely than before. *Probably pretty hot ten years ago.* Her plushness was leaning toward fat but she still retained some cuteness within. Short, with a dark coif, and . . . *Stacked,* he noted of the volume of flesh filling the bra. The otherwise boring face and eyes lit up with the elation of being so close to a "star."

"Come on in, let me get a pen. And sorry about the way I'm dressed, I just got out of the shower."

"You smell really good!" she enthused.

Collier frowned at the odd comment as he went to the desk, found a pen.

"Could you make it to Carol and Dan, please?"

"Sure."

"Oh, I can't wait to show my sister! She'll be jealous!"

Collier rolled his eyes and scribbled on the napkin. "Here you go, Carol," he said and turned around.

He gulped. She'd come all the way in and closed the door and was now divorced of her blouse. She sat smiling on the edge of the bed. "I'm game if you are . . ."

Collier just stood there.

The white bra cups blared. Her eyes were huge. "Come here," she whispered. "We don't have much time."

Collier hesitated, then stepped forward till he was standing right before her.

She rubbed his crotch, finagling her hand inside the robe. Collier hissed. Then, with one hand, she expertly reached around, was just about to unhook her bra, when Collier winced and said, "No, don't. I . . ." Then he stepped back.

Her shoulders slumped. "Shit. I'm sorry, I feel like an idiot." And then she blushed and put her blouse back on.

"It's just that"—his mind reeled. "I'm married," he said, as farcical as the notion was. There were dozens of reasons not to proceed with something like this, a giant liability chief among them. She could be crazy. But worst of all was that he'd actually been one hair's width away from going through with it. "It's not you," he mumbled. "You're very attractive—damn! But . . ."

"I understand." Now she was clearly embarrassed, keeping her eyes down. "Nothing wrong with being faithful. Guess that says a thing or two about me . . ."

"But here's your autograph," he said and handed the napkin to her. "I'm glad you like my show . . ."

"Thank you," she said and sheepishly took it. "'Bye," she began but Collier stopped her before she got to the door. It was the oddest sensation, but he pulled her forward and kissed her. She seemed surprised.

"If I weren't married, we'd be getting it on right now . . . Carol . . ."

Her embarrassment dissolved; she smiled. One finger traced up his leg through the robe. "Maybe you'll change your mind later."

Collier said nothing but the look in his eyes said, *Maybe you're right.*

She left the room.

Collier stood there, staring at the closed door. "Unbelievable . . ."

As more minutes ticked by, he twinged at pangs of guilt and regret. Guilt that he'd actually considered having sex with her, and regret that he hadn't. *It would've been a shitty thing to do,* he told himself. *It would've been exploitative.* But then a voice like an alter ego yelled, *What kind of a pussy are you? You'd have been doing her a favor by putting some spice in her drab, boring life. A REAL man doesn't say no to free sex, you asshole!*

Collier blinked, frowning. *No, I guess not.* But it simply wasn't like him to do something like that. If anything, he was on the shy side.

He banished the odd episode from his mind, then started to get dressed.

For a split second he thought he smelled something foul—the stench of old urine—but then he blinked and it was gone.

CHAPTER FIVE

I

"You're more than welcome to join us," Collier was telling Mrs. Butler at the front desk while he helplessly stole glances at her bosom, hips, and plush pelvis.

"Oh, thank you, Mr. Collier but I've got more folks checkin' in tonight. It's a wonderful little restaurant, though, and I doubt that you've got anything close to it in California." Her bosom jiggled a bit; she quickly rose at the sound of people entering the vestibule. "These must be my Philadelphians."

Collier stepped aside as another tourist couple stepped perkily to the desk. He found himself looking up at the oil portrait of Harwood Gast . . .

Stereotypical Southern plantation guy, he thought. The stern face had been painted with detail—the eyes seemed to look specifically at Collier with disdain. *What's so evil about this dude?* He was still piqued by

Mrs. Butler's comments. *Just an old racist slave-driving stick in the mud.*

Several old-wood bookshelves flanked the large portrait, and between two of them Collier noticed a recess, about a yard wide. He figured it used to be an alcove where one might put a statue, but instead there was an old veneered table there, with an odd arrangement of small drawers and letter slots. A tag read: ORIGINAL MAPLE WRITING TABLE—QUEEN ANNE–STYLE—SAVERY AND SONS—1779. When Collier looked harder, he noted an elaborate webwork of minute carvings. Yet on the side of the alcove hung a small oil painting he hadn't noticed before. *Strange* . . . It almost seemed to be hung in that spot so as *not* to be noticed. MRS. PENELOPE GAST, a tiny plaque read. *Gast's wife* . . . An attractive woman with eyes that seemed wanton looked off the canvas, standing before a landscape of trees. A bonnet, a great billowy dress, frilly knickers; the plunging neckline offered a creamy bosom. *So this was Gast's version of the American Dream? This woman, and this house* . . . Yesterday's version of a corporate magnate. *I guess they're all assholes when you get right down to it.* He wondered if they'd had kids.

Mrs. Butler's twang reverberated as she jabbered of the house's historical wonders. The man asked, "Would it be possible to get one of the second-floor rooms facing the mountain? We'd love that view in the morning."

"Oh, I'm terribly sorry, sir," the old woman informed, "all those rooms are taken. But I've got a lovely room for ya on the west wing that opens right on the garden. And you can still see the mountain a bit . . ."

The oddity struck Collier at once. The room right next to his faced the mountain. He remembered Jiff telling him they didn't rent that one out. *I wonder why* . . .

Another display case showed more relics; one caught his eye immediately. HAND-CHISELED STONE MOLD FOR WOOLING SHEARS, and there was a flat piece of stone with a recess shaped like half a pair of big scissors. Beside it lay an actual pair of shears. THESE SHEARS WERE MADE AT THE GAST IRON FORGE LOCATED IN THE BACKYARD—1859.

That's some real work, he thought. He couldn't contemplate how hard things were back then. Even something as simple as a pair of shears took many steps to produce. *Smelting ore, skimming slag, pouring molten iron into a mold without burning the living shit out of yourself or becoming brain-damaged from poisonous fumes.* More handcrafted items from the family forge lay in the case: nails, hinges, door latches. *That stuff must've been hard as hell to make.*

He overheard the Philadelphia woman whisper: "Oh my God! Is that the Prince of Beer over there?"

Shit! Collier had been made again. He acted like he hadn't heard them and slipped out the vestibule doors.

The sun was turning orange as it lowered, a blaze on the horizon. Collier gazed across the well-landscaped front court, smelling mint, moss, and wildflowers. The quiet beauty almost stunned him.

Jiff bopped down the porch steps a moment later, wearing the same jeans and work boots but now he'd put on a black button-down shirt. *Gussied up,* Collier thought, *redneck-style.*

"Ready when you are, Mr. Collier!"

"Okay, Jiff. But if you don't mind, could you show me that little furnace in the back first?"

"My pleasure, sir. *Lotta* interesting things 'round here."

"Yes, there are." Collier followed him around the side of the main house, where a trail skirted the additional wings. "I guess I've lived in L.A. too long, but coming to a place like this really opens your eyes. We take so much for granted these days. Even the displays in the lobby: handmade boots, tools, and even nails that someone hammered out on an anvil, carpet and clothing stitched by hand instead of processed by machinery. It reminds me that this country was built on hard work."

"Very hard work, sir," Jiff agreed. "You wanna build a

house back then, you had to dig the clay and bake the bricks, cut the clapboards from trees ya chopped down yourself, blow the glass for the windows, you name it. And while you're doin' all that hard work, ya gotta eat. So you till the land to grow your food, find a spring or river to water the seeds, and if you want some meat to go with it, you gotta raise the pig yourself, butcher it, and cut *more* wood to cook it. And while you're choppin' that wood you better find the right kind of bark to tan the hide so's you can make the boots on your feet. But a'course if you're gonna do *that,* ya better find some cassiterite to melt down so's ya can make a tin bucket to do your tannin' in. That was life back then. Now we just go to the grocery store and The Home Depot."

Collier chuckled at the parallel. The walk gave him a closer look at the additional four wings of the house. "Why are these wings so differently styled than the main house? It almost—"

"It almost don't look right." Jiff got his point. "The wings are all made'a wood while the main house is fancy brick'n stone. It's 'cos the South was piss-poor for a long time after the war."

"The War of Northern Aggression—"

"Yes, sir. Harwood Gast had a million in gold when he moved into town, and everyone figured he spent it all on his railroad. He finished the railroad in 1862, 'bout a year after the war started. Then he came home . . . and you know what he done?"

"What?"

"Killed hisself. Just after that last spike was drove at the very end of the East Tennessee and Georgia Railroad, way past the border in a place used to be called Maxon."

"Why did he kill himself?"

"Aw, who knows?" The younger man seemed to deflect the question. "But folks figured he bankrupted hisself layin' all that track, but you know what? Turns out he *still* had a million in gold in his accounts. Like he never spent a dime."

"Strange," Collier said, trying to keep the information sorted. "So it wasn't bankruptcy that urged him to commit suicide. I wonder what it was then?"

Jiff still didn't comment. "After the fightin' was finished, Lincoln's boys seized all Gast's gold, but they sold the house. Point I'm trying to make is that the new owners—some'a my ma's kin—could only afford cheaper building materials to do the add-ons."

It made sense. Collier knew that the South fared about as well as Germany after World War I; the people were kept destitute for a while—punishment for their attempted secession. But Jiff had still evaded the topic he was more interested in. *That's . . . curious . . .*

"We live in this wing here. Two'a the others are more guest rooms, and the fourth—you gotta see the fourth, Mr. Collier, since you're interested in this stuff. It's loaded full up with more things from the old days."

"I'd love to see all that."

"And don't forget the bath closet—that's the door just to the right of your room. That's one way rich folks back then showed how well-off they was—by havin' a bath closet and toilet on the second floor near the bedroom. Plain folks just had outhouses and washin' sheds outside."

I guess I even take THAT for granted, Collier reflected. *A pot to piss in.*

They passed the second wing—through a window Collier spotted the newest guests checking in, Lottie lugging their bags—then followed a path through the garden. A slight breeze shifted countless hundreds of colorful blossoms.

When they arrived at the small clearing, Collier found the old furnace larger than it had looked from his room. Flat rocks fixed by mortar formed the large conical structure, which sported several vents at various heights.

"This is incredible," Collier said.

"Yes, sir, it is." Jiff pointed. "That there's the charcoal chute, and there, the ore drop. That l'il one there is the outflow, and there a'course, is the airway," he said, pointing to the pipe that extruded from a bellows the size of a refrigerator. "The smith'd yank this chain, to pump the bellows"—he demonstrated, and they could hear the device whistling air—"and the air'd shoot into the bed. It'd get up to 2,300 degrees in there, turn iron ore or damn near anything else into a red-hot puddle."

Now Collier noticed other features: a cooling barrel, a tool hanger, a grinding wheel and stand. The anvil, which he'd spotted earlier, had a date engraved: 1856. Collier was finding himself staggered by the nostalgia. These weren't props; they were genuine relics of a long-dead way of life. *Real people built this thing,* he thought. *Some guy, in 1856, MADE that anvil with his own two hands.*

"Has anyone used it, I mean, recently?"

Jiff scratched at a mortar seam with a penknife. The material was still hard. "For iron forging? Naw. But there's no reason why it wouldn't still work. You melt the ore against a wall of charcoal while pumpin' the bellows. All we use it for now is cookin' during holiday weekends. Sometimes we'll hang a couple of pig quarters inside and smoke 'em for twenty-four hours with hickory. But way back when, they even had to make their own charcoal; they'd pile up twenty, thirty cords of wood, light the middle, then cover it all over with sod. See, when the carbon in the charcoal mixes with the pig iron, it becomes steel. They didn't even know it back then, but that's what they were makin'. All by hand."

Smart guy for a hayseed, Collier thought. "This is pretty specified information. How do you know so much about it?"

"Grew up 'round all this stuff, so I asked. Most folks in these parts all have ancestors going back to even before the war. You learn a lot when you ask the right folks."

"That you do." Collier was impressed. Behind the charcoal shed he saw a pile of blocks. He picked one up. "Oh, here's another mold like the one your mother has displayed. A scissor mold."

"Shears," Jiff corrected. "Probably took some poor bastard a full day just to chisel *one* of those things."

But Collier saw a veritable pile of them. "That's an awful lot of molds," he pointed out. "Two blocks for each single pair of shears? There must be enough there for fifteen pair."

"Yeah, that is strange. Shears were important tools, a'course, but I don't know why the smith would make so many molds."

"Almost like a production line. I'll bet he made hundreds of pairs with these blocks." Collier thought about it. "I wonder why?"

"Ya got me, Mr. Collier. But the funny thing is there was only one single pair of shears ever found on the property—the one in the display case."

It was an unimportant question but one that needled him. *What the hell did they need all those shears for?*

"Nice, uh, nice car," Jiff remarked when he got into the Bug. "What, it's foreign?"

Collier pulled out of the front court, chuckling. "I got stuck with it at the rental office at the airport. I know it looks ridiculous. It's a woman's car."

Jiff raised a brow.

The horizon darkened as they drove down the hill, the air getting cooler. Collier saw the sign again—PENELOPE STREET—and remembered something. "Would this road be named after Penelope Gast?"

"Yes, sir. You must'a seen the portrait at the house. She was Harwood's freaky wife."

"Why do you say 'freaky'?"

Jiff sighed as much to himself as he could. "Just more

bad talk. See, Mr. Collier, I love this town and got respect for it. I hate to spread garbage talk."

"Come on, Jiff. All towns have their folklore and their notorious figures—big deal. I have the impression there's quite a bit about Harwood Gast that's actually very interesting. To you, it's hundred-and-fifty-year-old gossip but to me, it's fascinating. Let me guess. She killed herself right along with Gast, and now their ghosts prowl the house at night."

"Naw, naw. It's just that she weren't the finest of ladies, if ya know what I mean. She got around."

"Promiscuous wives are part of every town, Jiff."

"Yeah, sure, but, see, she weren't no good at all if ya believe the stories. There's lots of 'em, and they're all bad. Makes me feel like I'm bad-mouthin' my home. We've always tried to tone down that kind'a stuff. It could give the town a bad name, hurt my ma's business."

Collier grinned, egging him on. "Come on, Jiff. Don't jive me."

Jiff shook his head. "All right. Penelope Gast didn't kill herself, it was her husband that murdered her."

"Why? Did he go crazy?"

"No, sir, he killed her 'cos he found out she'd been pregnant with some other fella's kid. What'cha gotta understand is that once the railroad construction started to get close to the Georgia border, Gast would be away from home for weeks at a time. And for months, towards the end."

"The more track they laid, the farther it took him from his house," Collier assumed.

"'Zactly. To get back home to visit, he'd have to take one of his own supply trains that kept feeding track and ties. But there weren't a whole lotta them. He'd have to wait."

"And while he was away—"

Jiff nodded, morose. "She'd take up with other fellas

and got herself pregnant that way three times. She also got herself an abortion three times. They had abortions back then, ya know. I suspect Gast knew all along but waited till the railroad was finished before her killed her."

"He wanted to see his project completed, in other words."

"The railroad was very important to him. He told people that he believed by 1863, the Confederate army would have secured Washington, D.C., and his railroad would be crucial in moving supplies father north."

What a strange way to phrase it, Collier thought. "When you say he 'told' people he believed that . . . do you mean it was just a sham, that there was some other reason he went to the monumental expense and effort of building the railroad?"

"Oh, turn here, Mr. Collier." Jiff leaned forward, pointing. "Cusher's is right there on the corner. Yes, sir, you're gonna *love* the beer they got."

"Yes, but do you think Gast might've—"

"Folks just *rave* about the beer, yes sir. And they got several kinds. Beer expert such as yourself'll really get into it."

Collier smiled. *He's ducking the topic again. That's really bizarre.* He thought it best to drop it for now, but in all, he couldn't have been more intrigued.

With the sun dipping behind the mountain now, the light was being sapped. Streetlights with carriage lamp tops were coming on; shop windows glowed bright. Now that they were downtown, Collier thought of a dollhouse community: spotless streets, storefronts and building walls shiny in new paint, picture-perfect flower displays. Even the people were immaculate, mostly married couples strolling the quaint streets, window shopping. *No riffraff,* Collier saw with some relief. Typically he'd see psychotic bums sullying Rodeo Drive and Crips and Bloods blemishing Redondo.

"And there it is."

Collier saw the cursive sign—CUSHER'S—topping a slat-shingled awning on the corner. CIVIL WAR CUISINE AND HAND-CRAFTED BEER. The building itself stood three stories, ideal for a brewery, which processed beer from top floors to the bottom, exploiting gravity. Large windows showed a full dining room.

"Wow, not what I thought," Collier admitted. "I pictured a small place, kind of a dive."

"Oh, no, sir," Jiff spoke up. "It's fancy inside, and, well, big-city prices, if you wanna know the truth."

"Makes sense, for tourists."

More passersby shot funky looks at the car when he parked. Collier just shook his head. As night beckoned, the little town seemed to bloom in crisp yellow light and smiling strollers.

He grinned the instant he got out of the car. *You can tell there's a brewery here . . .* He took in the familiar aroma: the mash of barley malt being heated.

Inside, waiters wore the Confederate equivalent to military dress blues; waitresses were adorned in white bonnets, billowy skirts, and frilled, low-cut white tops. A line formed at the hostess stand, and Jiff muttered, "We ain't waitin' for a table, not when I tell 'em we got a TV celebrity here."

Collier grabbed his arm, afret—"No, please, Jiff. I'd rather sit up at the bar."

"Cool."

Jesus, Collier thought. Brick, brass, and dark veneered wood surrounded them, while framed Civil War regalia hung on the walls. A tourist trap, yes, but Collier liked it for its divergence from L.A. big-time, and its effort. "Great bar," he enthused of the long mahogany top and traditional brass rail. Buried in the bar top's crystal clear resin were bullets, buttons, and coins from the era. Another familiar—and pleasing—sight greeted him at once. Behind the bar, service tuns—beer's final stage before consumption—shined with edges of gold light, cask-shaped brass vessels the size of compact cars. A chalkboard posted the specialties: GENERAL LEE RUBIN, STONEWALL JACKSON MAIBOCK, PICKETT'S PILS, and CUSHER'S CIVIL WAR LAGER. Collier started a tab with his credit card and ordered two lagers from a barmaid who would've been nondescript save for a bosom like the St. Pauli Girl.

"I guess them big things there are where they brew the beer." Jiff gestured the brass vessels.

"They're called service tuns," Collier explained. "The beer's actually brewed in bigger tuns upstairs called brewing vessels, but it all starts in the mash tun. There are about ten steps to making beer, and beers like these—lagers—take at least two months to ferment."

Jiff clearly couldn't have cared less; he was just looking for familiar faces.

He seemed to be searching the crowd for someone, to the point that Collier began to look around himself, hoping not to be missing something. *He must be eyeballing girls . . .* A moment later, an attractive diner in her twenties sailed by: tight stonewashed jeans and a tube top that satcheled prominent breasts. *What a hottie . . .* He got a crook in his neck watching her wend between tables. But then he saw that Jiff hadn't so much as cast her a glance.

Before Collier could focus his newfound sexism on other diners, two pilsner glasses were placed before them. Collier immediately expected a Samuel Adams rip-off when he noted the sharp amber color, but when he raised the glass and sniffed . . .

"Oh, man. Great nose," he said.

Jiff looked perplexed. "Who? The barmaid?"

Collier sighed. "No, Jiff. That's how beer writers describe a beer's aroma. A rich but tight aroma like this means the brewer uses good water without a lot of minerals. It's also a sign of extensive filtering and refusal to cut corners with pasteurization."

"Uh-huh."

Collier reexamined the beer's color, as if the glass were a scryer's ball, then, *Here goes,* and he took the first sip, holding it in his mouth.

The emergence of the grain was immediate. The astringency of the hops—six-row, he was sure—rounded off after the initial sensation that experts called mouth-feel. After the first swallow, Collier's palate delighted in the complex, if not perfect, finish. "This is outstanding," he said.

Jiff had chugged half of his already. "Yeah, good stuff."

Good stuff. This guy wouldn't know the difference between Schlitz and Schutzenberger Jubilator. But what did he expect? Two sips later, the beer continued to retain all of its character. "Oh, how about ordering us something to eat, Jiff. Have whatever you like; I'll just take a burger." But food couldn't have interested him less right now. Further sips drew the lace down low; then he let the last inch sit for a few minutes to see what characteristics appeared or vanished as the lager's open temperature rose.

"So you like it, huh?"

"Indeed, I do, Jiff." Collier sat calm and sedate, the awe of any beer snob who'd come across a surprise. "This might be one of the best American lagers I've ever tasted."

"Didn't you say somethin' earlier 'bout how you'd heard of Cusher's from someone else?"

"Actually, yes. A few friends in the field had tried it—but they couldn't remember the name of the town. So I did some Web searches to try to pin the place down. In fact—" Collier extracted a folded printout. "Maybe you could help me with something."

"Help ya anyway I can, Mr. Collier. Say, can we order two more?"

"Oh, yes, yes, of course." Collier opened the sheet of paper. "Like I said, I was Web-searching—"

Jiff's eyed scrunched up. "Web—You mean, like, spiderwebs? Thought you were beer searching."

How could Collier not appreciate that? "No, Jiff. The World Wide Web—"

"Oh, that 'puter stuff, information highway'n all," Jiff assented.

"Yes." He didn't know whether to laugh or cry. The sheet he'd printed out off the "dining out" section of an obscure Southern-tourist Web site. The passage he'd flagged read:

> . . . *some of the most extensive collections of authentic Civil War regalia in the South, not to mention Cusher's, the only restaurant in the South that features a menu of genuine Civil War cuisine and beers brewed from actual recipes dating back to 1860.*

The address was found at the bottom along with the name of the article's author: J.G. SUTE, AUTHOR OF FIVE BOOKS AND THE AREA'S HISTORICAL SCHOLAR.

"See, right here." Collier pointed to the bottom. "This man, J.G. Sute. It says he's a local scholar. Have you ever heard of him?"

For whatever reason, Jiff stalled. Then he blinked and answered, "Oh, sure, ole J.G. we call him. He's a townie, all right."

"Sounds like he's a successful author."

Another weird stall. "Oh, sure, Mr. Collier. He's written some books."

"About local breweries, by chance?"

Jiff still seemed off guard but was trying not to show it. "No, sir, not that I know of. He writes history books, mainly books about this town."

"Books about Gast?"

"Yeah, sure, and how the town worked into the war'n all. And also local history and such."

Damn. Collier was hoping for an area culinary writer who might point him in the right direction of any similar breweries. "I'd really like to talk to him but he's not in the phone book. Where might I find him?"

What's wrong with this guy now? Collier wondered after asking the question. Was it his imagination, or was Jiff uneasy about this man Sute?

"Well, he usually eats here every day for lunch, sometimes hangs out at the bar down the corner at night." Jiff wiped his brow with a napkin. "Uh, and he spends a lot of time at the bookstore durin' the day, hawkin' his books. The owner don't mind 'cos he's a talkative kind'a guy and he gets tourists to buy stuff."

Collier *had* to ask. "Jiff, you really seem bothered that I asked about this guy."

The younger man sighed, clearly ill at ease. "Aw, no, it's just—"

"He's a local gossip? You don't want him bad-mouthing the town?"

"No, no—"

"Then you don't want to bad-mouth *him?* This guy's like—what? The local jackass? Some old cracker-barrel kind of guy, mostly full of crap? The town dick?"

At least Jiff cracked a smile now. "He's a nice enough guy, but yeah, pretty much everything you just said. Ain't *that* old—late fifties, early sixties, I think. Drives around in his brand-new Caddy talkin' his malarkey. Nice set of wheels, though. One'a them fancy Caddy SUVs. Enchilada it's called."

Enchil—oh, the rube means Escalade. "So he *is* successful from his books. A brand-new one of those will set you back fifty grand minimum."

Jiff shrugged and kind of nodded.

"Do you know him well? Are you friends?"

Jiff sprang a gaze at Collier that was nearly one of fright. "Aw, no, er, I mean, I know him, sure, but—" He gulped. "But only 'cos I do odd jobs for him, handyman-type stuff. I do a lot'a work on the side for folks, includin' him. Trimmin' hedges, fixin' doors'n windows and such."

But it seemed like an excuse. *Jiff probably owes the guy money or something, doesn't want me talking to him and winding up with the scoop.* Again, Collier dropped the mysteriously sensitive issue after saying, "I'll try to find him at the bookstore, like you said. I just want to ask about local beers."

Next, Collier winced when the barmaid's low-cut bosom descended to serve them their burgers. *Do I have to lust after EVERY GIRL WHO WALKS BY?* he scorned himself. He tried to refocus.

The burger was fine, but he couldn't stop enthusing over the beer. By the time he finished his second glass of lager, Jiff looked sheepish at him. "Is it all right if—"

"Jiff, order as many as you want. I told you, tonight's my treat."

"Thanks, Mr. Collier."

Collier tried to cheer him out of his mope. "And I really appreciate you bringing me here." Collier pointed to his glass. "I'm sure that this is the beer I need to finish my book and make my deadline . . ."

Eventually, Jiff did cheer up, as drunkenness impinged. Collier's rule was generally to never drink more than three beers in a day, so that he could write down his impressions with a clear head. However, when his third glass was done—*Oh, to hell with it. I'm on vacation*—he ordered another.

"Careful there, Mr. Collier," Jiff warned. "This brew's got a kick that sneaks up on ya."

You're telling ME? "Five percent alcohol, I'll bet."

"Five point three," a crisp but feminine voice cut in.

It wasn't the barmaid but instead a woman Collier thought must be a cook, for she wore a plain full-length apron.

"Specific gravity or volume?" Collier asked pedantically.

"Volume," she replied.

"Wow, that is strong. But it doesn't taste that strong."

"That's because of the six-row Bohemian hops, the same hops that were brought here by Czech immigrants in the early 1840s."

The specific remarks reached through Collier's rising buzz. *She knows her beer.* And then he took a closer look. Hair black as India ink hung just a bit past her shoulders. She seemed small-framed but something in her eyes showed him a large-framed sense of confidence. Collier's sexism ranged his eyes over her bosom but the baggy apron wouldn't hint at her size. An ornate silver cross sparkled just below the hollow of her throat.

When he tried to say something, though, he caught her staring at him.

"I don't believe it. Justin Collier is in my bar."

"Dang straight!" Jiff announced a bit too loudly. "A bonner-fide TV star he is!"

Collier winced.

"Hey, Jiff," the woman leaned to whisper. "Mr. Collier probably doesn't want a lot of attention."

"No, actually I don't," Collier said, relieved.

"Oh, sure, sure." Jiff got it. "Say, how about a couple more?"

The woman poured two more glasses and set them down. Then she extended a small but somewhat roughened hand. *Probably from dishwashing,* Collier presumed.

"I'm Dominique Cusher, Mr. Collier," she introduced. "It's a real pleasure to have you here. If you want to know the truth, your show is about the only thing I watch on television these days. I really love it."

"Thanks," Collier said. "Pleased to meet you."

She held up a finger. "But, I remember a couple episodes ago, you were touting that new *Rauchbier* from Oregon. Whew! You actually *like* that codswallop? They cut their barley with *corn,* and I could swear I tasted Liquid Smoke in it."

Collier laughed at the surprising, bold remark. He didn't really care for the product, either, but the question nagged, *What the hell is a dishwasher doing drinking an obscure smoked beer?* "Well, sometimes business has its demands. Every now and then I have to give a nod to a beer that's not all that great."

Now she smiled. "Oh, I understand. Advertisers."

"Bingo."

"I have to do the same thing, too. It kills me to post a Bud happy hour . . . but if we run the special we get a discount. Don't know how people can drink it."

"But more people drink it than anything else," Collier noted. "Business is business. One has to accommodate the market. But let me just say that this house lager is excellent. Could you please pass my compliments on to the brewer?"

"You just did," she said.

Collier was stunned. "You—"

"That's right, Mr. Collier," she said with no arrogance. "I've got a master brewer degree from the Kulmbach School, and I took supplemental courses at Budvar in Budejovice and Tucher in Nuremberg." She pointed between two of the service tuns. There hung the certificates in plain view.

"That's incredible," he said. In fifteen years of beer writing, he'd never met any American to graduate from Kulmbach, and perhaps only two or three women with master brewer certificates from anywhere. Suddenly, to Collier, *she* was the celebrity. At once, he felt invigorated. *This fiery little woman with black hair and rough hands is the one responsible for what has to be one of the finest lagers in America . . . Dominique Cusher.*

Jiff seemed content to be out of the conversation as

he swigged more beer and shoveled in the rest of his burger. Dominique leaned over on her elbows, smiling. "I guess you're on vacation, right? I can't be arrogant enough to think you came all this way to try my Civil War Lager."

"Actually, I did. A couple of fellow beer snobs told me about it." He took another sip and found no trace of monotony. "It really is fantastic."

"Mr. Collier here's finishin' up a book," Jiff barged in.

Collier nodded. "I need one more entry for my Great American Lagers project. I don't want to jump the gun, now, but I'm pretty sure this is going to be it."

"That would be a true honor." She tried to contain the thrill. But her eyes sparkled. "No palate fatigue yet, huh?"

"None," Collier admitted. "I'm not finding any deficits. Let me buy *you* one. It's known as good luck—"

"To buy the brewer a glass of their own beer," she finished. "Goes all the way back to the Reinheitsgebot Purity Law." Dominique poured herself one, then clinked glasses with Collier and Jiff (though Jiff's slopped a bit out of his glass).

"Prost," she and Collier said at the same time.

"Who's he?" Jiff said.

"It's German for 'cheers,' Jiff," she informed.

"Aw, yeah, that's right . . ."

Collier smiled at her. "I'd try some of your other selections, too, but I should wait. I don't want anything to interfere with my initial impressions of the lager. Is there anything unique about the recipe that you could tell me?"

"It's a family tweak," she said. She seemed to nurse her glass in exact increments. "A variation of Saaz hops and some temperature jinks in the worting process. But please don't tell anyone that. My ancestors would crawl out of their graves to come after me."

"So you're a family of brewers?"

"Yep. This tavern's been here in various incarnations

since the beginning of the 1800s, and the Cushers managed to hang on to it all that time, even through the war. When federal troops captured the town in 1864, they burned every single building downtown *except* this tavern. When the Yankees tried the beer, they didn't dare put a torch to the place."

"Good sense."

"The only other structure they didn't burn was the Gast House, now Mrs. Butler's bed-and-breakfast."

"I wonder why they didn't burn that, too," Collier questioned. "They were pretty torch-happy once they started to win."

"Jiff can tell you that," she said.

Again, that pained look on Jiff's face. "Aw, come on, Dominique. I been tryin' hard not to let any of that creepy B.S. get ta Mr. Collier."

"I knew it," Collier said. "Ghost stories. Haunted folklore."

"The way it goes," the woman began, "is that when the Union commander sent a team of men up to the Gast House, he had to wind up putting them in the stockade."

"The stockade? What on earth for?"

"Because they refused to carry out their orders."

"They refused to burn the house, you mean?"

Dominique nodded with a mischievous grin. "They said they were too afraid to go inside, said there was an ungodly presence."

Jiff frowned, as expected, but Collier wasn't impressed. "That's all?"

"No. Then another squad of men were sent up to the house, and . . ." Her eyes shined at Jiff. "Jiff, tell Mr. Collier what happened."

"Shee-it," Jiff said under his breath. "The second squad never came back, so's the Yankee commander went up there hisself and saw that the whole squad hanged thereselfs."

"From the same tree that Harwood Gast had hanged himself a year and a half previous. The tree's still there, too, right Jiff? That giant oak next to the fountain."

"Yeah, but it all ain't nothin' but a bushel basket full'a horse flop, Mr. Collier."

Collier chuckled. "I've got to tell you, Jiff, it's a fascinating story, but . . . I don't believe any of it. So you can relax."

"Thank God . . ."

"Regional folklore has always interested me, but at the end of the day," Collier said, and paused for effect. "I don't believe in ghosts."

"But Jiff's right," Dominique added. "There are a lot of ghost stories around here, typical of any Civil War town. Funny thing is, *our* stories are a bit harder-edged than most."

"Harder-*edged?*" Collier asked.

Jiff butted in again. "So, wow, that's really interestin', that this beer's been around since the war. I didn't even know they *had* beer way back then."

Collier knew Jiff was desperate to change the subject. *But why would silly ghost stories bother him so much?* Another Southern cliché? Were people from the South more superstitious than anyone else? Collier doubted it. But the pedant in him couldn't resist the deflecting remark. "Actually, Jiff, beer's been around for at least eight thousand years, and in earlier civilizations, it was the main carbohydrate staple. Before man figured out that they could turn grain into bread, they were turning it into beer."

Dominique accentuated, "Early nomads discovered that they could boil ground-up grain, like barley, wheat, and millet, and eat it as a porridge. But when they accidentally let it sit around, or when rain would saturate their grain stores, it would ferment and become ale. It had the same nutritional value as bread but it wouldn't go bad, like bread does, because of the alcohol content. And let's not forget the additional fact. You don't get a buzz from bread . . ."

Collier and Dominique spent the next half hour bantering more about beer. When he offered to buy her another, she declined with a comment that struck Collier as odd: "No, thanks. I never drink more than one beer a day."

Collier found this astonishing. "But you're a brewer, for God's sake."

"Well, that's sort of the point." She said it all very nonchalantly. "I'm a Christian. I don't let myself get drunk. You know, the body's a temple of the Lord, and all that."

Collier's eyes shot back to the cross around her neck. *What an odd thing to say* . . . He struggled for a response that wasn't stilted. "Well, Jesus drank wine, right?"

White teeth gleamed in her grin. "Yeah, but he didn't get shit-faced and swing from chandeliers."

Collier had to laugh.

"And that's the kind of stuff that happens when *I* drink too much," she went on, "so . . . one's my limit. I figure the least I can do is not insult God by getting pissy drunk."

Collier was intrigued by the strangeness of it all. The mild profanity mixed with a matter-of-fact religious sentiment. "My own personal rule is no more than three a day; it's no fun to write about beer when you're hungover." Then he looked at his glass and realized that he'd just finished his fourth. "But I'm being a hypocrite today. One more please. And another for Jiff."

"Thanks much, Mr. Collier," Jiff said, slurring "much" as "mlush" and "Mr." as "Mlister."

When Dominique returned with two more, Collier felt the need to continue. "But I've never thought of having a few beers as much of a sin. At least I hope it's not."

"Inebriation leads to temptation," she said. She was unconsciously fingering her cross now.

"I've definitely been guilty of that," Collier admitted.

"Sure, and we all have. Making an effort to stay sober is a form of repentance"—she frowned as if irritated with herself—"but I'm not trying to Holy Roll you. It's just my personal view. Spiritual beliefs are individual. When you're in the bar business as long as I've been, you learn fast—"

"Never talk about religion in a bar." Collier knew.

"You got that right. Anyway, I don't want you to think I'm a Holy Roller. Telling other people how to live is the worst hypocrisy. I think it's best to show your faith by example, not chatter and finger-pointing. If you're a Christian, Jew, Muslim, Buddhist, whatever. Live it, don't talk it is what I try to do."

This girl is cool, Collier realized. He also realized he was half drunk. *Don't make a dick of yourself!* "You weren't telling me how to live, you were just explaining why you only drink one beer a day. Beer snobbery is a sophisticated science. If you drink too many, you might as well be guzzling domestic draft—"

"Because no one can appreciate the nuances of fine beer, not with a load on."

God, I really dig her, Collier acknowledged to himself. Even the way she talked—half colloquial, half philosophical—seemed sexy. She looked at her watch, then excused herself. "I have to go upstairs and check the wort. But please don't leave yet."

"Wouldn't think of it. I might even have to have a sixth glass of your lager. See, my rules go out the window pretty fast," he joked, "but I can only blame you."

"Me?"

"For being the purveyor of one of the very best lagers in America."

She smiled at the overt compliment, then slipped away through a door behind the bar.

Jiff leaned over, concerned. "Shee-it, Mr. Collier. She say she had *warts?* Man, you don't want none'a that."

Collier was quickly learning to frown and smile in amusement simultaneously. "Not warts, Jiff. *Wort.* Wort is beer before the yeast and hops have been added. After the solution ferments and is filtered of its excess proteins, it officially becomes beer."

"Oh, yeah, well, now that I thunk of it, I'm pretty sure I knew that, and, yes, it's a damn good thing she ain't got warts. Not that I ever had 'em—you know, the sexual kind—" Jiff pronounced it "sax-shool." "And I say it's plain as barn paint she got a serious torch fer you."

Collier's unconfident eyes looked at him. "You . . . really think so, Jiff?"

Jiff's head lolled back with a big shucksy grin. "Shee-it, Mr. Collier. Her face was plumb all lit up like a pinball machine when you and her was talkin' all that beer talk." Then Jiff wheezed a chuckle, and elbowed Collier. "And—aw, shee-it—I can tell ya someone else who's got a fierce likin' fer ya, but don't ya dare say I said so—"

"Lottie," Collier supposed.

"Aw, yeah, sure, but I ain't talkin' 'bout that silly string bean. I mean my ma."

Collier was duped. *This guy's telling me that his MOTHER is attracted to me?* "Uh, really?" he said.

"And I gots to tell ya, there's dudes twenty years younger asking my ma out all the dang time. Yeah, I know, she's a bit raggy in the face but that's some body on her, ain't it?" And then another elbow jabbed Collier in the side.

Collier couldn't imagine an appropriate response, so he just said, "Your mother's very nice indeed, Jiff, and very attractive for her age."

"Yeah, she is, and ya wanna know how I know she likes ya? Huh?"

"Uuuuuuum . . . sure."

"It weren't that she told me, now, but it's 'cos whenever a single fella checks in that she's got a twinkle for, she gives him room three. Your room."

Collier's brain chugged through preinebriation. *What the hell? What could my room have to do with* . . . "Oh, you mean because it's better than the other rooms?"

"Naw, naw." Jiff waved his hand. He elbowed Collier one more time and whispered, "It's 'cos of the view. Bet she even told ya that, huh? That room three's got the best view?"

"Actually, she did but—" The ridiculous conversation was growing *more* ridiculous. *I guess the view from my balcony is pretty good but it's nothing really special.* "The view of the mountain? The garden?"

"Naw, naw," Jiff wheezed in his own amusement. He slapped his knees. "I'm gonna leave ya in suspense, Mr. Collier." A glance to the bar clock. "I best git my tail back to the house 'cos I still got some work to do."

"Oh, well, let me drive you back."

Another dismissive wave of hand. "Naw, naw, wouldn't think of it. You stay here'n jaw with Dominique. It ain't but a ten-minute walk and tell ya the truth I could use some fresh air 'cos I am more hammered than a hunnert-year-old fence post." Jiff wobbled when he pushed his stool out. "But thanks again for treatin' me, Mr. Collier. You really are a swell guy"—he winked—"and one I'd be proud to see datin' my ma."

I don't believe it. This guy's trying to set me up with his MOTHER. "Uh, yeah, Jiff, thanks for coming out." He awkwardly shook Jiff's hand and bid him a good night.

Yep. Strange damn day—the bar clock showed him it was only nine P.M.—*and it's not even over yet.*

He turned on his stool just to people-watch but noticed Jiff walking the wrong way up the street. *The inn's in the opposite direction* . . . But what did it matter? *Probably bored shitless listening to Dominique and me talk beer facts.* Still . . .

Collier got up and walked to the front window; Jiff took uneven strides to the corner and entered a door under a neon sign. *Another bar,* Collier realized. The one

Jiff had mentioned earlier, where this man J.G. Sute frequented? But again Collier couldn't imagine why he cared. Jiff was a hardworking and no doubt hard-drinking Southern rube; not the kind of guy to spend much time in a tourist spot like Cusher's. Collier squinted through the glass. He thought he could barely make out the neon: THE RAILROAD SPIKE.

Dumbest name I ever heard for a bar . . . He turned back for his bar stool, hoping Dominique would return. *I can't wait to talk to her some more* . . . In Collier's business, he met few women he could relate to professionally. *And she's cute as hell* . . . But then he felt as though fate had just hit him in the face with a pie when he got back to his seat and found Lottie sitting in the stool Jiff had just vacated.

I thought she had to do laundry!

He put on his best face. "Hi, Lottie."

She gave him a big smile and waved.

"Finished your work early, I see."

She wagged her head up and down. She'd pinned her hair back and changed into a shocking tight evening dress that was diaphanous black. *Jesus,* Collier thought. *She looks like a slot queen on a casino boat.* Redneck housemaids needn't dress like this, but there was Collier again, supporting the stereotype. *Why shouldn't the poor girl go out to a bar?* He struggled not to shake his head when he noted her shoes: black high heels several sizes too large. Collier thought of an adolescent trying on her mother's shoes, to feel grown up.

But despite her petite frame, the rest of her *was* grown up, and the howlingly inappropriate dress spotlighted her body. Immediately, he noticed an absence of pantie lines . . .

A lot of dichotomies here, Collier pondered: Mrs. Butler, the equivalent of Raquel Welch's physique circa 1980 topped by an old man's head with a wig; Dominique, the beautiful European-trained brewmaster who only drinks one beer a day because she's a Christian; and now Lottie, a racehorse bod who couldn't talk and had a face that . . . wasn't the prettiest. But after all the quirks that had already befallen Collier today, what else could he expect?

Lottie crossed her legs in the tight gown, a foot rocking. Collier gritted his teeth after one glance at the athletic legs, and a spark came to his groin when he imagined them entwined about his back. *Oh, man* . . . Next, his eyes flicked to her top and noticed the pert, braless breasts free behind the shiny black fabric, nipples erect. Then a glance to her face . . .

Absurd, excited, half-crazy eyes and a warped grin.

"Uh, would you like to something to eat?"

Grinning, she shook her head no.

"How about a beer?"

She wagged her head yes.

Collier ordered her a lager from the first barmaid. He felt obliged to engage in conversation with Lottie but of course he couldn't do that, could he?

Please, Dominique. Finish checking the wort and get back here.

"Oh, you just missed Jiff," he thought to mention.

She nodded and slugged a quarter of the beer in one gulp. The glass looked huge in her little hand.

"Looks like he went down the street to another bar."

She put her hand to her mouth as if laughing. Her other hand slapped her bare knee.

"I . . . don't get it." He thought back. "Oh, do you know this local historian? J.G. Sute?"

Now she belly-laughed—silently, of course—but this time slapped Collier's knee.

"I still don't get it. What, is Mr. Sute a funny man?"

Another silent belly-howl, and her hand slid halfway up his thigh and squeezed.

The pig in Collier didn't really mind her hand there, but . . . *Not here!* Dominique would be back, and he didn't want her to witness this weirdo spectacle. Just as he contemplated a way to remove it, she slipped it higher, her thumb edging his crotch—

That's it!

He plucked the hand off and put in her lap. But she was still silently laughing.

"Come on, Lottie. What's so funny about this guy Sute? He's, like, the town fool?"

Lottie slugged more beer while roving her hand in a circle.

"You'll tell me later?"

More rapid nods.

Collier frowned. He knew it was his own flaw, though—his intent curiosity. *Why can't I forget about all this bullshit and just finish my book? That's what I'm here for, not gossip.*

Nor was he here to revel in all this lust. He tried to glance around inadvertently, but anytime his eyes fell on an attractive woman, his crotch tingled. It got to the point that he forced himself not to look anywhere. He pretended to peruse the cased uniforms on display but even this he couldn't do without catching a glimpse of someone. Eventually he pointed to a case of Confederate double-breasted frock coats. "Lots of uniforms here," he said, if only to not sit in silence.

Lottie tapped him on the shoulder, looked right at him, and mouthed *I love you!*

Somebody please shoot me, Collier thought. He struggled for *anything* to deflect his unease. "So, uh, are you, uh, sure you don't want something to eat?"

You! she mouthed and grinned.

He pretended not to understand. *I'm dying here.* His next errant glance fell on her foot in the too-big shoe, which she was still anxiously rocking.

Even her *ankle* was attractive. Even the *vein* up the top of her foot seemed erotic.

I need help! I need a counselor!

Relief emptied on him when Dominique reappeared behind the bar. She'd removed her brewer's apron, sporting full B-cups and a trim, curvy figure with wide hips and a flat stomach. The plain attire—jeans and a white cardigan—only augmented her unique, radiant cuteness. She seemed to repress a smile when she saw who was sitting next to Collier. "Hi, there, Lottie."

Lottie waved energetically, and gulped her beer.

"How's the wort?" Collier asked.

"Yeasting nicely. It's for the next batch of Maibock."

"I'll have to try that after I've notated the lager well enough." He watched her washing barley dust off her hands in the triple sinks behind the bar. *She's just . . . absolutely . . . adorable . . .*

Lottie's hand opened on his thigh and pressed down. Collier almost flinched until he saw that she was just pushing off his leg to get off her stool. *She's faced!* "Here, let me help you." He stood and got her to her feet. She grinned up cockeyed at him; the top of her head came to his nipple. She mouthed something and made hand gestures, then turned and clopped away in the big shoes.

"I guess she wants to leave now."

"I think she just wants to go to the bathroom," Dominique said.

Collier watched the tight buttocks clench with each drunken step. "My God, I hope she doesn't fall," he muttered. "Maybe I should help her."

"Probably not the best idea," Dominique replied. Now she was polishing some slim *altbier* glasses. "She'd pull you *into* the bathroom with her. She's a card, all right, but I guess you're realizing that."

"You have no idea." He retook his stool and sighed.

"The poor girl's so messed up. And you shouldn't have given her a beer; she can't even hold one."

Collier saw that Lottie's big pint glass stood empty.

"She'll be a handful getting back to Mrs. Butler's place, just so you know in advance."

He nodded grimly. "I'll get her out of here. Hopefully she won't pass out in the ladies' room."

Dominique laughed. "That's happened a few times. She's actually a very nice girl and handles her problems well . . . *except* when she drinks. You'll see."

Collier caught the attractive brewer grinning. *Oh, boy.* With no apron now to cover her upper chest, Collier's eyes were rioting to stare. *Don't stare!* He almost bit down on his lower lip. *And don't drink any more. You're drunk!* The need to make a good impression overwhelmed him, but now he knew that if he even talked too much, he might slur his words.

"Care for one more?"

"No, thanks. I've had a few too many already," he admitted. "If I had one more, I'd make an idiot of myself in front of you. I wish I had your moderation."

"You should've seen *me* in my younger days."

Another interesting remark. *I'll bet she was an animal.* As for the "younger days" comment—*How old can she be? She can't be much more than thirty.* When she polished the next glass, he noticed that all of her fingers lacked rings.

Ohhhhhhhhhhhhhhhhh . . .

"I'd really like to talk to you some more," Collier braved, "but I've got to get back to the hotel. Do you work tomorrow?"

"All day till seven. And I'd really like to talk to you some more, too, Mr. Collier."

"Oh, no, call me Justin." *She gets off tomorrow at seven. Ask her out, you pussy!* that other voice challenged. But even in his heavyweight-lager buzz, he knew that would be the wrong move.

"Here's your check, Justin." She had his bill in her hand.

Collier fumbled for his credit card, then exclaimed, "No!"

She ripped it up. "But this one's on the house."

"Dominique, please, that's not necessary." Collier got the same treatment in a lot of pubs, mostly from owners wanting mention on his show.

"And, don't worry, I'm not trying to bribe you for a good review. It's just nice to have you here."

"Well, thanks very much. But I'm pretty sure that I want to put your lager in my book, if you don't mind signing a release form."

"Oh, of course I don't mind, but wait until you get your secondary impression first."

What an overtly ethical thing to say. She smiled at him again—a reserved yet confident expression. The cross at her bosom shined like her teeth. "Actually, it *was* a bribe for something."

"Oh, yeah?"

"A picture, for our wall." She pointed to several autographed snapshots: some sports figures, a horror author he'd never heard of, a soap opera star, and, yes, Bill Clinton.

"I'd be happy to pose for a picture, just not tonight, please. Tomorrow, when I'm sober."

"You got a deal, Mr.—Justin." Dominique glanced aside. "Here comes your charge."

Lottie limped back between some tables, the perennial nut-job grin on her face. She'd lost one of the overlarge high heels. *What a nightmare,* Collier thought. "I'll see you tomorrow."

"Good night."

Collier rushed to Lottie and turned her toward the door. "This way, Lottie."

She objected, pointing behind.

"No, no more beer for you. Jesus, Lottie, your mother's going to think *I* got you drunk." He shouldered her out the door, an arm braced about her waist. She clip-clopped along on one foot bare and one shoed. She appeared to be giggling in silence. Crossing the street was so cumbersome, Collier stopped, pulled off the remaining shoe, and threw it in the bushes. "They're too big for you anyway. Lottie, you only had *one beer!* How can you be this drunk?"

Her finger roved through his hair; then she tried to put the other hand down his shirt.

"No, no, none of that! We're going home!"

In the parking lot he heard from a distance, "Hey, there's that Prince of Beer guy with that drunk girl!"

Shit! He fumbled at the passenger door.

"Let's go ask him for an autograph!" a woman's voice shrilled.

"Get in!" He dropped Lottie in the car like a couple of grocery bags, then huffed around, assed into the driver's seat, and sped off. He thunked over a curb—*Idiot!*—then realized he hadn't put his lights on. He thunked over another curb, then almost hit a corner mailbox searching for the headlights knob. *This fuckin' car!* Finally he snapped them on and veered onto Penelope Street.

Thank God it's not far . . . He could see the Gast House all alight at the top of the hill. *Nice and slow,* he thought, settling down. *Just another quarter mile—*

Suddenly Collier couldn't see. His heart shouted in his chest when the wheel slipped, and he felt the vehicle go off the hardtop.

Fwap! Fwap! Fwap! Fwap!

He was mowing down bushes on the roadside. All he could see now were Lottie's bare breasts in his face. She'd dropped her shoulder straps and was trying to straddle him in the driver's seat—

"Lottie, for shit's sake!"

One of her hands clamped his crotch and squeezed.

"You're going to get us killed!" He shoved her back, and—

Thud!

She slid across the dash and fell into the passenger-side foot well, flat on her back. Then—

No movement.

Collier had managed to stop the car a yard short of the largest oak tree in the front court. He backed up slowly, then realized this:

That's the tree Harwood Gast hanged himself from . . .

He pulled his eyes off the sprawling tree, then idled to the parking lot.

No lights lit the half-filled lot; only moonlight traced into the car. Collier let his heart settle down again. In the moonlight, he found both of Lottie's bare feet in his lap . . .

He put his hands on them, paused, then moved them off.

She wasn't moving. *Christ, with my luck she broke her neck when she fell!* He leaned down and felt her throat. *Thank God.* There was a steady pulse.

Feeling weird, he looked closer at her, then gulped when he realized that one bare breast was exposed, its nipple dark and pointed like a Hershey's Kiss.

Man . . .

The toned legs seemed radiant in the moonlight. Then he looked at her face: serene and peaceful.

The silly ditz is out cold.

Then . . .

Would it be, like, sexual misconduct if I . . .

He couldn't believe what he'd considered. *I wanted to feel her breast . . . An UNCONSCIOUS girl's breast . . .*

He didn't think about it, or at least tried not to, but then that other voice—the alter ego, the *id*—seemed to whisper, *Go ahead. What's the big deal?*

His hand reached down without any guidance from his mind . . .

He pulled it back.

What a wuss! Go ahead! Cop a feel! Any REAL man would!

He ground his fists together.

Come on! She'll never know!

It troubled Collier more than significantly: the amount of time it took to decide not to. *I'm REALLY screwed up* . . .

But then . . . something else occurred to him as the memory flashed: his keyhole this afternoon, and the immaculate, hairless pubis displayed in it, and the unique freckle.

It was probably Lottie, and . . . judging by her behavior tonight, I'd say there's a 99 percent chance.

More curiosity, then.

He already knew that she wore no panties beneath the tight, diaphanous dress . . .

I'm just seeing if it was her, that's all, he thought as if to offer an excuse.

He raised her motionless leg, angled it away . . .

The moonlight didn't reach that low so, very briefly, he turned on the dome light—thought, *Pervert!*—and glanced down between her legs.

Wrong again.

There was quite a bit of pubic hair down there, a veritable pie wedge–shaped *tuft* of it.

He took a breath, clicked the light back off . . . and found himself shaking slightly.

The other voice again: *Shit, she only weighs a hundred pounds. Take her in the woods and have a go. Who's going to know?*

Collier could imagine the headlines. TV BEER GURU RECEIVES TEN YEARS FOR DATE RAPE.

His mind swam. He was *mortified* that the idea had even occurred to him. *Got to get her back in the house. Now.*

Eventually he got her shoulder strap back up, hauled her out of the car, and was trudging toward the front steps.

Jesus . . .

After twenty paces, gravity turned this hundred-pound "pipe cleaner" into an armful of cinder blocks. Collier wasn't in the best physical shape, and being drunk only compounded his effort. *I wish I could just leave her on the damn steps and go to bed.* He was tempted. But, no, he'd already been enough of a scumbag tonight.

He opened the front door—

Oops.

—with her head and muscled through the vestibule.

A very agape Mrs. Butler sprang up from the desk and came briskly forward.

"Mrs. Butler, this isn't what you think," he started. "She—"

"Oh, that silly daughter'a mine," snapped the now-familiar drawl. "She got *drunk* is what she did."

"Yes, ma'am. And only on one beer."

"Lottie! What am I gonna do with you!" she bellowed at the unconscious woman. "You've embarrassed Mr. Collier!"

"Oh, no, Mrs. Butler, it wasn't much of a problem—"

The old woman plucked Lottie from Collier's arms and threw her over her shoulder like she was a straw doll. Lottie's bare bottom looked Collier right in the face, then was spun around.

"Please forgive this, Mr. Collier!"

"Really, it's no big d—"

"I would just *die* if you went back to sunny California and told all your TV friends like Emeril and Savannah Sammy that folks in Gast ain't nothin' but a bunch'a drunks'n crackers."

"Don't worry, I won't tell Emeril." He struggled for something to do or say, through some sudden obligation. *I can't very well let her old mother lug her back to her room.* "Here, let me help you."

"Wouldn't *think* of it! You been inconvenienced enough! You can bet corn bread to gold doubloons that she'll be punished rightly."

"No, please, Mrs. Butler. She was just trying to have a good time and drank too much—"

"See you in the mornin', and please sleep well!" The old woman was already hustling away, her own shapely backside shaking in a loose lavender dress. "And, again, I'm *so sorry* 'bout this!"

Mrs. Butler disappeared down a hall beside the desk. *What a night.*

And it was finally officially over, he realized, when the lobby grandfather clock tolled midnight. He began to trudge up the steps, amused now by the previous debacle. Mrs. Butler's upset had seemed a bit over the top. *So what? Her daughter got drunk in front of a small-time TV star. Not that big a deal.* But then he recalled Jiff's little bit of interesting info earlier. The younger man had literally been trying to set Collier up with his mother.

The only one I wish I could be set up with is Dominique . . .

But how preposterous was that? Just because she didn't have a ring didn't mean she wasn't married or involved, he knew. Brewers, just like cooks or masons, didn't wear rings for obvious reasons. *How could a girl that pretty and that on the ball NOT be taken?*

And why worry about it anyway? His TV "stardom" was at an end, he was over-the-hill, and soured by L.A. and a catastrophe for a marriage. Collier knew he wasn't exactly the Total Package.

Back in his room, he dropped his shirt on the floor, stepped out of his pants, and groaned into bed.

At least the bed wasn't spinning, and when he burped he did so as the genuine connoisseur that he was. The burp was light and hoppy, and had good "nose." It reminded him that he'd found what he'd been looking for right away: a preeminent American lager. So even with all of the day's disasters and absurdities, it had been a terrific success . . .

And I got to meet Dominique . . .

He felt like his first grade-school crush. *But it's just lust.* That other voice crept into his head.

No, it's not!

Yes, it is. All she is to you is what you relegate all women as: a Lust Object, a dehumanized arrangement of sexual parts.

Bullshit! I really like her!

You don't like anybody, you only "use" people for masturbatory head fodder. Just like the old lady, who's nothing but an ass and a pair of tits for you to stare at. Just like Lottie, and that Wisconsin tramp you were about to screw. Good job, Collier. At least admit it. Dominique's no different. You want to use her for a roll in the hay, and that's perfectly fine. Why shouldn't you? You're a man, and men are supposed to do that.

Fuck you! Dominique's nothing like that! Collier hurled back at his conscience. *This is different!*

He rolled over in bed, clenching the sheets.

Guilt flowed over him like a stinking fog. All humans were sexual animals, one side said, but there was always the other side, too.

Sexual animals domesticated by a progressive morality.

You either choose to be good or you choose to be bad. But then he regretted the fact when he considered some of his own thoughts today. Yes, the eyes of his lust had been using Mrs. Butler's body for a scratching post all day, and even worse were his deeds in the car. As for the Wisconsin woman . . .

I came really close, he knew.

For each hour that he was here it almost seemed like his sex drive was doubling.

Just go to sleep . . .

He thought of Dominique's lovely face and barley-grist tinged hands, hoping the image would lull him to slumber. The cross around her neck glimmered, a hypnotist's tool.

Just . . . go . . . to sleep . . .

A noise jostled the encroaching REM waves. He sat up, aggravated.

Did I really hear something?

Then it resounded again.

Water.

Not water running from a tap but . . . a long splash.

Like someone dumping water out of a bucket . . .

Then he saw the dot.

What the hell is that?

There was a dot on the wall, like a dot of light, or—

A hole?

He squinted at the wall.

Don't tell me there's a hole in the wall . . .

But when he got up, he found this to indeed be the case.

There's a light on in the next room, and there's a hole in the wall, he knew now. The hole existed between the closet on one side and a waist-high vase cabinet with a marble top on the other. As Collier lowered himself to his knees he was vaguely reminded of this afternoon when he'd knelt similarly to look through the keyhole.

The next room is that bath closet, he thought he remembered correctly. And that's exactly what Collier saw when he put his eye to the hole.

Soft yellow lamplight glowed over finished wood-slat walls. Directly in Collier's view was something he first thought must be a seat, because he noticed the high, curved back swept down to a lower rim with half-circle cutouts. Through his beer daze, then, he recalled what Mrs. Butler had said of this room when he'd checked in.

It's a tub for a hip bath.

He flinched at the sound again: gushing water.

I was right!

Through the hole he saw two hands bearing a bucket. The bucket was upended into the tub, then withdrawn. But . . .

Who was emptying the bucket?

He only caught the quickest glimpse, then . . .

Silence.

Next, he heard the slightest clattering, and a few footsteps. Then he saw a blur . . . *There she is . . .*

It was Mrs. Butler, or at least he thought so. He couldn't see her face, of course—the peephole only afforded a close perimeter. But now a woman stood before the tub, her buttocks to Collier's eye. A creped lavender dress jiggled as hands pushed it down by the waistband. Yes, it was definitely Mrs. Butler. *I know that dynamite old butt anywhere . . .* Collier's heart stepped up at the acknowledgment of what was about to happen:

She's going to strip and take a hip bath . . . and I get to watch.

He'd been lusting after her extraordinary body all day—now came the moment of truth.

He was looking at a pair of white cotton panties stretched out by the preeminent derriere. The view crawled up the lines of her back to her shoulders where it stopped. He could see the bra strap, too. Already, Collier's loins were tingling.

Don't get your hopes up, he reminded himself. *She's an old lady. Just because her body fills the dress right doesn't mean it won't be a wrinkled wreck once she's nude . . .*

The panties were pushed off and the bra removed . . .

And Mrs. Butler's body was not a wrinkled wreck by any stretch of the imagination.

Mama mia . . .

Now the hole circumscribed an hourglass of plush soft-white flesh. Midsixties be damned, Collier's eyeball was going dry staring at a rump, back, and shoulders that existed essentially without flaw.

Not a pock. Not a wrinkle. Not a mole, liver spot, pimple, nor blemish and not a single dimple of cellulite.

This old lady's not just a brick shit-house—she's the mother of ALL brick shit-houses . . .

Collier's arousal was plain at once, even in spite of the

influx of alcohol. It wasn't just the primal sight of this sumptuous bare buttocks just a few feet from his eye, it was the psychological effect: the anticipation. If he thought this side was good viewing, he could scarcely imagine the other side, and he knew in just moments she would turn around to let him see it all. And there was something else, wasn't there?

Collier knew—he felt absolutely 100 percent *certain*—that when she did indeed traverse her body, his eyes would be wide-open on a meticulously shaved pubis, which would hereby end the mystery of the Keyhole Flasher.

He felt his crotch without being conscious of it . . .

His eye went back to the peephole . . .

Mrs. Butler turned around at the exact moment. *Here comes the bald beaver,* Collier thought.

He froze.

Where he expected clean white skin and a pink cleft he saw instead a bounteous quantum of feminine thatch. *Another wrong number . . .*

At one point she appeared to lean backward—to grab something behind her?—which stretched the downy matt almost as if on cue. Collier didn't see any gray hairs in the mound, but he knew it was her. Then Mrs. Butler lowered herself into the hip tub.

Holy smokes . . .

Above the neck, he could only see her chin and some untied gray hair touching her shoulders. The rest was a vantage shot of her pubis, stomach, and breasts. What she'd reached back for was obviously a piece of the Civil War–era soap called ash cake. It was a grayish color in hand but when she glided it over her wet skin, it sudsed faintly like normal bar soap.

A voyeur's paradise now glowed back into Collier's eye: Mrs. Butler's hand soaping up her crotch, belly, and breasts.

Oh, man, this is better than my first Playboy when I was nine . . .

The image was so vivid, he thought of the most refined pornography. The light and her wet skin conspired to an image that seemed to just keep sharpening. And judging by the motions of her sudsy hand . . .

She was doing more than washing.

Only then was Collier even aware that he'd previously taken himself in hand. By then he couldn't help it. He felt *absurd,* yet the idea of stopping was beyond consideration. He kept staring with one eye through the hole, intent on the potent image, yet another part of his consciousness realized the absolute necessity that he MUST NOT make a sound. Mrs. Butler's slick torso wriggled in rhythmic waves. When her hips began to buck, her orgasm was apparent.

So was Collier's.

He slammed his eyes shut and closed his teeth hard against his lip. The sensation sidled him over on the floor, and there he cringed.

Cheek to floor, he lay for many moments, eyes wide in the dark, heart racing down. Impulse urged him to get up and watch the last of Mrs. Butler's private antics but he simply couldn't move.

Paralyzed . . .

When he put his hand down to push himself up, it landed on a damp spot. *Oh, sure, Collier, go ahead and jerk off on the rug. It was only handwoven in the 1850s and should probably be in the fucking Smithsonian.*

When he got back to his knees, he looked in the peephole but found it dark. He fumbled to his feet, turned on the bed lamp, and took some tissues to feebly daub up what semen he could.

The residue of his sperm left damp marks that could've been a gorilla's handprint. *It'll dry up,* he hoped.

Then, for some reason, he looked back at the hole.

Questions occurred to him now. Like: Who drilled it? *Some kink who'd rented this room before me . . .*

And now that he thought of it, the hole had obviously been drilled with some thought behind it. *A perfect dead-eye view of the hip tub,* he reasoned. The hole had even been angled down, to maximize the tub's position and ensure that the woman's crotch, belly, and breasts all fit into the circumference. *I guess you call that Pervert's Craftsmanship.*

He inadvertently touched the hole and found it splintery.

Hmm.

His ruminations started to tick, and he quickly redressed, left his room, and went to the bath closet's door. He knew Mrs. Butler wasn't in there anymore because he'd seen the light was off. The stair hall, both ways, stood empty. Collier entered the bath closet.

Warm air touched his face, and he smelled an expected soapy fragrance. His finger clicked the lights on.

The hip tub remained in place but had been emptied. The wall next to the window hosted a large sink and an old-fashioned wooden toilet seat with a chamber pot in a compartment beneath, the latter obviously for display only. There was also a large—and modern—janitorial-type sink.

On the other wall stood an identical vase cabinet, which seemed exactly opposite of the one in his room, and a yard to the left of that . . .

Collier leaned over and found the hole. He rubbed his finger against it and found it—

Smooth . . .

No splinters. *I was right,* he deduced. *The hole was drilled on this side, not mine.*

But what did it matter?

He squinted at his thoughts. *A former guest realized that Mrs. Butler takes hip baths, so one day he came in here, drilled the hole for the perfect view, and just waited till she did it again.* An unpleasing thought traced his imagination now: that Collier likely *wasn't* the first man to masturbate while peeping through the hole.

He shrugged, switched off the light, and slipped back to his room. When he climbed into bed, a weirder notion nagged at him.

What . . . is it?

Something Jiff had said . . .

. . . whenever a single fella checks in that she's got a twinkle for, she gives him room three. Your room.

Jiff had said that at the bar, hadn't he? Embellishing the offbeat remark about Mrs. Butler having some sort of crush on Collier.

Yes. He was sure of it.

But he'd said something else, too.

It's 'cos of the view. Bet she even told ya that, huh? That room three's got the best view?

Collier couldn't believe what he was considering. *Room three's got the best view, all right. The best view of Mrs. Butler's bare boobs and butt!*

But, no. That was ridiculous.

He couldn't possibly suspect that it was Mrs. Butler herself who'd drilled that hole, could he?

He shook his head against the pillow, aggravated now. Eventually, he let it all go and fell into a deep slumber . . .

. . . and had this dream:

CHAPTER SIX

I

The eye of the dream, like the eye of a camera . . .

Pitchforks flop piles of steaming brown matter to the ground. Female slaves rake the matter until it lays carpet-like. The bright, high sun beats down on it.

Why?

And what is it?

You look out farther and see that this odd brown layer of stuff covers roughly a quarter acre of land . . .

Slaves roll wheelbarrows of more of the stuff out from an old barn behind you. It's a constant process. The wheelbarrows come out, slaves with pitchforks empty the barrows, and then the barrows are wheeled back in.

"Rake it out nice and thin!" a Confederate soldier barks.

Then you know. Whatever this brown stuff is, they're raking it out under the sun, so that it will dry.

You follow the wheelbarrow trail back to the barn. More soldiers in drab gray guard the entrances, rifles—mostly Model 1842 Harpers Ferry muskets—shouldered. You hear some shouts, and the clop of hooves. Around the other side of the barn is a dirt road, which winds down the hill to a train depot. Soldiers surround the depot, and a white-washed sign reads GAST TERMINAL, MAXON, GEORGIA—C.S.A. *From the depot, wagons are departing.*

It looks like a lot of wagons.

You assume that some raw material for the war effort is being transferred from the train cars to the wagons—the mysterious steaming brown stuff.

It is peat? You scarcely know what peat is, just a crude fuel source that comes from bog marshes. Did they use it during the Civil War?

It occurs to you then that you don't really know much about anything. Nevertheless, you decide that the stuff drying out in the field must be peat, and that it is being delivered here by train.

Your eyes widen as you watch. Lines of horse-drawn wagons approach the barn.

You expect to see peat piled high in the wagons, but as they get closer you know you're wrong. The wagons are full of people.

Women, children, and old men.

They are naked, their wrists bound in front of them. They stand shoulder to shoulder in caged wagons that look medieval. Eventually the line of wagons stops at a barn entrance. You watch, appalled yet intensely curious. Soldiers wield bayoneted muskets and off-load the prisoners from the first wagon and file them into the barn. "Move it, Yankee bitches and grandpas!" one solider yells. "Single file!" another shouts. "Any of yous don't do as yer tolt, you're dead!"

When the wagon is empty, it turns and wheels over to an exit door at the other end of the building.

So where's the peat? you wonder.

There is no peat.

A Confederate major and two enlisted men on horseback approach the barn. They look weary and blanched by dust, but as they slow their horses, they stare at the barn.

"Halt and state your business, sir!" a sentry calls out.

The major dismounts and salutes. "I am Major Tuckton, First North Carolina Infantry, Sergeant. You may stand at ease as I present my orders." He produces a roll of paper and shows it to the sentry, continuing in an enthused ac-

cent. *"I am passin' through to the town of Millen to deliver important intelligence to General Martin."*

The sentry examines the orders and returns them. *"Yes, sir!"*

"And I need water for my men and horses, as Millen is still quite a trek and I must be there as soon as possible."

"Yes, sir, we'll take care of ya right away, sir!"

"And let me ask you something, Sergeant. Are you ready for some good news?"

"Yes, sir, you can surely believe that I am . . . We been hearin' rumors that the Yankees are fixin' to take Chattanooga . . ."

"Yeah, well that ain't gonna happen, and you can spread the word because our proud General Braxton Bragg just destroyed the Union division at Chickamauga Creek. Those goddamn bastards are fleein' north, Sergeant, 'cos they know they can't take the rail junctions in Chattanooga now, not with ten thousand of their men dead. We're gonna win this war now, Sergeant. Spread the word . . ."

The sergeant shouts in glee. He drops his rifle and runs toward the other sentries. *"Get water for the major and his men, and tell everybody that we just crushed the Yankees at Chickamauga!"*

The news spreads like a virus. Whistles, hoots, and shouts of celebration rock the air.

When the sergeant returns with a watering detail, the major's brow rises. *"Sergeant, what is goin' on here?"* and he points to the wagons and the naked crowd being filed into the barn.

The sergeant pauses. *"Prisoner processin', sir."*

The major removes his hat and brushes his hair back. *"But I thought we was sendin' all Yankee prisoners to that new place just south'a here, Andersonville."*

"These here are civilian prisoners, sir."

"But . . . I don't see no prison here, Sergeant. Just that big barn." The major starts to walk toward the barn. *"I'd like to know what's goin' on here—"*

"I-I beg your indulgence, sir," the sergeant interrupts and offers another roll of paper. "But here are my orders for you to examine. See, sir, this area is a restricted perimeter by order of the provisional deputy of engineering operations, a Mr. Harwood Gast."

"Who? A civilian issuin' military orders? I don't recognize civilian decrees—"

"Oh, no, sir, it's a military order, which is countersigned by General Caudill."

"Hmm . . ." The major reads the order, perplexed. "I see . . ."

"But thank you for the glorious news about General Bragg, sir! Lincoln'll surely sign an armistice now, won't he?"

The major seems distracted, looking quizzically at the barn. "Oh, yeah, Sergeant, he likely will, now that he knows he can't get his hands on the Tennessee railheads. Once Europe hears of this great victory, they will surely recognize the C.S.A. They'll threaten to stop trade with the North if they don't call a truce and recognize us as an independent nation now . . ." But he shakes his head, at the barn. "You may carry on, Sergeant."

"Yes, sir!" and the sergeant runs back to the sentry post.

Now the major is looking—

At you.

He walks up and you snap to attention. You do not salute because you are under arms.

"Good afternoon, sir!"

"At ease, Private." Behind him, the major's men are watering the horses. "Can you tell me what the hell's goin' on in that barn?"

"I'm sorry, sir, but I don't know."

"Strangest thing . . ." The major squints up. The prisoners previously filed into the barn are now coming out at the farther entrance, and getting back in the wagon. The wagon departs up a hill.

"And who is this man Harwood Gast? I ain't never heard of him."

"He's a civilian appointee, I believe, sir," you say but have no idea where that information came from. "A private financier I've heard him called. He built the alternate railroad that comes here from eastern Tennessee."

"Oh, yeah, the one out'a that junction in Branch Landing, right?"

"I believe so, sir. What I heard is he paid for it with his own money, laid five hundred miles'a track, sir."

"Hmm, yeah, okay. Just another rich guy in cahoots with the new government. Probably tryin' to buy his way onto President Davis's cabinet or somethin'."

"Yes, sir, I guess that's the case."

The major seems aggravated, fists on hips as he continues to stare at the barn, where the next wagonload of naked civilians is being off-loaded.

"Oh, well, orders are orders. Carry on, Private."

"Yes, sir!" you snap.

The major gets back on his horse. One of his men points behind him, to the field . . .

"Now what the hell is goin' on there I wonder?" the major mumbles.

"Looks like they're sun-dryin' peat," the other rider says.

"They use peat to make coal easier to light," says the third rider, "and the barrel works is just up the way."

"Yeah, peat," the major concludes, though without much conviction. "I guess that's what it is . . . Come on, men, let's get out'a here . . ."

They ride off.

You resume your post around the barn. Yes, the wagon is heading up a hill, and behind the hill you see smoke. You look back out to the field and notice slaves raking up some of the dark stuff off the ground and putting it in more wagons . . .

On your rounds you overhear other soldiers talking . . .

"Seems a waste'a time to me . . . And where do they go after this?"

"Other side of the hill it looks like."

"*The old rifle works?*"

"*Ain't old no more. Been completely rebuilt by that Gast fella. You seen him. I heard it's now the hottest blast furnace in the country. He was around a lot last month when they was finishin' the train depot down yonder.*"

"*Oh, the guy with muttonchops . . .*"

"*Yeah, and the white horse.*"

"*And there must be a big stockade somewhere beyond the works. As for what we're doin' here—shee-it, armies been doin' that for a thousand years. The spoils'a war is what it's called. Usin' the enemy's resources 'cos they sure as hell'd do the same to us. Shit, now that Lincoln won't exchange prisoners no more, what else can we do? I been hearin' some ungodly stories 'bout that Yankee prison in Annapolis. Starvin' our men, beatin' 'em.*"

"*Goddamn Union can go to hell, and we'll send 'em there. A'course what we're doin' here is all right. You heard that, Major. We just kicked the Yankees out of Tennessee. General Lee's army'll surely be capturin' Washington by December.*"

"*Yeah, and they got* cold *winters up there. Our boys need good sleepin' bags . . .*"

You still don't understand yet you march your post via some order beyond your consciousness. They're drying something in that field, *you realize.* And it's NOT peat. It's something coming from the barn . . .

Your perimeter march takes you around the other side. No doorways on this wall but there is *a half door, with the top half open.*

Go look inside . . .

As you approach, a stench rises. It's an appalling smell and also an incomprehensible one. These civilian prisoners probably hadn't washed in months but only part of the stench was body odor. Their clothes had all been stripped, obviously, to reuse the fabric for the war effort, but now that you thought of it, why go to all this trouble to confine and feed women, children, and old men? They were of no military value . . .

Then you look into the barn—

Large wood fires burn in each corner, and over each fire sits a kettle six feet wide. The kettles are boiling, gushing the foul-smelling steam, and each is being stirred by a male slave with a long wooden paddle.

"Boil it good, boys," a pistol-bearing officer barks.

But what are they boiling in the kettles?

"Gotta kill all that dirty Yankee lice 'fore it's fit for our men . . ."

You still don't understand . . . until you look to the center of the barn where there is an incessant snick—snick— snick *sound . . .*

The mostly nude prisoners are standing in a silent line. They're all very skinny, ribs showing, knees knobby. Some of the women show signs of pregnancy; in fact, so do some of the female children just entering puberty.

"Next ten! Come on, hurry it up!"

Ten at a time the prisoners are called to the center of the barn where ten grim-faced Negro women wait, each holding a pair of shears.

Their duty now is clear. They quickly clip all of the hair off the prisoners' heads.

"Arms up!"

Next, tufts of underarm hair are shorn off to fall to the ground.

"Feet apart! Hurry!"

Now each Negro kneels, shears poised. All pubic hair is similarly snipped off. Children too young to have any are merely shorn of their head hair and sent to the second door where they reboard the wagon . . .

They're boiling hair, *you realize,* wide-eyed. Then it's dried in the sun and used to stuff mattresses and sleeping bags . . .

After several cycles the hair sits in veritable piles. The cutters take a few minutes to scoop up the hair and drop it in the kettles after the previous batch is skimmed out and dropped steaming into a waiting wheelbarrow.

Hence, the process.

A farm for human mattress filling.

On several occasions, you see soldiers throw some women *into the kettles, who are left to churn for a minute and are then pulled out. The soldiers stand round guffawing as they watch these unfortunates shriek and shudder, red-skinned, on the floor, their eyes boiled and their faces steaming. You have the distinct impression that the soldiers are doing this simply for amusement.*

You step back gagging, a monstrous taste in your mouth. You stagger backward to see out of the corner of your eye the wagon heading up the hill, only now the forlorn captives are all bald.

The wave of nausea threatens to keel you over, and from a distance you hear some shouting.

"Get her!"

You look out but only see through a shifting vertigo of sickness . . .

"Private! Shoot that escaping prisoner right now!"

You're still staggering. When your vision clears, you see a bald and very naked little girl running away from the barn.

"SHOULDER YOUR WEAPON AND FIRE!" *a red-faced lieutenant is screaming as he approaches. You raise your weapon and sight the target in the V-notch. Your finger touches the trigger . . .*

"What are you waitin' for!"

"But-but, sir," *you stammer,* "it's just a-a little girl . . ."

A pistol barrel touches your temple. "Private, if you do not shoot that escaping prisoner, I will kill you right now and put* your *hair in with the next batch!"

I'm not going to do it, *you think but nevertheless you take a breath, let half of it out, and squeeze the trigger. The hammer snaps, striking the brass primer cap, and after a split-second delay, the musket tries to leap out of your hand. Black powder blows the .69-caliber smoothbore minié ball out of the muzzle with a deafening boom and a belch of smoke.*

Your eyes were closed when you squeezed the trigger but you hear a faint thwack! *and a child's shriek.*

The lieutenant is fanning gun smoke with his hat. "Fine shot, Private! You hit that kid right in the back even as she was turnin'!"

Your eyes sting like fire. You see the small nude body quivering in the grass. For a few seconds she hacks out some sobs—"Mommy! Daddy!"—*then:*

Silence.

"What's your name, Private?"

The answer grinds out, "Collier, Justin. Third Corp, sir."

Did the lieutenant's eyes seem tinged yellow? "Where'd you learn to shoot like that?"

Your throat is nearly squeezed shut, and in the back of your head a voice whispers, You killed a child, you killed a child . . . *and the words come out of your mouth with no awareness,* "Fredericksburg and both Bull Runs, sir." *But you only wish you could reload and kill yourself right there.*

"Damn *fine shooting, Private." A slap on the back.* "Now get some nigrahs to recover the body and resume your post."

You stare into the field and drone, "Yes . . ."

II

". . . sir . . ."

Collier lay atop the sheets in a trembling rigor, eyes peeled in dread. A cold sweat thick as honey seemed to sheen him. Confusion came first; then his stomach tightened when images from the dream illuminated in his head. *Holy SHIT, that was the most disgusting nightmare of my life . . .*

He tried to swallow but couldn't; then he found he couldn't move, either, the dream having crushed him like a collapsed ceiling. The image snapped brighter in his brain: a gut-sucked nude woman with parchment white flesh shuddering and in tears as a pair of iron shears identical to those he'd seen in the display intricately snip-snip-snipped off all of her hair. *Like the Nazis,* he thought.

Did the Confederates really do such things? Had he read that somewhere?

Or had his mind generated the entire atrocity?

I must really be fucked up to have a dream like that . . .

Indeed.

He still couldn't move; he felt half suffocated. His chest rose and fell as he heaved in air—

Holy shit!

—and immediately noticed a figure standing next to the bed.

Collier's heart quaked. His brain told him to roll off the bed and turn on the lamp but—

The dream paralysis only hardened around him.

Who are you! he tried to shout but his throat was just as paralyzed. Grainy darkness filled the room like smoke. The figure's head seemed bowed. It seemed to stand there looking down at him for full minutes, and then suddenly its pose snapped. The figure's head was leaning toward his face.

Collier's body clenched when a mouth locked to his and a fervent, hot tongue began to churn over his lips. His own lips parted against his will, to allow his tongue to be sucked. The action was fastidious, almost machinelike, and then petite yet insistent fingers toggled his nipples. The forced kiss sent wet smacking sounds about the dim room.

The clash of opposites couldn't have been more profound: terror and arousal. The shapely shadow figure manipulated itself above him; then eager, deft hands pulled his shorts down and dabbled with his genitals. *I've got to get up!* Collier thought. *I've got to find out who this is . . .*

But he couldn't. He couldn't budge.

Now the figure slid over his hips; he could tell—thank

God—that the intruder was a woman, and a rather insistent one. Collier's arousal *strained;* then the figure adjusted itself and suddenly he was engaged in intercourse with someone he couldn't identify.

The figure's hips began to stroke up and down over Collier's helpless member. He remained lain out on his back as this person *took* him in the dark. He heard the faintest moans as his own climax impinged. Bedsprings creaked as the rhythm rose . . .

The dream rigor released just moments before he'd orgasm; his hand shot out and turned on the light.

It was Lottie, grinning down at him.

Reason of the most unpleasant sort flooded his awareness once the paralysis was gone—

Lottie continued riding him, her grinning face bearing down, and he was pretty sure she mouthed these words: *Knock me up!*

More terror, then, as more awareness returned. Collier heaved her hips off him, severing the coitus. "Damn it, Lottie! You don't just sneak into a guy's room and start . . . *doing* him!"

She giggled silently.

He snapped his shorts back up over the straining erection. *Knock me up,* he thought in the worst dread. At least he'd interrupted the intercourse before he'd climaxed but still, he knew that was no guarantee. Errant sperms in preejaculatory fluid could indeed make women pregnant—couldn't they?—and making *Lottie* pregnant was a prospect he shuddered to contemplate.

"You have to get out of here, Lottie!"

She shook her head. Collier had to snatch her hand away when she reached for his groin.

"Get out, get out, get out!" he half shouted, but only now did he take full note of her trim, toned naked body. *Christ* . . . She leaned over him, still tipsy, and began to rub his chest.

"Just—stop. No more of this, okay? I'm not in the

mood; I just had an awful nightmare." But even as he said it, the ghastly nightmare's pall took a backseat to more primal impulses. "Go back to your room, just—" But his lust kept tipping. He stared slack-jawed at her bonbon-size nipples atop the ripe-fruit breasts. The tight stomach curved down . . .

Finish the job! that other voice said. *What's WRONG with you!*

His hand began to rise to a breast, but then retracted . . .

Have some common sense for once! he berated himself. "Lottie, no. We can't do this, it's not right. You're still drunk, and your mother's already mad enough at you, so just go back to your room!" He pushed her back with some urgency.

I love you! her silent lips told him.

Collier groaned. *There's always something, isn't there?* "Lottie, look, you can't possibly love me."

She wagged her head up and down.

"We've only known each other a few hours, and besides, I live in California, and I'm married."

She shrugged energetically, still drunk but enlivened by him. She got on her knees at the bedside and began to rub the inside of his thighs.

Collier grabbed her hands again. *This is a lawsuit waiting to happen,* he knew. *And—shit!—what if she really DOES get pregnant? I'd be ruined.* He wanted her out of here so he could simply go back to bed. But he didn't want to be caustic, and he didn't want to hurt her feelings. *What a pain in the ass.* "Lottie, you're a beautiful girl but this *can't* happen again. You understand that, right?"

Now she frowned, and the frown turned sad.

Collier got up, put on his robe, and wrapped her up in a clean bedsheet from the dresser. "Come on, you have to go." He opened the door and stepped out with her. It was his very best luck that no one else stood in the hall to see them.

"Just go to bed now," he began. "You had too much to drink tonight, and that's why this happened. You'll feel better tomorrow . . ."

But then he paused as the words left his lips because he heard something.

From the bedroom, he felt sure.

A voice from the bedroom. Very light.

A *woman's* voice. A drifting accent . . .

"Come on, sweetie, there's one more thing ya gotta do for me."

Then a rougher voice, a man's. "I'm done, now I gotta get out'a here."

"No, no, not yet. Do it—you know."

Collier's hands froze on Lottie's shoulders.

Who the hell is in my bedroom!

His eyes beseeched Lottie's. "Did you hear that?"

But all Lottie could offer was the familiar drunken grin.

Collier pulled himself back into the room. Looked around.

There was no one there.

But what did he expect? *I know I heard voices,* he told himself. It sounded like they were coming from here but . . .

Had someone come into the room, then left just as quickly, all in the few seconds he'd been standing outside the door with Lottie? Was there some alternate entrance?

All right. I'm just tired. I heard some voices through the air duct, from another room is all.

The stair hall remained clear. "Go to bed, Lottie," he whispered. "And hurry. Someone could see us out here."

Lottie, ever grinning, headed drunkenly down the stair hall.

"Do it! You know! Like last time . . ."

The drifting female voice again.

"Who the hell's here?" Collier barged back into his room.

The bedroom remained empty.

He brought his hands to his face, rubbed his eyes.

Jesus, I'm cracking up.

But now, *now,* he heard something else. A panting sound?

Like a dog panting.

Collier's hands slowly lowered.

By the baseboard, a small, ugly dog snuffled. Was it eating? Now came licking sounds . . .

Collier stared in disbelief.

How the hell did a dog get in here!

It was lean, mud colored, a mongrel. It didn't seem aware of Collier as it snuffled around the baseboard.

Collier, unmindful of how this might look, loped after Lottie and caught up with her just before she'd start downstairs. He grabbed her arm and looked right into her eyes.

"Lottie. Do you have a dog?"

She shook her head no.

"Do any guests have pets with them?"

Another shake.

He scratched his head. "There's a dog in my room, Lottie. First I heard it, then I *saw* it."

Lottie's grin disappeared. Very slowly, she shook her head no.

"Just . . . come and see so I know I'm not going nuts." And then he guided her sheet-draped form back to his bedroom door, opened it, and took her in.

No dog was present.

"That's . . . crazy," Collier mumbled. "First I heard voices, then—I swear—I heard and saw a dog."

Lottie tightened the sheets around her body, slipped back out of the room, and scurried away.

It was now that Collier's drunkenness crept up on him. *Don't think about it,* he begged himself. He relocked the door, checked the closet, checked every corner as well as under the bed to make *certain* there was no dog in the room.

When he went to bed, he left the light on.

Shapeless dreams haunted the murk of his sleep. Sounds:

Children laughing?

A dog barking?

And, later, the voices.

The woman: "Just do it!"

The man: "Good God, you are one dirty broad to want me to do somethin' like *that.*"

"Just . . . do it . . ."

CHAPTER SEVEN

I

1857

A rugged man in a leather hat by the name of Cutton rode them up the main street on a new two-horse wagon. The steeds looked strong and healthy, and the wagon had iron-spoked wheels and slat springs: more proof that Gast had a lot of money behind him. The air of the street cleared Poltrock's head quickly. He felt purged.

"So how far's the junction?"

"Not but two miles, just out of town," Cutton said. He sounded like a Marylander, or a Delawarean.

"It's a nice town," Poltrock observed of the clean streets and well-constructed buildings. Women in bonnets and bustle dresses strolled past shops with tidy men in tailcoats. Orderly slaves off-loaded goods from wagons.

"It sure is. We got a fine whorehouse here, and, well, I saw you in Cusher's Tavern last night so you know we got good liquor. The general store's always full up, and folks come from all over to buy boots from our cobbler. We even got a doctor and an apothecary."

Just then the horses pulled them past a sign: GAST— POP. 616.

"Yes," Poltrock said. "This town's got more to be said for it than Chattanooga. Strange I ain't never heard of it."

"Used to be called Branch Landing since we got statehood in '96. Weren't nothing but a little trading post then. Called it that 'cos three main roads branch out from here, one to Richmond, one to Lexington, and one to Manassas, the three biggest Southern rail junctions that have lines from Washington. But once Mr. Gast came to town, they just said to hell with it and named the town Gast. These folks worship the ground he walks on. He built everything here."

"Plantation money's what I heard," Poltrock said over the next bump.

"Owns thousands of acres, here and other states, too."

"What other states?"

"Don't know."

"This ain't Virginia, you know, or the North. How's one private man own all that land and manage the Indians?"

"Killed 'em. What did you think?"

Past the final buildings on the main street, they could see the Gast House.

Poltrock shuddered at a chill. His sickness had passed. He hadn't known what to make of any of it when he'd been inside. *That . . . house,* he thought. The vision, the smell. "Can't say I care for the house, though."

Cutton said nothing as he tended his reins.

"A fine house to look at, but I mean . . . there's just somethin' funny about it. I swear I was seein' things, hearin' things, even *smellin'* things."

Cutton remained silent.

Poltrock tried to push the memory out of his head. "Felt sick as a dog when I was in there."

"You was likely hungover," Cutton finally spoke up. "I saw you at the tavern last night, in your cups."

"Yes, that's right." *And that's all it is.*

"You meet his wife?"

"I did. Seems nice, sophisticated."

Did Cutton smile to himself? "She's somethin', all right. How about his kids?"

"I saw a blonde girl with a dog for a minute." And then Poltrock gulped at what he thought he'd seen next. "Like about fifteen, sixteen or thereabouts."

"That's Mary, and there's another one—nine, I think— a brown-haired little girl named Cricket . . ." Cutton stalled his next words, which Poltrock found curious.

"Yeah?"

Cutton gnawed off the corner of a tobacco plug. "Well, see, Mr. Poltrock, I understand that you're a man with some credentials. I heard you were the track engineer for the Pennsylvania Railroad."

"That I was, but what's it got to do with Mr. Gast's children?"

Cutton spat over the side. "I'm just an inspector—all of a sudden a very well-paid inspector but still. You're my boss, and I don't want to *lose* my brand-new job by sayin' something out of line."

This perked Poltrock up. He didn't know anybody here. "I appreciate any information you might be kind enough to render. Good men keep the details of their discussions to themselves. My word is bond, and I am certain yours is, too. An honest man is worth his weight in gold and, for instance, it will be an honest man as well

as a helpful man that I pick to be my line chief. Which
pays an extra five dollars per week."

Cutton nodded. "I just mean to say that without no
discourtesy to Mr. Gast, his children are a might peculiar and the same for his wife. It would do a wise man
service to keep a good distance from 'em all. They're bad
luck is all I'm sayin', Mr. Poltrock."

Cutton stroked his reins and drove on.

Poltrock thought he got it. But now that he was out of
the house, he could think clearly. *Gast just hired me to be
his number-two man on this job—that's all that matters.*

The horses drew the wagon down a byroad that ran
parallel to the track. The track itself appeared to be top
quality, as was the tie bed beneath. "How much track's
been laid so far?"

"Five, maybe six miles so far, and we only started a
few weeks ago."

Poltrock looked at him. "That's impressive, Cutton."

"Mr. Gast plans to have it completed in mid-'62. He
says the war will've already started by then, and the
South will likely be in Washington. Mr. Gast's rail line
will be a crucial alternate supply route."

Poltrock thought about that, and smirked. A lot of it
didn't make sense to him. *An alternate supply line . . . from
Maxon?* He figured it was best left alone. *Just do what
you're paid for, and let Gast think what he wants . . .*

A high gaze ahead showed him the layout. A steam engine connected to several pallet cars would haul the new
rail and ties up the current point of construction, then
go back to Virginia for more: a constant replenishment
of material. Each return run would find the newly lain
track a mile or two longer. *Five years,* was all Poltrock
could think. *Five years of goin' back and forth like that,
each trip back a little bit longer.* It would be hard work, for
sure—and Poltrock wasn't adverse to that—and by the
time the project was done, most of his formidable salary

would still be in the bank. *Ain't gonna have much time to spend it.*

The sun blazed. The closer they got to the site, the more apparent the sound: metal ringing as a hundred slaves brought hammer to spike. It was almost musical in Poltrock's ears.

"Gettin' close now," Cutton remarked.

At once a foul odor crinkled Poltrock's nose. "God in heaven, what's that?"

Cutton pointed beyond the track, to farmland. Poltrock saw cotton, corn, and beans being picked by complacent female slaves. But that's not what Cutton pointed to . . .

Poltrock thought of scarecrows when he noticed a couple of severed heads on stakes. The awful smell came from the rotting heads? "I heard some talk of executions," he mentioned through a half gag.

Cutton nodded. "Yes, sir. Plantation justice I guess is what you'd call it. When slaves get frisky, well . . . you gotta make an example of 'em."

"Any white men executed?"

"Oh, sure. Two or three, at least. One fella got caught tryin' to steal from Mr. Fecory—"

Poltrock stared at the odd name in his head. "Who's he?"

"One you'll get to know well, like the rest of us. Mr. Fecory is the paymaster. Shows up at the site every Friday with his ledger book and suitcase full'a money. Funny little man in a red derby hat. And he's got a gold nose."

"A gold *what?*"

"Nose. Rumor is he got his nose blowed off a while back when some fugitives tried to rob him, so now he wears a fake one made'a gold. But like I was sayin', one'a Mr. Gast's white laborers pinched some money out of Fecory's pay case and, well, that was that for him. Then another white fella or two got caught rapin' some town girls. They got executed, too."

Poltrock looked at the next severed head. "In the fields?"

"No, no. The white men got trials. They was hanged in the town square. Only the nigrahs are killed in the field. You're probably smellin' it right about now."

"Yes, I am. Hard to believe a couple of severed heads could smell that bad at this distance."

"Oh, it ain't just the heads," Cutton calmly went on. "Their whole bodies are threshed into the soil. Fertilizer. Turnin' somethin' bad into somethin' good. And they'll just leave the heads there till they rot down to skulls, a reminder for the rest of the slaves not to act up."

Poltrock gazed back out when several intermittent shadows crossed his face. *Jesus Lord,* he thought grimly. They'd just passed two more severed heads mounted in the field. He forced himself to look forward.

Down the line, he could now see the men working. White foremen measuring gauge and marking the next length of track bed to be dug and filled with ballast, then a hundred sweat-glazed slaves, either digging, hammering spikes, or dropping ties. Armed security men stood watch over the entire site, faces vigilant.

"Here were are, Mr. Poltrock," Cutton announced and slowed the wagon. "Everything you see, you're now in charge of. It's a pleasure to be workin' for ya."

You work for me, but I work for Gast, Poltrock reminded himself. "Thank you." Metal striking metal sang in his ears. "I must say, this appears to be a top-notch team." And suddenly he felt enthused. Maybe the job wasn't impossible after all. The operation was running like well-oiled machinery.

The wagon stopped. "Morris is the crew boss. I'll have him call a break, and then he can introduce you to the men."

"That would be in order."

They both dismounted the wagon. No one even looked at him when they approached the line. Each man, black or white, worked with focus and determination.

And the hammers hitting spikes rang on.

When Poltrock crossed the line, he stopped cold. Suddenly he felt bile bubbling in his gut . . .

The field seized his gaze, where he saw at least three dozen more severed heads on stakes.

II

"Quit actin' like you ain't never done this before," the younger man said, straddling the fat man's face. The fat man mewled.

This guy is the hardest trick I ever turned, thought the younger man, frowning, and this younger man, of course, was Jiff. To maintain his arousal, he forced himself to think of Tom Cruise in *Cocktail,* because every time he looked down at his obese client, he winced. Nothing arousing about *him.* The fat man remained strained and trembling on his bed, his XXX-large Christian Dior shirt opened, and his Bermuda shorts pulled off.

"Suck it right, fattie," Jiff said, and grabbed a hank of white hair beside the fat man's bald spot. "If'n you cain't suck better than that, I just might have to slap your big fat face."

The overweight "client" struggled to do as complied.

"Maybe if I kick your fat ass, you'll get the message," Jiff went on with his playact. He angled off the bed and—

CRACK!

—brought his open palm *hard* against the fat man's face.

The fat man was misty-eyed now. "I . . . I love you . . ."

Jiff couldn't have smirked more sharply.

Afternoon sun lit up the fat man's posh bedroom; Jiff found it amusing that a busy Number 1 Street bustled just outside that window, a story down. Tourists out for leisurely strolls and antique fanatics scouring the town's quaint shops. *And none of 'em would ever guess what's going on up here.* When the fat man brought his hands up to caress Jiff's ass, Jiff jerked away the fat man's cheeks with one hand, squeezing hard.

"Did I give you permission to touch my ass, girlie? Hmm?" He squeezed harder, and the fat man shook his head.

"I ought'a drag your fat girlie ass right out in the street with your little pants down like ya are, so's every one out there can see your little pansy pecker! And then piss on ya to boot!" Now he squeezed so hard, tears formed in the fat man's eyes, and—

Jesus, what a sick pup, Jiff thought.

Before the great mound of belly, the client's genitals hardened and he moaned.

How grim. It just reminded Jiff of the situation's strange psychology. *I tell the guy I'm gonna piss on him and he gets hard?* Jiff had been a male prostitute for a long time but even *he* had never seen a client this bad off. It wasn't the actual sex, nor even the pain and bondage—it was the sheer humiliation that the fat man was paying for. It didn't matter that this was fast money—the gig was getting *old.*

Get it over with, he thought, disgusted.

He put the rubber ball in the fat man's mouth and got to work.

A few minutes later, Jiff was finally done, his client ravaged. He removed the rubber ball. *Finally . . .*

"Help me! I love you so much!" came the desperate plea.

By now Jiff felt sorry for him. *Poor fat bastard's up'n fell in love with me.* "That's a good girl," he praised. "And now, for bein' so good, you know what I'm gonna do?"

Hopeful eyes glimmered up.

Jiff lowered his face and bit one of the nipples.

The fat man shrieked in glee.

Jiff climbed off the bed, nude. He knew that the fat man's eyes were on his body when he strode to the bathroom. Behind him, he pretended not to hear the forlorn whisper: "I love you so much . . ."

Jiff washed up at the sink. He felt skewed. He'd originally viewed this gig as easy money—thirty bucks for ten minutes?—but now it was getting too kinky even for him. The debasement? At least his other tricks in town were simple action. It was his body that got him the business. He appraised himself in the mirror, flexed his abs, shot a few bicep poses. Some of the guys down at the Spike would lay twenty on him just to flex while they jerked off. *Now I've got this tub'a lard with all his hangups.* Oh, well, he supposed it beat cutting yards.

He pumped his pecs once in the reflection. *Yeah. I still got it.*

Behind him, his client's voice drifted, "You're beautiful . . ."

Jiff frowned.

When he came back out, the fat man was sitting up in bed, his shorts still at his ankles. "I'd be a mess without you."

You ARE a mess! Look at yourself! You look like 300 pounds of vanilla pudding folded over in bed! Jiff ignored the remark.

He looked around the spacious room. A stone bust of some guy named Caesar stood on a pedestal by one wall, and another one of some guy named Alexander the Great stood next to the window. Jiff guessed these guys were relatives of Liberace, maybe helped get him started in Vegas. There was also a chess table made of checkerboarded marble and pieces that looked made of silver and gold. *Lucky bastard . . .* Jiff knew that his client's money came from an inheritance—he was the last of the line. *Ain't no way that fat pansy's ever gonna have a kid to inherit what's left.* Jiff knew he could steal a chess piece or two, but that wasn't his style. He was just a hayseed male hooker, not a thief.

An old, fancy armoire stood opened, revealing cans

of nuts and boxes of chocolates. "Hey, can I have some'a this?"

"All that I own . . . is yours."

I guess that means yes. Jiff knew he had to get the gears shifted fast now, otherwise the man'd just get all depressed and mushy. He opened a box of Trufflettes. "Wow, these are good."

"Take the whole box, I'll get you more. I order them special from France."

Jiff shook his head. The antique cupboard was *full* of such stuff. *The poor bastard. Aside from me comin' over here and treatin' him like dog shit, all he's got to look forward to is food.* "But, you know, you ought'a cut down on this stuff. It's bad for your heart'n all."

A grateful sob. "You care about me!"

Christ. Jiff knew that the sight of his naked body was just riling the old man up. He began to dress.

"I'm nothing," his client croaked. "I've got nothing."

"Aw, don't start talkin' like that now. Shee-it, you got quite a bit from what I can see. Nice car, nice place, money."

"Don't you understand? None of that means anything, not without love. I've got no true happiness at all . . ."

"Stop feelin' sorry for yourself!" Jiff snapped. *I gotta get out'a here!* "Come on, now, none of that. Look, I got work to do, so where's my money?"

A trembling hand pointed to an inlaid dresser. Jiff picked up the check and folded it in his pocket.

"At least, tell me . . . Tell me you like me! Please!"

"A'course I like ya—"

"Then love me, too!"

"We been over it'n over it. This ain't like that, and never will be. This is just fun and games. We're *friends,* that's it. You help me out, I help you out. We play a *game.* What's wrong with that? What's wrong with bein' friends?"

Teary eyes looked up. "Do you ever . . . think about me? I mean . . . when we're together?"

Jiff was getting sick of this. *Man, when I'm with you, all I think about is Christian Bale in his Batman suit, you pathetic fat slob* . . . But Jiff just couldn't be that much of a prick. The man was too harmless to be disgusted by. "A'course I think about you sometimes," he lied.

The client clasped his hands. "Thank you!"

Jiff needed to split. He needed to be around some real men. "Now you give me a call next time you want me to come by." And then he headed for the stairs.

Halfway down, he heard the plea: "Marry me! It'll be our secret! You can have as many lovers as you want! I'll give you everything! Just . . . marry me!"

Jiff hit the back door fast.

III

Collier woke at just past noon, a seam of sunlight from the curtains laying a bar across his eyes. *What a slug,* he thought. He felt sick from some inner confusion, then in bits and pieces everything resurfaced: the atrocious nightmare, Lottie, the hole in the wall . . . and the voices he thought he'd heard.

He frowned it all away and quickly showered, only now noticing a numb erection. *What a night.* The stair hall bloomed in the sun, flagging a distant headache that was no doubt the by-product of drinking too much. Just as he began to take the stairs down, he heard children laughing, and an excited voice like a little girl's exclaim: "Here, boy! Come get the ball! Here, boy!"

Like a kid calling a dog, he thought. He walked back up and looked but no one was there.

Mrs. Butler was dusting the banister down below. She looked up at him, as Collier was forced to look *down,* where his eyes targeted her cleavage. Today the stacked old woman wore a smart frilled blouse and blue skirt. Collier felt a covert thrill, now that he'd seen her naked in the peephole.

"Good morning, Mrs. Butler—er, I should say good afternoon."

Her withered face beamed. "Ya missed breakfast but I'd be happy to fix ya up somethin' for lunch."

"Oh, no thanks. I'm going to walk into town. I'll pick something up there later."

"And again, Mr. Collier, I'm so sorry about my silly drunken daughter bein' a thorn in your side last night—"

"Don't mention it. I was a little drunk myself, if you want to know the truth."

"So what'cha lookin' for in town? Anything in particular?"

She stepped aside as he descended; Collier's eyes groaned against her plush body. "Actually, the bookstore. Is that on the main street?"

"Yes, sir, right on the corner. Number One Street and Penelope. It's a fine little shop."

Something nagged at him—besides her blaring curves. "Oh, and I wanted to ask you something. Do you allow guests to bring pets to the inn?"

Her eyes seemed to dim. "Pets, well, no. But of course if you're thinkin' of bringing a pet on some future visit, I'm sure I could make—"

"No, no, that's not what I mean. It's just that—" Suddenly he felt foolish bringing it up. "I thought I saw a dog last night."

"A dog? In the inn? There aren't any here, I can assure you. And we don't own any pets personally."

What a mistake. I was seeing things because I was drunk and stressed out from her psycho daughter. "I'm sorry, I guess my head wasn't on straight last night. Let me just say that the beer at Cusher's was so good, I drank a few too many."

She tried to laugh. "Well, we want ya to have a good time, Mr. Collier." She paused and pinched her chin. "There is a stray dog 'round these parts that some folks see. What kind'a dog was it you thought ya saw?"

"I don't even know. A mutt, I guess, about the size of a bulldog. Kind of a muddy brown."

Did she throw off a moment of fluster? "Well, if some stray got in here, we'll have it out of here a mite fast. Lottie leaves the back door open sometimes. Honestly that silly girl runs me ragged, but you have a nice time in town, Mr. Collier."

"Thanks. See you later."

Collier went out the big front doors. Did her reaction strike him as odd, or was it just more overflow? *There's no dog. I'm the one who's overreacting.* He let the winding road out front take him down the hill, into warm sunlight.

After a hundred yards, he felt better; something more positive began to supplant last night's foolishness. He'd brought one of his boilerplate permission forms because he'd already decided that Cusher's Civil War Lager would be the final entry in his book. He'd found what he'd been looking for, and the brightest sideline was the brewer herself. *She's so cool,* he thought in a daze. "Dominique . . ." The name rolled off his tongue. He'd already assured himself that his professional motives were intact. *I'd give the beer a five-star rating even if the brewer were ugly.* Still, he couldn't wait to see Dominique . . .

Downtown, the lunch crowd was out, filling the picture-postcard streets with smiles and shining eyes. *Money first,* he reminded himself. He didn't have much cash on him, and right there on the corner stood a bank. FECORY SAVINGS AND TRUST. *Odd name,* he thought, but who cared? There was an ATM.

Several people stood in line before him. Collier waited idly, looking down the rest of Penelope Street. When he turned, he noticed a mounted bronze plaque bolted to the front of the building.

THIS BUILDING WAS CONSTRUCTED ON THE ORIGINAL SITE OF THE FIRST BANK OF GAST, AND NAMED FOR THE TOWN'S PAYMASTER, WINDOM FECORY. IN 1865, UNION SOLDIERS CONFISCATED THE

BANK OF MILLIONS IN GOLD THAT HAD BEEN HIDDEN BENEATH
THE FLOOR, THEN BURNED THE BUILDING TO THE GROUND TO
RETRIEVE ITS NAILS FROM THE ASHES.

Interesting, Collier thought, but now the only thing on his mind was Dominique. *I'll have lunch there today, and give her the release form.* "And I'd really like to talk to you some more, too, Mr. Collier," he remembered her saying. Collier was so distracted by the thought of her, he didn't even take note of the tube-topped/cutoff-jeaned Paris Hilton look-alike who was now bent over the ATM tapping in her PIN. Collier's resurgent lust, in other words, was thwarted by thoughts of someone else.

"Oh, hey there, Mr. Collier—"

Collier looked up, surprised to see Jiff standing right before him in line. "Hi, Jiff. Didn't even see you there. Guess I'm preoccupied or something."

"Hard not to be on a beautiful day like we got." Jiff stood lackadaisically in his work boots, scuffed jeans, and clinging T-shirt. "Out for a stroll?"

"Yeah, but I saw the bank here and thought I'd grab some cash first."

"I just stopped by to deposit a check real quick, and then it's back to work." He'd pronounced "deposit" as "deposert." "And thanks again for last night. I had me a lot of fun."

"Me, too. We'll do it again before I head back to L.A."

Jiff grinned ruefully, arms crossed. "Ma told me 'bout your little problem last night with Lottie. She can be a right pain in the ass, she can."

You're telling me? "It was no big deal. She's a good kid."

"Yeah, but it's too bad she's the way she is. Don't fit in proper with everyone else, not bein' able to talk and all, and a'course that goofy grin."

"Hopefully she'll come out of her shell someday."

Jiff waved a hand. "Naw, that'd just get her into more

trouble. She's best just doin' her work 'round the house'n stayin' put."

The poor girl's doomed in that house of bumpkins . . . But by now, Collier noticed the lithe blonde at the ATM, and several other men in line were eyeballing her, too. But when Collier looked to Jiff . . .

The man didn't seem to be aware of her.

Just like last night at the bar, Collier remembered. Then, very quickly, he noticed the top of the check in his hand.

JOSEPHAWITZ-GEORGE SUTE, the name at the top read. *The local author,* he thought. Collier hoped to be running into him today. He noticed that the check was made out for thirty dollars. *Side work,* Collier recalled. Jiff had already mentioned that he was also a local handyman.

The blonde left; then Jiff stepped up and deposited his check. "Guess you'll be stoppin' by Cusher's for lunch, huh?"

"As a matter of fact I am. I'm going to write up the lager in my book and I need Dominique to sign a release form."

Jiff grinned over his shoulder and winked. "It's a mighty fine beer, but you know, Mr. Collier, my *mom* makes her own spiced ale on occasion. I'm sure she's still got plenty in the fruit cellar, and I'm *double*-sure she'd love for you ta try some."

He's trying to fix me up with his sixty-five-year-old mother again. Collier squirmed for a response. "Oh, really? That's interesting. I enjoy homemade ales." But, sixty-five years old or not, he still remembered that body of hers, in the peephole—*Man* . . .—then the odd notion that Mrs. Butler herself had drilled that hole . . . "You're welcome to join me for lunch," he added, if only to blot out the image of the plush, large-nippled breasts all glimmering in lather.

"Aw, thanks much, Mr. Collier, but I still got some fix-it jobs around town 'fore I head back to the house." He flashed a final grin. "But you have a fine day."

"You, too, Jiff."

Jiff strode off, whistling like a cliché. Collier took money out of the machine and continued into town.

A quick look into Cusher's showed him a full house and full bar. *Shit. I've got to get a seat at the bar, otherwise I won't get to talk to her* . . . The lunch crowd looked heavy everywhere, so he decided to kill some time roving in and out of some knickknack shops, tourist crannies, and the Gast Civil War Museum. On the corner, then, he noticed the bookstore. *Might as well go in now and see if I can run down J.G. Sute* . . .

A bell jingled when he pushed through the door. It was a small, tidy shop, with more tourist buttons, shirts, and related trinkets than books. Several browsers milled about but none of them could be Sute. *Jiff said he was close to sixty* . . . Collier shouldered into a cove and found it full of Civil War tomes, mostly pricey picture books. *Wouldn't mind picking up a few books on Gast, though,* he told himself. One shelf was filled end to end with the same title: *From Branch Landing to Gast: A Local History.* The author was J.G. Sute, but, *No way!* Collier rebelled. The downsized hardcover was fifty dollars. Another book, more like a trade pamphlet, showed the title, *The East Tennessee and Georgia Railroad Company,* also by Sute. The same title filled the next shelf: *Harwood Gast: A Biography of Gast's Most Sinister Figure.* It was very thin, but, *That's more like it,* he thought of the five-dollar price tag. It was not a quality printing, and the photo-plate section looked xeroxed, but as Collier flipped through he found some curious tintypes of the town in the 1850s and through to the end of the war. One plate, of Gast himself, Collier found chilling in the way the subject's eyes seemed to burn through the photo's fuzzy surroundings. The well-dressed, mutton-chopped plantation baron looked exactly like the huge portrait in the atrium. Another plate showed a sturdy wooden building with the text below: THE FIRST BANK OF GAST. *I was just there,*

Collier thought. An opposite daguerreotype was devoted to MR. WINDOM FECORY: HARWOOD GAST'S CONTROVERSIAL BANKING OFFICER. *What could be controversial about him?* Collier wondered with a smirk, but the more he appraised the picture—a wiry, thin-faced man with a peculiar nose—the creepier he found the image. One surprisingly clear plate showed Mrs. Penelope Gast standing elegantly beside one of the house's entrance pillars; she looked demure and beautiful in an elaborate bustle dress and corsetlike top. The cleavage in the low-cut top couldn't have been more apparent. *What a rack!* Collier admitted.

The little book hooked him. *I'm buying this,* he knew, but as an author himself he flipped instinctively to the copyright page, to see who the publisher was. *Not a good sign, but I'm still buying it,* he resolved. The publisher was listed as J.G. Sute Publications.

"Let me guess what you're thinking," a crisp yet deep baritone Southern voice surmised. Sun from the front window reduced a wide figure to shadow. "You're thinking that it must not be any good since it's self-published."

"I—"

"But I can assure you, sir, that the author has no resort since all respectable publishing houses found the subject matter too controversial."

Collier, caught off guard, stepped aside and found himself facing a short, obese man in a tweed sports jacket with patches on the elbows. Balding, stout-faced, but with eyes that seemed serious and credible . . . and a white-gray mustache and Vandyke that reminded Collier of Colonel Sanders. It was the same man on the book's back cover. "Oh, you must be J.G. Sute. I've actually been looking for you. I'm Justin—"

"Justin Collier," the deep voice replied. "When a celebrity comes to town, I'm the first to know. Very pleased to meet you." He offered a soft but large hand. "I have seen your beer show several times but I'll have to admit, I'm more of a wine and scotch man myself. And you say . . . you've been looking for *me?*"

"Yes, yes," Collier returned and quickly got the Internet printout from his wallet. "It's actually this piece you wrote that got me here."

Sute looked at it and seemed pleased. "I do a lot of freelancing for local papers and the tourist Web sites. Oh, you mean my reference to Cusher's?"

"Right. And I'd just like to thank you because their lager turned out to be just what I needed to finish my current book."

Now the wide, squat man seemed to grow a few inches from the compliment. "I'm flattered my little piece could be of service. So . . . if you don't mind my asking, who's the publisher for your book?"

"Random House," Collier said.

Mr. Sute's extra inches dropped back down very quickly. "Well, regrettably, I've never been published by so lofty a house *but*"—he pointed to the fifty-dollar edition—"that one there is my pride and joy. Published by Seymour and Sons, in Nashville. It's sold a thousand copies so far."

Collier got the gist. *The poor sap's just a hack and I'm rubbing Random House in his face.* He decided to bite the bullet, and he took a copy down. "I planned on buying that one, too. Would you sign it for me?"

Sute blustered. "I'd be honored."

"I've only been here a day but I've become enthralled by all the local color. Harwood Gast and his railroad, for instance."

"It's quite a story, and as I was saying previously, a little too *harsh* a story for the big publishers. I've had to publish several on my own for the same reason—"

"Too *harsh?*"

"—and I don't think I'm being conceited to say that I am the only *true* expert on the local color and history of *this* town. All my works are based on original letters, photos, and estate archives. This one, for instance"—his finger gestured another slim paperback, entitled *Letters of Evidence: The Epistemological Record of Gast, Tennessee*—"and it's only five dollars."

Collier took down a copy. "I'll be digging into all of these soon, thanks. But I was also wondering, since you write for tourist and dining sites, are there any other brew pubs or regional taverns in the area? What I'm looking for are more places that might specialize in regional beers based on old recipes."

Sute seemed downtrodden that he could offer no more expertise. "Not really, I'm afraid. The South is more known for whiskey and mashes. There are a few taverns in Chattanooga that brew their own beer but I think it's more faddish than authentic."

Well, I guess I knew it was too good to be true. But at least Cusher's had been a stunning success . . . *And I suppose I owe part of its discovery to him.*

"I wish I could be more help."

"You've been quite a bit of help already, Mr. Sute. If it hadn't been for your piece, I might never have found out where Cusher's is located." Collier supposed buying several of the man's books—especially the fifty-dollar job—was gratitude enough. "Let me take these to the cashier, and then you can sign them."

Sute gushed behind Collier, and eventually signed the tomes with a confident expression. Maybe they'd be interesting, maybe not. But then something ticked in Collier's ear.

"You said this one book was too *harsh* for a New York publisher?"

"That and a number of others. Not even the local college presses would touch them, even though these are the only books ever written on this aspect of town history. And it's an important history, too—there are dozens of books on the railroads of Chattanooga during the war, yet the most *unusual* railroad of the same period was the one that Harwood Gast built. My book details, among other things, Gast's actual *use* of the railroad, which was . . . atypical."

The comment seemed bizarre. "I presume that any railroad during a war is used chiefly to transport troops and supplies."

"Um-hmm, but not *this* railroad, Mr. Collier—and my sources are firsthand evidence. No supplies, and not one single soldier was ever transported on Gast's railroad." Sute nodded sternly, and indicated the books under Collier's arm. "The railroad's actual use is touched upon in those books, however. I hope you find them interesting."

What is it with people in the South? Collier wondered, aggravated. *They deliberately evade the point.* The best storytelling ploy, keep the listener in suspense. "Come on, Mr. Sute. What was the railroad used to transport?"

"Captives," the obese man said.

"Oh, you mean they used it to take Union prisoners to detention camps? Andersonville and all that?"

"Not . . . Andersonville. That was on the other side of Georgia, and, yes, that's where most of the captured Union *troops* were sent. But I'm afraid *Gast's* railroad had an exclusive utility: to transport captive *civilians*. Women, children, old men. The innocent. It's unfortunate that the *complete* story was never published."

"Yes," Collier added, "because it was too harsh. You told me. But you've got my curiosity going. So . . . Gast transported captured Northern *civilians* on the railway—do I have that right?"

Sute nodded.

"And I guess they were transported to a separate detention camp . . ."

"In a sense, you could say that. It's a harrowing story, Mr. Collier, and probably not one you'd like to hear in detail on a beautiful day such as this. You're a celebrity,

after all, and it's wonderful to have you in our humble
town. I'd hate for such a story to spoil your stay."

Collier smiled. "It's some 'ghost train' or something,
then, right?"

A curt "No."

This guy is ticking me off now, Collier thought.

Sute shed some of the grim cast, and raised a finger.
"But if you like ghost stories, I'll admit, a few of those are
touched on, too. Some nifty little stories about the house."

The house, Collier stalled. *The Gast House.* "I knew it
all along! So the inn's a haunted house. I *knew* Mrs. Butler was bluffing . . ."

J.G. Sute's broad face turned up in a grin. "Well, I'm on
my way to lunch now, Mr. Collier, but if you stop by tomorrow I'll tell you some of the tales."

Collier wanted to bang the books over his head.
"Come on, Mr. Sute. Tell me one story about the house.
Right now."

Sute drew on a pause—of course, for effect. "Well,
without sounding too uncouth, I can tell you that many,
many guests of the Gast House—dating back quite a
spell—have reported a curious . . . influence. A, shall we
say, libidinous one."

Collier squinted at the thick mustachioed face. "Libidinous—you mean, *sexual?*"

The schoolmarmish cashier frowned over her glasses.
"Please, J.G.! Don't start getting into all that now. We
want Mr. Collier to come *back,* not stay away forever!"

Mr. Sute ignored the crotchety woman. "I'll only say
that the house seems to have a sexual effect on certain
people who happen to stay there. One of whom was my
grandfather."

The cashier was fuming, but Collier couldn't let it go.
"A sexual effect in what way?"

Sute's shoulder hitched up once. "Some people have experienced an inexplicable . . . amplification of their . . . sexual awareness."

Amplification. Sexual awareness. Collier's mind ticked like a clock. "You're saying that the house makes people h—"

Before Collier could say "horny," Sute polished up the inference by interrupting: "The house will incite the desires of certain people. Especially persons who are otherwise experiencing a decline in such desires. My grandfather, for instance, was in his eighties when he stayed there." Sute smiled again, and whispered, "He said the place gave him the sex drive of a twenty-year-old."

Collier had to make a conscious effort to prevent his jaw from dropping.

Just like me, from the second I set foot in the place . . .

"Mr. Sute? I'd be honored if you'd allow me to treat you to lunch," Collier said.

But why was Collier so fascinated? He didn't even try to discern it. Sute's strange comment about "amplified" sexual desire, and the fact that Collier had experienced exactly that, could have just been timeliness and coincidence—in fact, he felt sure it was.

Still . . .

The house *was* having some effect on him—probably due to his boredom and angst. They walked around a busy corner, Sute still ego-stroked that this "celebrity" was interested in his stories enough to actually buy him lunch. *Two birds with one stone,* Collier thought; J.G. Sute was all too happy to lunch at his favorite local restaurant: Cusher's.

"Would you mind if we sat at the bar?" Collier asked when he noticed two empty stools. Better yet, Dominique was tending the taps, cuter than ever in her dark, shiny hair and bosom-hugging brewer's apron. Collier looked up hopefully, and when she smiled and waved, he could've melted. *Oh, man. The perfect woman . . .*

"The bar's fine with me," Sute said, but just then—

You fuckers! Collier's thought screamed. *Get the fuck away from those stools!*

A middle-aged couple beat them to the stools.

Collier walked to the end of the bar. "Hi," he said to Dominique.

"I'm glad you came," she said. Caramel irises sparkled. "No room at the bar right now, but there's plenty of seats in the dining room."

Collier stammered, "I was really hoping to get to talk to you—oh, and I have that release form."

"Great. When you're done eating, just come by." Dominique glanced at Collier's unlikely lunch guest. "Getting an earful, huh?"

"Well . . ."

"Good old J.G. will keep you enthralled," she said. "Last night you did seem pretty interested in some of the town's folklore. Mr. Sute's the one to talk to about that."

"So I gather. But—" *Shit!* "I really wanted a seat at the bar."

Her eyes thinned, and she smiled. "I won't fly away."

Christ, I really dig her, Collier thought. A hostess seated them in the dining room. *I'm the one who invited this big dolt to lunch, so live with it. I'll have plenty of time to talk to Dominique later.*

"I'd recommend the pan-fried trout cakes in whiskey cream," Sute mentioned. "It's state-of-the-art here, and a Southern delicacy."

"I'll try it. Last night Jiff and I just had regular old burgers and they were great."

Sute's jowly face seemed to seize up. He looked at Collier in a way that was almost fearful. "You—you know . . . *Jiff? Jiff Butler,* Helen's son?"

More to gauge reaction, Collier said, "Oh, sure, Jiff and I are friends. He helped me check in." Collier remembered Jiff's similarly odd reaction last night, to *Sute's* name. "We had a few beers here last night. He was the one who told me I could find you at the bookstore."

The reference seemed to knock Sute off center, from

which he struggled to recover. "He's a . . . friend of mine as well, and a fine, fine young man. What, uh, what else did Jiff say?"

Yes sir, this place and these people are a hoot. What is going on here? Sute was obviously bothered, so Collier acted as though he didn't notice. "He had a few stories himself, though I'll be honest in saying that he was even more reluctant than you telling me them. The most interesting one was something about Harwood Gast hanging himself shortly after his prized railroad was finished."

"Yes, the tree out front," Sute acknowledged.

"And how several years later, just when the war was ending, several Union troops hung themselves from the same tree."

"Quite true, quite true . . ."

Collier leaned forward on his elbows. "Sure, Mr. Sute. But how does anyone really know that?"

Sute grabbed one of the books Collier had purchased, thumbed to a page, and passed it to him.

Another tintype in the xeroxed photo-plate section. The heading: UNION SOLDIERS SENT TO BURN THE GAST HOUSE HANGED THEMSELVES FROM THIS TREE INSTEAD, ON OCTOBER 31, 1864. HARWOOD GAST HANGED HIMSELF FROM THE SAME TREE TWO YEARS EARLIER.

The stark, tinny image showed several federal troops hanging crook-necked from a stout branch.

"That's . . . remarkable," Collier said. "Every picture really *does* tell a story."

"There are quite a few such stories, I'm afraid." Sute's forehead was breaking out with an uncomfortable sweat. "Did, uh, did Jiff say anything else? Anything about *me?*"

This guy is really sweating bullets, Collier saw. Sute's reaction to Jiff's name was as curious as the ghost stories. "Just that he did yard work for you sometimes, and that you were the local expert on the town's history." Collier decided to stretch some truth, to see what happened. "And, of course, he mentioned that you were a successful author and quite respected in the community. A local legend, he called you."

Sute gulped, staring at Collier's remark. "What a— what a generous compliment. Yes, Jiff truly is a wonderful man." Sute patted his forehead with a handkerchief, squinting through more unreckonable beguilement. "Say, Mr. Collier? Do you mind if I *drink?*"

You look like you need to, buddy. "Go right ahead. I'll be having a few myself."

Collier ordered a lager while Sute ordered a Grey Goose martini. *He's so flustered he needs booze.* Indeed, the mere mention of the name—Jiff—seemed to pack some hypnotic effect on this man. But Collier was getting sidetracked himself. Whatever odd vibe existed between Sute and Jiff wasn't the point. Collier burned to hear more about—

"And Penelope Gast, the wife? I believe Jiff mentioned that Gast *murdered* her. Is that right?"

Sute settled down when his first sip of the top-shelf martini drained a third of the glass. "Yes, he did, the day before he hanged himself. And if you want to talk about a person with amplified sexual desires? Mrs. Gast fits that bill quite nicely, and an interesting accompaniment to the nature of the house itself."

"Are you saying that the house was the reason for her high sexual state?"

Sute mulled it over, with another sip of his drink. "Perhaps, or perhaps the opposite. Some claim that the house didn't affect her—she affected the house. The sheer evil of her carnality."

Collier came close to laughing. "Mr. Sute, it sounds to me like she was just another cheating housewife who had the misfortune of getting caught. Being a floozy doesn't mean her house is possessed. If that were the case, the real estate market in L.A. would be in big trouble."

"Just another cheating housewife, or something

more? No one will ever be able to say for sure," Sute calmly remarked. "She was reportedly pregnant, and *not* by her husband. We know this because the local physician had her name in a ledger in his safe."

"So? Maybe she had an appointment for an earache."

"She had an appointment for an *abortion*. The way they did it back then was—" Sute peered up, mildly pained. "It's uncomfortable to talk about, Mr. Collier. It's an ugly, ugly story, and not one you'd want to hear before eating your lunch."

Collier chuckled. "Mr. Sute, my life is so boring in Los Angeles I can't even see straight most of the time. This is fascinating stuff; I'm really intrigued by it. And besides, it can't be any grosser than the crime section of the *L.A. Times* on any given day."

"So be it. If you want me to oblige you, I'll oblige you." The large man cleared his throat. "The way they aborted pregnancies back then was by injecting a distillation of boiled soapberry flowers into the uterine channel. This compound—very astringent—would cause a drastic PH shift in the womb, and usually result in a miscarriage within three days. The town physician's ledger—and keep in mind, this was a *private* ledger, for his *private* activities—plainly listed Mrs. Gast's appointment as a meeting for an abortion. And prior to that, Mrs. Gast had had three more appointments for the same procedure— at least three on the record; the ledger went back five years. Of course, she didn't live long enough to make that fourth appointment. Harwood came home earlier than expected—and killed her."

"How?"

Another pained look. "With an ax. "

"He axed his own wife to death, when she was *pregnant?*"

"Yes, and he did so in the very room she'd committed all of her infidelities. She had a special room for these trysts. It was kept locked for her—by the family maid, a slave named Jessa. I shudder to think of how many *other* secrets Jessa went to her grave with—though I don't suppose she ever really had a grave, not a proper one. See, Gast murdered her, too, when he became apprised of her collusions with his wife."

Collier peeped over his beer. "I almost hate to ask."

"She was . . . well, she was left out in the fields for the buzzards and the crows."

Sute's pause irked Collier. "Left? You mean Gast killed her and then left her body somewhere?"

Sute finished his martini, ordered another, and stolidly replied, "Gast had her raped to death, by twenty of his most loyal rail workers. *Then* her body was discarded in the fields behind the house. The mass rape, by the way, took place in the same room that Mrs. Gast would be murdered in later that day—"

Raped to death. Yeah, it's hard to get grimmer than that.

"—and I might add, since you insist on some of the more morbid details, that Mrs. Gast received similar attentions from Gast's roughriders, while he watched, of course."

"I don't get it. Mrs. Gast was gang-raped to death, too? I thought you said she was killed with an—"

"She wasn't quite raped to the point of death—this by Gast's particular order. After a few hours, and when she was just about to give up the ghost, *that's* when Gast put the ax to her."

"Then she was dumped in the field, like the maid?"

"No. He left her body to rot in the bed. Ironic that she should die by such means in the very room whose purpose she kept hidden from Mr. Gast. No doubt those four previous pregnancies by men other than her husband germinated in that room as well, and I suspect much else."

"You keep mentioning this *room*—I wonder which room it is exactly . . ."

"It's on the main stair hall. Mrs. Butler doesn't even rent that one out. Room two." Sute looked at him. "Which room are you in, Mr. Collier?"

Collier winced at a twinge. "Room three."

"You're in an interesting spot, then. To your left is the room where both Jessa and Penelope Gast were murdered. And to your right, the original commode closet and bathing room."

"What . . . happened there?"

"He drowned one of his foremen there, a track inspector named Taylor Cutton. Cutton had the bad luck of being one of Mrs. Gast's secret suitors. Somehow Gast discovered this and drowned Cutton in the hip bath, among other things."

Eew, Collier thought. *I hope it wasn't the same hip bath I saw Mrs. Butler washing herself in last night . . .*

The topic was at last getting the best of him. When the food arrived, it smelled delicious but he only picked at it. Several more pints of Cusher's Civil War Lager took some of the edge off the nefarious story that he'd essentially forced Sute to relate. But he did ask, "And this manuscript you wrote, the one too harsh for publishers—do you still have it?"

Sute's face was pinkening a bit, from a third martini. "Oh, yes. It's gathering dust on my shelf."

"And that's the entire story of Harwood Gast—the entire legend of the man?"

Sute nodded. "And I think a lot of it's probably quite accurate. Most of the sources are *very* authentic. Whether you believe the supernatural angle or not, Mr. Collier, you can believe this: Harwood Gast was purely and simply an evil man."

"Mrs. Butler said the same thing."

"And she's well advised. Some of her ancestors lived in this town when all these things were happening, and mine, too. I appreciate your interest, though. It's quite flattering, I must say. Here's my card." He slipped one across the table. "If you'd like to borrow the manuscript, or browse through it, don't hesitate to ask. But—please—call first."

"Thanks," Collier said. "I might take you up on that."

"I can also show you some of the original daguerreotypes that I didn't elect to put in any of my published books. There are a few nudes of Mrs. Gast, if you're . . . interested in seeing that sort of thing."

Collier's brows jiggled, but then he thought, *Nudes?* "Oh, come on, don't tell me she did pornography, too. They must not have even had it back then."

"No, nothing like that, but just as aristocrats of earlier eras would have their wives painted in the nude, the same went when photography was invented. Daguerreotypes and other early forms of photography were *very* expensive, and reserved only for the *very* rich. Well, Harwood Gast may have been the richest private citizen in Tennessee back then. He had several nudes taken of his wife, for his own viewing. She's quite a comely woman."

Collier continued to be astounded by his interest in this. And now . . . *Nude pix of Penelope Gast. I've GOT to see those.*

It took another moment for the next question to click in his head. "Mr. Sute . . . Was anyone murdered in *my* room?"

"I'm quite happy to say . . . no, Mr. Collier."

Collier—even though he wasn't sure he believed *any* of this—was relieved.

"And there you have it, the short version anyway." Sute's distraction continued. He seemed to keep peering over Collier's shoulder, out the restaurant's plate-glass window. "I won't bore you with certain other testimony—things said to have been witnessed in the house."

"Finally. Ghosts."

"Yes, Mr. Collier. Ghosts, apparitions, and every con-

ceivable bump in the night. Footsteps, voices, dogs barking—"

"What?" Collier snapped.

Sute smiled. "Yes, as well as regressive nightmares,
hallucinations—"

"What do you mean, *regressive* nightmares?" Collier
snapped.

"—and even demons," Sute finished.

Collier plowed his next beer. He didn't like to be taken
for a fool. Was this bizarre fat man a master storyteller?
Or . . .

He hadn't heard any dogs *barking* exactly, but he had
seen one, or so he'd thought. He'd found his own sexual
responses exploding . . . something Sute claimed to
have happened to others. And the nightmare he'd had?
It had *regressed* him back in time, all right, to a mind-
boggling atrocity that involved a railroad during the
Civil War.

And he'd heard voices, too, hadn't he? Children, a
woman, a man.

Now this.

"Demons?" Collier asked.

"I'm afraid so."

"Let me take a stab at it," Collier tried to mock. "Harwood Gast was really a *demon,* I'll bet. To do the devil's
bidding on earth."

Sute chuckled at the attempt. "No, Mr. Collier. It's actually something even more contrived than that."

"Really?"

"There's long been the suggestion that Gast sold his
proverbial soul . . . to a demon."

Collier rubbed his eyebrows, if anything, laughing at
himself now. That other stuff? It was just human nature,
plus too much beer. He was seeing what the fabulist in
him wanted to see. *People make any excuse to think
they've seen a ghost.* More human nature, *primal* human
nature. He was the Cro-Magnon listening to the scary

story in the cave, and just *knowing* that that sound he'd heard in the woods was a Wendigo or a lost soul.

And now Sute was professing demons.

"I'm glad you said that, Mr. Sute. Because now, your story isn't really that disturbing anymore."

"I'm glad. You don't believe in ghosts then?"

"No, not at all."

"Nor in demons?"

"Nope. I was raised in a Christian family—" Collier felt an inner gag. Peeping on a sixty-five-year-old woman taking a bath, coitus interruptus with Lottie, getting drunk to the gills, plus a burning, unabated, unrepentant LUST . . . *Jesus, what am I trying to say?* "What I mean is, I'm not what you'd call a practicing Christian, but—"

Sute nodded, with a cryptic smile. "You were influenced by the faith. They say that more than half of the Americans who even *call* themselves Christians never even go to church."

That would be me, Collier realized.

"But I think what you're trying to say is that some of your upbringing, in the midst of Christian values, has remained with you."

"Right. And I don't believe in demons."

"How about Christian thesis in general? Do you believe *that?*"

"Well, yeah, sure. The Ten Commandments, the New Testament, and all that. Blessed are the pure of heart. I mean, I guess I even believe in Jesus."

"Then you believe in basic Christian ideology," Sute observed more than asked.

His hypocrisy raged. *I'm profane, I'm lustful, I'm gluttonous, I'm a pretty serious sinner, but, sure, I believe it.* "Sure," he said.

Sute rose, and pointed at him. "In that case, Mr. Collier, then you *do* believe in demons. Because Christ acknowledged their reality. 'I am Legion, for we are many.' And on *that* note, I must excuse myself momentarily."

Collier watched him depart for the restroom.

The conversation's shadow hovered over him. In truth, he didn't know how to define his beliefs at all. When he turned, his vision was cut off by a pair of ample breasts in a tight white T-shirt, and a silver cross between them.

"Did I hear you right? You were discussing . . . Christian thesis?"

Collier looked up, slack-jawed. It was Dominique. She'd removed the apron and was standing right next to him.

Collier didn't know how to reply. He was hypocritically claiming a Christian ideal to explain why he didn't believe in demons? *I'd sound like a complete tube steak.* Dominique—at least it seemed—was a genuine Christian, not a phony. For a moment, he even thought of lying to her, just to impress her.

And she'd see through that . . . like I see through this empty beer glass.

Finally, he said, "Mr. Sute and I were just talking subjectively."

"About what?" she asked in a heartbeat. A little cat-smile seemed to aim down at him.

Collier tried to sound, well, like a writer. "Theoretical Christian interpretation of demonology."

She shifted her pose, to stand with a hand on her hip. "Well, Jesus *was* an exorcist. He cast out demons like he was a football ref throwing penalty flags."

Collier's thoughts stumbled. *This is the girl of your dreams, dickhead. Maintain conversation.* "So . . . true Christians believe in demons?"

"Of course!"

"And the devil?"

"Well, Jesus wasn't tempted in the desert for forty days by the Good Humor Man. If you believe in God, you have to believe in the devil, and the devil's minions. Lucifer isn't a *metaphor*—jeez, I'm so tired of hearing *that* one. He isn't an abstraction or a symptom of *mental ill-ness.*" She groaned. "God punted him off the twelfth gate of heaven—once his favorite, the angel called Lucifer—for his vanity and his pride. The friggin' *devil,* in other words, is a real dude, and so are his demons. If you don't believe in demons, then you can't believe that Christ cast them out, and if you don't believe *that,* then that's the same as saying the New Testament is bullshit—"

Collier sat stunned, by the variety of her animated explanation.

She finished up with a nonchalant shrug. "So if a person who calls himself a Christian doesn't believe the New Testament, that person is no Christian at all. Simple."

Collier could've laughed at her diversity, or remained stunned by her conviction. Before he could comment, she asked, "So what brought this conversation on? It's not exactly what I would expect America's premier beer chronicler to be yakking about at lunch."

Now Collier *did* laugh. "I guess some aspects of religion snuck their way into my curiosity about the town lore."

Dominique rolled her eyes at the empty martini glass. "Oh, so *he's* the one ordering umpteen Grey Goose martinis."

Collier craned his neck up at her. Sunlight sparkled off the cross on her bosom like molten metal. "Do you . . ."

"What?"

"Do you believe any of it, the lore, I mean?"

Her little cat-grin dropped a notch. "Yes."

For some reason, the tone of her response gave him a chill. *Is she jerking me around?*

"You only ate a smidgen of your trout cake," she noticed. "Do I have to go back to the kitchen and kick some ass?"

Collier chuckled. "No, they're great. But I'm a sucker for a good story, and Mr. Sute got the best of me."

"Mr. Sute . . . or Harwood Gast?"

"Well, both, I guess. But you know, last night you sounded kind of into it yourself."

She shrugged again, and tossed her hair. "I'm a sucker for a good story, too. Just, please, don't ask me if I've ever seen anything at the Gast House. It'd put me in a compromising position."

She's as bad as Sute, or do I just have a MANIPULATE ME *sign on my head?*

"Anyway, I have to go now, so I just came over to say 'bye."

Collier was wracked. "I thought you worked till seven," he almost exclaimed.

"I just got a call from one of my distributors. I have to drive up to Knoxville and pick up a hops order. I won't be back for several hours, and I'm sure you can't hang around till then."

Shit! Collier was pissed. He'd been so busy listening to Sute's ghost stories, he'd missed his chance to talk to her. "Damn, well. I'll come by tomorrow and give you the release form."

"That would be great," she said. "I really appreciate it."

"Don't thank me. You're the one who makes the lager." Collier's mind blanked, and before he knew what he was saying, he'd already said it: "Maybe we could go out to dinner sometime . . ."

What! he thought. *What did I just say? I didn't ask h—*

"Sure. How about tonight?"

Collier froze. "Uh, yeah, perfect."

"Pick me up here at eight. 'Bye!"

Dominique whisked out the front door.

Collier felt like a parachutist who just stepped out of the plane. His face felt like it was glowing. *I just asked her out . . . and she said yes!*

He barely noticed when Sute's bulk sat back down. Were the man's eyes red? *Either he's allergic to something,* Collier supposed, *or the guy's been crying.*

"You okay, Mr. Sute?"

The man looked absolutely disconsolate. "Oh, yes, I just . . . I've got several personal quagmires, that I'm not quite sure how to deal with." He ordered *another* big martini.

Well, that's one way of dealing with it, Collier thought. Even during their discussion's peak, Sute seemed haunted, even *pining* for something. Could it have something to do with Jiff?

Collier knew he shouldn't but . . . "Oh, yeah, that's another thing I was wondering about. The land. Yesterday when Jiff was showing me my room, I asked him about all that land around the town. It looks like perfectly good farmland to me. But Jiff says it hasn't been cultivated in years."

Sute swallowed hard, nodding. But the tactic had worked; both times the name Jiff had been mentioned, Sute reacted in his eyes—the same pained cast. It was everything he could do just to respond to the subject.

"The land hasn't been cultivated, actually, since Harwood Gast's death in 1862. It was great land, mind you, outstanding soil. There were rich, rich harvests of cotton, corn, and soybeans for as far as one could see." Sute's voice darkened. "If farmers grew crops there now . . . no one would eat them."

"Because the land is cursed?" Collier posed. "As I recall . . . *Jiff* said something along those lines."

Was Sute's hand shaking?

"Of course, Jiff didn't say that he personally *believed* the land was cursed," Collier went on for effect. "Just that that's part of the legend."

"It is, very much so." Sute finally composed himself. "People believe the land is tainted for what happened on it when Gast owned it. As the story goes, he executed a vast number of slaves on that land."

"Really? So this is fact?"

"Exaggerated fact, more than likely. Based on my own research, perhaps thirty or forty slaves were executed, not the hundreds that the legend claims. But still, men were killed there."

"Lynchings, in other words?"

"Yes, but not by hanging, which is the standard denotation. These men were slaves, of course, there was never any trial beforehand. Bear in mind, this was the era of Dred Scott—slaves, by law, were regarded as property, not citizens entitled to the rights granted by the Bill of Rights. Therefore, slaves accused of crimes never got their day in court. They were executed summarily anytime white men suspected them of something criminal."

"Legal murder."

"Oh, yes."

"These slaves—what were they accused of?"

"Some sexual crime, almost exclusively. If a white woman *willingly* had sexual congress with a slave—the slave was guilty of rape. If a slave put his hands on a white woman, or even looked at her salaciously . . . same thing. A number of these accusations were made by none other than Penelope Gast herself. There were even some accounts of slaves rebuffing her advances, which infuriated her to the point that she'd swear the man either raped her or molested her. Instant execution. And of course we know that she had many, many willing liaisons with slaves, a few of which no doubt resulted in very unwanted pregnancies. The entire ordeal was ghastly. I doubt that any of the slaves killed were guilty of forcible rape—ever."

Collier's eyes narrowed. "If they weren't hanged, how were these men executed?"

"They were dragged to death by horses, or sometimes butchered in place. And then they were beheaded while all of the other slaves were forced to watch. Harwood Gast very much believed in the principles of deterrence. The severed heads were mounted on stakes and simply left there, so to be visible, and some remained erected for years."

Collier's brow jumped. "Well, now I can see why superstitious people would believe the land was cursed."

Sute's martini was being drained in quick increments. "No, the beheadings weren't the highlight. After the unfortunate slave was decapitated, his body was crushed by sledgehammers, minced by axes, and then hoed into the soil. How's *that* for a 'haunted field' story?"

Collier's stomach turned sour. *Jesus. Gast was pure-ass psycho. He could make Genghis Khan look like Mickey Mouse.* "Now I know why the locals call Gast the most evil man the town's ever seen."

"Essentially, everything Harwood Gast ever did was in some way motivated by evil."

"Just building the railroad itself," Collier added. "Solely to transport captured northern civilians to concentration camps—that kind of takes the cake, too."

Sute popped a brow at what Collier had said.

Almost as if to reserve an additional comment.

Collier noticed that, too. That and the man's distress—from some "personal quagmire"—made Collier think: *I'd love to know what's REALLY going on in this guy's noggin . . .*

"They say evil is relative," Sute picked up when his next drink was done, "but I really don't know."

"Gast was insane."

"I hope so. As for his wife, I'm not sure that she was really *insane*—just a sociopathic sex maniac is probably more like it."

Collier laughed.

Over the course of their talk, Sute's face looked as if it

had aged ten years. Bags under his eyes dropped, while his lids were getting redder.

"Mr. Sute, are you *sure* you're all right?"

He gulped, and repatted the handkerchief to his forehead. "I suppose I'm really not, Mr. Collier. I'm not feeling well. It's been wonderful having lunch with you, but I'm afraid I must excuse myself."

"Go home and get some rest," Collier advised. *And don't drink a SHITLOAD of martinis next time.* "I'm sure you'll feel better soon."

"Thank you." Sute rose, wobbly. He shook Collier's hand. "And I hope my accounts of the town's strange history entertained you."

"Very much so."

Quite suddenly, a sixtyish man probably even heavier than Sute wended around the table: balding, white beard, big jolly Santa Claus face. "J.G.!" the man greeted with a stout voice. "Going so soon? Stay and have a drink!"

"Oh, no, Hank, I've had too much already—"

The hugely grinning man turned to Collier.

"And Mr. Justin Collier! Word travels fast when a celebrity comes to town, and I'm always the first to get the news." He pumped Collier's hand like a car jack. "I'm Hank Snodden, and I must say it's a pleasure to meet you! I *love* your show, by the way. I can't *wait* for next season!"

Sorry, buddy, but you WILL wait for next season, Collier thought. "Thanks for the kind words, Mr. Snodden."

"Hank is the mayor of our humble little town," Sute informed.

The ebullient man slapped Collier on the back. "And I'm also the county clerk, the town license inspector, and the recorder of deeds." A hokey elbow to Collier's ribs. "I also own the car lot on the corner. Come on in and I'll give you a really good deal!"

Collier faked a chuckle. "I love your town, Mr. Snodden."

The bubbly man turned back to Sute, then frowned. "J.G., you don't look well."

Sute reeled on his feet. "I'm a bit under the weather . . ."

"No, you're drunk!" Snodden laughed. "Just like me! Go home and sleep it off—"

"Yes, I'm leaving now—"

"—but don't forget chess club on Monday! I'll be kicking your tail!"

Sute sidestepped away. "Thank you again, Mr. Collier. I hope we meet again."

"'Bye . . ."

Sute finally made his exit, almost stumbling out the front door.

"He's a character, all right, Mr. Collier," the mayor piped. "I've known him thirty years and I don't think I've ever seen him that stewed. And speaking of stewed, please let me buy you a drink."

This guy's a little too high-amp for me, Collier realized. Besides, those lagers had buzzed him up but good. "Thanks, sir, but I've got to be going myself."

"Well, if there's anything you need, you just call up the mayor's office, tell them you're a personal friend of mine, and I'll get you fixed up in no time."

"Thanks, sir."

The big man's eyes beamed. "And I guess J.G. was talking about his books."

"Yes. I bought a few. But he mentioned that one of his books never—"

"—never got published because—well—he's not a very good writer! So that's what he was bending your ear about, Harwood Gast and his notorious railroad."

"Yes, it's pretty grim, but it's also a fascinating story—"

Another elbow in the ribs. "And pure bullshit, Mr. Collier, but you know how these Southerners are. They love to spin a tale. Horrible Harwood and Mrs. Tinkle, they called them."

Collier squinted. "Mrs. *Twinkle?*"

"*Tinkle,* Mr. Collier, Mrs. *Tinkle*—that was her nickname, among other things."

"Why'd they call her *that?*"

"Oh, there's my wife, Mr. Collier—I better go before she starts yelling at me—" He slipped a business card in Collier's hand. "But it's been a pleasure meeting you!"

"You, too, sir, but—wait—why did they call her—"

Snodden rushed away, to a sneering wife in a dress that looked like a pup tent with flowers on it.

Mrs. Tinkle? Collier paid the check, frowning. Here was something Sute had skirted in his indelicate description of Penelope Gast. It didn't take Collier long to assume between the lines. Sex maniac, indeed. *Water sports,* he guessed. *She was probably one of these kinky weirdos who likes guys to piss on her.* It wasn't all bonnets and mint juleps on the porch. Every age had its veneers.

He shook his head as he left the restaurant. *A piss freak . . .* But his guts sank when he reminded himself that he thought he'd smelled urine in his room.

The gorgeous day helped him get Sute's dreadful story out of his head. However—

Maybe I'll walk around town a bit, walk off this buzz. He knew he needed to be 100 percent sober when the time came for his dinner date with Dominique.

Wait a minute! he remembered now. *She won't want to eat at her own restaurant. I'll have to take her someplace . . .* Now a new kind of dread sank in his guts. *I can't take the woman of my dreams out in that lime on wheels!* He looked around for a car rental but wasn't surprised that a small town like this wouldn't need one. Suddenly the problem felt like a crisis.

I should've asked Sute. He probably would've loaned me his Caddy. It would be his prize at the chess club: to brag about how the TV star had asked to borrow his car. But Sute was gone, and too mysteriously distressed to call now. Then Collier thought: *Jiff! I'll bet he's got a car! I'm sure he'd loan it to me in a heartbeat . . .*

Collier was about to head back to the inn but stopped in the street. Two blocks down, he was pretty sure he spotted Jiff walking into a store.

He followed the clean street down, ducking whenever it appeared he'd been recognized. *This celebrity crap is getting on my nerves. I should've grown a beard . . .* When he got closer to the store, he realized it *wasn't* a store. It was that place he'd seen last night.

THE RAILROAD SPIKE, read the awning sign.

Just what I need, another bar . . .

A swing door with a circular window opened into murky darkness. Cigarette stench smacked him in the face, and the place smelled like stale Miller Lite. A long bar descended deep, with padded stools as though the place had once been a diner. Collier peered through murk but saw no sign of Jiff. A woman sat alone in a booth, applying lipstick, while several men eyed him from another booth. The bar itself stood tenantless.

What a dive, Collier thought.

A tall barkeep cruised slowly down to his spot. His apparel seemed off-the-wall and then some: a leather vest with no shirt beneath it, and he had a haircut that oddly reminded Collier of Frankenstein's monster. He held a shot in his hand, slapped it down on the bar, and slid it to Collier.

"That's a tin roof, just for you," the guy said in a wrestler's voice.

"A tin roof?" Collier questioned.

The keep rolled his eyes. "It's on the house."

"Uh, thanks," Collier said, dismayed. *Damn, I hate shots, and I don't want to stay if Jiff's not here.* But he'd feel rude in declining. He sat down at the cigarette-burned bar top. Collier downed the shot. *Not bad, even though I HATE shots.* "Thanks. That was pretty good."

"Glad you liked it, Mr. Collier, and like I said, that's on the house. I heard you got to town yesterday. It's damn exciting to have a TV star in my bar."

It never ends, Collier's mind droned.

"I love your show, and it's good luck, you being a beer man and all." The keep extended a huge hand behind him, to a row of beer taps. "We're not some redneck dump here, Mr. Collier. We've got the *good* stuff here."

Collier was almost visibly offended by the typical domestic beer taps. *I wouldn't drink that stuff if you had my head in a guillotine* . . . "Uh, actually, I was just passing through—"

"Oh, Buster!" a tinny voice called out from one of the booths. "He doesn't drink domestic beers! Give him a Heineken. On *my* tab."

Collier quailed. "On, no, really, thanks but—"

The green bottle thunked before him. "That's on Barry over there."

Collier slumped. His raised the bottle to the guy in the booth—whom he could barely see—and nodded. "Thank you, Barry." *Damn* . . . At least Heineken was a beer snob's Bud, which could be drunk in a pinch. But Collier didn't want to drink anymore. "Say," he addressed the keep, "I'm looking for Jiff Butler. Could've sworn I saw him come in here."

"Oh, that explains it now." The keep seemed gratified.

"Explains what?"

"Why you'd be coming into a place like this. I got a pretty good eye, you know? I pegged you as straight."

Collier blinked. "Huh?"

"But how can you be, if you come in here looking for Jiff?" The keep smiled and began polishing some highball glasses.

"Wait a minute, what do you mean?"

"This is a gay bar, and I didn't make you as gay."

Collier blinked again, hard. "I didn't, uh, know this was a gay bar . . ."

Suddenly the keep's friendly face turned belligerent. "What? You got a problem with gays?"

Jesus . . . "Look, man, I'm from California—I don't care what people's preferences are. But I'm not gay. I had no idea this was—" All at once, Collier considered the bar's name, and felt asinine. "Ah. Now I get it."

The keep looked quizzical. "And you're here looking for *Jiff?*"

"Well, yeah. I'm staying at his mother's inn. I wanted to see if I could borrow his car, but—"

"He'll be out in a minute . . . Say, do you know Emeril?"

I sure know how to pick 'em, Collier thought.

He almost knocked his Heineken over when an arm went across his shoulder. A handsome man in a business suit cocked a smile. "You say you need a car, Justin? Wanna borrow my BMW?"

"Uh, uh—no. Thanks—"

A squeeze to the shoulder. "Love your show." He shot a finger at the keep. "His next one's on me."

"Oh, thanks, but—"

"That Ken doll who just bought you the beer is Donny," the keep told him. "Donny, leave Mr. Collier alone. He's *straight.*"

"Oh . . ."

The man disappeared in murk.

Collier leaned forward and whispered, "Hey, tell me something. If this is a gay bar, why's that woman sitting over there looking like she wants to get picked up?"

The keep chuckled. "That woman's name is Mike. I'll call him over if you want."

"No, no, no, no, no, no, no, please. No." Collier's heart surged. "I was just curious." He tried to clear his head. "Did I misunderstand you? Did you say Jiff was here?"

"Yeah, he's in back. He won't be long."

"Oh, you mean he works here?"

The keep grinned, revealing a Letterman-type gap between his front teeth. "Sort of. And now that you mention it, he owes me some money . . . but that's another story, Mr. Collier."

This was too weird. *I'm sitting in a gay bar drinking mass-market beer,* Collier realized. And another thing: *Jiff's obviously gay—why else would he "sort of" work here?* No wonder the young man hadn't been interested in the eye candy at Cusher's last night. *And Sute . . . Could he maybe be an ex-lover of Jiff's?* Sute had seemed distraught enough, but the rest didn't add up. *Jiff's young and in good shape, Sute's old and fat . . .* Collier didn't care—he just wanted to borrow Jiff's car. He stood up and looked at his watch—one thirty. Still plenty of time to be ready for his date tonight. "Say, where's the bathroom?" he asked the keep.

"You're *standing* in it!" a voice called from the back booths. Laughter followed.

"Don't listen to those queens, Mr. Collier." The keep pointed. "Down that hall, last door on the left."

Collier smiled uncomfortably when he passed the other booths. Men barely seen in the shadows all greeted him and complimented his show. The hallway was even murkier; he practically had to feel his way down. *Did he say last door on the left, or right?* Only a tiny yellow makeup bulb lit the entire hall. He saw a door on either side.

Then he heard, or *thought* he heard, the words: "Get it, come on."

Collier slowed. *That sounded like Jiff . . .* But where was he? In the bathroom?

Dark light glowed in an inch-wide gap at the last door on the right. *That's not the bathroom, is it?* There was no sign.

Then he heard: "Yeah . . ."

A man's voice but definitely *not* Jiff's. Collier peeked in the gap.

He didn't know what he was seeing at first, just . . . two shapes in the murk. Only a distant wedge of light lit the room, which looked like a lounge of some kind. There were several ragged-out couches, a table, and some beanbag chairs. The shapes he'd seen were moving.

Jiff's voice again: "Ya better get it soon, your thirty bucks are runnin' out."

Collier's vision sharpened like a lapse dissolve in reverse.

You've got to be shitting me!

Jiff was in there, all right, bent over like someone touching their toes. He was also naked. Another man stood behind him, buttocks pumping . . .

Then, "Yeah . . ."

The motion slowed, then stopped, and the shadows separated. The other man, exhausted now, gushed, "Thanks, that was great."

"Glad'ja had a good time," Jiff's voice etched from the dark. "So where's that thirty?"

Collier pulled away and slipped into the bathroom opposite. *Now I've seen everything.* He backed against the bathroom wall, squinting from the sudden change of dim light to bright light. *Jiff's a male prostitute. He turns tricks, and J.G. Sute must be one of his clients.* It was an age-old story that worked for gays and straights alike: the Fat Older Man falls in love with the Hot Younger Prostitute—then gets rebuffed. *That must be why Sute was nearly in tears during lunch.*

The bathroom was more like one in a gas station. Collier relieved himself, then washed his hands, thinking, *I guess Jiff's mother doesn't pay him enough at the inn.* He wasn't as shocked as he would expect, but suddenly a curdling image assailed him. The scene he'd just witnessed in the little lounge room, only with J.G. Sute as Jiff's customer . . .

He waded back through the darkness toward the bar.

"You don't mind, do you, Mr. Collier?" the keep said, surprising him at the end of the hall.

"Whuh—"

The keep put his arm around his shoulder, then—

"Say cheese!"

snap!

Somebody took a picture of them. The sudden flash left Collier blind.

"Thanks, Mr. Collier," he heard the keep say. A hand on his arm led him back to his bar stool.

"That'll look great, framed behind the bar. Our first celebrity!"

Collier could barely see. *I better get out of here and sober up before tonight.* He reached for his wallet.

"Oh, you can't leave yet, Mr. Collier. Frank and Bubba bought you beers, too."

"No, really, I have to—"

"Aw, come on. It's not every day we have a TV guy in here."

I guess one more won't kill me, Collier thought, but was still semishocked by the revelation of what Jiff's "handyman" work really was.

He spent the next hour trading banter and TV stories with the keep and other patrons. The beers slid down fast, and God knew how many autographs he signed. "Oh, that's right," the keep eventually remembered, "you wanted to see Jiff. Mike, go back there and see what he's up to, all right?"

The beautiful female impersonator rose from the booth, went down the hall, then reappeared a few moments later. "He's not there, Buster," Mike said in a silky voice. He hoisted his bra beneath a tight blouse.

They seemed to be shielding the conversation from Collier, but even through the alcohol haze, he could hear traces: "He's supposed to slip me a ten each time." "He probably went out the back." "How do you like that!"

The extra beers were exactly *not* what Collier needed. He felt narcotized. "Problem?" he asked, when the keep came back.

"No, no biggie, Mr. Collier. But I'm afraid Jiff's gone; he must've left out the back door. If he comes in later, I'll tell him you were looking for him."

"I'm sure I'll see him back at the inn . . ."

A Pabst clock told him it was past two thirty now. *Less than five hours and I'm on a date with Dominique . . .* The fact buffed off the weirdness of his current situation. He was determined to leave soon; he needed some time to nap off his buzz. He had one more beer to be polite, but then his head was spinning. He put a twenty down for a tip, took another fifteen minutes saying good-bye to everyone, and at last stumbled out into daylight.

Holy smokes, I'm drunk out of my gourd . . .

He had to concentrate on each step. *Focus, focus!* he ordered. If he fell down on the sidewalk, everyone would see. By the time he got to the end of the street, that last beer was overriding his liver. Collier walked as though he had cinder blocks tied to his shoes. *Don't fall, don't fall, don't fall,* he kept thinking.

When he looked down Number 3 Street, he saw a drove of tourists moving toward him. *There's no way I can fake it,* he knew, *and with my luck they'll all want autographs. I'm so stewed right now I doubt that I could sign my name . . .* He made a forty-five-degree pivot on the sidewalk—*Here goes!*—and walked right into the woods.

I'll walk through the woods around the hill. No one'll see me, and that's a good thing because I'm pretty damn sure I'm gonna fall on my face a couple of times.

Among the trees, he found a convenient footpath, then—

flump!

—fell flat on his face.

The town buffoon, he thought. *Me. Washed-up TV has-been alcoholic wreck and L.A. burnout useless waste of space! Gets shit-faced in the middle of the afternoon* . . . Collier hoped there was no afterlife. He didn't want to think that his dear dead parents might be seeing him now, lamenting tearily, "Where did we go wrong?"

He dragged himself up, then lurched from tree to tree for about a hundred yards. He could only sense where the inn was. *Over there someplace,* he thought, and gazed drunkenly left. He squinted through double vision, saw that he still had about four hours before his date . . .

I can't make it, I need to sit down for a little while. His butt thunked to the ground, and he thought he heard the seat rip open. He heard something else, too, a steady disconnected noise . . .

Running water?

He shot his face forward and thought he saw a creek burbling through the woods. *I ought to go put my face in that,* he considered, but now that he was down, he wasn't getting up. There was no bed to spin here, only the woods.

He nodded in and out. The steady sound of the creek reminded him of those sleep-machine things that supposedly offered calming sounds but only wound up alerting the sleeper. He nodded off again, quite heavily. He felt as though he were being buried in sand.

Pieces of dreams pecked at him: the clang of railroad workers, and men singing like a chain gang. He dreamed of Penelope Gast fanning herself in a posh parlor as female maids tended to her, and then he dreamed of the smell of urine.

A splendid horizon, into which a steam locomotive chugged briskly, smoke pouring, and a whistle screeching as it disappeared into the distance . . .

"I wanna do it, too," the voice of a young girl whined.

"Don't be stupid!" insisted another older-sounding girl.

The brook burbled on, but beneath it crept a fainter sound:

scritch-scritch-scritch

"Then let me do it to you . . ."

"You're too little, stupid! You'd cut me!"

"No I wouldn't!"

Something like alarm pried open Collier's eyes. The voices weren't from a dream. He craned his neck and stared forward, at two young girls doing something near the creek. One dirty blonde who looked about thirteen or fourteen, and the other about ten, with a ruffled helmet-cut like a 1920s flapper, the color of dark chocolate. They were both barefoot, wearing white smocklike dresses.

Shit! Two little kids, and they don't know I'm here, Collier realized. It would likely scare them if he announced himself. The young one stepped into the water and continued looking down at the other, who sat with her back to Collier and seemed to be leaning over.

scritch-scritch-scritch

What the hell is she doing? Then Collier almost screamed when a feisty mud-colored dog trounced in his lap and began licking his face. "Jesus!"

Both girls looked over, and the younger one said, "Look. A man's there," in a sharp Southern accent.

The blonde's accent seemed more lazy. "Hey, mister. That's just our dog. Don't worry, he don't bite."

"He's a good dog!"

Collier had to palm the dog back. He wasn't sure, but in the animal's enthusiasm, he thought it might be humping his leg.

"Leave the man alone!" one of them squalled.

The mutt broke off, running excited circles in the clearing. But Collier knew at once: *That's the dog I . . . think . . . I saw in my room.*

"What are you doin' there, mister?" the dark-haired one squawked. She had smudges of dirt on her dress, and there was something about the way she stood and the way she looked at him that seemed hyperactive.

"I, uh, oh, I was just taking a nap."

"Too much whiskey, huh, mister?" supposed the older one. She kept her back to him, and was leaning over as if looking into the creek.

"An alkie!" the younger girl half shrieked. "A rummy, like Mother says! Says there's lots of 'em."

Collier's head thunked. "No, no, I'm staying at the inn." Then he lied. "It's nothing like that. I was just taking a nap in the woods, because it's nice out."

"Rummy! Rummy!" The little girl danced in the water, while the mongrel joined her.

Precocious little shit, Collier thought.

"Shut up, Cricket. Don't be disrespectful . . ."

scritch-scritch-scritch

Collier felt he had to prove something now. Very carefully he stood up, and noticed that he'd slept off some of the drunk. Some but not all. *Careful.* He walked over. "What are you girls doing over here? I hear this noise."

The dirty blonde looked up, smiled with a doughy face that seemed to droop. Her eyes looked dull in spite of the big, proud smile. "I'm shavin' my legs, 'cos I'm a young lady now, and I gotta do ladylike things."

"That's what our mother says," the younger one seemed to regret. "I can't wait till I'm a young lady, too, so I can shave my legs."

Collier almost winced at the sight. A cup of shaving lather sat beside the blonde, and indeed, she was shaving her legs in the creek, with an old-fashioned straight razor.

scritch-scritch-scritch

Then she splashed the lather off with creek water.

"Oh, wow, you should be careful," Collier warned. "You ought to do that at home. If you cut yourself, you could get all kind of germs from that water."

Both girls traded bewildered glances. Now the blonde splashed off some more, shot her gleaming legs up. She wriggled her feet in the air, and seemed pleased with the effect. "There," she drawled. "All smooth now, just like a real lady." The doughy face beamed back up. "My name's Mary, and this here's my sister, Cricket. I'm fourteen, she's eleven."

"Hi," Collier said, and tasted a waft of old beer.

The younger girl jumped out of the water and poked him with a finger. "What's your name, mister?"

"Justin."

A toothy grin turned Cricket's face into a lined mask. "You ain't one'a them fellas who messes with little girls, are ya? Ya don't look like it."

Out of here! Collier thought. *Kids these days—they see all this molestation stuff on* Oprah. "No, no, but you girls have a good day, I have to go."

"Aw, Cricket! What'cha say that for? Now you got him scared. Don't go, mister. She's just teasin'."

"No, I've got to—" He winced again. "Please, Mary, be careful with that razor—"

Now she was doing her underarms, rather obliviously. *Scritch-scritch-scritch.* She shaved the lather out of one armpit, then flipped it off the blade into the water. Collier noticed a thread-thin line of red.

"See, you've cut yourself—"

"Aw, it's just a nick, but I can't do it right with this hand." She held up her index finger.

First glance made Collier think she was wearing a fat dark ring but then he realized it was a bruise.

"I got one, too, but not as bad." Cricket showed her own finger. "I stole a piece of sugarloaf from the store and got caught." A manic giggle. "But that ain't as bad as what Mary got caught doin'—"

"Shut up!"

The gritted-teeth mask again. "She got five minutes 'cos she got caught kissin' a boy at school!"

Mary laid a hard hand across the back of her sister's thigh. The sound cracked through the woods.

"Ow!"

"Serves ya right. Mister, don't listen to her."

Collier's mind churned over too much at once. Who were these girls? Were they staying at the inn? Collier doubted it. *Probably a trailer park nearby*. Then: *Those bruises,* he pondered. He couldn't forget Mrs. Butler's painful demonstration of the "Naughty Girl Clips" in the display case . . .

scritch-scritch-scritch

"Oh, please, you really shouldn't do that . . ."

Now the blonde was shaving the other armpit.

"Do mine next, do mine next!" Cricket insisted.

"There ain't nothin' to shave!" Mary almost wailed. "You ain't got no hair yet!" Another gleeful smile shot back to Collier. "She's jealous, mister, 'cos I got hair and she don't. I got the blood, too."

Collier's throat thickened. "The . . . blood?"

"The Curse of Eve, like our mother told us 'bout. Eve did somethin' bad in the Garden of Eden, so now all girls get the curse. But the curse gives us hair. Ain't that right, mister?"

Collier stood speechless. He cleared his throat and asked, "Are you, uh, are you girls from town?"

"Oh, yeah. We was born here."

"Where are your parents?"

Cricket wriggled her toes in creek mud. "Our father's away workin' and our mother's at home. Where *you* from, mister?"

"California—"

Both girls traded another glance that seemed in awe.

"—but I'm just visiting here. I'm staying at Mrs. Butler's inn."

Mary splashed off her other armpit. It occurred to Collier just then that, for sisters, the girls couldn't have looked more different.

"We don't know no Mrs. Butler."

Must be from a nearby town, and wandered over here.
But . . . had it really been that dog he'd seen last night?
No. It was just a dream. Just a hallucination . . .

Yet it wasn't *too* far-fetched to think that the dog may
have gotten inside. Mrs. Butler had even suggested the
possibility.

"Oh, yeah," Mary informed. "There's a man at the coo-
per's named Butler, but he ain't got no wife."

Cricket piped in, "One time he was all drunk and he
offered us half a dollar to show him our—"

"Cricket! Be quiet!"

Collier's contemplations stretched like taffy.

"Hey!" Cricket wailed now. "What'choo doin'?"

The dog frolicked in the water, chasing plops of floating shave cream. It seemed to be trying to eat them.

"He's a silly dog," Mary offered.

"Sometimes *real* silly . . ."

Now the dog yipped, thrashing circles in the woods.
At one point it stopped abruptly, to defecate. It seemed
to look right at Collier.

"He's poopin'!"

"I have to go—good-bye," Collier said quickly and began to walk off.

"Don't go yet!" Cricket objected. "Don't'cha wanna
watch Mary shave her . . ."

Collier lengthened his strides.

As he made off, he heard:

scritch-scritch-scritch

He walked straight in spite of the dizziness: half drunk,
half hungover. He slowed his pace up the hill he hoped
to God would take him back to the inn. *White-trash kids
or something,* he guessed. *Poor, negligent parents, no decent role models.* It happened everywhere. Then he
thought: *Or maybe . . .*

Maybe it was another hallucination.

*The finger clips? The dog? A young girl shaving her legs
in a creek?*

The half-heard sound of giggling stopped him. But he must be a hundred yards away now.

Some perverted gremlin in his psyche made him turn against his will.

And peer back down into the woods.

The girls were still at the creek. "Dirty dog!" Cricket reveled amid a flood of more giggling that could only be Mary's.

Collier's stomach turned at what he saw, or *thought* he saw. Then he jogged as best he could for the inn.

CHAPTER EIGHT

I

1861

"Good work, men!" Morris barked to slaves and white men alike. He stood before the work site on the back of the rear guiding car for the pallet train. Then he shielded his eyes and looked down the line as dusk approached. "I say it looks to me like some *mighty* good work! Wouldn't you agree, Mr. Poltrock?"

Poltrock stood aside, distracted. He was looking at the numbers: how many iron track rails and fish-bolt plates the crew had consumed since last Friday. *Can that be right?*

Morris grinned at him, hands on hips. "I guess Mr. Poltrock didn't hear me—" All the rest of the men, the Negroes included, laughed.

Poltrock snapped out of it. "Yes, Mr. Morris. Perhaps even better than mighty fine . . ."

Morris's long hair lifted in a breeze. "Until Sunday mornin' then"—one of the strong-armers clanged the bell—"we are all off shift!"

Roughly a hundred and fifty men disbanded from their ranks, shining in sweat, bent by fatigue, but cheering as they broke away for the campsites. The bell clanged on, jarring Poltrock's brain.

"End of another week." Morris rubbed his hands together. "Hard to believe we're deep in Georgia territory now. Goin' on four years, ain't it? Seems like 'bout six, eight months, if you ask me."

Poltrock barely heard him. Only then did he notice a long side-knife in a tin scabbard flapping on Morris's hip. "Mr. Morris, what *is* that thing on your hip? Looks part sword, part D-guard knife."

The blade whispered when Morris unsheathed the fourteen-inch tool. "It's called a saber-bayonet, sir. Fancy, ain't it? It's made'a folded steel from the Kenansville Armory. They add somethin' called chromium to the metal—shit won't rust even if ya leave it in a bucket'a water overnight. And the brass hilt's so hard you can use it for a hammer."

"Why's a crew chief need a knife that long?"

"Don't really need it at all—" Morris turned the blade till it flashed. "It's just . . . pretty, I guess. Women got their fussy jewelry, but men got their guns and knives, I suppose."

The point had never crossed Poltrock's mind, but it was novel. "Now that you mention it, I guess I feel much the same 'bout my Colt .36," he said, and gestured to the revolver on his hip. "Don't have much real use for it neither, not with this army of strong-armers Mr. Gast's hired on. If the slaves were gonna rebel, they'd've tried that a long time ago."

"They'd have to be crazy to rebel," Morris said. "They'll be free men when we're done. A'course, there are still some Indians who get their dander up. All of us'd be wise to always carry somethin' for protection."

"Forearmed is forewarned . . . Or is it the other way around?"

"Speakin' of Indians—" Morris peered out past the work site.

Poltrock saw some figures straggling toward them.

"Beggars, probably. Or maybe some whores for tonight," Morris presumed. "But gettin' back to what we were talkin' 'bout—time's goin' by so fast. I wanted to ask how many miles'a track have we laid so far? Bet we're surely past 350, don'tcha think?"

"I only add the monthlies up twice a year, but—shit—yeah. Fast as it seems we're goin' we could be close to 350. We could be."

"You fixin' to count up the week now?"

"Yes, but don't let Mr. Fecory leave till I get back. Probably take me a half hour."

"I'll tell him," Morris said. He was squinting at the slow approaching figures. "It'll take him more than that to pay the white crew anyhow." Now Morris slapped some dust from his beard. "And I am *ready* for some whiskey tonight. How 'bout you?"

Poltrock closed his notebook, still perplexed by his numbers. "What's that? Oh, yeah, maybe . . ."

Mr. Gast gave everyone Saturday off, but Poltrock often wondered about the man's choice of days.

Sunday was the typical day of rest.

Nevertheless, things could get fairly wild. Whiskey was brought in, and several head of cattle. And some squaws were allowed on the grounds, too. *Eshquas,* they were called. Mr. Gast didn't mind some whore tents being set up for Friday nights, for the whites to use to relieve their tensions.

Poltrock's mind snagged on something. "Wait a minute. Now that I think of it, I remember the quartermaster tellin' me earlier that no whiskey had been delivered today. I didn't see any supply train come in earlier, did you?"

"Damned to hell. No, I didn't." Morris appeared as though a bad taste had come into his mouth.

"I know that a coupla times, Mr. Gast bought kegs of whiskey from the nearby towns. Don't make sense to train it in from home every week—"

"In Georgia? Shit, Mr. Poltrock. Georgia don't know from whiskey any more than goddamn Massachusetts knows from cotton."

Poltrock smiled, perhaps for the first time in a week. "I guarantee, after a week'a hard work like this, it'll do just fine."

"I hope you're right. Probably tastes like somethin' from a piss barrel." Morris sighed, putting a closer eye on the figures coming forward. "But a coupla whores will surely get the ticket. Here come some now, I'd say."

Poltrock could see them even in the dimming light: some Indian women in stitched leggings and sleeveless yokes fashioned from tattered hide. Their eyes looked huge on flinty faces. "Just what kind'a Indians are they anyway?"

"Nanticoke," Morris answered. "They was mainly in Maryland until the state militias killed 'em off 'bout fifty years ago. Most of 'em headed north—and froze to death—but some of 'em drifted south. Georgia gave 'em some reservations just like they done up in New York with the Iroquois. Some'a these here squaws look damn good, too. They fuck for ten cents and a swig, then take the money back to their men." Morris rocked on his tiptoes a moment. "Yes, sir, I'll have my cock in some'a *that* tonight."

Poltrock had to credit the strange women for their resilience at least. He counted exactly four of them, and he knew they'd be taking on fifty horny white men till late tomorrow night. A lot of the men would go four or five times. *Like Morris,* he knew. Morris had a thing for whores. A lot of the men did.

"Look at that 'un there," Morris said. "That's the one I'se gettin' first . . ."

Poltrock squinted. It was easy to tell which squaw Morris was highlighting. Three looked older and weatherworn, but a fourth appeared quite a bit younger and more endowed. The girl/woman's breasts were so large they strained the rawhide strings that held the yoke together.

"That's some tits on that Injun, huh, Mr. Poltrock?" Morris made the useless query. "A fella could do all *kinds'*a things with some tits like that." Morris waved mockingly at the girl, and said under his breath, "Hey there, ya dirty little bitch. You's'll be all full up with my spunk a right shortly."

Poltrock felt tired, and maybe coming down with a cold. He didn't share his colleague's lusty zeal at all.

"Here comes Cutton," Morris noticed.

"I need to talk to him," Poltrock said, and stepped down off the guiding car.

"Afternoon to ya, Mr. Poltrock," the younger man greeted. "Or—damn—I should say good *evenin'!* Where the days been goin' lately?"

Poltrock pulled out a panatela that he was entitled to from Mr. Gast's private stock. They came all the way from Florida. Before he could reach for a match, Cutton had one burning for him.

"Thank you," he puffed. "And I wanted to ask you somethin', Mr. Cutton." He held up his record book. "We seem to be goin' through rail and fish bolts a right fast. Did somebody increase the order for the last shipment?"

Cutton nodded, then took a chew of tobacco himself. "Yes, sir, they did."

"Who? The supply master?"

"No, sir. Mr. Gast. He mentioned to me—oh, I'm not exactly sure when—but he said he'd been bringin' in 10 or 15 percent more the past coupla weeks. Rail, too, a'course. There's a new iron works in Kentucky he's buyin' it from, he told me. Tredegar's runnin' 'round the clock makin' cannons in case there's a war."

Poltrock filtered out the useless details. "Ten to fifteen percent more? No wonder my figures didn't seem right . . ."

"The men are workin' hard, so far as I can see. If you were a slave with freedom at the end of the line, wouldn't you work extra hard?"

"Yes, I surely would—" Poltrock scratched his ear. Hard work was one thing. *But . . . this?* He knew he'd need to work the numbers again. This could be very interesting . . .

"Would you round up my horse, please, Mr. Cutton? I'm going to go count the rails."

"Yes, sir. We all know it's Friday when Mr. Poltrock counts the rails. Sure I can't be of assistance to ya?"

"No, no, it's somethin' I need to do by myself."

"I'll fetch your horse . . ."

Cutton jogged off. Morris cut him a silent grin, then climbed down himself. "What's that about fish bolts, Mr. Poltrock?"

"Oh, nothing. Probably just some bad accounting."

A big man with a pistol in his hand followed a small man in a red derby. *Mr. Fecory,* Poltrock saw. Fecory's face looked shriveled, and his odd gold nose flashed.

"Well, I say hey there, Mr. Fecory!" Morris greeted loudly.

"Mr. Morris," the little man replied. He nodded as if he had a kink in his neck, and carried a leather suitcase that everyone knew was full of cash. "Are you happy to see *me,* or just happy that it's payday?"

"Why, I'm happy to see *you,* sir!"

"Um-hmm." The weaselish man nodded to Poltrock, too.

"I don't suppose you could just slip Mr. Poltrock and

me our pay right now so's we don't have to wait in line," Morris gestured next.

"I am certain, Mr. Morris, that you work as hard as everybody else; therefore, you can wait in *line*—like everybody else."

"I *knew* you'd say that . . ."

Fecory dipped a finger up and down like a teacher. "This isn't a chow line, you know. You need to sign your receipt, sir, just like—"

"Everybody else," Morris finished. "Shit," he muttered to Poltrock after the paymaster crossed the track toward the camp.

"We're in no hurry, Mr. Morris," Poltrock reminded.

"I know, sir. It's just that we'se rail men—we live for our Fridays, and I can tell you that I am *all* riled up for some drinkin' and carryin'-on."

Poltrock was no different from any man, but since he'd signed on with Gast, he seemed to notice some conflict within himself. He barely drank on Fridays—hadn't in months—and he couldn't remember the last time he'd solicited a whore. Even during the three-day respites Gast granted them the first of every month—sometimes Poltrock would retreat to the bunkhouse and recheck his inventory book, leaving the revel to everyone else. *Guess I'm just gettin' old,* he told himself too often, or was it something more? Behind his spirit, something glowered, as if to whisper, *This is all wrong and you know it. You ain't the Christian your fine upright parents raised. They'd be ashamed . . .*

Would they? What *was* it?

Morris's mood was feisty as always, but his eyes looked dark. Poltrock didn't know if it was his imagination but sometimes the eyes of the other men shined in a dull brown-yellow cast . . .

"And you can bet," Morris continued, "that I am lookin' forward to the next respite."

"Ain't even been two weeks since the last one," Poltrock reminded him. "Honestly, Mr. Morris, you're like a kid in a rock candy shop."

Morris's grin sharpened. "Yeah, but it ain't candy that this rail man needs to get his hands on." Morris was about to say something else, but then his eyes shot wide. "What the *hell?*"

"Something wrong?"

"Look at that there—that strong-armer—"

One of Gast's big security men seemed to be rousting the four squaws, waving them off and yelling, "Not tonight! Get your asses out'a here!"

"What the hell's he doin' runnin' off our whores!" Morris exclaimed. "Hey, you there! Don't run them Injun girls off! We need 'em for tonight!"

The strong-armer held his long rifle out like a barricade. "Mr. Gast's orders, sir," he shouted back. "No whore tents tonight, and no whiskey . . ."

Morris was outraged, his anticipations punctured.

"You heard him," Poltrock said.

"Well—damn it all! It's *Friday!* It ain't like we don't deserve it, hard as we worked this week. Why's Mr. Gast cancelin' our fun?"

"'Cos he's the boss, so the reason don't matter."

The squaws jabbered back in their own language, clearly irate.

"I said get out!"

Another security man rushed to assist. *"Dahdeeya!"* he yelled at the women, and pointed back to the range. *"Nahah!"*

Finally, the women got it, and began to skulk back the way they came.

"Aw, ain't that a bust in the chops," Morris lamented. "Now I might not *never* have a turn with that big-titter . . ."

I wonder why Gast ordered them off, Poltrock thought. The sound of slow hooves grabbed his attention; Cutton was walking his horse over. "Here she is, sir." He dismounted and passed the reins to Poltrock. "Too bad 'bout Mr. Gast callin' off the Friday cookout'n all. Hope he ain't disappointed with our work of late."

"So you heard about it, too," Poltrock said. "I'm a bit curious myself. It's looking to me like this might've been one of our most productive weeks."

"Feels like it in my bones, at least." Cutton smiled forlornly. "Sure you don't want me to help ya count rail, sir?"

"No."

"Okay, then, Mr. Poltrock. I'm off to get my pay, not that I got anything to spend it on with no whores or whiskey tonight." Cutton flagged Morris. "Come on, Morris! Let's get in the pay line less'n we'll be standin' at the end of it!"

The two men departed. Poltrock could see across the track where Fecory and his security bulldog had set up the pay station. A rowdy line formed fast.

Poltrock walked his horse off. Was there something strange in the air tonight? In a sense, there always was; he could never put his finger on it.

Two younger white laborers bantered as they unloaded boxes of spikes from a ten-foot handcar. "So he told me he could *see* her up there in the window, prancin' 'round stark nekit."

"Yeah?" the other kid said with a pervert's leer.

"Said it looked like she were talkin' to someone in the room, but he knowed that Mr. Gast was down South on the line—'bout the same time we startin' laying the first track across the border—so he got to thinkin'—"

"If her husband ain't in town, who's she talkin' to?" the second kid calculated.

"Yeah, and *nekit* ta boot!"

Poltrock hadn't been listening at first, but as the boy yakked on, he halted the horse and canted an ear.

"And he already had a few in him when the shift broke and went to Cusher's, so's next thing he knowed, he's climbin' the trellis up to the balcony."

"No!"

"Ain't lyin'. Then he get up there'n looks in."

"Well, damn, come on! What he see?"

The storyteller lowered his voice behind a sharp grin. "She's buck nekit, all right'n; then she sits down in a big fancy armchair drinkin' some wine and she's sittin' there with her legs spread, and ya knows what?"

"What? What!"

"She was all *shaved* down there. Not a single hair on her pussy nowheres."

"You're lyin', Jory!"

"'S'the truth, so help me! And whiles she's sittin there talkin' to whoever it were she was talkin' to, she gets to playin' with herself a bit . . ."

"Aw, shit, man, I can't stand it—"

"Then finally—" He leaned closer. "Finally, she walks over to the bed'n gets to fuckin' a fella, like, real hard . . . and that's when he seed that it was one'a the slaves."

"Oh, man . . . What he do? Did he tell?"

"HELL, no, ya dimwit! If he done that he'd have to 'splain what he was doin' up on Mrs. Gast's balcony in the first place."

"They'd put him in a pillory fer that, fer a week at least."

"Think he didn't know that? So, shit, he couldn't say *nothin'.* But he did stay'n watch a whiles, and the—"

"You men!" Poltrock yelled. Both laborers looked up in dread. "You stop that trash talk right now, and stop it for good, you hear me?"

"Yuh-yes, sir, Mr. Poltrock. We was just—"

"*Bullshit.* You're spreadin' dirty, undignified talk like a coupla crackers, you were." Poltrock jabbed one in the chest with his finger. "You don't talk like that *ever* again.

You don't say *nothin'* like that, to *no one!* Never! Things're hard enough out here, and we don't need no slander'n barroom talk. You boys are bein' paid well so don't you be disrepectin' the fine man who's payin' you. Less'n you want me to tell him myself."

One boy looked close to tears, while the other stammered, "Oh, no, no, sir, Mr. Poltrock, please don't do that—"

"I've a mind to."

"Please, please, by God we won't never say nothin' like that ag—"

"The strong-armers'd put a nine-tails across both your backs, then ya'd be fired and banished with no way to get back to Tennessee. You'd have to go live in the woods with the Injuns'n eat dog meat and grubs, and that's only if they decides not to scalp your dumb white ass and eat *you*."

"We swear, sir, we swear to God on high, we'se'll never talk no trash like that again."

"Ya best not. Now stack those fuckin' boxes'a spikes and git into that pay line."

"Yes, sir, yes, sir, yes, sir—"

Poltrock mounted his horse, glared at them, then headed down the line. *Put the fear'a God in 'em at least.* He'd heard much of the same, though; the work site was a rumor mill, and so was the town, whether the entire crew was on respite or not. A number of men had been executed for daring to take a chance with the promiscuous Mrs. Gast. Then Poltrock thought, *Mrs. Tinkle . . .* He'd heard those rumors, too, and had even smelled piss anytime he'd had occasion to be in the house.

He cleared it from his head, taking the horse slowly north. It was time to get his mind off all the things that had been bothering him for the last four years—all the things he knew were wrong . . .

* * *

Pullin' two miles plus per week, Poltrock realized. His eyes followed the track, subconsciously counting each piece of rail. He'd done this every Friday night since 1857 when they'd started. Even the horse knew the task; it maintained a slow gait up the track bed as its master sat in the saddle, counting. Every so often, he jotted down the figures in his book, then blinked. *This is some progress. Last week, we did 2.4 miles, and this week . . .*

Poltrock pulled the horse to a stop at the sound of faster hooves. The Indians had been pacified in these parts, yet he'd already unholstered his .36-caliber Colt just in case. The sun was almost gone now, but after a moment he could see who it was: Morris.

"Hold up there, Mr. Poltrock!" Morris waved. Did he have a rider with him? "Just somethin' I wanted to ask . . ."

Poltrock wasn't interested. "Have you seen Mr. Gast?"

"Why, no, sir—"

"So you haven't heard the reason for him cancelin' the usual Friday night festivities . . ."

"No, sir, I ain't, but—" Morris seemed giddy about something, and that's when Poltrock noticed that he was indeed sharing his horse's back with another rider.

That squaw . . .

The young Indian woman held fast around Morris's waist.

"I caught up to them Injun whores 'fore they could get back to their reservation, and plucked me up this 'un here."

"So I see," Poltrock replied.

"Couldn't stand the idea of a Friday night goin' by without a whore." Morris pulled alongside and stopped. "Ten cents a roll is what she charges, same as them other ones who're older'n ugly . . ."

Poltrock couldn't have been less in the mood, yet his eyes flicked up all the same. The squaw hugged against Morris's back, shapely legs splayed, smooth unscarred skin showing in the wide-stitched seams of her leggings. Her bosom was overflowing in the deerskin yoke.

"She's a looker, ain't she, sir?" Morris acted like a dog bringing its owner a bone. He dismounted quickly, the long knife on his hip flapping, then lifted the girl down. "I mean, sir, you really need to see what she got under here," he said, and then yanked open the yoke.

He turned her like a display piece. The desirousness of her youth seemed to glow beneath the smudged skin. The bare breasts raved, large as a pair of baby heads but buoyant, big nipples puckered up like dark gooseflesh.

Morris jiggled a breast with his hand. "Ain't that somethin', sir? I mean, have you ever *seen* a pair like these? Oh, and this is even better—" Morris twirled her around, pushed her pants down to bare her rump.

Morris whistled. "Shee-IT! Would you *look* at that!"

The girl knew what was going on; she leaned forward to intensify the display. Her rump was large and shapely, but tight, bereft of a single blemish.

"For the life'a me, Mr. Poltrock, I can't tell which is better, her tits or her ass!"

Poltrock felt confounded. "Mr. Morris, did you bring that woman damn near two miles down the track bed just to show me her bosom and ass?"

"Well, I mean, I'se plannin' on havin' some fun with this 'un more than a few times, but since you're my boss, I thought I'd offer you first crack."

Amazing. "I appreciate your professional courtesy," Poltrock responded. "That's quite considerate—" Then his eyes went from the Indian woman's fresh bosom to her face.

Wide, shining eyes on a dirty face. Wantonness reflected back through a smile that could only be described as counterfeit.

"No, no thank you, Mr. Morris," Poltrock eventually said. "I'm not feelin' up to it tonight. Got to finish counting these rails."

"Aw, you sure, Mr. Poltrock?" Morris ran his hands over the plush rump. "This is prime stuff."

"She is quite a handsome girl, Mr. Morris, but still, I must decline. You go have your fun now."

Morris shrugged, astounded by his superior's rejection. "Whatever you say, sir." He looked aside and spotted a clearing in the high brush. "Right here, I say . . . I got me couple'a squaws last week in this selfsame place." Morris shoved the girl toward the clearing, tying his horse off to a slim tree. Poltrock just shook his head as they disappeared behind the brush.

That's one randy man, he thought, then gently stirrupped his horse. He continued down the track bed and resumed counting.

The figures still weren't adding up. He'd built railroads all over the country, and he knew full well what a certain number of men could lay in a certain period of time. He knew that the marker for the beginning of the week must be coming up soon . . .

The horse shimmied; Poltrock looked up at the sudden tremble. A distant, rising roar; then the tracks began to vibrate, and at last, the sound of a steam whistle.

Poltrock knew a train was coming. He guided his horse off the track bed, then steadied it at the tree line. "Easy, easy now." He tried to calm the animal, all the while thinking, *The pallet train's still at the end of the line. What's THIS train coming?*

The ground shook; it was all Poltrock could do to keep his horse from bucking. In moments, a very fast train tore by. It was back-riding; in other words, the engine was pushing the cars rather than pulling them. Poltrock had only a few seconds to count one coal hopper, five passenger cars, and a guide car up front. It was gone moments later in a great wake of dust and concussion, and in another minute he could hear its whistle blowing again as it slowed to stop at the work site.

What the hell's goin' on? He couldn't imagine why Gast would bring up another train when their own supply haul was still parked at the site.

He supposed he'd find out in due time. He let his horse calm down a few minutes more, then continued to count the last rails of their week of work.

The sun had just sunk behind the mountain when Poltrock got to the red-flagged stake he'd sunk exactly one week ago. He had to focus on his figures now, so he dismounted and tied his horse off. He lit an oil lantern he'd brought along, then sat down on the very first piece of rail that had been spiked last Friday.

Jesus Lord, he thought, staring at his notebook.

It was just simple math, and by now he'd gone over the week's numbers at least five times. Every single piece of rail was exactly twenty-two feet and six inches long. There could be no irregularities.

He was never aware of the figure looming over him.

"Working by lamplight," the voice intoned. "A sign of diligence, I must say."

Poltrock's heart jolted. He looked up in shock.

It was Mr. Gast looking down at him from his great white steed.

"The rest of the men are preparing for revel, but you, Mr. Poltrock, are here working the numbers past dusk. I do not forget the men who give me their very best work."

"Thank you, Mr. Gast," Poltrock uttered.

"I feel great things, wonderful things tonight." The low moon was rising just behind Gast's head, cutting his features in blade-sharp blackness. The steed stood still as a statue. "Do you have the week's account for me yet, or have I interrupted you?"

Poltrock stood up and dusted himself off. "No, sir, in fact you've arrived at the perfect time. I have indeed finished my account of this week's work, and . . ."

"And?"

Poltrock sighed. "I don't know how to say this, Mr. Gast, but unless the rail you're buyin' is shorter than it's supposed to be, we done laid 3.1 miles of track this week."

A pause. Gast's high silhouette didn't move. "That's outstanding."

It's either outstanding or just plain impossible, Poltrock thought to himself. "For the past two years, in fact, the crew's been layin' a minimum of a quarter mile extra per week, and some weeks more, like a half mile or six-tenths. Last week we laid a full mile more than quota, and now this week . . ." Poltrock stared at the numbers in his book. "An *extra* 1.2 miles. Just in one week."

Gast's voice was like a low throb. "What does this mean, Mr. Poltrock?"

"It means several things, sir. For one, it means that each man workin' for you is doin' the job of two. And when you add it all up, since we started, we're fifty or sixty miles ahead of schedule."

More silence. Silence was how Harwood Gast showed his jubilation. All he said was: "Thank you, sir."

Poltrock stowed his book back in the saddlebag. "Mr. Gast, what was that train I just saw flyin' by here a little while ago? We ain't scheduled for no deliveries anytime soon, and, besides, it looked like a passenger train."

"It is. I just bought it from the yards in Pittsburgh. It'll move thirty miles an hour, they say."

"I believe it, sir. So you'll be going back home tonight for a visit?"

"Yes, and so will we all. I've decided to give the men another respite. The men deserve it . . . as you've just verified with your spectacular account of their progress."

Well . . . Poltrock could use some rest. "That's very generous of you, Mr. Gast. We was all wonderin' why the usual Friday night cookout'n all was canceled."

"The train boards in a hour, Mr. Poltrock, and it will

be takin' us all back to Gast for a week of relaxation. Why, I haven't even seen my own wife and children in several months. And as fast as that new steam car goes? We'll be back home before noon tomorrow."

"That's great news, Mr. Gast. The men will be beside themselves."

"So you best get back to the site soon, Mr. Poltrock. Oh, and here . . . A token of my appreciation for your work thus far."

Poltrock took a small leather case from him. "Why, uh, thank you, sir."

Gast looked to the stars. "Good things will continue to befall us, Mr. Poltrock. I can feel it down to the roots of my very soul. I can see it in the stars . . ."

Maybe he's been drinkin', Poltrock mused. The man sounded wild, loony even. But now that he thought of it, Poltrock had never once seen Mr. Gast take a drink.

"It's the night for it, I can tell," Gast went on with his obtuse talk. He looked once more down at Poltrock. "Yes!" he whispered. "Tonight!"

Gast turned his horse and trotted off.

Poltrock shook his head after the man. *Well ain't that the damnedest . . .* He hefted the leather case.

When he looked inside, he couldn't even speak.

The case contained five stout cigars, an ink pen studded with diamonds, and $500 in cash.

My God . . .

It was a fortune, added to the lofty salary he was already being paid. *When this is over, I'm going to be a very rich man, and I owe it all to . . . Mr. Gast.*

He climbed back on his horse and headed back to the site.

It's the night for it, I can tell, Gast's words came back to him.

A mile or so down, the horse stopped for no reason. "What's the matter? Come on, I got a train to catch." he said. But then he realized exactly where he was.

He was looking to the left, into a little clearing in the side brush.

That's where Morris took the Injun girl . . .

Something compelled him to dismount, and he never even considered what it might be. Next, he was walking into the clearing, his oil lamp raised.

Morris must have already left; Poltrock could hear nothing within. When he entered farther, he stopped and stared.

He wasn't sure what he was seeing at first. It was the girl, he could tell, but . . .

Something didn't seem right.

The girl lay naked. He could see the backs of her legs, the bottoms of her bare feet, as well as her buttocks, which Morris had fussed about so.

But . . . Poltrock could also see her breasts . . .

He stepped closer. His cognizant mind shut off when he leaned over to see what had been done. Indeed, the well-endowed Indian girl lay on her belly. He need only lift her shoulder to realize exactly what Morris had used that fancy bayonet for.

She'd been skinned from collarbones to pubis, and it was an intricate job. Morris had managed to slough off her breasts and belly skin in one clean sheet, after which he'd flipped her over and laid the sheet across her back.

So he could sodomize her and look at her bosom at the same time . . .

Poltrock stared at the strange corpse for untold minutes, and as he held the lamp higher, he noticed several more dead Indian women deeper in the clearing.

He couldn't think for the loud drone in his head that suddenly threatened to push his skull apart from the inside out. *My God . . .*

He was staring at the dead girl . . .

My God, he thought again. *What am I . . .*

The roar in Poltrock's head began to abate when he

realized he was unfastening his belt and lowering his trousers.

As Poltrock was stepping onto the train car, he noticed Morris sitting in the very first seat, the long brass-handled knife and scabbard hanging off his belt. "Mr. Poltrock! Now we know why no whiskey was delivered tonight!"

"Yes . . ."

"They say we'll be back to town by noon tomorrow." Morris winked as Poltrock passed.

He mentioned nothing of what he'd found in the clearing, nor what he'd done afterward. He preferred to fantasize that it was all a bad dream—of course it was. Since the moment he'd signed on with Mr. Gast, in fact, his *life* was a bad dream.

He followed the aisle down to the last block of seats, which were reserved for Mr. Gast and himself.

Bones creaked when he sat. Yes, it had been a hard week; moreover, it had been a hard four years. Poltrock suspected that once they got back to Gast, he'd spend most of the respite sleeping, while everyone else made revel. He sighed at the fancily cushioned seat and footrest, let himself sink.

Bad dream . . .

Through the window, he could see strong-armers with lanterns walking along the cars; only a few would stay behind to guard the work site and its heaps of construction materials. The lanterns cast misshaped yellow circles to and fro in the darkness. Poltrock squinted. When one of the strong-armers glanced up at him, his eyes looked a sickly yellow.

Poltrock pulled down the curtain.

Next, he looked across the aisle and saw Mr. Gast fast asleep in his seat. Minutes later, the whistle blew, and the train chugged off. Far enough away now, he reopened the curtain and stared into the nightscape sliding by. An oblong moon followed him, tingeing the countryside. When he found himself scrutinizing his reflection in the glass . . .

Did his own eyes look yellow?

The train clattered gently over the newly lain track; Poltrock could feel their speed. He could hear the Negroes singing from the last car, while the white men in the remaining cars sat in edgy silence. Poltrock slept in jags and fits, each time wakened by an impossibly sharp image: his own lips desperately sucking the nipples of a pair of severed breasts. Each time his eyes snapped open, he was terrified to look to his side, expecting to find the skinned Indian sitting next to him, holding his hand like a lover.

Later, he dreamed inexplicably of a great blast furnace . . .

The train chugged on, deep into the night. Many behind him were asleep now, too. *Maybe I'm the only one awake,* he considered.

"Yes!"

Poltrock's eyes darted right.

It was Mr. Gast. He'd remained asleep as well, and had sleep-whispered the word.

"Yes!" Mr. Gast muttered again. "Tonight!"

When Poltrock got off the train the next day at noon—that's when they all learned that Fort Sumter had been besieged two days ago by Confederate forces in South Carolina. The fort's commander had surrendered last night.

At last, the war had begun.

CHAPTER NINE

I

Collier had passed out in his bed the minute he'd returned to the inn, and when his alarm went off at six o'clock, his brain felt like a lump of garbage. *Shiiiiiiiit,* he thought. Bad judgment was one thing, but now he was truly beginning to suspect he might be a serious alcoholic. *I got trashed in a gay bar,* he remembered. *And I have a date tonight . . .*

The shower shocked him awake. He was still half drunk and half hungover when he struggled into his clothes. The memories crept back . . .

Jiff turning tricks at the bar, and . . .

Those two little girls with the dog . . .

Mary and Cricket; he remembered their names. As he brushed his teeth and gargled he tried to convince himself it was all a dream he'd had when he'd passed out but he knew he'd only be lying to himself. No doubt they were two sisters from a poor family.

They had to be.

Collier spat foam into the toilet; several more gargles couldn't dispel the hangover taste. Next he stuck his mouth directly under the faucet and filled his belly with water.

Then he remembered that little dog—the feisty mutt—and what he thought he'd seen it doing as he left . . .

Collier shoved it from his head and left his room but before he could take his first step down the hall, he stopped.

Sniffed the air . . .

Is it my imagination, he wondered sourly, *or do I smell urine?* He frowned and walked away.

Sluggish steps took him down. No sign of anyone in the lobby, but then he recalled that Jiff and the rest of his family lived in the rear wing.

Where am I going?

Two hallways branched off the east side of the lobby but both appeared to be rental rooms. Instead he slipped out an exit door into the backyard. He looked down a line of sliding-glass doors, hoping for a clue. If he saw guests, then he'd know it was the wrong wing. He took an adjacent footpath that allowed him to get a look through each glass door without appearing conspicuous. A large spiny bush sat at the end of the wing, and as he was about to pass it, to the next wing, he heard:

"Shit! Come on, girl!"

Jiff's voice, for sure, but where was it coming from?

"Hold still, Lottie—Jesus!"

Collier turned back and noticed the last unit's door was opened all the way, while the screen door was closed, and a quick glance into the room showed him . . .

A face. A big face.

Collier rubbed his eyes. *It looks like . . . George Clooney.*

He frowned till his vision sharpened and then realized it was indeed the face of the Hollywood star. *A poster,* he realized. It was tacked to the wall. Clooney's big smile and big white teeth shot through the screen door larger than life. *What the hell's a poster of George Clooney doing in there?*

"Tighter . . ." Jiff's voice again. It was coming from the room.

This must be the family's wing after all. At first he

thought that he was likely looking into Lottie's room, and that she was a Clooney fan but if so, why Jiff's voice?

Collier took one step to the side, which increased his vantage point. The shock of what he saw so suddenly almost knocked him into the bush.

No, no, no, no, no, he thought.

Lottie had her shorts off, her bare legs spread in a V as she stood bent over at the waist. Was she wearing a man's shirt? Jiff, also nude from the waist down, stood right behind her, his hands on her hips. His tight, muscled buttocks slowly pumped.

"Shit, Lottie, you could at least have some hair on your ass—"

Collier thought he'd seen *everything* when he'd witnessed one of Jiff's tricks at the bar. He was wrong.

"Damn, cain't you make your butthole tighter?"

No, no, no, no, no, Collier thought again.

More than the jolt of incest was the mere ludicrousness of the scene. Now he understood that it was Jiff's room, and he'd positioned his sister quite deliberately: so that he could gaze at the Clooney poster while he sodomized her.

Next, Jiff muttered, "Yeah . . ."

Collier's brain told him to walk quietly away, but how could he? He'd been quite the Peeping Tom of late. He continued to watch, peering just around the bush.

"Tighter—yeah . . ."

Jiff's stokes slowed, then stopped.

"Thanks, Lottie. Shit, I needed that. Them johns at the bar got me *all* gunned up. Turned me three tricks today."

The outrageous scene was over quite nonchalantly. *I do not believe it,* Collier thought. Jiff perfunctorily pulled his pants back on, then got to tying up his bootlaces, while Lottie threw the shirt into a laundry hamper and redonned her shorts. Collier saw now that she wore a tight, nipple-revealing Tennessee Titans T-shirt. She sat down on the bed, brushing her hair back.

Jiff disappeared for a few moments, apparently to wash his hands, then strutted back into view. "Aw, dang, that's right, I forget to tell ya. After I got done doin' Richard in the lounge, I come out to get myself a beer, and guess who I see sittin' right up at the bar? Mr. Collier hisself."

Lottie's eyes shot wide, and she mouthed *No!*

"Ain't kiddin'. Like ta shit my pants when I saw that. The Prince'a Beer throwin' 'em back with Buster, Barry, Donny, and the rest of 'em. I snuck out the back so's he wouldn't see. But I never would'a thunk in a coon's age that he was gay."

Lottie burst into a round of silent giggles, all the while shaking her head.

"What? You sayin' he ain't? Then what's he doin' drinkin' at the Spike? He's *gotta* be queer."

Lottie just kept shaking her head, mouthing *No he's not, no he's not!*

Jiff gave her a stern look. "Don't tell me *you* got it on with him!"

Lottie kept smiling, then grabbed a piece of candy off Jiff's dresser and began to unwrap it.

"Hey! That's my Chunky!"

Lottie gave him the finger, then opened her hand.

"Oh, right. Here." Jiff gave her a five-dollar bill. "Thanks."

Five bucks! Collier outraged. *What a rip-off!*

It just kept getting nuttier. *This really is a different world.* Collier slipped away and went back into the inn. His watch told him he only had fifteen minutes. *I can't ask Jiff to borrow his car when he just got done having anal sex with his SISTER,* he lamented. Back in the lobby, Mrs. Butler's old face beamed up.

"Got'cher self a hot date, huh, Mr. Collier?"

Unbelievable. "Actually, yes."

"Well I hope ya have a wonderful time." Mrs. Butler

was clearly braless again, this time beneath a sleeveless
snap-front blouse that shined iridescent pink.

"Thanks, Mrs. Butler."

Her pose at the desk proffered a wedge of creamy
cleavage. Unbidden, Collier's brain put a younger woman's head on her shoulders. "Oh, I did want to ask. Are
there any other towns nearby?"

"Oh, sure. Roan's not ten miles west, and they got
some nice restaurants there—"

"No, I meant—well, are there any *poor* towns nearby.
Run-down, low-income areas? The reason I ask is because when I was coming back earlier, I saw these two
young girls in the woods, and they simply struck me as
not from around here. Like girls from a ghetto or something."

Mrs. Butler looked perplexed. An unconscious finger
traced the edge of her blouse top. "None too many poor
folk 'round here. Mostly just old money and ritzy tourist
places."

"No trailer parks or anything like that, low-income
housing?"

"No, you'd have to get out a speck for that . . . Two
girls you say?"

"Yes. Sisters. They were playing by a ravine on the hill
out here." The more Collier explained, the sillier he felt.
What's my point, anyway? "And, well, they had a dog—a
little mutt—that looked like the one I asked you about
earlier."

"I had Lottie'n Jiff look high'n low for any dogs that
might'a snuck in but they didn't find none," she said.
"None'a the other guests seen it either."

When Collier thought of mentioning the other
oddity—the sisters' reference to the finger clips—he
suddenly determined: *Forget it!* "Never mind. It was just
sort of odd. I was wondering something else, though. Do
you . . . have a car I could borrow for a few hours?"

* * *

In the parking lot, Collier winced like someone who'd just discovered their fly open. Mrs. Butler's "car" was a dented Chevy pickup truck that couldn't have rolled off the production line after 1955. Rust riddled the flat-black paint like eczema. *It looks like that hunk of shit on the* Beverly Hillbillies . . . He glanced, next, to the lime-sherbet Bug, sighed, and got into the truck anyway.

The dashboard had holes where most of the gauges should be. *I asked for it, I got it,* he reminded himself. He jammed the wobbly three-speed shifter, backed out of the lot, and headed for Cusher's.

Whenever he looked in the rearview, he saw a sheen of blue smoke following him. Nothing happened when he turned on the radio. *Another smart move by me.* But at least on the main drag he got fewer looks of hilarity than his airport rental.

At the intersection, a tap on the glass startled him; then the passenger door was creaking open.

Dominique slid in.

"Hi! Right on time . . ." She assayed the vehicle's interior. "Isn't this the truck Mrs. Butler's father bought to celebrate Eisenhower's election?"

"I'm sure it is," Collier groaned. When he looked at her, though, he felt like someone in an inner tube floating at a sudden swell in the surf. *Oh my God she's so beautiful . . .*

Dominique wore a white satin summer skirt with rosette accents and a lacy white bra-cami. The top ran down to just an inch above the skirt's hem, providing a gap from which her navel could peek. She couldn't have looked more classily casual. Just below the hollow of her throat, the silver cross flashed.

Collier attempted an explanation. "My rental car looks—"

"Yeah, I heard. Some funky green thing like in a cartoon." She tossed her head, the predusk sunlight shining orange off each separate strand of hair. "But it's actually kind of fun riding in a car this old. A whole lot of butts have sat on this seat."

Collier chuckled. "I never thought of it that way. Posterity measured by posteriors."

"So how was your day?" she asked, and seemed to be examining her nail polish.

Collier drove through town, frowning each time the truck hiccupped smoke. "Great," he lied.

"Get much work done on your book?"

"Oh, yeah," he lied again. What could he say? *I got drunk in a gay bar, passed out in the woods, then watched an act of incest.* "The book's nearly done, and I'm happy to say I'll make the deadline. Speaking of which . . ."

At the next light, he extracted the permission form from his wallet. "All I need is you to sign this release. It gives me your permission to comment on your beer."

She signed it without even reading most of it. "This is wonderful. Now more people will know about it than these yokels—Oh, where are we going for dinner?"

Good question. "Since I'm new in town, how about you make the choice?"

"Do you like Korean?"

"Love it." Collier hated Korean cuisine. It always sat in his belly like a corrosive.

"Good. There's a great little Korean joint at the edge of town. You'd think you were eating in Seoul it's so authentic."

Don't they eat dog in Seoul? Collier didn't care—he was with her. They chatted about beer as he followed her instructions to a tiny restaurant squeezed between a hardware store and—Collier raised a brow—a dog salon. An aroma strong as a stench greeted them once they entered: spiced cabbage and lemon grass. But Collier knew it was a good sign that every other patron in the place was Asian. "The *bulgogi* is terrific," Dominique enthused at their booth, "but so is the *bibimbop*. I can never decide which to order."

"I happen to love both of those, too," Collier lied, "so why don't we order both and split them?"

"You're so accommodating!"

"And since we're both beer snobs," he continued, "I guess it's OB."

"I like OB with Korean food. It's probably my favorite Asian beer that's not brewed here on a license," she was quick to add. "Oh, and it's great with rice."

You're great with rice, Collier dopily thought. He couldn't believe he'd been given this opportunity. As one of the most credible beer writers in the country, Collier never needed to be told that genuine brewmasters knew more about beer than anyone, including him. He gauged her plain but vibrant beauty as she perused the menu for appetizers. *Why couldn't I have met her ten years ago?* he scorned himself. *Why couldn't I have NEVER met Evelyn and met Dominique instead? We'd be the perfect match. We have everything in common . . .*

The glittering cross around her neck suggested otherwise.

When the waitress arrived with their beers, Dominique said, "Here comes my one beer of the day."

Collier sulked within himself. How many had *he* had today? *Jesus . . .* "I'll have to try your method some time," he said. "That is *if* I have the willpower. That's never been my strong suit."

"It wasn't mine, either, until . . ." She half smiled and half smirked. "Sorry, I'll shut up."

Collier didn't get it. "What?"

"You'll think I'm Holy Rolling you again."

"Go ahead and Holy Roll me."

"Okay." She took a sip of beer. "Nobody has willpower, not on their own. God knows we have weaknesses that are destructive, so that's why he gives us an out. I'm not just talking about salvation, I'm talking about the shit we've got to bear while we're here—"

I love it when she says shit, Collier mused.

"Half the apostles were probably alcoholics and whoremongers before they met Jesus. So what did they do?"

"I . . . don't know."

"They gave their burdens to God," she said very casually, "and were freed. That's what I did."

Collier unwrapped his chopsticks. "How do you give away a weakness?"

"Ask God, that's all. And he'll answer." She shook her head. "You should've seen me in college. I was an asshole, I was a tramp. I couldn't tell you how many scumbag guys I had sex with. Every night was a party: beer, booze, dope, and sex."

Her candid talk astounded him . . . and the gutter that was his mind tried to picture the scenario. It was thrillingly crude.

"I was so hungover in college," she admitted, "I don't know how I ever graduated. Don't know how I managed to not get pregnant, either. I'd read things about myself on bathroom walls, and the worst part was"—she shot him a cunning look—"they were all true."

Collier felt impacted and aroused at the same time.

"Then one day it occurred to me that I was letting my weaknesses destroy a child of God. So I asked God to relieve me of my burdens so that I could one day find salvation, and he did."

"Is it that simple?" Collier asked, then noticed that his own beer was half drained already. He knew he was only listening in part, but trying to act like she had his full attention.

"It's not like rubbing a magic lamp and then the genie grants your wish, no. Look at it this way. God's forgiveness is a million times bigger than our sins, so we're covered. You just have to do some stuff in return."

Collier wanted to make out with her under the table, on the floor. *In my case,* he thought, *God's forgiveness would have to be TWO million times bigger than my sins.*

Suddenly his falseness seemed as solid as the chair he sat on. If human beings really did have auras, he knew that his was black with lust. *Say something, you moron* . . . "Stuff in return? What kind of stuff? Go to church? Give to charity?"

"No, no. Deeper than that," she said. She crunched on some spicy bamboo shoots and pickled radishes. "That's between you and God. But it's like charging on your credit card. You have to pay for it someday. And declaring bankruptcy doesn't cut it."

Her analogies were interesting. He wanted to be engaging, he wanted to be involved with what enlivened her, but his lust nagged at him. And that's when the truth hit him, rearranging her own words: *My lust is a million times bigger than my desire to be forgiven* . . .

Every time he looked at her bosom, his eyes were repelled by the cross, like a vampire.

"But enough of that," she said, beaming. "Here comes our dinner."

The waitress set down fragrant, steaming entrees. They'd also ordered a dish of squid flanks in scarlet hot sauce. "Be careful with that." She pointed a chopstick to the latter. "It'll torch you up."

Collier was already torched up, by the lust boiling over his psyche, which only made him feel more fake, more despicable. *She could pick a phony like me out in a crowd,* he knew. *The worst thing I can do is pretend* . . . He tried a piece of some kind of sweet barbecued beef. "Great *bibimbop.*"

"That's *bulgogi.*"

"Ah, of course. It's been a while for me." The *bibimbop* looked like a hodgepodge of greens and meat submerged in broth, with a half-cooked egg on top. He tried some squid instead, which was tender, delicious, and—

"Wow, that's really—" He chugged his entire glass of water.

"I told you it was hot. It's better to eat it with some rice."

Collier followed her lead with the food, eating it in the same way.

"So how was your lunch with the venerable J.G. Sute?"

"Do I detect sarcasm in your tone?" he asked after his mouth cooled.

"Just a tad," she laughed. "He's a legend in his own time—just ask him. Actually he's quite a nice man, and he does know more than anyone about this area's importance during the Civil War."

"Well, his knowledge of regional history seems very detailed," Collier said. "But I wasn't asking him as much about the war as I was—"

"About the house," she guessed. "And the legends. The cursed fields, the murdered slaves. The mansion of evil, and Harwood Gast and his railroad to hell."

"Sute told me it was built privately by Gast, with his own funds."

"Funds that were never depleted, by the way," she added.

Collier remembered. "Oh, yes, he talked about that, too. So what did he pay his men with? They weren't all slaves."

"No. The white workers on his crew were paid a small fortune, and the slaves were well clothed, well equipped, and well fed—all thanks to Gast's money."

"So how did he buy the materials? All that track and railroad ties, spikes, tools, supply cars?"

"Nobody knows." Dominique smiled. "Some say Gast sold his soul to the devil."

The word flagged him. "And you said that there really is a devil."

"Um-hmm."

"So if there *really* is a devil, maybe people *really do* sell their souls to him."

"People sell their souls to the devil every day, for a whole lot less."

Collier found that if he ate the food without looking at it, it was much less radical. When Dominique excused herself for the restroom, his gaze covered the back of her body as effectively as a paint roller. He ordered another beer from the waitress and had her take the other bottle after draining it, then drank the new bottle down to the first bottle's level. *Yeah, that'll fool her, all right . . .*

When he saw Dominique coming back, he dug his fingernails hard into his leg. *Don't look at her boobs anymore, you sexist pile of shit!* Instead, he sensed her breasts riding ever so slightly in the clinging cami-top.

"What were we talking about?" she asked. "Oh, yeah. Deals with the devil."

But the idea seemed to taint the power of the legend. Could it really be that bland? "Satanism, then. The Gast myth is just a painted-up version of that?"

"Probably. Inventing stories is part of our nature, I guess—as the highest animal. Detractors of religion say the same thing about Christianity. It's just a caveman legend: the savior comes and plucks the good people out of their hellhole existence and takes them to paradise."

"A fair point, for people who consider religion objectively."

"Of course it is. But seeing is believing. Those detractors never get a chance to really *see,* because they don't believe in anything strong enough to ask to be *shown.* They believe in concrete and steel and Ford and Mercedes. They believe in Starbucks and Blockbuster and Super Bowl Sunday and reality TV. Brad Pitt and Angelina Jolie are all the saviors they need. And their paychecks, of course. All that shit in their lives prevents them from seeing anything everlasting."

"Money and fashion is the new god?"

"The new golden calf," she said. When she crossed

her ankles under the table, her toes brushed his leg. "Sorry. Wasn't trying to kick you."

Baby, you can kick me anytime you want . . . and I'd LIKE it . . . "So with your caveman analogy, and objectively speaking, we create ghost stories because we've always been intrigued by them—"

"Not just intrigued. We need them," she said. A squid tentacle slipped between her lips into her mouth. "Cavemen *wanted* to believe there were ghosts, because the idea reinforced ancient myths of the afterlife."

Collier's brow furrowed.

"Not only are ghosts proof of an afterlife, but they're also proof of a netherworld—or hell. If the caveman really believes there are ghosts haunting the woods, what else can they be but unsaved spirits? And if there are *unsaved* spirits, then surely there must be saved spirits, too. Follow the code and you go to heaven. Don't follow the code, and you're a ghost prowling the woods at night."

Collier tried to make more observations without being the devil's advocate. "So . . . *not* objectively speaking?"

"I don't worry about it because I see the reality of God every day."

"What does that look like, exactly?"

"You have to ask God to *see,* Justin," she nearly exclaimed. "It's personal. It's between God and the individual. If I say anything more, I'll only sound like a Holy Roller again. I don't have to explain why I believe that Christ is my Savior—"

"No, no, I wasn't asking you to do that," Collier hastened. "I understand that it *is* personal." He feared the conversation was growing too touchy. If he touted any serious Christian ideals himself, Dominique would smell him out as a fake. "I believe in the Ten Commandments and the Sermon on the Mount and all that. My problem is following them. Back to what we were talking about earlier. Weakness."

She just looked at him and nodded. "Humans aren't strong—not since Eve bit the apple. That's why God gives us an out. We either find it or we don't."

He tried to assimilate. "Then what did Harwood Gast find? You say that you know there's a God because you've seen evidence of him in your life—"

"Sure. A bunch of times."

"So if you know there's a God, then you know there's a heaven, and if you know there's a heaven, then you know there's a hell?"

She laughed. "Yeah."

"So then maybe all those cotton fields *are* cursed. Maybe the Gast House really is haunted, and maybe Harwood Gast genuinely made a pact with the devil, or, well, a demon, which is what Sute suggested. Maybe all those stories are *true*."

She shrugged. "I agree with the possibility."

"So what about you? I believe you when you say you've seen evidence of God in your life. Have you ever seen any evidence of anything else?"

Her gorgeous eyes narrowed. "As in what?"

"At lunch, didn't you imply that you *had* seen something at the inn? I just want to know if you've ever witnessed anything around here that might suggest it's not all a bunch of—"

"Bullshit? Well, in all honesty I can say . . . maybe. But I won't say what it was."

Collier sighed.

Now she was grinning. "I know. I hate it when people do that, too. But I don't want to say anything 'cos then you really will think I'm a crackpot."

"I swear I won't," he about pleaded. Collier was getting the same jive from everyone around here. "There's no way I'll think you're a crackpot."

"Well . . ." Her gaze darted up to the waitress. "Oh, here's the check. This is Dutch treat—"

"I'm not Dutch." Collier gave the waitress cash, with a big tip. Then he leaned into the table. "Tell me."

Her reluctance was genuine. "All right, but not here. You paid for dinner, so I'll get dessert . . ."

A hot fudge sundae on top of . . . squid, Collier thought in disbelief. He opted for a large shortbread cookie and followed Dominique out of the corner ice-cream parlor. They sat on a bench facing a semicircular half wall of old brick and mortar, which highlighted a large cannon. The cannon had no wheels but sat on a round track and swivel; a pyramid of fat shells rested beside it. Collier half noticed one of the omnipresent historical plaques: LONG-RANGE ARTILLERY BARBETTE BUNKER AND MODEL 1861 6.4-INCH PINTLE-MOUNTED CANNON. *A world of hurt,* Collier thought. Beyond them, tourists seemed to emerge from the settling dusk.

Dominique dug into the sundae as if ravenous. As each spoonful was savored, Collier saw the wet shine of her lips and tongue-tip in a Daliesque clarity; nightfall hovered around the radiant face and the gem-shine of her eyes. "I'm such a pig, but this is so good," she reveled. "You sure you don't want some?"

"No, thanks, I'm stuffed." When he imagined his stomach's reaction to ice cream mixing with Korean spices and squid, beef, and half-cooked egg—plus all the beer he'd had today—he shivered. In all, he had to force himself to eat the cookie.

Then he imagined something else: when she raised the next spoonful to her parted lips, she froze. Suddenly she was topless and sitting spread-legged on the bench, the quirky Christian reverting to her college-tramp roots . . .

Her mouth sucked the ice cream off the spoon, where it sat on her tongue till it melted, and then her lips expelled it. The slew of white cream marbled with hot fudge began to run a slow line down her chin, over the hollow of her throat, and between her breasts. It stopped to pool in her belly button, and that's when the fantasy put Collier on his knees licking it out. His hands molded her hips and slid up her ribs as his tongue followed the track in reverse. He evacuated the adorable navel, then sucked upward over a quivering stomach. His mouth could feel excited blood beating in vessels beneath succulent, perfect flesh. No thoughts formed in his own mind, just the carnal craving. She had become his own ice-cream sundae. When his tongue laved her cleavage, her breasts vised his cheeks.

When his tongue slathered over the fudge-covered cross, he recoiled—

It burned like a tiny branding iron.

"—and, see? Those are some of the very first tracks, right there."

Collier's head surfaced from the dirty delusion like a bubble breaking sewer water. She'd been talking but he hadn't heard any of it.

"What's that?"

She pointed past the cannon, to the brick-paved street. Two parallel lines crossed the quaint lane, and the lines seemed sunken beneath the bricks.

"Oh, railroad tracks," he finally recognized. "Gast's railroad, I presume."

"Right. See that plaque there?"

Another old brick wall sported the plaque: ORIGINAL SITE OF DEPOT NUMBER ONE, OF THE EAST TENNESSEE AND GEORGIA RAILROAD COMPANY—1857.

Collier looked at the strangely rustless rails. "So the original track still exists?"

"Oh, no. Most of it was taken up after the war—for reparations. But they left these here, and there are a few more sections around the town, even with the original ties. But this site, right here where we're sitting, is where the madness of Harwood Gast officially began in 1857. It ended less than five years later in an area in Georgia called Maxon."

"Maxon," Collier uttered. "I don't think I've ever heard of the place."

"That's because it doesn't exist anymore. The Union army razed the entire area. There's nothing there now except scrub."

Collier thought back. "Mr. Sute told me that Gast actually built the railroad to take prisoners to some sort of concentration camp. Was that this Maxon place?"

"Yes," Dominique grimly replied. "And the prisoners weren't captured Union soldiers, they were—"

"Civilians. I remember him telling me that, too. Doesn't make a whole lot of sense, from a military standpoint, I mean."

"Neither did Dachau and Auschwitz, until you consider the motivation behind it all. It wasn't logistics or efficiency—it had to be evil."

"So Harwood Gast was the Hitler of the Civil War?"

"Maybe worse, simply because Gast was never political. He was a private citizen," she said. "He was never in office, and he never bid for office. He simply built his railroad and killed himself."

Collier smiled darkly. "His service was done, the pact complete: building a railroad that had no military use during a war. Himmler answered to Hitler, but Gast answered to a higher—or I guess I should say—"

"A lower authority," Dominique finished. "At least that's if you believe the legend."

"Which, by the way, you haven't really said if you do or don't," Collier added, "but just a little while ago you told me you didn't necessarily *dis*believe the stories . . . which leads me to my next point . . ."

"You are one persistent beer writer," she laughed. "All right. I'll tell you what I saw that night."

They walked the fringes of the main drag as the town turned over to nightlife. Carriage-style streetlamps drew floating lines of light down the street.

"Just, please," she said halfheartedly, "don't tell *anyone* this because it makes me look idiotic."

"You have my word."

Her shadow angled before him, a sexy cutout. "Several years ago a wedding party hired the restaurant to cater their reception. They rented the atrium at Mrs. Butler's inn. It all went fine, but at one point just before we brought out the desserts, I looked in the far corner of the room. There are a lot of little nooks on the sidewalls where Mrs. Butler keeps all those bookshelves and display cases full of Civil War stuff. Between two of those bookshelves, there's a little alcove that's hard to notice—"

Collier remembered immediately. "Right. And there's a desk there, with very elaborate carvings and little drawers and compartments."

Dominique nodded. "And also a tiny portrait of Penelope Gast on the side, like someone hung it there to keep it hidden. Anyway, I'm counting heads for the desserts— some of the wedding party had already left, so I wanted to get the number right . . . and I see someone sitting there."

"At the desk?"

"At the desk. It's this guy hunched over the desk writing something. I hadn't seen him before, so I figured he was a late arrival and maybe he sat down at the desk to fill out a wedding card or something. I go over there and ask him if he wants a homemade Napoleon for dessert."

"Yeah?"

"He stops writing and looks up at me—and this guy is, like, really ugly. Real pale face, crabby hands, big hooded eyes—and something messed up about his nose— looked like it had gold foil on it or something—and there's this bizarre-looking red hat sitting on the desk, too. He looks at me like he's pissed off I interrupted him, and he says, 'Napoleon? I met him in Egypt, and he was absolutely deplorable.'"

"Huh?" Collier emphasized.

Dominique's bare white shoulders shrugged. "That's what the guy said, so I'm thinking he's drunk and making some strange joke. I ask him again if he wants dessert, and he kind of grimaces and says, 'Can't you see I'm busy? I have to pay more to Harding, out of the railroad account. Mr. Gast just put in an order for fifty more, to send to Maxon. They're wearing them out down there.'"

"Wearing . . ." Collier began.

"That's what he said, didn't explain. But I didn't care, the guy was a snot to me, so I left him there and went to help my people serve dessert. I ask my assistant manager if she saw when the guy had come in, and she says 'Who?' and I point to the alcove. 'That weirdo sitting at that desk,' I say. But—"

"When you looked again, he was gone," Collier supposed.

"Right. Gone."

Collier thought as much. "A creepy story, for sure. But . . . is that all?"

She playfully slapped him on the shoulder. "No! That's just the beginning. See, I shouldn't tell you the rest— you'll just make fun of me."

"Tell me the rest!"

They turned a darker corner, a side street of shops that had closed earlier, and just one candlelit bistro with people having cocktails at outside tables. Dominique's bright white apparel and lambent skin made her ghostly now in the lower light.

"So the reception's a big success, and the bride's father pays the bill and tips hard. Most of the people are gone by midnight, but a few stayed past that for drinks. I let my people go home after they got everything loaded up, and I stay to serve the drinks and listen to these drunk people in tuxedos jabber. At one point I look out the window and I see someone walk by—two little girls in white dresses."

Collier's throat tightened. "Was . . . there a dog?"

She looked at him funny. "A *dog?* No. Just the two girls. But then something else catches my eye, on the stair hall. *Another* figure. Guess who?"

"The guy at the desk?"

"Yeah, and now he's wearing that imbecilic red hat. I see him go down the hall. I'm *positive* I saw him. He even looked down at me and scowled. Could be wrong about the two girls in the window, but I'm *sure* I saw him. I figure he's a guest staying at the inn, maybe the crotchety old guy with the nose was the kids' father or grandfather or something. No big deal, right?"

"Okay."

"By one, everybody leaves, so I'm just doing the last-minute cleanup, shouldn't take me more than an hour. I want to get out 'cos I'm tired. Mrs. Butler shows up to see if I need a hand, so I ask her how many guests are staying at the inn that weekend, and she says none."

"Oooooo," Collier remarked.

"Um-hmm. Ooooo. She tells me she's going to bed and I can lock up when I'm done. If I need anything, I can just call out for Jiff 'cos he's around mopping the floors."

Collier errantly touched her shoulder. "Please tell me you went upstairs to look around."

"Of course I did. But by now I have to admit I was a little freaked. Most of the lights were out, and the place was *real* quiet. I'm positive that no one came *down* the stairs because you can see both stairwells from the atrium. So I go up . . ."

Collier was becoming intrigued. "Yeah?"

"It's dark up there. The minute I set foot on the landing, I regretted it. But I look anyway. All the doors were open to air the rooms . . . except one. It was locked."

"Room two?" Collier asked.

She looked surprised. "Yeah."

"That's the room next to the one I'm staying in. It's also the room where Penelope Gast and her maid were murdered."

Dominique's look of surprise darkened. "I didn't know that. How do you—"

"Well, I mean that's what Mr. Sute told me," Collier amended.

"Wow," she paused, reflecting.

"So—come on—what did you see upstairs?"

"Nothing," she said.

Collier felt cheated. *"Nothing?"*

"Nothing *yet.* I didn't see the guy and when I looked out the windows I didn't see the two girls but—and this is the unsettling part—I did smell something."

An irrepressible chill swept up Collier's back. *Please don't tell me you smelled*—

"I smelled urine. Jeez, I'll never forget it. Old urine, like when you walk under an expressway bridge where homeless people pee. It seemed to emanate from that door—room two. I actually got down on my knees to look in the keyhole, and that's where the smell was coming from—right from that hole."

Collier didn't know what to say, or what he might add to corroborate.

"But the funniest part? It was gone a minute later."

"The smell, you mean."

"Right. One minute the hall *reeked,* and the stench coming out of that keyhole was so strong it was like *steam.* And the next minute . . ."

"Gone like it was never there."

She nodded slowly.

Collier remained silent for several steps; then her face turned mischievous.

"Either you just swallowed a frog or . . . something's bothering you all of a sudden."

Collier decided what the hell. "I've smelled the same thing a time or two myself."

"I love it!" But then her enthusiasm lapsed. "But, you know, it's probably just a rotten carpet or something. Mildew."

"Yeah, maybe. That would be a much more sensible reason why Mrs. Butler never rents that room. It's just unserviceable, not haunted," he said, but continued in thought: *Haunted . . . by urine?*

"Sure. Or maybe it was something else. Maybe I'm more impressionable than I think, and I simply *thought* I smelled it."

Collier pushed his hair back. "Your mind *invented* it, in other words?"

"Yeah."

"Dominique, what reason would your subconscious mind make you *think* you were smelling . . . *that?*"

"Because of the story!" she exclaimed as though it were obvious. "You know. The whole 'Mrs. Tinkle' thing. I'm *sure* J.G. Sute told you about that, didn't he?"

"No, but Mayor Snodden did. Some kinky 'water sport' fetish is what I assumed."

"No, no, that's not it."

"Well then what is?" Collier insisted. "Why did people call her Mrs. Tinkle behind her back?"

Dominique almost blushed. "Same reason they called her 'Penelope Piss.' You don't know?"

"No! So tell me!"

She seemed coyly uncomfortable now. "That's what she'd always have her secret lovers do. You know. You never heard of Redneck Birth Control?"

"What?"

"A Southern Douche? Jeez. I guess I have to explain everything . . . as gross as it is. Whenever her lovers were . . . done . . ."

Collier finally put the pieces together. *They urinated in her after they came, to wash the sperm out. For shit's sake!* "All right, I get it."

"And the rumor is she always took her lovers to the

same room—the door marked room two now—and that's why it always reeked of urine."

"How charming," Collier muttered. *Yes indeedy. A Southern Douche.*

"It didn't always work, of course," she added. "Penelope had several abortions."

"Sute was kind enough to point that out."

A stasis passed as they walked. Collier presumed her story was over. "Oh, look," she said and immediately stood on her tiptoes.

Collier's sudden leg fetish raged. Her shapely calves tensed as bare heels elevated in the sandals. Then he pictured her standing like that bent over nude . . .

Pervert. The word clacked in his head like two stones smacking. *Pervert, pervert, pervert . . .*

"The moon," she said. "Tell me *that's* not creepy . . ."

They'd walked to the end of the side street. There were no streetlamps here. Crossing the road at an angle was another length of track sunken in the bricks. It extended past the street and seemed to continue into scrubby grassland. Collier walked out farther with her and actually found the rail still mounted securely on century-and-a-half-old railroad ties. An oblong moon the color of brick cheese glowed eerily in a shallow sky.

In the oddest vertigo, like a snippet of nightmare, Collier saw a woman's face, grinning in a wanton evil, then skeletal hands rising up toward the moon.

The face of the mirage belonged to Penelope Gast . . .

"I second that," he finally said. "Perfect setting for your ghost story."

"And that's the land, right out there. God knows how many acres, not used for anything anymore."

He realized after the fact that they were holding hands.

Something almost like a hidden terror trembled in him. *Who did that? Me? Her?* He didn't know . . .

"And it never will be," she continued, gazing. "People

really do believe the land is hexed by what Gast did out there."

Staking the heads of slaves and hoeing them into the earth, he remembered. It was monstrous, but . . .

Collier wasn't particularly focused on town history anymore. *Oh my God, this girl . . .* His blood felt like oil heating up on a stove top, just from the warm sensation of her hand.

"And in a way, even though all that scrubland out there is pretty ugly . . . there's still something beautiful about it."

"Yes, there is," Collier agreed without even getting it.

The low moonlight on her face surrealized her features, leaving lines and wedges black but luminescing the rest. Now her eyes looked bottomless, the swell of her bosom and the moonshine on her legs a threshold to something that transcended the reality of his lust. Collier had never seen a more beatific face in his life.

Who turned whom, then? Collier didn't know. She remained on tiptoes when he suddenly found himself kissing her. Her grip on his hand tightened and grew hotter; the tips of their tongues met. Her other hand stole around his back and urged him closer, and when he slid his mouth off her lips and ran it down the side of her neck, she sighed in what could only be desire.

Collier felt he had stepped into a precious demesne, a place where desire was more than instinctive brain cells firing to compel reproduction. He was overjoyed to be in that special place—the first time, truly, in his life. But he also knew it was a place he did not deserve to stand in . . .

Her could feel her nipples go rigid against his fake Tommy Bahama shirt; he could swear he even felt his own nipples sensitize. Another hot, liquid sigh, and she pulled his mouth back to her, and sucked his tongue, inhaled his breath . . .

Her hand opened on his chest and she pushed back.

"Time to stop—"

SHIT! "I don't want to," he said, and tried to recaress her. But her opened hand remained firm.

She seemed disappointed and awkward. "Justin . . . I've only explained some of myself, not all. There's stuff you don't understand about me. I'm just the way I am, I can't help it, and I don't want to."

Collier felt like a popsicle that had just been run over on Arizona asphalt. He grabbed her hand and squeezed it. "I want to know what you mean. I want to know everything about you."

"It just wouldn't be fair."

"Fair? To who?"

"To you."

The reply stunned him. Next, she was leading him by the hand back to the bench. "It's too soon."

"Okay, that's fine," he nearly pleaded. "I'm very patient—"

Her chuckle fluttered in the dark. "Yeah, right."

I'm fucking crazy about you . . . "I can wait till it's *not* too soon."

"No, you can't. Shit, in this day and age there's probably no guy anywhere who'd wait that long . . . and you're distracting me, anyway."

"Distracting you?"

She turned on the bench, still grasping his hand. "You're the one who wanted to hear my story. I didn't want to tell you, but you insisted."

"And you told me. It's a great story, and I believe it. But what's that got to do with—"

"My story's not over," came the abrupt information.

Damn it . . . "There's more?"

"Everything I've told you until now is *squat* compared to the rest. Now. Do you want to hear it, or not?"

"Yes . . ."

So this was how she checked her boundaries. *I don't care,* Collier thought. He was content to sit with her hand in his, their shoulders touching . . . that is, *he* was content, but the same wasn't holding true for a certain part of his anatomy. *Deal with it! Don't be an asshole and piss her off* . .

"The stench from room two, like I was saying, disappeared so fast, I honestly don't see how it could've been there. I must have imagined it."

You didn't. Collier kept the correction to himself.

"And I found no trace of the old guy with the screwed-up nose, so I told myself that was my imagination, too. Shit, it happens sometimes. Tired, long day, hadn't eaten much—it happens. No big deal, right?"

"Right."

"But I told you, except for room two, the other rooms had their doors open, and the second-floor rooms on the stair hall all have balconies overlooking the garden, the courtyard, and then all that scrubland past it."

"I know, it was the first thing I noticed about my room when I walked into it. So . . . what happened?"

For the recital's entirety, Dominique had maintained a smooth, none-too-serious composure, as though she were fine with the likelihood of it all being imagination. Now, though—

Collier's gaze on her face hardened.

It was akin to a Hollywood morph the way Dominique's expression went dark. Her eyes, at once, looked troubled, and she almost stammered a few times. "In one second, there was—was—orange light, real bright—"

"Orange light? Where?"

"In the French doors right when I was standing at the doorway of the room you're staying in."

"Dominique, I don't understand. Orange light?" Alarm. "Was part of the house on fire, or the fields?"

"That's what I thought at first, but no, and then I thought I must've fallen asleep and woke up at the crack of dawn." She paused. "But my watch said it was going on two in the morning."

"So you went to the balcony, right? And looked out—"

A stifled nod. Was her hand shaking? "I went out the French doors, and saw that it was a fire, all right. And I heard a ringing sound, too. The entire backyard was lit up, and shifting. I could feel wafts of heat . . ."

Now something began to nag in Collier's mind—

She spoke in front of her, not to him. "There's an old Civil War–era iron forge out there. I don't know if it's *still* there but—"

"It is," Collier spoke up. "I saw it the day I came. But Jiff told me it's never used for anything but a barbecue nowadays, for holidays and parties."

"Jiff wasn't there, and this was no barbecue. Ore was being smelted in that thing. Every time the bellows pumped the orange light doubled . . . that and the intermittent sounds of a hammer made the whole thing feel maniacal. There're several different chutes on the walls of the forge, and all that light and heat just *poured* out of them."

Collier remembered the look of the thing, and the vents, one quite large. "What next?"

"There was a man down there, too, of course, but I couldn't really see any details. He seemed to be working in cycles: pumping, hammering, pumping, hammering, like that. But every so often he'd disappear around the other side of the forge, and the light would go down some 'cos he wasn't pumping."

"Probably skimming slag or whatever it is they do."

"He was pouring molten metal out of a little crucible," she verified, "but I didn't find that out till I got down there."

Collier considered the scenario. "Must've been pretty scary."

Another slow nod. "The whole thing was so crazy, I

had to go out there. Somebody smelting *iron* in a bed-and-breakfast garden at two in the morning? You've got to be kidding me. I was freaked out, yeah, but I was also mad. I ran down there—"

Collier couldn't help but anticipate. "And the guy was gone and the forge was cold."

She nudged him. "Hey, *I'm* telling the story!"

"But am I right?"

"You're dead wrong. By the time I got down there, if anything, the light was brighter, the air even hotter. The guy'd come back around, pumping the bellows and hammering something on an anvil, but now . . . I could *see* him . . ."

Was she doing it on purpose? Collier didn't think so. He used the old line: "You sure know how to keep a jackass in suspense. *Tell* me. Who was the guy?"

She looked directly into his eyes, straight-faced. Now her hand was slick with sweat. "What did you think? It was a blacksmith—circa 1860. High leather boots, canvas pants, a slick rawhide apron. He was hammering a strip of metal, and alternately yanking the bellows chain. So I said, 'Hey, what the hell are you doing?' and I said it loud. But he didn't hear me, just kept whacking away."

"What did he look like, I mean, his face?"

"Big bushy mustache, and the skin on his face was like pitted leather. He wore this hat that was sort of like a leather cowboy hat but without the sides curled up, and the front flopped down. I yelled at him again, and he kept ignoring me. He walked back around the side of the forge and that's when I saw him dipping the crucible into the vent. He took it out and poured it into a stone mold that looked like it had wax or something in it, and he did it very carefully. Then he picked the mold up with tongs and dunked it in a tub of water."

Collier could feel the pulse in her hand pick up.

"He brought the mold around, knocked the metal out

with a hammer, and started beating on it—the cycle beginning again."

Collier felt dour when he asked, "Was it a mold for shears?"

She looked at him, startled. "Yes. Why do you ask?"

He knew he couldn't possibly mention the morbid nightmare. "I saw one in Mrs. Butler's display cases. A mold chiseled out of stone, for wooling shears."

"Well, that's what these things looked like. They were big, like tin snips. He had a mold for each half, and after he'd banged on them a while, he tossed them aside with the tongs. There were two piles of them on the ground, sizzling."

"Did you tap him on the shoulder, give him a nudge to get his attention?"

Dominique seemed tired now. "To tell you the truth, that's the first thing that came to my mind, but I didn't. Because I was afraid if I touched him—"

"There'd be nothing there."

She nodded. "I shouted at him one more time, and I mean at the top of my lungs . . . He obviously didn't know I was there, but when I shouted, he kind of paused and stood up straight. Then he turned around and looked right at me."

"I thought you said he didn't know you were there."

She made a nullifying hand gesture. "Or I should say, he didn't look right *at* me, he looked right *through* me."

Collier thought on that.

"Then"—she visibly gulped—"I noticed the rest."

"What!" Collier nearly yelped in frustration.

"His eyes," she said in the lowest tone. "The whites of his eyes. They didn't look human. The whites were yellow, like someone with a disease, with darker smudges like soot. His face, right just then—the way his eyes looked, I mean . . . I was more terrified at that moment than I've ever been in my life—that one second of looking in his eyes. Because I got the sickest feeling that for maybe a sliver of a second, he saw me."

Collier was keyed up. "What did he do next?"

"He grimaced, and it turned that pocked, leathery face into the grossest mask. Then he starting pumping the bellows again." She let out a long sigh. "So there. That's my story."

Crickets chirruped around them. The night had deepened and grown more humid; Collier felt clammy at his armpits.

"Wow," he said.

"I forced myself to walk back into the inn, all that light and heat raging behind me. It was a *wall* of heat. I got back inside, looked out the window, and—of course—the backyard was dark. The furnace was cold, and there was no one there."

Collier believed her at once. Unlike many he'd met thus far, bullshitting wasn't her style, nor was exaggeration. But he'd seen some things, too, hadn't he?

He elected not to mention them.

A question popped up. "Was this . . . back in your drinking days?"

She smiled. "Fair question. And, no. This was years later. Hallucination? Sure, it could be, but I don't think so, and I don't think it was lucid dreaming or any of that stuff, and I wasn't on medication for anything. I'll never know the answer"—she pressed a hand to her heart—"but in here, I think it was a ghost. A revenant, discorporate entity, or whatever it is they call it these days."

"'Ghost' works just fine for me. And that was the last time you ever took a catering job at the inn?"

"Oh, no," she said. "I've done a bunch since then. But that's the only time I ever saw anything funky."

Funky is right. I've got voices, piss stench, dogs, nightmares about SHEARS, and some woman flashing my keyhole with a shaved crotch. Could we BOTH be crazy?

Collier dropped it.

She half laughed but it didn't sound convincing. "Anyway, now that I'm done telling it, it all sounds pretty silly."

"You're wrong about that," Collier argued. "The Gast House is a pretty chilling place if you're in the right frame of mind—or, I guess in this case, the wrong frame of mind. Mr. Sute said that many, many people have had unusual experiences there."

She tossed a shoulder to dismiss it, but it was obvious her retelling left her discomfited.

"Enough of all this ghost stuff, though," he said more softly now. Her hand remained clasped in his.

He was looking at her again. He drew her back to him—had the story kindled her desires?—and found she was even more eager to kiss than before. Each tongue played around in the other's mouth with more fervor this time. Her breath seemed hotter now, if that were possible, and a bit of that push-back barrier had lessened. Her hand ran up his arm and over his chest as her tongue seemed desperate. Collier fell into a luscious void right then. Dominique was the fresh-baked bread still warm from the oven, and he was the butter melting into it.

The words in his head arrived like a zombie's drone: *I could really fall in love with her . . .*

Next she draped one leg over his to afford closer contact. For a moment he expected that smooth, bare leg to slide over his groin . . . but that never quite happened. Instead her hand around his back pressed him tighter to her.

He began to slowly suck down the side of her neck, and when his tongue laved over her jugular vein, he could feel her pulse beating like a hummingbird's, but as his tongue continued to glaze her throat and bare shoulder, the taste of her sweat, plus the commingling scents of body spray, soap, and shampoo magnified his rising horniness. He had one hand around her side, part of it over the gap between the clinging top and waist of her skirt. He knew he was testing her now, encroaching her obscure boundaries, but she didn't flinch when his hand pressed flat against her belly and the tip of his pinkie slipped an inch beneath the waistline of her skirt. Collier's Evil Twin voice returned: *Congratulations, stud! Right now your finger's about four inches from Party Central!* but Collier was too fevered to listen. He didn't move his hand but let his tongue trace the rim of the cami-top. Something told him not to slide the top down and expose the breasts he'd sell his soul to see, but he very gently ghosted his lips over the top of the ruffly fabric.

Then his lips inched closer to the nipple . . .

"Oh, jeez!" came a frustrated whisper.

Collier brought his lips away, but his hand remained in place. "What?"

"This is my fault," she sighed. "I know better. I need to tell you the rest . . ."

Collier was almost indignant. "No more ghost-story stuff!"

She paused to collect her breath. "No, more *me* stuff."

Collier didn't relieve his embrace. "If you don't want to go all the way tonight, that's cool." He tried to sound understanding.

"I should've explained everything earlier but I don't want to go all the way *ever.* What I mean is I don't have sex—at all—anymore. I probably didn't make that clear before."

Collier contemplated a thoughtful response but couldn't.

"I'll put it bluntly," she continued in a wearied tone. "I don't fuck. I haven't since college."

Collier tried to manage his reaction. "I understand," he assured her but really didn't. A small chuckle. "We weren't *fucking,* you know."

"I *mean,*" she added, "I'm never going to have sex again until I'm married. Making out is one thing, but . . . that's all I do. No sex out of wedlock, ever. That means any kind of sex—coitus, anal, oral. It's part of what I was telling you before. It's part of how I pay off that credit card I used to get my life back."

Think! Collier thought, but the alter ego piped in, *She's just making an excuse so she won't feel guilty after you ball her from one end of the street to the other! Keep feeling her up! In a few minutes you'll have her so hot she'll turn into a great big bowl of Do-Me Stew . . .*

Was that really it? *We were making out pretty heavy.* He replied like a trained actor, "I understand."

There was a fret in her eyes. "I don't think you do, and I realize that most guys don't—they can't. It's not reasonable for me to expect them to. And the part that sucks the worst is I really like you."

Evil Voice: *It's bullshit, buddy! Just stoke her up some more!*

He squeezed her hand. "Now it's my turn to be blunt. I'm so fuckin' crazy about you I could howl at the moon."

Her face looked childlike when she laughed. Then that expression of seriousness-merged-with-frustration drained back to her eyes. "I don't want you to think I'm a teasing bitch—"

"I don't."

Evil Voice: *Not only are you a teasing bitch, you're a teasing bitch who's about to get serious blocks put to you . . .*

"It's a hell of a lot to ask of a guy," she admitted, "even a hard-core Christian."

"I'm not a hard-core Christian, but I've got it covered."

"And for God's sake, I don't expect you or anyone to live by my personal spiritual standards. It's just *my* thing."

"Just trust me," he whispered into her neck. They kissed some more. Collier was so intent on her that he wasn't sure *what* he planned, and he had no idea how closely he'd been listening to his own dark side. He whis-

pered, "Is this too much?" and lowered his mouth to her
waist and teased her navel with his tongue. He licked a
ring around it, then daintily pressed his tongue in and
sucked.

Well . . . she didn't say no . . .

He sucked harder, and was overjoyed by the way
she flexed, squirmed, and moaned. Her hands came to
his head; he expected her to push him off but it didn't
happen.

He was also getting away with his right hand half cup-
ping a buttock, which squirmed and tremored as well.
And again, "Is this too much?" before his tongue slowly
licked a line straight up her several inches of bare stomach to the bottom of the cami but when he tried to hook
his tongue beneath the hem, her hands nudged him off a
moment and replaced his mouth back on the fabric. Collier continued to move up . . .

Testing more boundaries, he knew. His lips roved
over the meager fabric that covered her breasts, and he
replaced his hand over her belly, one pinkie returning to
its previous position an inch beneath the waistband.

Her skin felt so hot now, and shedding sweat. The pinkie roved in the sweat but when he tried to slide it down
another half inch, her hand pulled it back.

*The bitch is still playing with you. Once you start suck-
ing her tit through that cheesecloth tramp-wear she's got
on, she won't stop you then, brother . . .*

Collier wondered. But she allowed his mouth to proceed farther up the bottom of her breast. His lips felt
sensitive as a stethoscope; they could detect the swell-
ing heat, the racing pulse.

Keep going . . . But were they his words, or his id's?

Collier's mouth kept creeping up. Through the corner
of his eye, he spotted an elderly couple walking by, but
even in the dark he could see their eyes wide in shock.
To hell with 'em, he thought. They hurried by.

At last, Collier's lips found the very distended nipple, and began to slowly suck it through the cotton top.

Her back bowed, and she huffed in a breath.

But she didn't stop him.

She's all yours now. You just turned her stiff Christian starch into pudding . . .

Was Collier listening?

He sucked more fervently, and precisely; her breast was a pulsing bag of excited nerves and hot blood. When Collier took his mouth off, he could see how he'd sucked a dark, wet circle into the fabric, her inflamed papilla standing hard. In the next blink, he switched to the other nipple and began to suck even harder.

Dominique's hands fisted in his hair. She was breathing through her teeth, inhaling her next words: "Oh, shit, I can't believe how good that feels . . ."

That's when Collier's hand slipped between her legs and let his middle finger dip into the flooded vaginal groove.

"Damn it!" she yelled and yanked his hand out like someone pulling a snake out of a hole. "I *knew* it!"

When she jumped off the bench and strode off, Collier was thrown back. "What the hell? Dominique!"

Her heels clacked so loud down the brick street they sounded like a hammer smacking slate. Collier jumped up after her.

"Wait!"

She was walking real fast. Collier had to huff after her.

"What the hell is wrong?"

"I should've known!" she seemed to sob and yell at the same time. "It's always the same. No one gives a *shit* how someone else feels!"

"What are you talking about?" he pleaded when he finally caught up and grabbed her arm. He wanted to collapse when he saw tears welling in her eyes.

"What, I guess you just thought you'd get me horny

enough and I'd decide to fuck you? Right after I just got
done telling you I didn't want to?"

"I-I—"

"Past a certain point all women are just bitches in
heat? They're all asking for it? 'No' really means 'yes'?"

"No-no—"

She turned and resumed her strut.

"Wait! Please!"

When Collier grabbed her arm again, she almost
hauled off and hit him. But he had to stop her, he had to
find out what had happened.

"Why'd you have to ruin it?" she wailed in the street.

"What? My *hand?*"

"I told you, no sex, and you said okay!"

"It was just my hand! My finger!"

"That's just great." Her glare mixed with heartache.
"Let me spell it out. If you put your penis into my vagina,
that's sexual contact. Why? Because my vagina is my *sex
organ*. If you put your mouth on my vagina, that's sexual
contact, because my vagina is my sex organ. So tell me,
Justin. If you put your finger in my SEX ORGAN, what is
that?"

Collier's jaw froze open.

Now she was wiping her eyes. "I'm leaving. Good-bye."

"Wait!"

His shout cracked down the street. He was sure anyone within a block had heard it. Now he was squeezing
her arm hard.

Let her go, man, insisted the Evil Voice. *She's the Tease
from Hell. Forget about this nutty bitch. Go back to the hotel and use Lottie for an oil change . . .*

Collier was getting sick of that voice. "Listen," he
began.

"Let me go. You're hurting my arm."

"At least give me a chance to talk. This isn't fair at all."

He released her arm. Now the street stood in total silence, like the silence after a machine-gun volley. He

could see several late diners at the bistro craning their
necks at them.

"I'm sorry," he said. "I didn't understand—"

"Come on, you were working me—"

He pointed his finger right in her face. "Let me talk,
damn it. Give me two minutes, and then you can split
and think whatever you want. But I'm *sorry.* I didn't understand. You gotta admit, your rules are a little weird."

"I know they are!" she yelled. "But they're still my
rules, and I explained them to you, and you said that
was okay, but five minutes later you've got your hand
down my—"

"All right!" he yelled just as loud. "I get it! I guess it was
my male instincts or something. But you were letting
me . . . do . . . other stuff, so . . ."

"So you figured it was okay to stick your finger in my
pussy?"

Those words, too, echoed down the street. *Jesus,* he
thought. *This is too hard!*

So why didn't he just leave?

"We were just making out, Justin," she said, "and it
was wonderful. It was passion, it was desire. But that's
never enough for you guys, is it? If two people are making out, then that's carte blanche for the guy. Everything's got to be a *nut.* Everything's got to be a *piece of
ass.* If a woman makes out with a man, even after she's
told him she doesn't want sex, all of a sudden she's got
an *obligation* to fuck him—"

"Now you're being a cynical smart-ass," he countered.
"That's not how I feel at all." He felt the *need* to convince
her. "And look at it this way. I *know* now that I'll never get
to have sex with you. Right?"

She peered at him with suspicion. "Yeah."

"So if I'm just your typical cock-hound, if all I'm out for
is a *piece of ass* . . . then why am I still standing here?
How come I'm not long gone?"

Dominique couldn't answer.

"Tell me that you'll go out with me again," he insisted.

"I don't think that's a good idea, Justin—"

"Bullshit. It's a great idea." He squeezed her arm gently this time. "Tell me you'll go out with me again."

She sighed. "All right."

"When?"

"Tomorrow."

"Great. What time?"

She grinned. "Seven thirty in the morning."

What! "That's really early."

"Take it or leave it."

Collier's shoulders fell. "All right. Seven thirty in the morning. Where?"

She pointed across the street.

Collier couldn't see the building very well, for the shadows. But he could see the sign just fine: ST. THOMAS METHODIST CHURCH. JOIN US FOR OUR EARLY SERVICE!

CHAPTER TEN

I

"Please!" wept the nasally voice. "I'm begging you . . . My love!"

Jiff frowned, his feet kicked up in bed before the television. "But I was just there earlier today. You want me to come over again, tomorrow morning?"

"Yes, yes!"

"I—" *Sheee-it!* "I got too much work to do tomorrow," he semiled. "My ma's pissed at me fer not gettin' to all my chores today."

Sniffling. A croak. "I'm . . . worthless."

You got that right.

"I love you."

"I done *told* ya. Quit talkin' like that!"

"I need . . . to be utterly debased. I'm not worthy of your love because, I know, I'm shit. I'm begging you. Come here tomorrow morning and humiliate me. Treat me like the garbage I am."

It was getting pathetic. "No. I told ya. I cain't."

"I need to be *profaned.* I need to be *debauched.* Please, my love."

"No!"

"I'll pay you a hundred dollars . . ."

"I'll be there. What time?"

"Thank God!" Another sniffle, and something like a yelp of joy. "Come at nine, and . . . Jiff?"

Jiff was trying to watch Home Shopping Network. "Yeah?"

"I need it . . . to be real bad. Because *I've* been real bad. I'm so unworthy of your love that I need to be treated like common scum, do you understand?"

Jiff waved his hand. "I gotcha, J.G.," he almost yelled. He was getting to hate the pitiable fat old man and his masochistic kink games, but . . .

For a hundred dollars?

"Don't worry. I'll surprise ya. Now go to bed, I'll be 'round at nine."

"I love y—"

Jiff hung up. At least business was picking up. He'd made over a hundred dollars today just at the bar; another hundred tomorrow just from one trick with Sute would cash in a fine week. Things could be worse.

It was going on midnight; Jiff hoisted himself up and left the room. He still had to empty the ashtrays and take the trash cans outside, then make a final window check before going to bed. When he passed Lottie's room, he thought he heard her bed squeaking. *Sounds like she's humpin' her pillow again,* Jiff figured.

The next contemplation aggravated him. *Sute wants something extra hard tomorrow.* But Jiff couldn't imagine what. He was being left to his own creativity, and as much of a pain in the ass as it was . . .

A hundred bucks is solid bread.

Jiff knew he'd think of something rough.

When he left the wing, he didn't notice the pallid brown dog snuffling around at the other end of the hall.

II

Collier came back to a lobby empty and barely lit. *Damn, didn't realize it was so late.* He felt like looking around at more of the display cases but thought better of it. *Need to go to bed right now,* he reminded himself. *I need to be in CHURCH at seven thirty tomorrow morning . . .* He could still scarcely believe it. *I'm pussy-whipped for a girl who will never go to bed with me.* Collier thought hard about that, but didn't feel any different after doing so.

He was really looking forward to seeing Dominique.

The incident on the bench seemed so absurd now, he almost laughed out loud. *Smart move. Great way to really impress her.* But his nerves still felt vibrant from being so close to her. He could still smell her hair, could still taste the clean sweat he'd been allowed to lick off her skin . . .

God . . .

He left Mrs. Butler's truck keys behind the counter. *Mental note: NEVER borrow her truck again.* He'd walk to the church in the morning. He was about to turn up the stairs but noticed a display for the first time: an oblong glass display case on end, almost as tall as he. It held a woman's dress, a rich burgundy, in something almost like velvet. BALLROOM DRESS WITH STOMACHER AND PANNIERS, the plaque told him. WORN BY MRS. PENELOPE GAST. Collier stepped back to assess it, as one might a painting. *She wore that,* he abstracted. *A hundred and fifty years ago, her flesh and blood was standing in that dress—in this house . . . the wife of a twisted killer.* The notion gave him a chill.

Mrs. Gast. Mrs. . . . Tinkle . . .

He stepped away, unnerved, but not before noticing a much smaller case hanging on the sidewall of the stairs. It looked like a pair of crude pliers next to an old hat, but then he read, HAND-FORGED IRON COOLING TONGS—1861—AND REGULATION PATTERN 1858 "HARDEE" HAT, OWNED BY R. HARDING, THE FAMILY BLACKSMITH.

Collier remembered Dominique's story, the midnight blacksmith in the floppy hat. *That's it,* he thought, looking at the hat. *If the guy she saw really was a ghost . . . that's the hat he wore. Same guy that made the shears in the other case . . .*

Another chill followed him up the stairs. He hadn't noticed that the "Naughty Girl Clips" in the other case were now missing.

The floor creaked with every other step upstairs. Several wall-mounted electric candles were all that lit the stair hall. Did he hear a door click shut somewhere? Collier gazed through grainy dark. When he passed room two, he couldn't help it. He bent to sniff the keyhole but noticed nothing. Then he whisked into his own room and locked the door.

Why am I so creeped out tonight?

It was Dominique's story, of course, and the power of suggestion that would follow most anyone who'd heard it. Something in the house was building up, some unnamed psychic residue, and Collier was picking it up like a lint trap.

When he stripped and turned out the lights, impulse took him to the curtains over the French doors. He looked out at the old forge, which, in the sinking moonlight, looked like nothing more than a pile of rocks.

Sleep impelled him once in bed. *God, I'm tired.* But when he tried to drift off, his brain betrayed him with images of Dominique: her eyes in the moonlight, her bare legs shining, her nipples plump beneath the thin fabric he'd sucked a great, wet circle in. His penis erected at once, but he shouted at it, *No!*

He thought about her force of will—to abstain from sex—and then thought about his, which barely existed. He determined himself not to use her to assuage his own lust. The voice of his id kicked in yet again, *You got her so torqued up, she's home right now with her feet sticking up in the air with a twelve-inch dildo stuck in her, you asshole!*

Collier, somehow, doubted it, and he sloughed off the voice.

Right now she's hauling some other guy's ashes 'cos you didn't have the balls to go for it . . .

Collier smiled and shook his head.

He fell into black sleep and began to dream at once. *Please let me dream about her . . .* Instead he dreamed of lying prone in a lightless void; darkness lay on him like great rolls of pitch-black cotton.

No sex dreams tonight, he begged his mind in the dream.

Because he knew this was a dream.

He dreamed that someone was looking in *his* keyhole . . .

Who was it? And what were they seeing?

The blackness prevailed. A soft hand ran up his chest. *Shit . . .* There was no relent to his lust, even in sleep. It stained him like wine on white linen. Another pair of hands landed on him, one rubbing the other pectoral, the other slowly sliding toward his groin. His hips squirmed but he couldn't move—of course not—as the hands softly molested him. It was as though two women knelt at either side, to tend to him.

Even his dream was goading him to masturbate. But why not with images of Dominique? Was Dominique one of the women, and if so, who was the other?

Eventually the tongues and hands retreated.

Did he hear a giggle?

That's when it occurred to him how *small* the hands on his body seemed . . .

A lively whistling, then a girl's Southern drawl whispered through the utter blackness, "Here! Come on! Here!"

The bed rustled a bit; then someone else began to ravenously lick his face. It was frenetic, unabating . . .

More giggles.

The voice on the right: "Look at him go! Good, good boy!"

The voice on the left: "Don't lick him *there,* Nergie! Lick him down there!"

"What a dirty dog!"

This is no dream! Collier's mind stormed, and he lurched up, shoved his hands through the dark, and pushed two unseen forms off the bed. His legs mule-kicked outward, and his heels shot something lean and hairy off the mattress. After a *thump!* he heard a dog yelp.

He snapped on the bed lamp—

The room stood empty, but . . .

Bullshit!

The door was ajar.

"I know I locked that!" he stated to no one. He got up uncaring that he was naked, and he closed the door and locked it. "I'm *positive* I locked it . . ."

But was he really?

Damn it. He sat on the bed's edge. He felt his face and chest and, of course, there was no trace of wetness.

I gotta get out of this house . . .

Collier wished he smoked just then, because it seemed the perfect time for a cigarette. *Should I leave? Should I just pack my bags right now and get out of here?* But he'd barely written anything on the book. And where would he go at this hour? He'd have to pay his bill.

tap, tap tap . . .

His eyes shot wide. He looked at the door but—

tap, tap tap . . .

The tiny tapping sound came from the other side of the room.

What in the HELL is going on now?

tap, tap tap . . .

It was coming from the wall. *Low* on the wall.

Even with the lights on, he could just make out the peephole.

He switched off the lamp and found himself kneeling at the wall. Now the hole was lit.

He looked in.

He could tell at once that the sleek physique sitting in the hip bath belonged to Lottie. The circle encompassed her spread thighs, belly, and tight peach-size breasts. *Oh, Jesus . . .*

The strange girl's hips writhed in the bathwater, her hand frenetically plying her sex.

Collier's teeth chattered; he watched for many minutes, even as he thought, *She's knows I'm watching. She WANTS me to watch . . .*

His hand inched toward his own crotch. *Not this again,* he thought, wincing, but then his face blanked when he imagined what Dominique would think if she knew he was doing this, on the verge of masturbating while peeping on a whack-job exhibitionist.

She'd think I was scum.

He pulled away from the hole and sighed. *Madhouse,* he thought. *A house full of sexual weirdos . . .* But did this solve his most current dilemma? Did Lottie enter his room with a master key and feel him up before slipping away to the washroom? It made perfect sense, except . . .

There were FOUR hands on me . . .

And what could explain the final observation, what could only have been a *dog* lapping his face and chest and, very nearly, lower?

He remained there on his knees for several minutes,

and through the wall heard Lottie's obvious climax, then the hip bath being emptied, then the door click shut. A few moments later, and not much of a surprise . . .

tap, tap, tap . . .

It was from his door now.

"Gimme a break, Lottie," he hefted his voice. "Go to bed."

tap, tap, tap . . .

Don't answer it.

He felt absurd sitting on the floor, in the dark. He was hiding in his own room. But he knew what would happen if he let her in.

A few more taps and evidently she got the message. He heard her footsteps pad away.

You really are Man of the Year, huh? his id voice complained. *What kind of MAN says no to a horny woman?*

Collier didn't answer the voice.

thunk!

Collier's head jerked upright. The sound he'd just heard . . . had come from the other side of the wall. The bath closet.

Had Lottie returned, to tempt him further with more exhibitions of her body?

And the next sound? A rapid *gurgling . . .*

Collier looked back to the peephole.

A dark blur crossed his pinpoint field of vision. The gurgling sound continued, heightened, then stopped. When the blur moved off again, Collier blinked, and in the space of the blink thought he saw a man . . . *with his head in the hip bath . . .*

Impossible! he yelled at himself.

Another blink, and then he heard a vicious *gnawing* sound.

Collier jerked his eye back from the hole. He took repeated deep breaths, staring into the dark. Then he jumped up, pulled on his robe, and bound out of the room and over to the bath-closet door.

He paused, hand on the knob.

I know that when I open this door, no one will be inside.

He opened the door and found the small room unoccupied.

Madhouse, he thought again.

He returned to his room and went back to bed, disgusted, exhausted, and no longer capable of considering the latest absurdities.

Go to sleep. I have to go to church tomorrow . . .

Exhaustion and unease sucked him deep down into sleep . . .

III

Just as the sun sinks, you notice the man hanging by his neck. That's the first thing you saw when you turned the corner at the bottom of the hill . . .

Then you blink, and you're a little girl again.

Your spirit has transfused. Your name is Harriet, and you know this because you read it in your mother's diary that you kept for five years after she died. You remember: When you were seven, you came back from picking boysenberries in the woods and saw the Indians ripping off her clothes. She was screaming, and the Indians took turns lying on top of her and moving funny. They chopped off the top of her head with a great war hammer, then peeled off her scalp. You were terrified but you knew you must be very quiet. You looked around for your father but quickly saw that the Indians had done the same to him. After that one Indian cut off your father's thing, too, and put it on a cord around his neck; the cord had the things of many men on it. Another Indian had a curvy French knife—you knew it was French because your father had one just like it. He'd told you once that he got it from his own father, who'd killed lots of Indians in a war a long time ago. In this war, French soldiers gave lots of these knives to the Indians and paid them for parts they cut off of colonists. But anyway, right now this

Indian used the knife to cut off the fur between your mother's legs, along with the skin, and he put it in a bag.

Then the Indians burned the camp, but they never caught you.

You were in a place called the Ohio Territory, and this happened in 1847. You thought you were going to freeze to death that winter but some federal soldiers found you and took you with them. They took you south. You lived in a supply wagon, and it was your job to wash the soldiers' clothes, and at night they'd all come into the wagon and take turns lying on top of you and moving funny the way the Indians did to your mother.

That's how it went. You got used to that part. The soldiers always smelled horrible but they gave you food and left you alone most of the time. By spring, they arrived at an army post in Tennessee called Camp Roan.

There you lived with a lot of children whose parents were killed during various Indian wars or died from diseases. It was mostly widowed women who taught you how to sew, cook, tan hide, and any other duty that was needed around the camp. These women also taught you how to read. That's when you were able to read in your mother's diary about your name. "Walter wanted to name our wonderful baby Harriet after President William Henry Harrison, the hero of Tippecanoe. 'He'll be the finest president we ever have,' Walter always said, 'and it'll be good luck to name our beautiful daughter after him.'" At least your luck had lasted longer than President Harrison's. He died during his first month of office.

Because the camp had calendars, you always knew what day it was. On your sixteenth birthday, you snuck out of the camp and never came back. You got real skinny living on roots and berries but eventually you were taken in by a charcoaler. He was a strange little man who lived in a sod hut and spoke almost no English—he was from some weird place called Germany. You cooked for him and sewed his clothes while he spent the whole day chopping *up wood and turning it into charcoal to sell to blacksmiths. He was always smeared black with soot. Every night he put his thing in you just like the soldiers but he also taught you how to do other things to his thing, too, with your mouth. You guess you did it very well because sometimes he'd bring you little presents from the nearby town called Branch Landing where he sold his charcoal. Several times you got pregnant but the baby usually died in your stomach and came out early, but one time it lived, and you were overjoyed. By then you understood that this happened most of the time to pregnant women, so to actually have a baby that lived was a great gift. You named your baby Henry, after President William Henry Harrison, and maybe that was bad luck, because a week later the German man took the baby to town and sold it to a couple who just lost theirs. They gave the German man thirty dollars, a big sack of flour, a brand-new cast iron skillet, and a pig.*

That night you killed the German man for selling your baby. He fell asleep after you used your mouth on him, and then you collapsed his head with the skillet. You buried him in the giant ash pile and let the pig go, and then you left. You're not sure how old you were then but you were probably around nineteen, because a trapper's wife you met on the road to town told you it was 1859.

You didn't know how pretty you were. You hadn't seen a mirror since the camp. When you got to the town, a jolly fat woman named Bella took you in. You were dirty and covered with charcoal soot. She washed you vigorously in a tub, chattering, "Oh, my good Lord, aren't you just the most precious thing to ever walk in here!" It was a wooden building with two floors, which you never knew existed, and it had a swing sign out front that said BELLA'S. *There were a lot of other girls there who didn't look very happy to see you.*

When you'd crushed the funny German man's head, you took the thirty dollars he got for Henry, plus more money he got for his charcoal, but Bella took it. "It's for housing and training, dear," she told you. "All the girls have to pay, but lookin' at you I can tell you'll be earnin' your keep a right fast." This was when you learned what a whorehouse was.

You learned a lot more here than the camp. You learned that there were men who pay money to pretty girls who let them put their things in them. You learned that if a girl squirted vinegar in herself after a man put his thing in you, then you sometimes wouldn't have a baby. You learned there was a thing called an abortion that would kill a baby growing inside of you, and lots of girls did this because they could make more money at the whorehouse. There was a doctor in town who could this for a girl but it had to be a secret because it was against the law.

You also learned that the town wasn't called Branch Landing anymore; it was called Gast, after a tall man in nice clothes who brought lots of money to the town. Most of the men who came to Bella's worked for Mr. Gast, and they got paid lots of money because they were building a railroad for him. Mr. Gast never came to Bella's whorehouse, though, but he did build it, so his men would have a place to put their things in girls.

The other girls didn't like you, and one day you learned why. "It's 'cos you suck better," one of the rail workers told her one night after she'd done just that for two dollars. "And, shee-it, girl, you're the best-lookin' whore in this place." You figured that was a compliment, and it must be true because you seemed to make more money than the other girls. Some men paid extra for . . . other things, like putting it in your bottom. One time a nutty man with a beard even paid you to let him squirt his jism on your feet, and he paid three dollars! But the funniest one was a little man weirder-looking than the German. He had a nose made of gold and wore a red hat that looked stupid, and he paid to watch you move your bowels into a bucket. That's when it came to your mind that lots and lots of men were really weird.

Then there were other men who were bad . . .

* * *

"You take him, bitch," Jane snaps, glaring at you. "You the only whore here that likes suckin' it. So go suck his."

"Fuck you!"

You go to hit her but she runs away.

"Yeah, you best run! Ain't no man wanna pay you with two black eyes'n I'll knock the rest'a your teeth out to boot!"

"That's enough'a that, Harriet," Bella orders from the velvet couch. She was eating sugar balls from the baker's.

"Is it that man I keep hearin' 'bout?"

Bella just raises her brows and keeps eating.

"The one that's so mean?"

Bella licks her chubby fingers. "Oh, Mr. Morris is a good customer, and he pays good. He just gets a little rough sometimes, but you'll be all right. You're a tough girl, 'cos that's how I taught ya."

"I don't want him," you declare.

Bella lurches up and slaps you hard across the face. "Do as you're told, girl. Don't get high'n mighty just 'cos you're the favorite 'round here. I made you, remember? You were eatin' grubs'n drinkin' creek water when I brung you in. And I remember that day well, hon, how you were all covered with soot. I never told that to no one, even after I heard 'bout that charcoaler they found in the ash pile near 'Bethstown."

You wilt.

"Am I gonna get any more sass out'a ya?"

"No, ma'am."

"I need my girls to be reliable. Bunch of Mr. Gast's rail men come back a few days ago so's we'll be busy. I need girls who wanna work, ya hear me?"

"Yes, ma'am."

"So get in there'n take care'a Mr. Morris." Then she shoots you a big, jolly smile. "He'll probably give ya five dollars, and he'll only last five seconds!"

You share a phony laugh, then turn for the waiting parlor. But as you're walking you glance in the pantry and notice Teeta, who's mulatto. She's dipping a tin cup into the spring barrel, and she's only got one hand. "Mr. Gast's railroad's done is what I heard," *she says.*

"Really?"

"They'se all comin' back over the next few days, so we'se'll be gettin' lots of business."

"Oh. Good."

"Some's back now."

"I know. Bella told me."

The mulatto girl's eyes widened with something scary. "I heared they killed all the slaves when they was done. Near a hunnert of 'em. In Maxon."

"That can't be true," *you say.*

"Hope it ain't."

"We hear things all the time that ain't true. Like the Yankees gettin' close. Our boys whup 'em anytime they get near Chattanooga. So don't believe most'a what'cha hear, Teeta."

The girl smiles a little, then walks away after taking down a jar of vinegar. But now that she's gone you can see the calendar on the wall. You notice that it's May 3, 1862.

"Aw, yeah, I done heard about you," *the voice seems to grind out of the air when you enter the sitting parlor.* "'S'bout time I had me a crack at'cha."

You smile and bat your eyes, reeling in a sudden nausea. The man sits spread-legged in pants of tent canvas and wears a raggy hat. Several gold teeth interspersed with rotten ones sparkle.

"We'se finally back. Five years'a hard work'n for the last four I ain't been back home but once a month. To top it off me'n some of the boys've been workin' up the house past few days, diggin' and such. I need me some relaxation." *He peers closer.* "You ain't even been workin' fer Bella a year, have ya?"

"About that, sir." You take his roughened hand and lead him through the crimson curtains to the hallway. You immediately notice that his hands are gritty with earth.

"And that's a mighty fine ass on ya."

You can't think of any reply. One of his hands claws your bottom when you lead him into your room. A short, scruffy beard makes his face indescribable, but you notice . . . something—

Maybe it's just the way the light is in the room, but his eyes look yellow, like a piss stain on a white bedsheet.

Even before the door closes, his hands are up your dress yanking down your linens. Fingers like file stones tweeze the tender folds between your legs.

"Yeah, that's real nice, too . . ."

Finally you speak, as he's bending you over the daybed: *"Puh-pardon me, sir, you gotta—you gotta tell me what'cha want'n then pay me first—"*

A ten-dollar gold piece hits the floor, spins like a top, and lands tails. Part of you could squeal with delight—you've never been paid that much for just one go with a man, but then your belly continues to sink because you know that this man Morris will make you earn it. You can't help but notice the very long knife and scabbard on his hip.

"Sir, thank you—"

A knuckled fist hits you in the back of the head. *"Shut up,"* he says, and continues to fiddle with your sex like a baker working dough. His pants are already down . . .

You can't even think about the thing he does to you. Oh, God, please, you beg over and over. Let him be done soon . . .

A half hour later, you fall back on the floor.

"There, that weren't so bad, was it, sugar?"

You look up through misting eyes and see him sitting on the couch, his trousers still unfastened. The taste in your mouth combines with the smell coming off your lips. It's so foul it seems evil, and just as bad is the malodor wafting *off his exposed groin. On the couch arm lay a pretty cotton smock you've been sewing; it's about half complete. You could howl when he picks it up and wipes himself off with it, then drops it to the floor. He winks at you, and lights a long, thin cigar that smells like burning garbage.*

"Come on up here, pretty girl. I need my money's worth."

You remember the ten-dollar piece, and tell yourself that this will be worth it.

"I ain't got much more time," *he says rather distantly now.*

You reluctantly sit next to him. "Pardon me, sir?"

His yellow eyes stare into space, but then he smiles again. "Gotta get back to the house a right quick. One more thing I gotta do fer Mr. Gast. He's already gone, but he trusts me'n a few others to do what he wants."

"He's left town again? I heard he just got back . . ."

"See, only important men are invited to do his bidding. Men like me." *His yellow gaze slowly turns to you.* "Do you believe that? Do you believe that I am an important man?"

He sounds so strange now. You know you must ingratiate him. "Oh, yes, sir, I do, very much so. I understand that you are one of Mr. Gast's most important foremen."

"Yes . . ." *He nods.* "Yes, that is true." *Then his eyes focus.* "Do you like me? What I mean is, do you enjoy my company?"

You shiver. "Oh, yes, sir. You're a very handsome and rugged gentleman."

"Now, I realize that I just put you through the wringer a mite hard. So you've probably had enough. Right?"

You're not sure how to figure him. You don't know what to say. You know he's very, very violent. "Only if you feel you've had your money's worth, sir . . ."

He blinks. "Hmm. Yes. And I suppose I have. But . . . you just said that you enjoy my company . . ."

It's getting too strange. You don't like it at all.

"So . . . I'll tell you what. I'll leave it up to you. If you'd

*like me to stay a bit longer, then I will. Or'n if you'd rather I
leave now, then I'll leave."*

*He's plotting something, you can feel it. You know that
your next response is very, very important.* If I ask him to
leave, then I just know he'll beat me'n take the ten-dollar
piece with him . . .

"Well, sir, I would like it if you stayed . . . a bit longer . . ."

*The man shrugs, then grins. "Whatever you say, honey."
And then—*

smack!

*—the web of his hand catches your throat and slams
you off the couch to the floor. He moves in a blur and pins
you down. He's got one knee across your throat and the
other on your belly.*

*"I'm always one to oblige the request of a lady," he says,
and then he laughs so hard and dark that you think it's
more like a caterwaul from hell. "Don't'cha move, now,"
he warns, "less'n I might have to break your windpipe." So
you lie perfectly still, breathing fiercely through your nose
as the pressure of his knee on your throat increases.
Then—*

swish!

*He slides that long knife out of the scabbard. "I skinned
me a lotta women with this, and cut off a lotta ears'n tits.
Mostly Injuns'n creek people. You work hard as me, you
need some sport." The tip of the blade tickles up your thigh.
"Does this scare you?"*

"Yes, it does, sir." You choke out the words.

*"I like a honest gal," he says, then laughs and puts the
knife back in the scabbard. "Don't'cha worry none—you're
too pretty to cut. But I'll be cuttin' on someone else with it
real soon. Now . . . Let's see this apple-dumplin' cart," he
says and jacks down the top of your ruffled blouse. The terror makes your breasts quiver. His hand plays with one;
then his fingers begin to pinch the nipple. You look up
through slits for eyes and see his cigar smoke ringing his
head like an unholy aura.*

"Let me put a little spark in your day, huh, pretty girl?"
His forefinger and thumb begin to vise the tip of your nipple until it hurts. Then, *"What we got here—ahh, perfect,"* but you can't see what he's reaching for, and then, *"Look it. Think this'll liven ya up?"*

With his other hand, you see now, he'd taken a long sewing needle out of the pincushion on the end table.

"Oh, my God, please, Mr. Morris, I'm beggin' you not to—"
He sticks the needle directly into the tweezed tip of your nipple, and the sound that comes out of your throat is like an animal's shriek. Your body bucks beneath his weight as you watch the entire two-inch-plus needle disappear into your breast.

The shriek reels out of your throat like ribbon. *"What?"* he asks. *"Does that hurt? Awwwwwwwww . . . I'm sorry."*
He removes the needle, and your body goes limp.

"See, some gals like a little spark . . . but I guess you ain't one of 'em."

You're breathing so fast you can barely understand him. His face looks blurred through your tears.

"Guess I'll be on my way. I done told ya. Got a chore or two up the house . . ."

Please, leave! Please, please, please!

But if he's leaving . . . why does he still have the end of your nipple pinched between his fingers?

One last grin and he says, *"Honey, aren't ya glad ya asked me to stay?"* And then he puts the lit end of the cigar to your nipple and begins to puff.

You drown in the instantaneous wave of pain, and then your mind turns black.

The room is darker when you wake up. Your left nipple burns in a slow, thudding pain. It doesn't take you long to remember what happened.

"At least he's gone," you whisper in relief.

The end of your nipple is inflamed beneath a scab. You carefully re-cover your breasts and collect yourself, then *crawl around the couch to where he'd dropped your ten-dollar gold piece.*

It's not there now.

You bolt out of the room. You haven't felt this enraged since the time the German man sold your baby. When you storm into the parlor, Bella looks up surprised from a plate of chocolates.

"Why . . . Harriet! What—"

"That shitty man burned my nipple and stole my money!" *you wail.* "Do you have a gun I can borrow?"

"Calm down, dear! My, oh my, you ain't gonna be shootin' no one. Now just you sit down and—"

"No! I'm gettin' my money!"

"Harriet? Honey? Listen now. You just have to accept that these things happen to a gal in this line sometimes. Sometimes we get took advantage of—"

"I earned that money and I'm going to get it!" *you bark.*

"Settle down! You just leave that Mr. Morris alone, girl! He's crazy! Lotta them rail men are awful rough with the girls, but he's the worst. He'll kill ya—"

"He can try!" *you scream and tromp out of the house.*

Bella calls after you but you don't listen. You're running up the hill . . .

To the Gast House.

Your rage sends you running up but then you begin to slow down and eventually stop, because that's when you notice the man hanging by his neck from the biggest tree in the front yard.

The rope creaks as the well-dressed corpse turns very slowly. You see that it's Mr. Gast.

My . . . God . . .

You keep stepping back, because it almost seems like the corpse turned by a will of its own, to look at you. Mr. Gast's face is pressed with a dead grin, and you can see yellow in the slits of his eyelids. The scariest thought sends a chill up your back: that those yellow eyes will fly open and he'll begin to laugh . . .

The lowering sun covers the yard with dark molten light. You hear a snuffling and notice several stray dogs nosing through some bushes. A brief shadow crosses your face and you look up, still stepping backward, and see a lone raven gliding silently overhead.

"Ohhh!" you yelp, and turn just before you'd fall. You'd been stepping back farther from the corpse, and now you see what you'd almost fallen in: a hole.

A deep trench had been dug into the yard, six feet long and probably six deep. A grave? you wonder. But you know the hole was recently dug because the turned earth is fresh, and several shovels are lying around. You remember the fresh dirt on Mr. Morris's hands and his reference to "diggin'." Could he have been the one who'd dug the hole?

"Jumpin' Jesus!" a voice cracks like a pistol shot. "Mr. Gast has up'n hung hisself!"

"Oh, my holy shee-it!" booms another.

"Looks like he's been hangin' a few days . . ."

Several townsmen are running for the house, and you see that one is the marshal. He glares at you and points. "You! You see what happened here?"

"Nuh-no, sir . . ."

"What's that hole dug there?"

"I don't rightly know, Marshal Braden . . ."

Something like recognition flashes. "You one'a Bella's whores, ain't ya?"

"Yes, sir," you speak right up. "And I come up here 'cos a man inside owes me money."

"Forget about your money and come help us!" he orders, so you do as you're told.

You follow the two men into the house. "Ain't no one seen his wife or kids for several days. Girl, you check upstairs, and we'll check—" But the other man was already groaning.

"Marshal, in here. You ain't gonna believe this . . ."

In the study two men are sitting in brass-studded armchairs. They're both grinning but not moving.

"It's Mr. Morris," you gasp.

In his hand is the long knife you saw at Bella's, and it's clear what he'd used it for: to cut his own throat from ear to ear. A gush of blood had run down his chest to pool on the floor.

The other man is older, and has a long mustache. Half the side of his head is gone. A pistol dangles from his fingers.

"What in God's name happened here?" the marshal mutters.

"Looks like they both kilt themselves, like Mr. Gast . . ."

"We gotta find Mrs. Gast and them two kids'a theirs. And where's that damn maid?" The marshal points to you again. "Upstairs! Give a shout if ya find anything," he says, and then both men stomp through the room toward the back of the house.

But you stay to stare at Mr. Morris. Part of you wants to rummage through his pockets to retrieve your money but you know you can't do that. You know that if you did, he'd reach up and grab you.

So you scurry back to the foyer and go up the stairs. The first thing you notice are dirt tracks going up. On the landing you falter—your heart is pattering—because there's something about the silence that terrifies you even worse than when you watched the Indians killing your mother.

The tracks lead to a door in the middle of the stair hall. You try the knob but it's locked.

Maybe this one. The door clicks when you turn the knob.

You don't scream. Instead a pressure jolts in your chest and your heart stops for a moment, but you steel yourself to remain composed. Another of Mr. Gast's rail men lay dead. You don't know his name but you've seen him at Bella's. It's a bath closet that you've entered, a fancy one that even has a wooden commode.

A hip bath sits on a heavy wooden table, water still in it.

You notice that the dead man's hair and face are sopping wet, but only after you see his trousers open, and there's a big splotch of dried blood there.

Something in your mind that's not really your will makes you lift the wooden lid on the commode cabinet. You look in and see the man's thing floating in the chamber pot water.

You back out of the room. You pass the locked door and move to the one next to it.

When you open it, you're knocked down.

Oh! Lord! What IS that?

It's not a person who pushed you to the floor, it's the stench that plowed out of the room. It's an awful hot rotten smell mixed with another stench like latrine dirt on a sweltering day.

You pick yourself up and look into the room—

—and that's when you scream a hundred times louder than when Mr. Morris was pushing the sewing needle into the tip of your nipple.

You're looking down at a naked woman dead for days, spread-eagled on a blood-caked bed. A large ax had been dropped right between her legs.

Just before you fall backward, you think you noticed one more thing: A bloody fetus on the floor, but it's tiny, not much bigger than a field mouse. It looks like someone had squashed it under their shoe.

Footsteps thunk up the stairs, and now you think you also hear a dog barking.

The second man gags, "In the name of—What's that stench? Piss?"

"What the hell—" The marshal looks into the room.

The other man helps you up, but looks like he wants to throw up over the stair-hall rail. They all got enough of a look.

"Guess we done found Mrs. Gast . . ."

"Somethin' pure evil's goin' on in this place." He jerks his head. "Where's that dog barkin'?"

The other man leaves you to lean against the rail. "This door here."

You bring a hand to your chest. "It's locked . . ."

Ka-KRACK!

His booted foot implodes the door. More meaty rotten stench gusts into the hall, so dense it's like a cloud, and a skinny mud-tan mutt tears out of the room and disappears down the stairs. But the man is already on his knees and then he sidles over. He's passed out.

The marshal looks in the room but when he turns back to you it's with a face leeched of all color, and though it can't be true you could swear that in the time it took him to look into that room, some of his hair turned gray.

He puts his hand across your eyes and turns you around. "You get out'a this house, girl. You get out right now, and don't come back."

"But, sir, what's in the—"

"You get out now! You run to the town square'n ring the bell and tell every man to get on up here to help me."

"But—"

"Go!" *He shoves you toward the steps. You stumble down the staircase. You can hear him weeping,* "God, protect us, my dear God, protect us . . ."

Downstairs, the spacious foyer seems smaller now, and very dark.

When you turn, your heart freezes again and you almost scream.

There's a man sitting at a desk, scribbling. He looks up at you as if irritated.

"Who are you, child?" *a creaky voice asks.*

"Harriet . . ."

"Oh, yes. The whore . . ." *He gets back to scribbling. You recognize him a moment later from the stupid red hat and metal nose: one of Mr. Gast's employees, who once paid to watch you shit.*

"You should leave here," *he mutters without looking at*

you. "*Even in the grievous sin of your whoredom, you are more blessed than anyone to ever set foot here.*"

You don't understand him at all.

He stands up at the desk. In his hand is a sheaf of oblong papers, which he slips into one of the desk's many letter slots. "I won't be needing these anymore"—his tiny eyes scan the dark room—"just as this place will no longer be needing me."

Now his hand is extending, his palm full of gold coins. "Take this. I'll write you a receipt."

Your mouth hangs open as you shake your head no.

His fingers pluck up one coin. "At least take this ten-dollar piece. It belongs to you, does it not?"

"No . . ."

"My time here is at an end, and so is yours." He removes his false nose to reveal gnawed holes. "Say your prayers, fornicatress. You've much to be grateful for. You will live a long, long life, and you will have children and grandchildren and great-grandchildren, and you will die on the day before Trotsky is murdered."

Your stare gapes. "What?"

He walks away into a side hall.

It's as if the house ejects you; you nearly fall down the front steps. Mr. Gast's corpse has turned on the rope again, to face your exit. You stumble down the path, exhausted by your witness. Before you begin to run, you see the last edge of the sun melting over the distant cotton and soya fields, backlighting so many skulls on sticks, and you also see the tan mutt that escaped the room upstairs humping the other stray dogs in the yard, and that's when you feel as if Lucifer himself has just blown you a kiss . . .

You fall to your—

CHAPTER ELEVEN

I

—knees before the toilet to vomit harder than he ever had in his life. *Holy ever-living HELL,* Collier thought in the mad, wincing turmoil. He didn't remember stumbling to the bathroom, but he *did* remember the nightmare . . .

With each pulse of vomit, the alarm pulsed in the bedroom. The images from the nightmare assailed him, and ghosts of discomfort throbbed at his anus and his left nipple. When he was done, his stomach squeezed dry, his vomit floated in the toilet like an inch of oatmeal.

The worst dream of my life . . .

He sat on the bathroom floor, head between his knees.

It was the first time he'd ever dreamed he was a woman—

Not just a woman, a Civil War whore . . .

When he could bear the buzz of the alarm no more, he straggled up and smacked it off. It was twenty-five before seven. *Oh, shit,* he recalled. *Church.* While showering, the distress in his belly sharpened when he recalled the ludicrous incident with Lottie and, worse, the awful hallucination of those four small hands titillating him . . .

And the dog.

I got the triple whammy last night, he groaned to himself as he dressed. *And didn't J.G. Sute say that someone was murdered in the bath closet?*

And was that trace smell of urine his imagination or . . .

Downstairs he heard early risers chatting over the light breakfast Mrs. Butler served every morning. Collier stepped quickly past the dining room door, so not to be seen. Then he turned for the door and noticed—

The fancy antique desk sat recessed within the wall, close to the small portrait of Mrs. Gast. *The same place it was in the dream.* Collier knew his dreaming mind had been quite creative last night, producing the morbid dream out of pieces of things he'd heard. *My name was Harriet and I just got raped every which way, and then I saw that weird little dude sitting at that desk, the guy with the messed-up nose.* Of course his mind had remembered Dominique's story of a similar man sitting at the same desk during the wedding reception. He reread the tiny metal plate: ORIGINAL MAPLE WRITING TABLE—QUEEN ANNE–STYLE—SAVERY AND SONS—1779. It was no big deal, he knew, but . . .

In the dream, I saw the guy put a stack of papers . . .

His fingers fished around one by one through the letter slots. The slots were quite deep. In one he found an inexplicable business card that read PHILTY PHIL'S BAR! ST. PETE BEACH, FLORIDA. The card was obviously new. He forced his fingers down deep into the very next slot—

Something there . . .

With finesse and some aggravation, his forefinger and middle finger managed to seize something and pull it out.

A sheaf of very old, heather gray sheets of paper, oblong-shaped, about seven inches by three. The same things he'd seen the man in the dream put in this self-same desk.

Don't freak out, Collier warned himself. Up front, it seemed impossible, but coincidence more easily explained it. *I noticed them when I first saw the desk, but wasn't consciously aware of it . . .*

Or so he hoped.

The stack seemed about sixty pages thick, and some were white instead of the heather gray. He'd seen one before already, in one of Mrs. Butler's displays. They were paychecks from the era, and he supposed they might even be moderately valuable to a collector. He read the first one.

RECEIVED OF: *Mr. R.J. Myers*, AGENT OF THE EAST TENNESSEE AND GEORGIA RAILROAD COMPANY, *Fifty* DOLLARS.

The date: *April 30, 1862*, and at the bottom was scribed a signature: *Windom Fecory.*

Windom Fecory, Collier thought back. *The man whom the bank is named after. The man with the gold nose . . .*

Collier peeled off a few of the checks and put them in his pocket. *Maybe Mr. Sute knows exactly what these things are.* The rest he put back in the slot.

But what of the rest of the nightmare?

Morris, the john in the whorehouse, he thought. *Didn't I see his name on something in one of the display cases?* One of Harwood Gast's rail workers, no doubt. But it could still be explained by a subconscious recollection; even the dull but precise pain in his left nipple could be explained. Collier had to wonder if he was *hunting* for proof of something supernatural now. *I wonder what a therapist would say. "Well, Doctor, last night I dreamed I was a woman and I got corn-holed by a rugged railroad worker. Oh, and I also got drunk with a bunch of gay guys earlier."*

Why bother trying to figure it out?

The morning air outside refreshed him; he was at the church in less time than he thought. As he waited for Dominique, some other people standing outside the church door seemed to be eyeing him, so he moseyed away so not to seem abrupt.

"What are you doing over here?" Dominique asked,

appearing around the corner. Collier was stunned. She wore a refreshing camel tan wrap-dress with a smart belt. Her eyes glittered in the morning light.

"Oh, I—"

"I keep forgetting, the Prince of Beer doesn't want to be made," she giggled.

"Exactly. Especially at church."

Collier wasn't prepared when she gave him a peck on the lips. Her soap and shampoo, as usual, turned him on in a big way; even her mouthwash and toothpaste seemed enticing.

"I . . . missed you," he uttered, and then felt ridiculous afterward.

"Good," she said, and took his hand. The chattering precongregation—mostly middle-aged and elderly couples—began to enter the church when the steeple bell began to clang.

She said very chirpily, "Let's go in now and ask God to forgive us for our sins."

"Sure," Collier said. *In my case, it better be a long fucking service . . .*

II

"All right, bitch. You want it bad, so you're gonna get it. Bad."

"Yes, yes!" J.G. Sute had huffed.

That's how it had started, but how it had ended was another story . . .

Naked on the bed, the 300-pounder looked like an obese cartoon. It was less than an inspiring image, and worse were the dream fragments that haunted Jiff from last night's nightmare. Jiff had dreams like that sometimes, and never understood it. *Civil War* dreams, along with the most awful images, and last night had been the worst. He'd seen wagons full of people so skinny they looked like living skeletons. Most were naked but the ones still clothed were stripped by slaves. Several male Indians stood around, waiting, with knives in their belts, their eyes keen and patient. The place was so *hot*. Next thing Jiff knew he was shoveling coal into a vast furnace, and he'd been able to see *people* bubbling inside . . .

Jiff bit his lip till the images were gone.

He stood naked in front of his prone and cringing client. For the course of the next hour came pleas, like: "I love you, I love you," then a hard *slap!* and "Please! I deserve it! I deserve the pain because I'm not worthy of your love," then a harder *smack!* and, "Jiff, my love. I need you to *hurt* me . . ."

Like that.

Throughout the regimen, however, shreds of Jiff's nightmare kept pecking at his mind: women and old men, plus children, bald and starving, standing in a line but—

A line for what?

Aw, God . . .

Exactly what use Jiff made of the rubber glove need not be mentioned, nor need it be mentioned what and how many areas of J.G. Sute's corpulent body he'd used the "Naughty Girl Clips" on. His client had wanted pain this time, and it was pain he'd received, until he was a sobbing, sniffling, quivering mass.

Debasement, too, was on this morning's one-hundred-dollar agenda; hence, the wine goblet. It need not be mentioned what fluid other than wine Jiff filled it with and then forced Sute to consume.

"I'm so unworthy—I'm scum! Shit on me if you like!"

Even for a hundred bucks, Jiff was not quite up to *that*. As a "grand finale," however, he slapped his client up a few more times, then took a big hock in his face, but while he was engaged in these final tweaks, he swore he could still see the stoked flames from the dream furnace, thought sure he could still hear the screams . . .

When services had been properly rendered, J.G. Sute sobbed tears of joy as his elephantine body shuddered.

"My love, I could die now . . ."

Freak show's over. Jiff loped to the bathroom sink to wash up. *I just cain't do this shit anymore.* When he returned to the bedroom, he was relieved to see that Sute had wiped his face off and donned his robe. The man looked dreamy-eyed now, his demented needs slaked. "That was wonderful," he sighed.

"Yeah, yeah." Jiff stood listlessly at the liquor cabinet. He wasn't going to tell the man that this was his last trick with him. "Mind if I have a shot?"

"What's mine is yours, my love."

Jesus. Jiff's eyes scoured the shelves: Asombroso tequila, Macallan thirty-year-old scotch, Johnnie Walker Green. *Shit, he ain't got no Black Velvet?* He poured himself an inch of something and sat down bare-assed on a William and Mary wing-back chair.

Now that his perverse duties were over, his nightmare filtered back into his head.

"Jiff, you look inconsolable."

The liquor bit hard. "Huh?"

"You appear to be troubled by something . . ."

"Bad dream, is all. I get 'em sometimes—don't rightly know why." The horrid images felt like bruises in the back of his brain. "Dreamed I was a coal shoveler, back durin' the war."

"Heaver," Sute corrected. "That was the official job title in those days. A coal *heaver.* They shoveled sixteen hours a day, for about fourteen dollars a month." Sute's "afterglow" left him relaxed, or perhaps it was just Jiff's presence. It was a conversation, not a demented sexual scenario. "A contributing factor to the C.S.A.'s surrender was its inability to mine coal as effectively as the North. You were a Confederate coal heaver I take it?"

Jiff's nude pecs popped when he rubbed his brow. "Naw, and I weren't paid no fourteen bucks a month, neither. See, in this dream, I was a black man. I was a slave."

Sute's bulbous face creased in concern. "You seem

terribly upset, Jiff. It was only a dream. But this is interesting. Where were you working?"

"What's that?"

"Where were you shoveling this coal? A supply ship? A locomotive?"

Jiff shook his head. "A big furnace, and I mean *really* big."

Sute's attention became more focused. "And how do you know it was during the war?"

"On account'a the place was full up with Confederate guards all walkin' 'round with bayonets on their rifles. They was all callin' me nigger'n tellin' me I'm dead meat if I don't keep shovelin'. Bunch'a other black fellas with me doin' the same thing. Seemed like the dream went on forever: me throwin' in one shovel fulla coal after the next. Place was so hot I could feel my skin blisterin'." Jiff took another inch of scotch and sighed. "I been havin' weird dreams every now and then long as I can remember, always durin' the war, but each time I'm someone else, and it's always horrible."

"Slavery was a horrible thing, Jiff."

"Aw, shit, that ain't what I mean. The really horrible part was what they was usin' that furnace for."

"Smelting ore, I presume."

Jiff shook his head. "Weren't no ore in the place that I could see. It was more like a prison camp. See, we was shovelin' the coal into the fuel chutes on one side, but on the other side, the soldiers was throwin' *people* into the furnace."

"What?"

"Yup. They'd bring folks in a few at a time; women and kids, mostly, and most of 'em were naked—see, they come offa these wagons outside. Some still had their clothes on but they was all shit'n puke-stained and fulla bugs. Then every now'n then some Indian fellas'd bring in *more* women, and each time they done so, a soldier'd give 'em some money."

"Delivery fees," Sute said. "Same thing as a bounty. Gast's deputies frequently recruited nearby Indians to round up civilians who'd fled their homes as the Union forces encroached. Strange that you should dream something so accurate."

"Aw, shit, but that weren't the worst part," Jiff went on, beating down his disgust with the liquor. "Lotta the women they brung in was pregnant, and the kids, too, just little girls, all starin' out with big hollow eyes in their skinny faces like they ain't et in weeks. And the soldiers just fed 'em all right into the furnace. Didn't even think twice about it."

Sute went silent.

"Babies, too, they was throwin' in. We could see inside'n the fire was so hot sometimes the person they throwed in would just explode. Others looked like they was *melting*. Like they'd just turn into vapor."

Sute lumbered up and began rubbing Jiff's shoulders. "You're letting the legends get the best of you. Come and lie down with me . . ."

But Jiff was spacing out. "Finally, I fall down. I'm so weak, see, that I can't shovel no more coal, so . . . so—"

"What happened?"

"The soldiers throwed *me* into the furnace . . ."

Sute stroked Jiff's face from behind. "It's just the legend, Jiff, it's the legend. Put it out of your mind."

"That's just it, J.G.—my *mind*. Why in hell would my *mind* serve up somethin' so vile? And after I got tossed in, I just kept burnin'. I could see the flesh *smokin'* right off my body, but the nightmare *still* wouldn't end. Finally I did wake up, and I was screamin' bloody murder. And you know what? 'Bout a minute later, I heard Lottie screamin', too—her bedroom's right next to mine. How fucked up is that? Lottie cain't talk, can't barely make no sound at all. But she was screamin', too, like she was havin' a nightmare herself. Jesus H. Christ, I hope she didn't have the same one as me."

"I'm sorry to see you in such duress, Jiff." Sute was nearly in tears. This was the first time that Jiff had ever confided in him, the first time he'd ever regarded Sute as more than just a kink trick. "Stay with me. Let me make you breakfast."

Shit, Jiff thought. *What am I doin'?* He snapped out of it. *He's right, it was just a dumb dream, and I'm all actin' like a baby about it.* He pulled away from his client and began to dress. "Naw, I gotta go. Got work at the inn." He blinked away the remaining dream fragments yet still felt his stomach souring.

Sute sat back down on the bed, morose that the love of his life was leaving. "If it's any consolation, Jiff, a long time ago I spent the night at the inn when my roof was being reshingled. You were just a teenager then. But I had a nightmare, too, that's similar to yours in some ways."

Jiff paused to look at him.

"I dreamed that I was a Confederate general, who'd sold his soul to the devil, and the first man I met after making the pact was Harwood Gast."

Jiff felt as though a tarantula had just skimmed up his back. He didn't want to hear anything about the devil. But he had to ask, "J.G.? You think a place can make nightmares, 'cos of what happened in it in the past?"

"Well, that's one endless rumor about the Gast House, Jiff. But in truth . . . no. I really don't think so."

"I hope not."

"It's ironic, though: the content of your nightmare as well as the history of your mother's inn. That man from the TV show is quite interested in the topic. He's almost obsessed with the Gast legend."

Jiff eyed his client with suspicion. "Yeah?"

"Seems quite odd, doesn't it? A book writer and celebrity from California, so taken by a Southern ghost story."

Yeah, I guess it is . . . "He's a nice guy and all but this town definitely ain't the place for him."

"Southern pride." Sute managed a smile. "I'll call you again soon."

For a split second, he had the most noxious vision: Jiff was shoving *Sute* into the furnace's fiery maw. His hand was shaking when he grabbed the doorknob. And, no, he wasn't going to tell Sute yet that he was dumping him as a client. The tricks were so much easier at the Spike. He'd simply had enough. *I'll tell him next time he calls,* he decided, and just said for now, "See ya later." Then Jiff turned to leave.

"Gracious, Jiff. You really *are* out of sorts, aren't you?"

Jiff turned. "Huh?"

"You were about to do something you've *never* done before."

Jiff was getting irritated. "What'cha talkin' about?"

"You almost walked out of here without your money," Sute informed him and smiled. Then he gave Jiff a check for one hundred dollars.

CHAPTER TWELVE

I

"There's no gray area here, folks," the minister said. "You can't get more cut-and-dry than the Ten Commandments. There's no *interpretation* necessary to understand Christ's Golden Rule, 'Do to others as you would have others do to you.' When Jesus said on the Mount, 'Blessed are the merciful for the merciful shall be shown mercy,' we don't need a literary analyst from Harvard to tell us what that *really* means. The Word of God is simple. It's like boiling rice. If you follow the instructions on the bag, it *works*. God's Word works, too, but our problem is we don't really listen. We may try to, or we tell ourselves that we're listening, but we really aren't because as humans we exist in error. We're unworthy in the shadow of our sin . . ."

Collier felt inhibited throughout the service, as out of place as a Washington Redskins jersey in a Dallas sports shop. The minister reminded him of the Skipper on *Gilligan's Island* but was bald as Telly Savalas. He interestingly mixed fire and brimstone with lackadaisical good humor: "We're all premeditated sinners worthy of nothing but hell, but God's a pretty cool guy and he cuts us slack if we earn it. He *knows* we're all screwed up but he loves us anyway! He doesn't want heaven to be full of nothing but stone-faced boring pilgrims and monks who haven't cracked a joke in their entire lives!" Collier figured heaven would indeed be Dullsville if exclusively populated by such folks.

Dominique held his hand through the entire service, save for intervals for hymns. She as well as most everyone there listened to the minister with the same attention that Collier had paid to those *Girls Gone Wild* commercials: with rapt veneration. Maybe that was the difference.

The minister pointed his finger at the congregation, like an accuser, then slowly aimed it at himself. "My friends, there really are seven deadly sins: wrath, lust, pride, greed, envy, sloth, and—my personal favorite—gluttony . . ." He stepped away from the lectern and hoisted a considerable belly beneath his vestments, which summoned laughter from the pews.

"But the other day I was thinking that maybe that's why God put seven days in the week—a day for each sin. Why don't we reserve each separate day to atone for one, and stick to it. Monday can be pride, Tuesday can be envy, Wednesday can be sloth, and so on. And today?

Sunday? Let's assign greed to Sunday, and use the Lord's day to try to redeem ourselves of this sin. Let's remember Jesus' story of the widow's mite, how a destitute woman gave her last two leptons to the offering box— only a fraction of a cent. That's not much money but to Christ that woman's selfless sacrifice was worth more than a mountain of gold."

Collier grew suspicious. *Here it comes. Open up your hearts and open up your wallets . . .*

"Let's remember that for every dollar we give, we get back a hundred in spirit. Let's remember the word of James: 'Every act of giving, with every perfect gift, is from above,' so that when we give in the name of God, we become *like* God. And the words of Matthew: 'Freely we have received, so freely we must give.' Just go out and *give*—let's do *that* today instead of watching TV or washing the car—"

The collection plate'll be making the rounds any minute now, Collier thought.

"—and for you wise guys out there who think I'm just pumping you up for the collection plate, I'm asking you to not give a penny to this church today. Give it to someone else instead—"

Collier frowned.

"—and if you've got no money, give your time. Or maybe we can follow our best examples"—he pointed to someone in the pews—"like Mr. Portafoy who spends every Friday night helping terminal patients at the hospice, or Janice Wilcox who runs the local clothing drive, or Dominique Cusher who prepares a hundred meals before her restaurant opens and drives them all the way to the Chattanooga homeless shelter every Sunday—"

Collier looked at her . . . then wondered if he'd ever given anything as charity in his life . . .

"Let's be like those wonderful people, and also remember Corinthians: 'God loves a cheerful giver.'" Next the minister stepped away from the lectern again, hoist-

256   Edward Lee

ing his belly. He seemed to be looking right at Collier when he said, "And for you wise guys out there wondering what *I'm* going to give? I'm not going to eat today, but instead I'm going to go drop a hundred dollars on pizzas and take them to the Fayetteville soup kitchen. I'm gonna drive those people at Domino's *nuts* . . . and I'm not even going to snitch a slice for myself. I swear!"

More chuckles from the crowd.

"Go to the hospital and give a pint of blood! Go to the underpass and dole out a backseat full of Quarter Pounders! Go online and throw some of that MasterCard at the Red Cross, or fill out that organ-donor form and drop it in the mail. You're not gonna need your liver when you're dead, are you? So go on and do it!" Then he scanned his finger across the pews and barked like a game-show host, "And until next week, go in peace to love and serve the Lord!"

Everyone said "Amen" while they were still laughing, then a jazzy organ kicked in to signal the final procession.

"Wow," Collier whispered. "Church has changed."

"When was the last time you went?"

"Ah, you would ask. I'm too ashamed to say. *When* was Oliver North shredding documents for Reagan?"

Dominique chuckled. "Being here is a start, isn't it? And, yeah, Father Grumby gets a little gung ho sometimes but he's a great pastor."

Collier's throat felt thick when he noticed two young girls in white dresses filing out behind their parents. *Couldn't be,* he thought. He still wasn't sure if he'd really seen the girls or if it was a booze-triggered phantasm.

Then his belly twitched again when he recalled the *other* mirage: the four small hands playing with him . . . and the dog . . .

"Let me ask you something," he said on a completely inappropriate lark. "Does Harwood Gast have any descendants?"

"Nope." She smiled at him. "Why do you ask?"

"I bought a bunch of books from Mr. Sute but I haven't read them yet. Isn't it kind of curious that the Gasts never had kids?"

"Oh, they had kids, two of them, two girls."

Collier felt a twinge. "But you just said he didn't have any—"

"No descendants, that's right." She seemed to stall on a thought. "But his two daughters died in their teens, during . . . the war."

Collier watched the backs of the two girls. One was dirty blonde, the other drably brunette. *Just like . . .*

Before they exited the nave, they turned for moment to wave to some other children. Collier saw that it clearly wasn't them.

"Did . . . Gast's daughters have a *dog?*"

"Justin, how would I know *that?*"

"Well, you know a lot about the legend. How did the two girls die, exactly?"

She nudged him. "I don't think *church* is the best place to talk about Tennessee's version of Ivan the Terrible. If you insist on obsessing over it, go ask your friend J.G. Sute. He'll tell you all the facts and all the B.S. you want to hear. If anybody's more obsessed with this stuff than you, it's him."

Collier felt foolish now, but what she'd said spiked him. *Maybe that's what I'll do today—give Sute a call.* Suddenly he felt intent on learning about Gast's two children.

He followed Dominique out as she spoke briefly to acquaintances. Outside he said, "So I take it you're busy this morning."

"Yeah, like the man said, that's what I do on Sundays before work."

"It's quite a gesture."

"No it isn't—it's no big deal. I use all the leftover side dishes from Saturday, then make some kind of meat dish with overstock or specials that didn't sell. It's actually kind of fun. One time I made chimichurri pork tenderloin with a banana-pepper drizzle and wasabi mashed potatoes for a hundred homeless."

"I'll bet that made their day," Collier said.

"They loved it. Another time my supplier was trying to get rid of eight-count sea scallops, so I bought a bunch on the bulk discount and did them up over penne quill pasta with truffled cream pomodoro sauce. It was a riot. The only real hassle is driving all the way to Chattanooga and back."

Collier felt a stab of obligation. "Let me help you. I've got nothing big to do today."

"No, no, it's something I do by myself. You heard Father Grumby; you've got to choose your own manner of charity." She grinned. "You'll think of something."

Collier felt relieved beneath his falseness. The last thing he'd actually want to do is cook for homeless people hours away. But at least he felt like less of a schmuck for offering.

He pulled on her hand and stopped her. "I hope I can see you later."

"Of course you can. Anytime after five at the restaurant, but I've got to run now. Today I'm taking chicken marsala and saffron rice to the shelter." She kissed him briefly but not so brief that she didn't have time to run the tip of her tongue across his lips. Collier tried to retrieve her for a longer kiss but her arms pressed him back.

"If you keep messing around with me you're only going to wind up pissed off and aggravated," she said with a coy smile.

He already knew what she was clarifying. "How do you know I don't *like* being pissed off and aggravated?"

Her smile dropped down a notch. "Justin, I've already told you, I'm *never* going to have sex out of wedlock. I don't put out. Get it?"

"As a matter of fact, I received that impression very distinctly last night—"

"If you're looking to get laid, you've got the wrong girl."

"How do you know I don't *like* not getting laid?"

She shook her head, amused. "What I'm saying is I'll understand if you don't show up tonight."

"Great. I'll see you tonight."

She kissed him one more time, then pulled away. "'Bye . . ."

He watched her traipse off in the morning light; he was speechless. Even in the distance, her beauty poured off her. He watched after her until she disappeared around the corner.

Collier considered his plight. *Over the past few days I've turned into a hell-bent, primo-perverted, lust-obsessed sex maniac . . . and I'm falling in love with a girl who will never have sex with me.*

"Oh well," he muttered aloud. He started back to the inn, to retrieve the phone number of Mr. J.G. Sute.

II

Lottie had dreamed she was being raped in the dirt by soldiers in gray uniforms. "Don't bust her belly," one of them laughed. In the dream, Lottie was very, very skinny but also very, very pregnant. "Keep the baby in the bitch 'fore we get her up the hill . . ."

She'd been shorn of all her body hair in a strange barn full of boiling vats, and though she wasn't sure, she thought she'd been naked for several months. Outside, the men took turns raping her on her hands and knees, while the rest of the prisoners were packed back into the wagon. "Give that bastard baby some Tennessee jism to swaller!" one guffawed, hoisting up his trousers. "Ain't gonna be no milk waitin' fer him when he comes out!"

The soldiers all laughed. When they were done, they

squashed her back into the evil-smelling wagon with the dozens of others. Lottie could see through the slats that the wagon was taking them up a winding path, to a great smoking hill.

The sound that throbbed from the wagon was a crush of children's sobs and desperate prayers. Lottie looked down at herself and saw that she was little more than a skin-covered skeleton but with a big, tight stomach sticking out; she could feel the rape-baby kicking in horror from within. Many of the other women there looked identical to her, but the worst sights were the children, who looked like smaller versions of herself, and some just as pregnant.

The sound of rifle fire cracked down the hill. What was happening? In between volleys, she heard shouts, then more volleys. The distant rifles fired for a long time, then sputtered out.

That's when the wagon stopped.

Lottie and the other prisoners were dragged out and forced into a line. They now stood before a compound formed by a great wooden fence, and spiring above the top of the fence was a brick-and-mortar structure that tapered to a tepee shape, at least forty feet high. Lottie knew this was a blast furnace, but she'd never seen one this big.

"Don't send these in yet," a soldier barked. "We gotta let Mr. Gast's men finish up . . ."

Finish up what? And who was Mr. Gast? In the dream Lottie didn't know . . .

Next, a soldier who seemed to be in charge ordered, "Send a couple'a these 'un's in to collect the boots'n clothes." And then Lottie and several of the women less close to death were pushed through the fence gate by more soldiers with bayonets.

Inside the compound, she could not comprehend what she saw. The base of the furnace had to have been a hundred feet wide, and into various vents shirtless black men shoveled coal. But in the compound's open areas dozens and dozens of more black men lay moaning while their clothes and boots were pulled off by still more slaves. The heat was so hellish, Lottie almost lost consciousness.

Baskets were shoved at Lottie and the others. "Collect it all up and pile it by the gate," they were ordered.

The floor of the compound was like a field of dying men—all black slaves. Lottie could see they'd been shot, and at the far wall stood several dozen white men with big rifles. They weren't soldiers, though. They looked like rail workers.

Lottie stalked between the fallen slaves and gathered up their clothes. At one point she noticed a well-dressed man in coattails looking on with the rail workers. Their eyes all seemed to have a yellow glaze.

Someone shouted, "One's got out! Don't let him get away!" and then several soldiers ran to a window. Lottie got one glimpse outside as she hauled a basket: she saw a black man running in the distance, then—BAM!—a soldier on horseback dropped him with a pistol shot.

When all the clothes had been gathered, Lottie helped transfer it all outside, where another wagon waited.

That's when she began to hear the screams.

They didn't sound human; they sounded like rough animals.

Lottie and several of the other younger women were raped yet again by more soldiers. She wished she could die now, but she sensed that there was something here— something in the air—that wouldn't let that happen.

Then a solider grabbed her from behind. "Here's some payback fer Fort Donelson," he said, and then began to sodomize her. That's when Lottie passed out.

When she regained some facsimile of consciousness, she was back inside the compound, but she noticed that all of the fallen slaves were gone. Shrieks and chuckles fluttered about like birds. Then her head lolled to the other side. She stared for a moment and thought, *I'm in hell* . . .

With pitchforks and bayoneted rifles, soldiers were feeding the other naked prisoners into the furnace. One young pregnant girl caught a pitchfork in the belly, was raised for all to see, then pushed back-first into one of the fiery openings. Several other soldiers skewered bloody babies with their bayonets, then heaved them in. When numb fingers touched her stomach . . . it wasn't there anymore. That's when Lottie noticed that her belly had been sliced open, the fetus pilfered and similarly incinerated.

"Here comes the next load," a voice called out. "Don't forget that 'un there."

Steam, blasting heat, and a smell like cooked pork hung like fog about the compound. Two fingers popped Lottie's eyeballs, then began to drag her by the sockets toward the furnace . . .

That's when she awoke in her bed, shivering in sweat. Had she screamed her way out of the nightmare? She thought she'd heard a shout from Jiff's room, too.

Yes, every now and then she had nightmares that were utterly horrific. She knew about the history of the town, and Harwood Gast, and she also had an idea what the power of suggestion was. "Everybody has bad dreams," her mother had told her in the past. But the one Lottie had suffered through last night was positively the worst.

She felt as though her entire body had been sucked by something vile; even her sweat felt evil. She showered desperately, scrubbing herself raw . . .

"The hell's wrong with you?" Jiff asked her later. She sat glum on her bed, still shaking a little.

"Huh? Looks like someone shot yer dog, and you ain't even *got* a dog."

Her eyes felt bloodshot when she peered at him. *Bad dream,* she mouthed to him.

Jiff's upbeat demeanor faltered when he read her lips. "Yeah, well, join the club. Last night I had me the worst of the bunch."

Lottie had no qualms about sitting naked before her brother. As gay as he was, why should she . . . just so long as he wasn't horny and there were no pictures of handsome men around. *It's the house,* she mouthed.

"Huh?"

The house. Sometimes I hate this HOUSE!

"I know, Sister. Like Ma told us a long time ago. Everyone has bad dreams here sometimes. Always been that way, since . . . back then." The low mood in the room felt dense as the summer humidity outside. "But check this out." Jiff tried to change the temper; he whipped out a check. "J.G. laid a hunnert on me. Kinkiest trick yet, but, shee-it."

Lottie sat limp in a lotus position and shrugged.

"You seen Mr. Collier this mornin'?"

Lottie shook her head.

"*Still* don't know what to make'a him. Yesterday he's drinkin' it up in the Spike with half'a my tricks, and now Ma tells me he borrowed her truck to take Dominique on a date—"

Lottie smirked.

"Still don't rightly know if he's bi, queer, or straight." Jiff chuckled. "A'course, he's got another think comin' with Dominique. Poor bastard'll need knockout drops and a crowbar to get into *her* Holy Rollin' panties."

Lottie errantly diddled her fingertips through the bedsheets. *It's my day off,* she mouthed. *What are you doin' today?*

"Ma tolt me to weed the whole motherfuckin' garden out back." He popped a brow at her. "How's about givin' your brother a hand?"

Sit on a gerbil, she mouthed.

"Funny. Come on, I'll give ya . . . ten bucks."

Eat a pile of corny shit, you homo whore!

Jiff glared. "Yeah, yeah—hey, Lottie, don't *talk* so loud. Someone might hear ya." Jiff ripped out an uproarious laugh, slipped out of the room, and slammed the door in her face.

Fucker! Lottie thought.

III

"Thanks very much for making the time, Mr. Sute. I'll be over in a half hour," Collier said and hung up. His eyes swept the bedroom for a reason he couldn't identify, and he quickly felt chilled, but the chill magnified when he looked at the bed and recalled not only the noxious nightmares he'd had on it, but the obscene hallucination last night. *Nergie,* he recalled the detestable mutt's name.

"Oh, hey there, Mr. Collier," Jiff greeted the instant Collier stepped into the hall. "How'd that inline handle?"

"Inline?" Collier asked, miffed.

"My ma's inline 235—her old Chevy pickup. She tolt me ya borrowed it. Bet there's a million miles on that baby. Like to see them Japs do that with one'a their Toyoters."

"It ran great, Jiff."

"Anything I can help ya with?"

"No, thanks. Right now I'm on my way to Mr. Sute's—"

Jiff looked at him weird.

"—to look at one of his book manuscripts," Collier finished. He'd mentioned Sute on purpose.

"Oh, you mean one'a his books about Hardwood Gast."

"Right. Don't really know why but I'm becoming intrigued by the whole town legend. I've even had a couple of nightmares about it."

Another weird look. "That so? Well, funny as it might seem, I've had a few myself and so's my sister. It's mainly just 'cos this house seems a lot creepier once ya hear all them stories."

"I'm sure you're right," Collier said. "But I'm still really fascinated. What do you know about Harwood Gast's children?"

"Aw, his kids? Nothin'." But the question clearly knocked Jiff off center. "I don't know that much about it. I gotta get started pullin' weeds out back . . . but have a great day," he finished and rushed off.

Collier smiled at the reaction he'd come to expect by now.

A leisurely walk took him back through town, which seemed to brim with more tourists than ever. Much spun through his head during the trek—the dreams, the mysteries of the Gast legend, his outrageous sexual ponderings—but most of the thoughts invariably returned to Dominique.

God. What I wouldn't give.

She contradicted his most apparent motivation—lust, essentially—or could it be true that Sute's cryptic impressions were more on the mark: that many folk who stayed at the inn experienced a rampant upsurge in libido? *Can't be true. Ridiculous,* he thought, yet a few minutes later he found himself matching the address on the business card to the numbers on the transom of a handsome Federal-period row house right in the middle of Number 1 Street.

"Come in, please," the globose man greeted with a handshake. Sute wore, of all things, a crimson smoking jacket and white slacks. "Don't mind the mess. I'm not known for my tidiness."

"Not many writers are," Collier said, instantly looking around. "Fascinating place." The living room was dusty and a bit unkempt but full of fine antiques, wall tapestries, and polished stone busts.

"Upstairs is a bit nicer, and that's where my manuscripts and sundries are."

Collier followed him up, wondering how many male prostitutes had done the same. Ahead of him, almost face-level, Sute's backside left little play on either side of the stairwell.

The upstairs was mostly master bedroom, plushly carpeted and walled with books. More stone busts on pedestals adorned the large room, along with sumptuous old oil paintings.

"Would you care for a drink?" he asked, opening a wide liquor cabinet.

"No, thanks. I've been doing a little too much of that lately, but feel free."

Sute poured himself something in a tiny snifter. "Mind if I smoke?"

Collier laughed. "Of course not, it's your place." He quickly regretted his answer when Sute whipped out a big pipe and began packing it up. "On the phone, you inquired about Gast's daughters—I guess I neglected to mention them when we had lunch." After a few gaseous puffs he handed Collier an opened box full of paper. "Here's one of my unpublished books, which details the children. But like most of this tale, it's a very unpleasant one, so be forewarned. Page thirty-three."

"Are there any pictures of them, photo plates?" Collier asked, flipping through. "Didn't you mention you had some old-style photos—ferrotypes, or whatever they were called?"

Sute sat down in an oversize reading chair, toking the nauseatingly sweet pipe. "No photographs of the daughters are extant, I'm afraid. Just some daguerreotypes of Mrs. Gast."

"Isn't that strange? Gast goes to that considerable expense to photograph his wife but not his children?"

"Normally that *would* seem strange. But Gast didn't like his daughters. They were very much mama's girls; they took after Penelope exclusively, and this I mean in some regrettable ways." Before Collier could ask for elaboration, Sute continued, "And it must also be said that Harwood Gast was very suspect of them."

"Suspect in what way?"

Sute pursed his lips. "Gast suspected that neither girl was necessarily sired by his loins."

Collier nodded. "The element of promiscuity. I almost forgot."

Sute leaned back, puffing. "If I may, why an interest in Gast's daughters?"

Collier half laughed. "If I told you, Mr. Sute, you'd think that I was a California loony."

"Please. I've indulged you, haven't I?"

The man was right. *I'm not gonna be here much longer anyway, so what difference does it make what he thinks?* "All right. Since I've been staying at the inn I've been experiencing some . . . things . . . that I'm hard-pressed to explain."

"But I told you at lunch, so have *many* of the inn's guests."

"Right, but, specifically? I'll just go ahead and tell you. You can laugh me out of here, and I'd deserve it, but . . ."

The mass of flesh that was Sute's face creased from a smile. "I'm listening."

"There have been a few times when I swear I've heard children's voices at the inn—two young girls."

"And according to Mrs. Butler, there aren't any children staying there," Sute presumed.

"Exactly."

"And if you heard the voices of the children, you must've heard the dog as well."

Collier thought his face had just hardened to the density of the Caesar bust.

"The dog is heard more at the inn than the children."

"Was it brownish, sort of a dark mud color?"

"No references to its color, coat, or breed. It was the girls' pet. Its name was Nergal."

Nergie. Nergal. Collier sought a link to logic but could find none.

"Peculiar name for a dog, but when you consider that

the farthest extremes of the Gast lore are founded in demonology, you have to wonder. The name 'Nergal' is referent to a Mesopotamian *demon*. A devil of pestilence and perversion, though I don't put much credence in that."

Collier had to ask the next question right away. "Were the girls named Mary and Cricket?"

"Yes."

He's lying. He's jerking me around for fun.

"But of course someone else could've told you their names," Sute added.

"No one did."

"Are you absolutely certain?"

"I swear."

Sute pointed to the box of paper. "Look on page thirty-three."

Collier turned to it and saw the heading.

CHAPTER TWO

DAUGHTERS OF DARKNESS: MARY AND CRICKET GAST

"Cricket, of course, was a nickname. The birth certificate cites Cressenda. She's described as dark-haired and mildly retarded. She was fourteen when she died, while Mary was chubby—more squat-bodied—and blonde. Four years older than Cricket. They both died on the same day, incidentally. April 30, 1862. And, yes, they were murdered by Harwood Gast. Their bodies were discovered on May third by the town marshal." Sute's eyes thinned. "Where did you see the girls? In the hotel?"

"I never said that I *did* see them," Collier commented, feeling sick.

"I'll be blunt, Mr. Collier, if you don't mind. My impression is that you're a very intuitive man . . . but your face is easy to read."

"Great."

"The girls' ghosts are typically only *heard* inside, but they're usually only *seen* outside. Where did you see them?"

Collier could only peer at the man. "You're talking about ghosts as though you personally believe in them."

"Oh, I do. Very much so. And though I may not have been totally honest with you during our lunch, I very much believe that Mrs. Butler's inn—the Gast House—is full to bursting with ghosts. I believe that it is *permeated* with the horrors of its original owner. A moment ago you were confident I'd be 'laughing' you out of here, but as you can see, I'm not laughing."

Collier rubbed his brow. "Well. At least I don't feel so idiotic now."

"No reason to. You see, Mr. Collier, it's pure human nature. Even for those who don't admit it, human beings *love* a good ghost story." Sute smiled. "The only problem is that some of them are true."

Collier sighed in a strange relief.

"And some *people* are more susceptible than others— you for instance. But I'm most curious now. I take it you saw them outside the building somewhere?"

"In the woods," Collier admitted. "There's a creek. And the dog was there. But I was really drunk, so—"

"You doubted your perceptions—a normal reaction, I'd say."

"But I guess the question I have to ask most"—Collier could refrain no more—"is . . . was the room I'm staying in either of the daughters' bedroom?"

Sute nodded. "It was both of theirs."

I knew it. "But at least they didn't die there," he said, relieved.

"I guess I should tell you now what I deliberately neglected to mention previously. Both Mary and Cricket's dead bodies were found in that same room on May 3, 1862."

Collier fumed. "You told me no one died there!"

"No one did. Gast murdered them on the property, on April thirtieth, then had some of his men transfer the bodies, to their beds." A low chuckle. "Don't fret. The bed you're sleeping on isn't one of them. The original beds were burned."

Collier felt accosted now by sickness and confusion. "Why would Gast kill them somewhere else and then move their bodies to their beds? Where exactly did he kill them?"

Sute pointed again to the manuscript. "It's the absolute *worst* part of the story, Mr. Collier. But you can read it there. Flip to the account in italics. It's the marshal's. But if you're certain you want to do so . . . then, please, let me advise that you have a drink. Something stronger than beer."

Collier slouched. *It's not even noon . . .* "Sure."

"What'll you have?"

"Scotch on the rocks."

Sute lumbered up to the cabinet, while Collier's eyes flicked down to the dusty manuscript. Several paragraphs down on page thirty-three, he found a transition heading: EXCERPTED FROM THE PERSONAL JOURNAL OF MATHIAS C. BRADEN, TOWN MARSHAL, MAY 3, 1862. But before he could begin, Sute brought him his drink. "Thanks," Collier said after the first cool sip.

"Those papers there in your pocket," Sute noted. "It looks like alkali rag."

Collier had no idea what he meant.

"A lot of printing paper during the first part of the nineteenth century was part rag pulp mixed with wood fibers. An alkali-soda base was used in the process. It bears a distinctive appearance."

"Oh, these, yeah." Collier reached to his breast pocket and withdrew the checks he'd discovered in the desk. "I brought them to show you. I found a bunch of them at the inn. They look like paychecks—from Gast's railroad company."

Sute examined the ones Collier had brought. "Oh, yes. Mrs. Butler has one of these on display, doesn't she?"

"Right."

"And you say you found a lot of them?"

"Yeah—fifty, sixty, maybe. They were stashed in an old writing desk, probably overlooked all these decades."

"I'm sure they were. I'll have to ask Mrs. Butler to let me examine them all, for the various names."

"Gast's employees, you mean?"

"Exactly. To cross-reference them with the other sources in my archives." He held one up. "See here, this man here? N.P. Poltrock. He was Gast's chief of operations. And Beauregard Morris—the crew chief. These men probably killed themselves on May second or third. Gast himself was already dead by his own hand—on April thirtieth—but it may be that Morris and Poltrock forestalled their own suicides to finish up a few of Gast's final requests, and to have a last hoorah in town. They both died in one of the parlors."

Collier tried to fix a chronology. "Gast hanged himself on the last day of April—"

"After he murdered his wife, his maid, Taylor Cutton, and his children."

The sickness continued to churn. "Do you know how the first two guys killed themselves? Morris, and the other guy?"

"It's in the same account by the marshal." Sute gestured the manuscript again. "Morris cut his own throat, and I believe Poltrock shot himself in the head."

The awareness thumped in Collier's blood like a slow heartbeat. He recalled his nightmare: he was a prostitute named Harriet. *The guy who raped me . . . Wasn't his name Morris?* He remembered the dream all too vividly.

Harriet never reclaimed the money he owed her. She'd seen his body in the parlor. With his throat cut.

I can't tell Sute that, I just can't!

"They look like paychecks . . ."

"The system was a little bit different back then—the workers were always paid in cash, often on the job site, but, yes, that's essentially what these are. Once it's endorsed it becomes a receipt for payment. I'm sure the company's treasurer kept these to maintain an accurate accounting. That's this man here—" Sute's stout finger tapped the bottom of a check. "Windom Fecory."

"The guy the local bank's named after."

"Yes." An expression of amusement touched Sute's face. "If the current bank president had known more about the real Windom Fecory, I suspect he'd have chosen another name."

"Why?"

"You'll recall the more abstract elements of our discussion—the supernatural element—"

Collier tried not to smirk. "Gast selling his soul to the devil, you mean."

"Not necessarily the devil, but possibly an adjunct to the same entity. That would indeed be Fecory. He produced a seemingly limitless flux of cash without ever once depleting Gast's personal account. That's how the more far-fetched extremes of the story go, at least."

"You just said you believe in ghosts. Do you believe *that?*"

"I can't say," Sute replied, still eyeing the checks. "But I must mention, if only in passing, that the name Fecory bears a suspicious resemblance to what you might think of as a demonic acolyte or serf, if you will. The archdemon who guards Lucifer's netherworldly treasures is called Anarazel, and his acolyte is called *Fecor.*"

"Fecor, Fecory." Collier got it. "But I don't buy the demon stuff, it's too hokey."

"I agree, but say that it's true. Windom Fecory was

Gast's paymaster; it was his job to remunerate cash in exchange for services. The demon Fecor can be likened to *Anarazel's* paymaster, to remunerate *Satan's* treasure . . . to those worldly men who serve him."

Collier tossed his head. "Fine."

"And I'll add that there is no accounting for Fecory after April thirtieth, not only the day that all these checks have been dated but also the day that the railroad was officially completed, and Harwood Gast came home for the last time." Sute maintained a clear interest on the checks. "Ah, and here's one for Taylor Cutton, the foreman."

"Don't tell me he knocked himself off, too . . ."

Another smile sunk into Sute's face. "You're not very attentive, Mr. Collier. I've already informed you that Taylor Cutton was *murdered* in the house—"

The memory sparked. "The guy Gast drowned in the hip bath."

"Yes. Also on April 30, 1862."

Collier couldn't help but recall the gurgling sound from the bath closet last night, and the gnawing sound . . . *I'll just have out with it. What the hell?* "Look, Mr. Sute. Since I've stayed at the inn, I've had a—"

Sute interrupted, "An accelerated sexual awareness, yes. You've implied that. Certain people have experienced the same thing while staying there."

Collier probably blushed. "Yeah but I've also had several nightmares where I'm *someone else*. Two nights ago I dreamed I was a Confederate sentry. I was guarding prisoners who were being deloused in a converted barn. It occurred to me that these people—civilians—were being *processed* for something—"

Sute didn't seem surprised. "Indeed they were. They were being processed for their extermination."

The word struck a black chord. "Extermination as in incineration?"

"Before I answer, tell me exactly why you ask."

"The nightmare," Collier implored. "The detainees were all naked and malnourished, and their hair was all cut off. Then they were packed back in a prison wagon—a wagon that departed from a nearby *train* depot—and taken up a large hill. In the dream, I couldn't see what was at the top of the hill, but I saw smoke, a steady, endless plume of smoke. Like they had a big bonfire up there."

"It wasn't a bonfire, it was the former Maxon Rifle Works, once the largest blast furnace in the South. It was closed down in the 1820s after superior facilities were built in North and South Carolina, but before that time, Maxon produced more rifle barrels than any other metal works south of the Mason-Dixon. It was a technological marvel during its heyday—the coal bed was fifty feet in diameter, and it possessed a high-efficiency bellows system that was operated by a water wheel."

Collier's mind filled with confused murk. "So the detainees were slaves, laborers forced to work at the furnace?"

"No," Sute informed. "It was Gast who refired the barrel works, but not for weapons production. He built an entire railroad to Maxon and refired the furnace solely to incinerate the innocent."

Collier felt tinged with evil. In a sense, it explained everything he didn't know, all at once. If . . .

"Why would he do that?"

Sute sat back down, fingering the old checks. "Either because he was insane, or because it was part of the deal. Riches in exchange for service. Mr. Collier, ritual atrocity and the sacrifice of the innocent are nothing new in the history of the occult. An oblation to the devil by the spilling of innocent blood is a powerful brew. Maxon was the Auschwitz of the Civil War . . . and almost nobody knows about it. The furnace's obscure location kept it in operation even for weeks *after* the war ended. How's that for evil, Mr. Collier? How's that for Satan protecting his flock?"

Collier wanted to leave. He'd heard enough. If it was all true, or all bullshit, he was done.

"Toward the end, the coal stores gave out," Sute went on. "Union troops were only a few days away, but there were still a hundred or so detainees awaiting incineration. So with no way to burn them, a slaughterfest ensued . . ."

Collier stared at him.

"It was a grim scene indeed that awaited the federal forces. They discovered locked prison wagons that had been set aflame with their charges still inside. But children had been pulled aside and beheaded, the heads left in neat piles for the troops to find. Dozens more were pitchforked to death, or simply hanged. Heaps of bodies were found rotting in the sun. It was a c*elebration* of evil, Mr. Collier. Truly the devil's jubal."

Collier finished the strong drink, craving a good beer now, but before he could bid a curt farewell, Sute asked:

"But back to your nightmare. Is that the only nightmare you had at the inn?"

The recounting of atrocities made Collier forget the actual reason he'd come. "Well, no. You don't seem surprised or suspicious that I'm having dreams that detail past events that I was previously uninformed of."

"I'm *not* surprised," Sute said as baldly as his pate. "I've spoken to *many* people who've had similar experiences there. Transpositional dreams are commonplace in haunted-house phenomena, Mr. Collier . . . if you believe the technical mumbo jumbo that's often affixed to it."

Collier tried to synopsize in his head: *Gast burned innocent women and children to death in a giant blast furnace . . . to pay his debt to Satan . . .*

"One thing I forgot to mention," Sute intervened, "is

how Gast spiced up his supposed reverence to the devil. The railroad was finished on April thirtieth, and even minutes after the final spike was driven, the first contingent of captives were transported to Maxon. Before Gast and his men returned to town, however, there's the matter of the slaves who worked so devotedly for him."

"You're going to tell me that the slaves sold their souls, too?" Collier couldn't help the sarcasm.

"Not at all. Gast promised them their freedom when the job was complete, but he executed them all instead, a fitting final touch. His security team opened fire on all the slaves at once, firing low body shots so they'd be incapacitated rather than killed on the spot. He wanted them *alive* for the furnace. It's ironic that the slaves who built the railroad were among the first into the coal bed, Gast's *first* payment to his benefactor."

Collier sat numb. He felt as though he were sinking into a morass of distilled putrefaction.

"Sorry, I've strayed," Sute admitted. "You were going to tell me about another nightmare?"

Collier had no good judgment left. "Last night I dreamed I was in the house. I was a woman—I was a *prostitute*."

"One of Bella's, no doubt. Bella Silver, but nobody knows her actual last name. She was the madam at the town bordello."

Collier nodded, gulping. "I went up to the house, and the marshal was there—"

"Braden."

"—with a deputy. We were the first to discover Gast's body hanging from the tree out front—"

"Then this would be May third."

"That's *exactly* the day, and I know that because I saw it on a calendar at Bella's—" Collier wheezed choppy laughter, knowing how mad he must appear. "There was a hole in the front yard, and shovels, and anyway the marshal ordered me to help him search. We were searching for Mary and Cricket Gast."

Sute sat large and immobile, listening.

"You told me about Cutton yesterday, and how Penelope was murdered, and also about Gast hanging himself," Collier continued almost breathlessly, "so that part of the dream could've been suggestion, but I didn't know about the other two suicides—"

"Poltrock and Morris—"

"Yes, yes, but last night I dreamed what you told me today, and I'm *positive* I hadn't heard it elsewhere." Now Collier's fingers were digging into his thigh. "In this goddamn nightmare I went inside and saw the same thing— I saw Morris with his throat cut and I saw Poltrock with part of his head blown off, and then I went upstairs and I saw Cutton in the washroom where someone drowned him in the fucking *hip* bath, and then I looked in another room and saw Penelope lying naked on a blood-drenched bed with an *ax* in her privates—"

Sute looked alarmed. "Mr. Collier, relax. These kinds of tales can get under anyone's skin. Let me get you another drink to calm you down."

"I don't want another damn drink," Collier harped. "I want to know what was in the children's room, the room I'm renting now. In the nightmare I went to open it and it was locked. So the marshal's deputy kicked it open, but they wouldn't let me look! Mary and Cricket were in there dead, right?"

"Correct."

"But they weren't killed in that room—you already said so. So where were they killed? And why were their *dead bodies* moved to that room after the fact?"

"For an obscene effect, I'm sure." Sute's voice seemed to vibrate in a grim suboctave. "It was Gast. He wanted *horror.* He wanted the children to be *found,* don't you see? Read some of the excerpt . . ."

Collier's eyes surveyed the italics:

. . Gast and his first team had already arrived back in town a week ago, according to the station master. There was no difficulty in discernment, after I'd spoken to Richard Barrison, a plowman, who testified that he saw several of Gast's men digging a large hole next to the front court. Not thirty minutes later, when returning, Barrison reports that he saw the same men refilling the hole. This was shortly before one o'clock in the afternoon. Further deliberation was hardly necessary when we discovered the bodies of those poor girls . . .

Collier rubbed vertigo from his eyes. "My God . . . You mean he—"

"Gast buried his two daughters alive, then went about the business of murdering Jessa and seeing to the gang-rape and sequent ax-murder of his wife. Cutton was murdered sometime after one in the afternoon as well." Sute diddled with another drink. "Just before sundown, he ordered Morris and Poltrock to exhume Mary and Cricket's bodies and place them in the bedroom. He closed the door, and locked the dog in with them. He knew that it would likely be days before the bodies were discovered. He wanted them to rot down a bit first, which is why he closed the windows. And the dog, of course, having nothing to eat . . ."

"The dog ate the girls' bodies," Collier droned.

Sute looked a bit sick himself now. "Not . . . just that, I'm sorry to say . . ."

"What do you mean?"

The obese man pointed again to the manuscript in Collier's lap. "Perhaps it's best that you *not* read anymore. An abridged version might be less offensive." Sute cleared his throat. "The girls were pregnant when Gast put them in the hole, probably considerably so."

"He buried them alive and they were *pregnant?*" Collier almost shouted his outrage.

"I'm afraid so."

"Rape-related pregnancies?"

"Hardly. See, these young girls weren't so innocent themselves. With a mother like that for a role model? They were notoriously promiscuous and quite willing, at least according to the plethora of letters and resident diaries. And what you're not comprehending is this: Gast wanted their punishment to be *rich*. After several hours under the ground, the girls were dead and the fetuses miscarried. The corpses were then exhumed—*four* of them, mind you—and lain in their beds. Hence, the dog's first pangs of hunger were satisfied by the fetuses and afterbirth, and when there was none of that left . . . it started on the girls. That's the scene that awaited Marshal Braden and his deputy when they forced open that door, and no doubt the same scene *you* would've witnessed in the nightmare had you looked in the room." Sute sighed. "Rumor has it that the dog escaped, never to be seen again. But you can be sure . . . it escaped with a full stomach."

And all of that, Collier regarded, *happened in the room I'm staying in now . . .*

Was Gast simply a man gone mad, or was it really something worse, something which, for all intents, was impossible? The silence that followed made the room seem darker; Collier's brain felt like nerveless meat. *I'm some kind of an antenna,* he thought, *and the inn is the power source.* But did he really believe it was a power source charged by the evil of the past?

He felt older when he pushed up from the chair. "I have to go now."

"It's a harrowing story, Mr. Collier. But now you know all of it. Of course, knowing what you know now, you're probably sorry you ever asked."

"It's my nature." He tried to laugh, and handed back the manuscript.

"You're sure you don't want to borrow it?" Sute asked.

"No. I wouldn't be able to hack it. I'll be leaving soon anyway."

Sute rose to put the manuscript up; then he returned the checks to Collier. "I'm sorry to hear that. I hope it's not the town's ghastly history that's sending you away."

Collier lied. "No, no, I've got to get back to L.A." There was a discomfort that continued to itch at him. What did it matter what Sute might say when he was gone? *Nothing,* he realized. Still, he didn't want anything getting back to Dominique, even though he realized that he'd probably never see her again after tonight.

"Mr. Sute? Please don't tell anyone what I've said today—the nightmares and all."

Sute stood half in shadow now, a smoking-jacketed hulk. "It's all in confidence, Mr. Collier. As I said before, you're an intuitive man. You don't want me to repeat what you've told me. And as with any agreement between good gentlemen, I trust that you'll keep *my* secret as well."

It was the first time that Collier had noticed the five-by-seven framed picture of Jiff, on the nightstand. *I guessed that one right, too . . .*

"I understand. It was nice meeting you—" Collier shook hands. "Thanks for satisfying my curiosity. It's definitely killed this cat."

"It's only a story, Mr. Collier." Sute tried to sound jovial.

"But one that we both know is true . . ."

Sute shrugged with a smile.

As Collier made to leave, his psyche felt like a watch spring that had popped. *I'm not the Boy Who Cried Wolf, I'm the Boy Who Asked Too Much.* But he knew this: he'd heard more than he could stand, and now he was going home with his tail between his legs—

"Not just yet!" Sute was back at a bookshelf, and slid out some heavy folders. "You wanted to see these."

"What . . . are they?"

"The daguerreotypes."

A rigor seized Collier.

"Mr. Collier, I know you've had more than your fill of the local lore . . . but after hearing it all, can you really walk away without ever seeing the only existing photographs of Penelope Gast?"

You bastard, Collier thought. He remained unresponsive for several more moments, then said, "All right. Let's see."

Sute carefully slid some metal sheets from various protective folders. "Take care to only touch the edges," Sute requested.

Collier found the first stiff sheet obscurely bordered in black; within the border the image seemed to float. Ghostly was the best description of what Collier's eyes fixed on: Penelope Gast gazing askance in a ruffled French-style bustle and petticoat. The embroidered bodice piece hung unlaced down the front to reveal a plenteous white bosom, starkly nippled. Collier gulped. Even in the grainy photograph, she was infinitely more beautiful than the modest oil portrait at the inn.

"Genuine daguerreotypes were hard to come by," Sute explained, "and outrageously expensive for private citizens."

Collier thought of Hollywood producers who had professional sculptors cast their wives' nude torsos and hang them on the wall. This was the same thing for rich men of the mid-1800s. Putting one's wife on a pedestal.

"Tintypes were more common during and after the Civil War, but the images were inferior and tended to lose detail after time. Gast spared no expense to immortalize the image of his wife."

And then have her gang-raped before he dropped an ax between her legs . . . Collier looked at the next, this one even more racy. Mrs. Gast stood poised with a togalike garment snaking up one leg, between her legs, then around her neck. Her legs were model perfect. The toga covered one breast; her right hand cupped the other. The light long curls of her hair seemed to illuminate about her head. Did he detect the faintest freckles in her cleavage?

He never saw it coming. The next sheet showed Penelope Gast lying totally nude across a reclining settee like an odalisque in a Turkish harem. The detail was shocking, as well as his ability to make out a single freckle just above the clitoral hood. And the woman's pubis had been completely shaved.

CHAPTER THIRTEEN

I

Collier drove. He had to clear his head. He wasn't sure where he was driving—the airport for all he knew.

For all he knew he was leaving Gast and its questionable horrors without even a good-bye. He could abandon his luggage, he could even abandon his laptop. Mrs. Butler already had his credit card number for the room bill.

I'm actually afraid, he realized.

Collier didn't want to go back to the inn.

The Bug swept around the snakelike turns of the side roads out of town. Did *it* want to get out of here, too? Then Collier's mind jagged:

What am I doing?

It's ridiculous to leave my laptop and luggage just because of a ghost story. Could he possibly spend one more night in his room, knowing what had happened in it? And the rooms on either side? *Sandwiched by murder . . .*

Then a more rational reality touched him on the shoulder. *I can't just leave town without saying good-bye to Dominique . . .*

She'd think he was an imbecile, or worse, just another drooling, insincere cock-hound who fled the scene when he realized he'd never get her in bed.

Even if he never saw her again, he couldn't have her think that.

I need something good to happen. He laughed and the wind mussed his hair. *Hey, God, can something fucking GOOD happen to me today?*

But why should God do anything for him?

His stomach rumbled. He hadn't eaten today and it was well into the afternoon. But when he considered the mutt's last meal in the Gast House, he doubted he'd have any appetite for a long time . . .

A sign told him the interstate exit for the airport was only five miles distant. *Christ, do I even know what I'm doing?* He pulled into a last-chance rest stop with a gas station and Qwik-Stop. *At least try to eat something,* he forced himself.

He thought of the most racist clichés inside; the clerk wore a turban and could've passed for a suicide bomber. "One dollar six cents!" he was yelling at an unkempt woman with smudges on her face. She had four quarters on the counter and was trying to buy a hot dog in a foil bag. "But it says a dollar each!" she cried. A dirty toddler stood at her side. "I just want to split a hot dog with my kid!"

Collier watched as he poured himself a coffee from the back of the store.

"Tax!" the clerk sniped in his radical accent. "Now get out! You cannot pay so you must leave or I call police! You homeless go somewhere else! Why you come to my store? In my country you be sterilized and put on work farm!"

"Fucker!" she wailed. She grabbed a handful of ketchup and relish packs and ran out with her kid.

Collier's hand went unconsciously to his pocket, for change. But then his cell phone rang. *Shit! I told Evelyn I'd call her!* For most of the time he'd been in Gast, he'd left the phone in his room, but now he saw a dozen missed messages stacked up. Several were from his soon-to-be ex-wife but he also noticed even more from Shay Prentor, his producer. And that's who was calling now.

"Hi, Shay—"

"Justy," came the distant voice. "Been calling for two days, my friend. Does the Prince of Beer not want to talk to his good friend and producer or does he not know how to charge his cell?"

"Sorry—" *Why's he calling?* "I'm out of town right now."

"Yeah, your lawyer told me, said you were in some bumfuck place in Arkansas, or West Virginia—"

"Tennessee."

"Justy, Justy, it's pretty much the same thing. Moonshine and incest, cruelty to animals . . ."

"It's not quite that bad. A town called Gast . . ."

"Oh, yeah, you can bet I've heard of that. Jesus Christ, Justy, what are you doing there?"

Collier knew something was wrong; Prentor only called him "Justy" when he wanted something. "I'm finishing a book—you know, for my *other* career, which I need desperately now since you're dumping my show. Why are you calling? You need me to clean out my desk, like, *right now?*"

"Oh, Justy, Justy, you're a regular bebopper with that wit. I just wanted to tell you the bad news—"

"What could be worse news than 'you're fired'? You laid that line on me a week ago."

"No, no, the bad news is *Savannah Sammy's Sassy Smokehouse* just dropped from number three to number four."

Collier frowned. "Shay. How is that bad news for me?"

"Not for you, for him! That cocky cracker!" Prentor

unreeled fuzzy laughter. "The good news for you is that we just tabbed the ratings for your last six shows, and you're now number three."

Collier almost dropped the phone in the coffeepot. "I thought I was eleven—"

"Not now, my friend. Your show has officially caught on. I'm not jiving you, Justy. You're actually only a few points off of number two. Emeril ain't happy, I can tell you that."

Collier couldn't think straight. "So I'm getting renewed?"

"How's this for an answer, Justy? Fuck yes. Three-hundred-thousand-dollar re-sign bonus and an extra half point in your kick, and that's from the VP. I'm looking at the piece of paper that guarantees it. It's this thing called a *contract,* which we really need you to sign right now. So when am I going to have your smiling face on the other side of my desk, and a *pen* in your hand? Fly back now. What, you have to be in *Tennessee* to write a book about beer? My daddy always told me there wasn't anything in Tennessee but steers and—"

Collier stood in shock, the phone printing against his ear. "I'll be back tomorrow, Shay. But . . . what about the guy you hired to replace me, the *San Francisco Seafood Psycho?* I heard you signed him up for twenty-six episodes right off the bat."

Prentor gusted another laugh. "We canceled the asshole's contract on character breech. *You* get the twenty-six episodes."

"Character breech?"

"It's hilarious, man! Turns out the guy really *is* a psycho. Last week some critic from *Gourmet* came to his restaurant and complained about the crab Wellington, said the crabmeat was that fake surimi stuff. So the Psycho's so offended he *comes after* the guy with a meat cleaver! No lie, Justy! It was in the paper! Almost got him, too. Took three cops to haul the Psycho out of there and

book him for assault with intent . . ." Prentor kept bubbling laughter. "Forget about that loser, Justy. *You're* the
big news at the network now."

Collier's hands were shaking as it finally sunk in: *I'm
getting renewed! I've still got a show!*

"And, Justy, are you ready for some *really* good
news?"

"I can't imagine anything better than what you just
told me—"

"According to our latest viewer survey, the reason
your ratings just tripled is because housewives are
starting to watch the show with their husbands—"

Collier frowned. "Shay, housewives walk out of the
room when my show comes on. They couldn't care less
about craft beer."

Wheezing laughter chopped up Prentor's next line:
"They're watching your show because they think *you're*
sexy! Emeril ain't happy, let me tell you. And we know it's
on the mark 'cos last week we did a Web site poll for sexiest man on the network? You won—"

Collier dropped his phone into the coffeepot.

Shit!

The clerk's back was turned. Collier dumped the pot
in the sink, and tried to pat the phone dry with paper
towels. *This is the best day of my LIFE!* Excitement drove
his heart rate so high, he knew he'd have to calm down—
he could scarcely think. He rushed his coffee to the
counter, fumbled for money . . .

A glance out the window showed him the homeless
mother sitting at the parking lot's edge with her kid.
They were sucking the ketchup and relish out of the
packets. *Jesus* . . . At once he thought of Dominique
spending half the day running food to the homeless, and
the sermon by the minister who looked like the Skipper.

Collier grabbed several bottled sodas, then told the
turbaned clerk, "Give me ten hot dogs and ten of those
cheese roll things."

The clerk shook his head, ringing it up. "Sir, sir, these dirty people, they are all addicted to the drugs and on welfare. It is not good to give them things. They must earn them like us."

Collier hated conversations, but he knew the difference. "Buddy, that woman out there's no drug addict. Not *every* homeless person is a drug addict." Being from L.A., Collier knew the difference. The panhandlers wore $200 sneakers. Homeless addicts didn't drift to remote areas like this.

"You are silly man to give *anything* to such scum—"

"Just ring me up." Collier held his tongue.

The clerk shoved the bag at him. "That's why this country is so fucked up, you give to dirty people who don't want to work hard like I have to. In my country, we make the useless work and sterilize them so they cannot bring more babies for more welfare!"

More stereotypes flared, but Collier just grabbed the bag and headed for the door.

"You don't come back to my store!" the clerk added. "You are a silly, ignorant man!"

Collier turned. "Listen, dickbrain. I'm not silly and I'm not ignorant. I'm Justin Collier, Prince of Beer, and I have the number-three show on the Food Network, and you can pack *that* in your hookah and smoke it all the way back to whatever freedom-squashing, terrorist-harboring, dictatorial SHITHOLE you come from," he said, then walked out.

"Fuck you! I say to you—*fuck* you!"

Collier was hardly bothered at all by the unpleasant confrontation. All that mattered to him right now was Prentor's phone call. *I've got my show back!* his thoughts kept trumpeting. But his cell phone was still hot. As he strode across the lot, he tried to shake the coffee out of it. *Got to call him back right now . . .*

The homeless woman and child were still sitting on the curb sucking ketchup. "Excuse me, miss," Collier said and set down the bag, "but I heard what that guy in there said to you. I got you some hot dogs and stuff."

The smudge-faced woman looked in the bag, then burst into tears. "Oh my God, thank you, thank you! We haven't eaten in a day! Finally someone nice comes along! God bless you!"

They began tearing into the food.

"Do you need a ride to a shelter or something?" Collier offered.

"Oh, no, thank you," she sobbed, cheeks stuffed. "They won't let us into the shelter so we live at the underpass right down the road. Usually the Salvation Army truck comes by and gives out sandwiches but they didn't come last night. But thank you so much for this food!"

Collier felt overwhelmed. *Damn. What should I do?* He took a hundred-dollar bill out of his wallet. "Here, why don't you take this?" he said and gave it to her.

The woman almost sidled over in her tears of joy. "Thank you! Thank you so much—" She leaped up and hugged Collier.

The toddler looked cross-eyed stuffing another hot dog into his mouth.

"God bless you, sir! God bless you!"

Eventually Collier had to urge her back. "You're quite welcome, but I have to go now. 'Bye . . ."

"Thank you, thank you!"

Collier walked off. Was this the type of charity the minister had called for? *Or did I just do it to feel good?* he wondered.

It didn't matter.

The exuberance of his show's renewal slammed back. *Yes-sir-ee! The sexiest man on the Food Network!* He opened and closed the cell phone several times but the screen never turned on. *I gotta get back to the inn, call Shay and tell him not to date the contract until after my divorce . . .*

Collier was five yards away from the homeless woman when he heard her voice behind him:

"Pokey? This is Dizzy—yeah, yeah, yeah, and don't you hang up this time, you shit!"

Collier turned and was astonished to see the woman talking on a cell phone that looked even more expensive than his.

"I know, I know, you told me a million times, no more rock on credit. You just meet me at the underpass and bring five rocks. That's right, five!"

What the hell . . .

"I'm not shitting you—yes, I've got it! Some guy just gave me a c-note so you MEET ME in twenty minutes and bring five rocks! Holy SHIT, am I gonna crack it up to-night!"

Collier felt excreted on by crows. A hot dog flew out of the kid's hand when the woman yanked him by the arm and strode off, the bag of food forgotten.

Collier stumbled back to the car.

"You see! You see!" railed the clerk out front. "Ignorant, silly man won't listen! You—how you say? Kiss my ass!"

Collier wanted to run back to the car.

"Yes! Yes—oh, look, now silly, ignorant camel's ass of a man is getting into car painted *woman's* color!" He cracked out accented laughter. "And I *see* your show on your stupid American television and is—how you say? Piece of SHIT!"

Collier didn't say a word. He simply got into the Day-Glo green vehicle and drove away.

He didn't go to the airport. It seemed overreactive to just bug off. He'd stay one more night, check out properly, and say good-bye to Dominique.

Which only left his fears . . .

Back in town, he checked every other hotel and bed-

and-breakfast: no vacancies. He didn't even hesitate to admit it now: *I'd really prefer NOT to spend another night in that haunted-to-the-max mansion.* He supposed he could sleep in the car. Or . . .

Maybe Dominique would let me spend my last night at her place . . .

A much more promising idea, but would she go for it? Did she trust him to respect her celibacy?

Collier didn't dwell on it, or anything else. Sute's final revelations about what had happened in room three back in 1862 packed too much of a wallop. Maybe Mrs. Butler could give him another room for his final night. The memory of Sute's daguerreotype only added weight to his decision not to return to the room . . .

Do I really believe in ghosts? he asked himself.

It was going on five o'clock now. *Dominique'll be on duty soon.* When he next checked his phone, the lights came on, but the screen read NO SIGNAL. *I could go back to the inn, call Shay from there,* he knew, but when he pulled into the parking lot, the house seemed to grimace back at him.

Damn.

Did he hear a dog barking when he got out of the Bug? His gut clenched.

It seemed to come from down the hill, where the creek coursed through the woods.

Collier walked in the opposite direction, into town . . .

When he passed the bank, he saw Jiff standing in line, evidently to deposit another check. Collier could guess whom the check was from, and for what.

Collier walked quickly, so not to be seen. He followed Penelope Street to the main drag and pushed into the sudden coolness of Cusher's. He took a stool at the half-filled bar.

"Hi, Mr. Collier!" the St. Pauli Girl barmaid greeted. "How's your stay so far?"

"Fine, but it looks like I'll be going home tomorrow."

"Oh, that's too bad." She put a pint of lager before him. "That's on the house. And congratulations!"

"Congratulations for what?"

"Come on, don't be so modest." She winked, then hustled to some other customers.

What the HELL is going on now? Within seconds three housewife tourists appeared and apologetically pleaded for autographs. One put a hand on his thigh and whispered, "You really ARE the sexiest man on the Food Network . . ." and another whispered, "If my husband wasn't here, I'd wear you out."

Then Collier got it. *Shay wasn't jiving me.* Obviously the news was out about the viewer survey. His eyes followed the housewives—all attractive and well built— but turned away when he saw several husbands scowling back.

Collier didn't care. He had to decide what he was going to do.

"Is Dominique in yet?" he asked the barmaid.

"She's running late, said she had a problem at her condo."

A problem at Dominique's condo?

He sipped his beer and tried to relax. *How late is she going to be?* When he looked up at the television in the corner, he saw Savannah Sammy basting a brisket. *How's it feel to be number four, you two-faced Jersey slickster?*

Collier's belly growled for food but every time he thought of asking for a menu, his mind recalled the nightmare: his bedroom door kicked in, the dog running out, and . . . the stench. He was glad the dream hadn't shown him the details Sute had only verbalized. He tried to divert himself; without thinking he'd taken the old railroad checks out of his pocket and began looking at them. *Some guy named Fecory filled these out almost 150 years ago.* The paper felt so fine, so thin.

Sute thinks these things are contracts with the devil . . .

He got a chill and put them away. He didn't notice that

the check on the bottom had been signed by Fecory but otherwise remained blank.

Am I going to sit here all day? Whenever he looked to the TV, he winced. When the barmaid walked by, he flagged her. "Miss? You said Dominique had a problem at her condo? What's the problem?"

She leaned forward on her elbows, highlighting the bosom. "Contractors or something. She forgot about them when she took the food to the shelter in Chattanooga."

"Did she say *when* she's coming in?"

"Soon, she said, didn't give a time."

"Oh." He sighed. "With my luck it won't be for hours." As soon as he'd said it, he was spun around and kissed on the lips.

"Hi, sorry I'm late," Dominique told him. "I didn't have your cell number so I couldn't call you."

"I heard something happened at your condo."

"The association tents the building every couple years—fumigators—and I forgot they were doing it today. So I had to rush back, seal all my cabinets, and get out. Can't go back for twenty-four hours."

Collier realized only then that he was clinging to her, arms around her waist.

"I really like it when you hug me," she giggled, "but if you don't let go, I can't do my work."

"Oh, right—"

"And congratulations: sexiest man on television."

"Just on the Food Network."

"I don't know about that." She kissed him again and slipped away.

Collier felt forlorn watching after her. *Yeah, I've got it bad* . . . But her condo closed till tomorrow nixed the possibility of him staying the night with her. *I am NOT spending another night by myself in room three,* he knew. He also knew that what he felt for Dominique, he'd never felt for any other woman in his life. A revelation socked home: Dominique had a lot of virtue, while he . . . didn't. *She makes me see my real self. But I don't like what I see and I want to be different. Dominique makes me want to be a better person . . .*

Was is that simple? Collier felt confident.

A better revelation: *I could've gotten it on with Lottie last night but I didn't because I wanted to be faithful to a girl who'll NEVER sleep with me.* His finger tapped the bar. *That's GOT to mean something.*

Dominique returned. "You should try tonight's special. It kicks butt."

"What is it?"

"Country-fried squid steak with curry tartar."

"Maybe, uh, next time." He reached across and grabbed her hand, instantly realizing a solution. "Since you can't get into your condo tonight, you should stay with me at the inn."

She looked relieved. "I was hoping you'd ask."

Collier stalled. "So that means . . . yes?"

"Of course—" Her eyes shot to the door. "Oh, I have to go seat this four-top."

She pulled away but Collier didn't let go. "So that means you trust me now?"

She laughed. "If I didn't trust you, I wouldn't be staying with you tonight. You know what *won't* be happening, so it must not bother you—"

"It doesn't," he said before he could think.

"Look, I have to go seat these people! I'm the boss, remember?"

She whisked away.

Her body's outline in the apron was killing him, and whenever she appeared behind the bar to get something, her cross glittered on her bosom. Collier felt so skewed. *I have to go back to L.A. tomorrow, but I'm sitting here fantasizing about having a relationship with a Christian celibate . . .*

At least the beer calmed his nerves. And now he wouldn't have to spend the night by himself in the room. She'd be with him the whole time . . .

He'd kept the cell phone open on the bar, hoping it would dry. NO SIGNAL it still read.

"Try these," Dominique said. She'd reappeared with a plate. "It's a misorder."

It was a knockwurst with mustard dip, which seemed bland enough. "Thanks."

"How was your day?"

A mess . . . and terrific. "Fine." He didn't bother telling her the show had been renewed, because he'd never told her it had been canceled. "Didn't really do much, actually. Went for a drive is all." He skipped the other details.

"Have you been drinking coffee?" she asked. "I smell coffee."

Collier hesitated, then pointed to his cell phone. "Oh, it's the phone."

Her brow scrunched. "Your *phone* smells like coffee?"

"Uh, don't ask."

"How's the book coming? Finished yet?"

Had he even written a single word? "Almost there. I have to fine-tune the last entry, Cusher's Civil War Lager."

"People will think it's favoritism." She tossed her head and laughed. "But the joke's on them."

"Huh?"

Her cross dangled when she leaned and whispered, "They'll think you're screwing the brewer, but they don't know that the brewer is celibate."

Again, Collier spoke before thinking. "The brewer is beautiful. I'm *falling* for the brewer, celibate and all." He reached to grab her hand again but one of the cooks called her away.

What a corny-ass thing to say, he thought after the fact.

Collier ate the bland sausage and found he felt better; his stomach felt less queasy from Sute's horror story.

A shapely shadow hovered—the barmaid. She got him another beer, then noticed his plate. "How did you like the Roadkill Sausage?"

"The *what?*"

"It's smoked possum and muskrat—a Southern delicacy."

Collier stared. "You've got to be kidding me! I just ate—"

"Relax!" she said. "They're farm-raised and corn-fed. You've never been to the South before, have you? An even better Southern delicacy are the Smoky Mountain Oysters. Want to try them?"

Mortified, Collier shook his head.

"Hey, everybody! Look!" someone called out. Everyone was looking up at the TV.

"The results are in!" a voice-over announced. Multiple clips of Collier's show flashed on the screen. "There's a new hunk in town! Justin Collier, the Prince of Beer, has just been voted the sexiest man on the Food Network! Look for his brand-new episodes coming soon right here!"

Damn . . .

Applause rose like the roar of a waterfall. Collier blushed. A bunch of women were whistling. When he jerked around, he found Dominique standing right next to him, clapping as well.

"I'm falling for you, too," she whispered and walked back to her work.

Collier signed autographs for the next several hours, and he didn't even mind. *When you're a star, it comes with the territory.* A number of women made some rather brazen suggestions, but Collier turned them all down without regret. All the while, he kept watching Dominique as she busied through her duties, and he realized just how hopelessly in love he'd become.

Many beers were bought for him, perhaps a few too many, but one thought kept his head clear. During his autograph foray, he'd made a decision . . .

The dinner rush was over. It was going on ten o'clock when Dominique said, "I'm almost done. Just give me a few minutes."

"I'll wait for you outside," Collier said.

His phone had finally dried out; the screen read READY. While Collier waited for Dominique outside the restaurant, he called Shay's number. When the answering machine came on, Collier left a message that he wouldn't be returning to the show.

II

Collier suggested they walk back to the inn rather than take her car. "I like that," she said, looking up. "Another full moon. It's romantic."

"Of course it is," he said, but the main reason he wanted to walk was to clear his head some more with the fresh air. And—

He was in no rush to get back to room three.

But at least she's with me . . . Was he really that scared now?

"The place really does look spooky at night, doesn't it?" she said.

They could see the inn atop the hill, darkened to a silhouette by the moon.

"You would say that."

"Huh?"

Collier laughed at himself. "I'll be honest with you. Mrs. Butler's quaint little bed-and-breakfast is really beginning to get to me."

She squeezed his hand. "You've been listening to way too much J.G. Sute."

"Oh, I know that, and it's my fault. I've reached the saturation point for ghost stories."

He didn't tell her of Sute's final revelations: that of all the atrocities that had taken place there, the very worst had happened in the room he'd just invited her to share. Nor did he tell her of his decision to quit the show.

A wind whipped up, and behind the house the clouds turned bruised. Before they even got to the parking lot, the sky released several loud rumbles.

They both laughed at the coincidence. "Isn't that fitting?" Dominique said.

"Just what I need. A dark and stormy night."

"I swear the weathermen flip coins for their forecasts. They said sunny and clear all week."

Another louder rumble seemed closer. Seconds later, the clouds blacked out the moon entirely.

Collier didn't like it.

When more wind rustled through the trees, he felt certain he heard a voice call out—"Over here!" or something like that. It sounded like a young girl's voice.

Dominique slowed and looked down into the woods.

"You heard that voice, didn't you?"

"What voice?" She seemed to be peering down. "I didn't hear a voice but . . . there *is* a sound coming from down there, don't you think?"

"There's a brook that runs along the wood line . . ."

"Let's go look at it."

Collier tensed. "No, that's crazy. It's pitch-dark down there now, and it'll be storming any minute."

When more wind blew up the hill, Collier thought he heard a dog barking . . .

Dominique stopped. "What was that?"

"Leaves rustling . . ."

"Sounded like a dog."

Collier pulled her by the hand. "Let's just get inside."

A belch of thunder cracked, and then the sky ripped. A torrent of rain fell just as they were jogging up the inn's front steps. Collier felt chilled and sweating at the same time. "Just made it." He reached for the door.

Dominique tugged his hand. "Hey. Are you all right?"

"Well, yeah, sure—"

"Justin, you're *shaking*."

Was he? "I've got . . . got a chill, that's all. From the rain."

She looked convinced when he held the door for her. The last thing he noticed before entering was the great craggy oak tree out front. A whiptail of lightning flashed, tingeing the tree's dead branches bone white, like malformed skeletal appendages.

Collier pulled the door closed.

The atrium shined bright from all the lights, but that didn't feel right in the vast room's emptiness. "It's not that late," Dominique observed. "Where are all the guests?"

Collier kept his eyes averted from the large portrait of Hardwood Gast, but it occurred to him then that Gast's eyes in the painting were looking out directly at the tree from which he'd hanged himself.

A clatter startled them.

Lottie stood in the corner, fiddling with something.

"Hi, Lottie," Collier greeted.

She looked over, smiled briefly, and waved.

They walked over to find her changing the bag in a vacuum cleaner.

"Are all the guests in bed this early?" Dominique asked.

She shook her head and pointed toward town.

The moment was awkward. Lottie seemed diffuse, not the high-energy nut she usually was.

"Good night, Lottie," Collier bid.

She waved without looking at them.

"Weird," Dominique whispered when they moved away. "Doesn't seem herself tonight. Usually she's bouncing off the walls . . ."

Dominique stopped again, tugged on Collier's hand. She was looking at the old writing table.

Remembering what she saw there during the reception, Collier assumed. A man uneasily similar to Windom Fecory. The added coincidence gave Collier a shiver.

He'd found the old checks in the same desk.

All signed by Fecory on the day Gast hanged himself in 1862.

Next her eyes crawled up the cubby's wall, to the tiny portrait of Penelope.

"There she is," Dominique mumbled.

The old oil painting seemed crisper than Collier remembered, eerily more detailed than it should be. More bothersome was that the details of the woman's soft yet seductive face were identical to the old daguerreotypes he'd already been shown.

Lightning flashed in the high windows, and more thunder rippled.

"This is ridiculous," Dominique griped.

"What?"

"Now *I'm* getting spooked."

Collier pulled on her. "Come on, let's go . . ."

As they wound up the curved stairs, Collier took a glance over his shoulder.

Lottie was now standing at the writing table, as if in a trance.

She seemed to be staring at Penelope's portrait.

Eyes dull. Mouth open.

When more thunder cracked, Dominique chuckled. "Now all we need is for the lights to go out."

"Don't even say that!"

She touched her cross. "Don't worry, my cross will protect us from the bogeyman . . ."

When Collier looked again, Lottie was gone.

Bogeyman, he thought. *Or Bogeywoman . . .*

III

Sute sat in his upstairs room, in tears. He sat before the bow window, letting each crackle of lightning turn his face stark. He felt tinged in ruin . . .

He'd called Jiff earlier, pleading for another illicit rendezvous tomorrow but had had to leave a message. When Sute returned from dinner, this reply awaited on his machine:

"J.G., I'se sure ya recognize my voice. Sorry to have to tell ya this but . . . I just cain't do it no more. What I mean's I ain't gonna do no more business with ya. It's too much fer me, ya know? I make easier money other places. Sorry, but that's it."

That's it, Sute had been repeating in his mind for hours now.

"That's it for my life . . ."

His town house shook with the next eruption of thunder.

He sobbed to himself. "This is what . . . all love comes to."

The room's darkness made him feel even more worthless. Everything was for nothing. The lightning turned his tears into a sad liquid glimmer.

Sute knew he was not a strong man. He wondered how long he'd last, sitting here like this, before he killed himself.

IV

"You dirty dog! Dirty, dirty dog!" A pair of wee voices impossibly disappeared around the corner. Just voices, with no children to go with them.

Giggles faded to nothingness, along with a single feisty yap, like the bark of a dog.

Mercy. It's bad tonight.

Mrs. Butler walked slowly along the main stair hall, then went down to make a last-minute check of the kitchen. She'd always known it was the house, and she was sure her son and daughter knew, too. The acknowledgment always passed across their eyes with nary a word. The only thing she'd ever said about it to Lottie and Jiff was: "It's just the past kind'a seepin' through. Don't happen much, just ever now'n then. Just you two always remember . . . what ya cain't see cain't hurt ya . . ."

The inn was full up; tourist season here ran nine or ten months sometimes. It was a good life. And folks rarely stayed long enough to ever notice anything funny. A couple now and then, sure—some people got it worse than others (and Mrs. Butler could never imagine why) but generally things ran well.

Mr. Collier, of course, had it bad. She could tell by his eyes. *He'd heard the dog, and the girls.* Perhaps she should've been more convincing when answering his queries about the building's past. *If I weren't so all-fired hot for the man, maybe I'd be a better host!* She often believed that something in the house made her so pent up for men, even at her age.

The kitchen was fine, everything prepped for the morning's light breakfast. The overhead lights wavered through the next peal of thunder. *Danged storm!* They rarely lost power here, but when they did, her guests were none too happy. *Please stay on, dang ya!*

She didn't want to have to suffer though complaints tomorrow and—her worst concern:

This ain't the night to lose the lights in THIS house . . .

She left the kitchen and went back to the family wing. Lottie'd already gone to bed. *Poor girl was all out'a sorts today.* Mrs. Butler knew it was just the house going through one of its cycles. When she peeked into Lottie's room, she saw her daughter tossing fitfully, bedsheets twisted into a snake that coursed her naked body. *More bad dreams,* Mrs. Butler realized. Lottie, though asleep, was pawing desperately at her sex.

When she peeked into Jiff's room, she wasn't surprised to find the bed empty. *Honestly, what IS that boy into?* She'd heard some things, but like many mothers, she ignored the rumors. *He's a grown man!* she kept telling herself. Drinking way too much, though, but . . . he always did when the house was like this.

Mrs. Butler felt a hundred when she trudged into her own room. She stripped and slipped into a sheer nightgown. *Jesus Lord, I am SO tired* . . . She sat on the bed, was about to switch off the lamp, but faltered. She didn't want to be in the dark . . .

Last night she'd had the most awful dream, and it was one she'd had before. She'd dreamed that she was a lissome black woman being raped one by one by a line of strong white men with big grins but eyes that looked dead. When they each had a turn, they took *another* turn.

Then another.

By the time they were finished, she lay ravaged, bleeding inside and out, organs ruptured. The hot room reeked so horribly of urine it could've been a sauna where piss had been poured over the hot stones instead of water.

Mrs. Butler knew what room it was . . .

In the dream, she'd died, yet her last breath had escaped with her consciousness only to rise above the horror and watch the men drag her corpse out of the house to the fields where it was minced with hewers and hoed into the soil . . .

When Mrs. Butler finally turned off the light, a volley of thunder ripped the air so violently she shrieked.

She shivered beneath the covers, terrified, yet impossibly moist between the legs, nipples aching to be sucked. When more lightning flashed, she shrieked again because she thought sure she could see the shapes of figures on the wall, as though someone was outside the window, looking in.

It's just the house . . . *It cain't hurt me* . . .

And she was right. The house *wouldn't* hurt her. It was only going to use her for a while.

Jiff walked home from the Spike when Buster closed. "Shit, Jiff, you shouldn't have stayed so long—you're drunk as a skunk!"

"Yeah, shee-it, I know."

"Something bumming you out?"

"Naw—"

"You're bullshitting me, Jiff, but—hell—it's none of my business," the big bartender said. The rain pattering the roof sounded like marbles.

"Let me call you a cab. It's pouring."

"Naw, I'll walk—" Jiff pushed open the door and let himself be swamped by the rain. He walked in hitches, staggering.

Yes, he was drunk, all right.

Truth was, he hadn't left the bar because . . . he was too uneasy about going back to the inn.

The rain fell in sheets but he didn't care. He had plenty of cash for a cab but he elected not to call one because he really was in no hurry to get back.

The house was having one of its fits, and Jiff could guess what kind of dreams awaited him once he went to bed. *If I'm drunk enough, I'll pass out'n might not remember 'em . . .*

Desperate logic.

With every whiplash of lightning, Jiff froze and grabbed a streetlamp to keep his balance. Had anyone ever been hit by lightning in this town?

With my luck, I'll be the first.

Eventually the awnings along Number 1 Street gave him some cover, which only allowed him to focus more on his dim and seedy life. Jiff was tired of two-bit tricks in a gay bar, and buffing his mother's floors . . . but he also knew he didn't deserve much more. *Why cain't I just make some decent money like other folks?* Drunk as he was, though, he had the presence of mind to step in closer to the shops. J.G. Sute's town house was right across the street. He walked as quickly as his stumble would allow, head down. A side-glance upward showed him Sute's bedroom window—all dark—but after another flash—

Jesus! Is that him sittin' there?

Jiff walked faster.

When he was far enough down the street, he thought, *Yeah, some hustler I am.* Sute was his most regular client, with the most dependable money, yet Jiff had pulled the plug on the poor bastard. He just couldn't hack the gross-out kinks anymore.

The poor fat slob's probably up there cryin'.

Too bad.

Outside of a bathtub, he'd never been more drenched than when he finally stumbled up the hill and rushed into the vestibule.

He looked through the glass panels of the inner door and saw the portrait of Harwood Gast looking right at him.

Why ain't I got the balls to just up'n move out'a this crazy place?

Behind him, the thunder sounded like it was crushing the sky. Had he ever heard anything so loud?

Jiff remained in the vestibule for another half hour, before he actually found the courage to enter.

VI

"What a nice room," Dominique commented when Collier took her in.

You'd be surprised, he wanted to say. But he found that her being here with him dulled some of the edges of his fear.

Something snapped; his head jerked around.

Dominique lit one of several candles that sat atop the armoire. "Just in case the—"

All the lights went out with a thunk, in time with the worst shot of lightning so far.

"It's a good thing you're smart," Collier said.

An orb of light floated around the wick. Dominique lit two more. "You got your wish," she joked.

The switch from lamplight to candlelight frayed a few of Collier's nerves. "My wish?"

"Haunted house, dark and stormy night, and now . . . no power."

"That's not exactly my wish." The atmosphere couldn't have been more potent now. The storm was rattling the French doors to the balcony.

Dominique walked around to the bed and quite by surprise, kissed him. "I'm so tired I can't believe it." Then she sat, and kicked off her shoes.

Is that her way of telling me she's too tired to make out? Collier, in all honesty, wasn't in the mood. "Well, of course you're tired." He tried to get his mind off the house. "You were in church at seven thirty, fed a hundred of Chattanooga's homeless, and worked the dinner rush."

"I'll fall asleep so fast . . ."

She unbuttoned her blouse with no hesitation.

"Want me to turn around?" he offered.

"No. I told you I trust you. But I won't sleep nude like I usually do. Then you really *would* think I'm a tease."

"Oh, no, no, no, I wouldn't—"

She smiled in the candlelight, and shouldered out of the blouse to expose the perfect breasts cupped in a sheer white-lace bra. Then she stood up and skimmed off her work slacks.

This is killing me . . .

When she turned in the candlelight he could see her nipples beneath the lace, and a tuft of pubic hair. The light chiseled her body's contours into a wonderwork of flawless feminine lines, razor-sharp shadows and flesh.

She flopped on the bed and bounced on it. "What a great bed!"

It's not the bed that's the problem with this room, he reminded himself.

"And these pillows!" The back of her head sunk into the middle of one. Another she embraced, a little girl with a teddy bear. She grinned up at him. "I can't wait to sleep with you."

Unfortunately, Collier knew what that meant: sleep. He lost his thoughts. "You're . . . beautiful . . ."

The grin turned serious. "I'm sorry this can't be what you really want."

"You might be surprised what I really want . . ." He almost groaned when her legs extended, her toes flexing atop the sheets.

"Come to bed. Let's spoon."

Collier strode to the bathroom with a candle, stripped down to shorts, then brushed his teeth, hoping to get rid of what must be awful beer breath. When he came back out, she was under the sheets up to her navel. Her cross sparked like a tiny camera flash in the candlelight.

"You want me to put out the candles?" he asked.

Thunder rumbled, then more loud lightning.

"Probably not," she admitted.

"I agree."

Collier crawled in, and they at once wrapped themselves up in each other. Her body's heat and the feel of her skin buzzed him more than all those lagers. Her hand opened on his bare chest, right over his heart. Collier knew it was racing.

They kissed, sharing each other's breath. Even after a day's hard work, her hair was so fragrant, it hit him like a drug.

"Oh, damn it," she muttered.

Collier's head was spinning, just from the feel of her. "What?"

"You must really hate this. It's not what most people are used to. It's not considered normal."

"I'm fine . . ."

"I know I'll never break my celibacy, but if I were going to, you'd be the guy I did it with."

It was the worst thing she could've said, but even more so, the best thing.

Then her voice turned joking, "Or you could always marry me, but I definitely wouldn't recommend that. It'd be hazardous."

"Hazardous?"

"I'd probably screw you to death on our wedding night."

Her thigh was between his legs, and when she'd said that, she moved it off because his penis had gone hard at once.

I love you, I love you, the words in his mind seemed to flicker up the walls with the candlelight.

He should say it. He *knew* he should say it.

"I . . ."

But she'd already fallen asleep, her head on his chest.

The thunder and lightning had at least subsided enough that he didn't quake with each flash. Sleep was inviting him within minutes, but images and words kept snapping him back to a tense wakefulness: his dream of the whore named Harriet, "Dirty dog!" the *scritch-scritch-scritch-scritch-scritch* as a young blonde girl shaved her legs and, presumably, her pubic hair in the brook, "Gast buried his two daughters alive, then went about the business of murdering Jessa and seeing to the gang-rape and sequent ax-murder of his wife," horses hauling caged wagons toward a plume of smoke, "I heared they killed all the slaves when they was done. Near a hunnert of 'em," an irate man with a gold nose scribbling checks, "He built an entire railroad to Maxon and refired the furnace solely to incinerate the innocent," a daguerreotype of a beautiful nude woman with a shaved pubis and a single freckle an inch above the clitoris, "Rumor has it that the dog escaped, never to be seen again. But you can be sure . . . it escaped with a full stomach . . ."

Collier audibly groaned at the imagery, eyes pressed shut. But more details focused. *In the room to my left, some guy was drowned in a hip bath and got his dick spat into the toilet, and in the room to my right, Penelope Gast got an ax between the legs.*

And in THIS room . . .

Collier could feel bubbling in his belly. All of Sute's stories and all that beer was suddenly boring a hole. The muskrat sausage probably hadn't helped either.

Even with the thunder, he could hear his own heartbeat along with Dominique's, and he could even hear his watch ticking. When he closed his eyes he couldn't shake the idea that a mutt was in the room, and when he opened them, the patterns on the wallpaper seemed to shift into something like train tracks. *Go downstairs and get something to eat,* the idea came to him. Something bland might settle his stomach.

But did he really want to cross that big portrait of Harwood Gast? Or what if he saw Windom Fecory scribbling on checks at the writing table?

Jesus . . .

He knew it was his imagination when he thought he smelled stale urine.

Collier carefully slid out from under Dominique, hauled on his robe, and slipped out of the room, candle in hand.

It was late now, but certain sounds in the hall comforted him: voices of guests, television chatter, even some bedsprings creaking from the Wisconsin woman's room. Some rumbling followed him downstairs—he didn't look at the portrait or the desk—then he crossed the dining room to the kitchen.

There were no lights, of course, and the candle made the long kitchen seem cubby-size. Collier helped himself to a piece of shortcake from the fridge, took one bite, then—

Shit!

—dropped it.

He'd heard a dog bark from somewhere deep in the house.

Bullshit. I didn't hear anything . . .

He was staring into the black entryway, which led to the back wings. The voice of a little girl said in a cattish, snippy tone: ". . . ritual atrocity and the sacrifice of the innocent are nothing new . . ."

Then the patter of bare feet running away.

It was no mistake. *I heard that . . .*

Sute's words from earlier, but definitely not Sute's voice.

Collier's eyes bloomed as he held the candle out and walked through the entryway.

The hallway felt like a catacomb. The dim candlelight wobbling on the walls lent the impression that the hall was moving past him rather than he through it. A window at the far end lit briefly from a throb of lightning. He could barely detect the dark paintings along the walls, and a row of closed doors.

Collier came to a dead stop.

Another voice, just a whisper: ". . . an oblation to the devil . . ." and then a trailing laugh.

Not a child's voice this time but a mature woman's, with a rich, wanton Southern accent.

What followed was the most complete silence he'd ever experienced.

Hands snapped out of the dark, grabbed Collier's robe collar, and yanked him into a suddenly open doorway—

Collier bellowed. The candle flew out of his hand and extinguished.

"Come in here!"

The terror jolted his heart in time with the next flash of lightning. He fell over on a bed with whomever had grabbed him. His fear sealed his throat.

It was Mrs. Butler who shuddered next to him. She put her arms around him, in sheer terror.

"Jesus, Mrs. Butler! You almost gave me a heart attack!"

"Mercy, I'm so scared! The lightning . . ."

Collier, infuriated, tried to calm her. "Just take it easy. It's only a storm . . ." He looked around at what was obviously her bedroom, done up nicely with antiques. Candles wavered from each corner.

"Mrs. Butler. Did you say something when I was in the hall? Something about the devil?"

"The—Mercy, no!" Her arms tremored around him. "But someone else did . . ."

"You heard a voice?"

Sweat adhered the cotton nightgown to her bosom. "It was her . . ."

Her. *She heard it, too,* Collier thought. "Her? Who?"

The woman rose, her gray hair astray to her shoulders. Something forced Collier's eyes to fix on the old woman's breasts and belly printing against the damp nightgown.

She walked dreamily to the window.

"Mrs. Butler?"

The next lightning flash framed her crisp silhouette in the window. "I just love these storms . . ."

Collier frowned. "Mrs. Butler, are you all right?"

"Oh, yes, Mr. Collier." As the words ran out of her mouth, she flipped off her straps, peeled down the nightgown, and stepped out of it. A moment later, she stood right before Collier.

Collier stared at the candlelit flesh glittered by sweat. *No . . .*

"It's just . . . the house is all," she drawled.

"What?"

Her fingers laced behind his head and urged forward as she leaned over slightly, till a nipple was in his face.

Without thinking, he took the nipple into his mouth and sucked.

"Aw, yeah, just like that . . ."

He let his face and mouth revel in the midst of her breasts for several minutes before he twinged from an inner jolt and thought, *What am I doing!*

You're priming this old sleaze for a GREAT roll in the hay—that's what you're doing, you moron, his bad side answered.

But Collier knew he couldn't continue, even with his own arousal more than apparent. *Dominique,* he thought.

To hell with that highbrow frigid ho, damn it! Now be a MAN and GIVE IT to this old bitch!

Mrs. Butler sighed, then straddled Collier's lap and pushed him back. "Suck 'em harder now, hon. I know ya been dyin' to, since that night you was watchin' me through the peephole'n jerkin' yerself." She slid upward and pressed her breasts more deliberately in his face.

Instead of resisting . . . Collier did as she'd instructed.

"Yeah, you like that, don't'cha?"

Regardless of her age, these were the best breasts he'd ever seen. He entered a dream world now, where nipples equated to deliverance.

Then he snapped again: *This is crazy!*

She began to pull him down onto the bed.

"Mrs. Butler, this is crazy!" he yelled. "We can't do this!"

"We'se *already* doin' it, hon . . ."

"There's some serious shit going on here. This house—"

"Shhh . . ." She was already on her back, her hands pulling at him.

No! "Mrs. Butler! You said you heard a voice before. What did you hear?"

Her legs were parting. "Voice? Aw, don't mind that . . ."

Collier was about to bolt until her hands touched him more urgently . . .

"Come on, come on . . ."

Collier shivered, then let himself be pulled down atop her. At one point he looked up and saw Lottie standing naked in the doorway. She was watching, eyes fixed. She was touching herself . . .

Yeah, man! his id celebrated. *Looks like it's gonna be a two-fer night!*

The idea frenzied Collier. He tried to get up, but . . .

The house wasn't letting him.

Collier's face fell back down into the old woman's bosom. Then the bed creaked, as Lottie climbed on.

"Little whores, the both of you," a man's voice blacker than coal croaked. "Look at you. You've let men fill your bellies with their seed—men who *work* for me, men who *take my money* and then *betray me* behind my back. But what should I have expected, with a harlot mother as abominable as yours? We must not suffer harlots to live . . ."

Collier clenched his teeth.

Don't listen! Just get down to business!

A young girl: "Please, Father, no!"

"Oh, no, I won't kill you. I'll let the earth do it . . ."

The voices seemed to come from everywhere in the room.

Then he heard the sound of shovels biting into dirt.

Don't listen!

Then muffled children's screams . . .

He looked up again, and this time, saw Jiff standing in the doorway: naked, aroused. Then, he, too, climbed onto the bed . . .

Just as Mrs. Butler, Lottie, and Jiff's hands all began to

caress him, Collier grabbed his robe and lurched for the door.

"Where you goin'!" Mrs. Butler yelled.

"Aw, come on, Mr. Collier," Jiff complained. "We can have us a four-way the *right* way . . ."

Collier ran out as if fleeing a blaze. Without a candle now, he stumbled in the nearly lightless hall. He blindly got his robe back on and felt his way to the atrium. *What's happening to me?*

Then the answer came to him.

Not me. It's the house.

He stopped when he found himself in the middle of the atrium. The storm seemed to be dying off now, the lightning less intense. But in each diminishing flash, he caught himself looking up at the portrait of Gast.

The house . . .

Was it merely suggestion, or had Harwood Gast changed his posture and expression? The plantation baron seemed to be grimacing now, and instead of looking out at the tree, he was looking to his left . . .

Collier looked left.

And saw the old writing table . . . and the smaller portrait of Penelope.

Slow steps took him over, his eyes widening. The next throb of lightning was all he needed to discern the small painting's only necessary detail.

The oil painting only showed a landscape of trees in the background—the image of Penelope Gast wasn't to be seen, as though her likeness had never been painted in it.

Was the rich Southern accent in Collier's head?

"It's not the house," it whispered from everywhere.

Collier stumbled for the stairs.

"It's me . . ."

Both of his hands let the banister guide him up. His eyes had barely adjusted—after feeling his way through more grainy darkness, he found his room.

He closed the door and leaned against it. *I've really had enough of this place,* he thought, almost hyperventilating, but in only a moment, he sensed something wrong.

The candles . . .

There'd been two lit candles when he'd left the room earlier. Now there was one.

He grabbed it, dipped it toward the bed.

Dominique wasn't there.

Collier cursed himself. *Damn it! The storm probably woke her up; then she saw that I wasn't here so she got scared and left!*

But—

Her work slacks and blouse were draped over the chair. Then he noticed with more alarm that her silver cross was hanging off the bedpost.

And so were her bra and panties.

Collier made the cold, unbelievable deduction. *She's not here but all her clothes are. Which means she's somewhere in the house . . . naked.*

The storm had faded. Collier tried to think—

Then he heard something like a long splash, like a bucket of water being emptied.

Collier had heard that sound before.

It came from the room to the left. *The bath closet . . .*

By now, Collier knew the drill.

When he blew out his candle, he wasn't surprised to notice a dot of light on the wall: the peephole. He got to his knees and looked in.

Candlelight flickered, not much, but enough. Dominique's beautiful pubis appeared, the triangle of dark thatch ever apparent. She lowered herself into the hip bath.

Collier watched, his eye frozen open on the hole.

It wasn't a bar of soap that she held in her hand, it was Collier's can of Edge Gel. Her finger squirted a few curls into the plot of hair; then she began to massage it into a thick white froth.

She's going to shave her crotch, came the slow acknowledgment. That was fine with Collier but . . .

Why shave your crotch in a goddamn Civil War hip bath, during a power failure!

Another sound he'd heard came to his ear next.

scritch-scritch-scritch

But it wasn't Collier's disposable razor she was using. It was an old-fashioned straight razor.

When the task was complete, she got out and patted herself dry with a towel.

Even in the candlelight, the clean, hairless crotch seemed to radiate its fresh *whiteness,* but . . .

What's she doing . . . now?

Now something else occupied her fingers, a small flat box that she quickly snapped open.

It was eyeliner.

Collier could bear no more. *What's she doing NOW?*

Then—

thunk!

The power snapped back on; the room blared in light.

Reason returned. Collier bolted out of the bedroom and turned right into the bath closet.

"Dominique, what the hell are you—"

She stood facing him but with her head pitched down; she hadn't noticed him enter.

But Collier was too taken aback by the shock of seeing her naked. All he could do was stare, his mouth drawn open.

The bright lights brought out every detail of her curves and feminine features, the sleek legs, wide hips joined by a flat white stomach. Plump white breasts jutted outward firmly as implants.

And what was she *doing?*

Two fingers wielded the tiny eyeliner brush, dabbed it

into the circle of dark makeup, then very daintily left one single tiny dot on her pubis, about an inch above the clitoris.

She dropped the plastic box and looked right at him.

Collier—thick in the throat—got the effect. Shaved pubis? With one tiny freckle above the opening?

The daguerreotype glared in his mind.

She made herself look like her . . .

"Who are you?" she asked as if put off.

Dominique didn't have a Southern accent, yet the voice that came out of her mouth did.

"I asked you a question, sir. Who the blazes *are* you, standin' in my house uninvited?"

"Come on!" he gruffed and shoved her out of the small room.

"This is no way to treat the lady of this house, and you can be assured—"

"Shut up and get in there!"

Collier hauled her back into his room. "We're getting out of here—" He grabbed her clothes and heaved them into her arms. "Put those on!"

"These are not my clothes, sir! And if you're one'a my husband's workers, you can wager that he'll hear about this unmitigated intrusion!" She dropped the clothes. "In fact, I am going to tell him right now! And where is Jessa, damn her? Did *she* let you in the house?"

She brushed past him, stark in her nudity, but when her hand landed on the doorknob . . .

"Oh, dear, well now . . . maybe I am being hasty." She turned back around. When she leaned against the door and straightened her posture, her bare breasts stood even more erect.

Holy moly . . .

Her eyes drilled right into him. "And, if I may be so forward, you are a *handsome* man. I'm sorry we haven't previously met. Are you one of my husband's foremen?"

Collier could have wept when he forced himself to

look away from her magnificent body. "Dominique, we have to *leave*."

She raised a delicate finger. "You must work for Mr. Cutton, am I right?" She pronounced "right" as "rat." "Or perhaps you work over him. He is a marvelous man, I must say . . ." She slowly traipsed over, her innocent expression shifting into something sly. "So tell me, sir. How marvelous are *you?* And by what manner?"

Collier cringed when her warm hand slipped into his robe and slid up his chest. Her touch electrified him, and next she was kissing him . . .

The voice of his id returned, *Looks like you gonna get a slice of the celibate weirdo after all . . .*

Her mouth sucked his tongue.

It's not her, it's not her, he insisted to himself.

You better haul this one's ashes right now . . .

But Collier knew he couldn't.

Just then her hands slid down to his groin.

"Mmmm, yes," she murmured. "You're clearly a man who senses the needs of a lady." Then she opened the robe and pressed against him. Her nipples felt like hot coins.

"But this is my daughters' room—and God knows where they are at this hour. Out being little girls, I suppose, with that annoying dog of theirs. But we had to get them the dog. They don't have any friends to speak of, and don't mix well with the other children in town, due to our elevated social standing."

Collier shivered with his eyes closed as her hand kept playing with him.

"Oh, but I've digressed," she whispered into his neck. "Let's retreat to the next room, shall we? It's my . . . *secret* room, reserved for my pleasures alone." She tried to pull him toward the door.

"No," Collier said through gritted teeth.

She paused through a sigh. "You might be a bit nervous, which I understand—many of my men are at first.

But you needn't be worrying about my husband. He's halfway to Maxon right now, and only comes back every month or so."

Now she pressed harder against him.

He could sense the outrage of his darker self.

Listen to me, buddy boy. If you don't ball the daylights out of this hunk of angel food cake, you'll be a disgrace to all of masculinity—

"Put your clothes on," he told her, pushing her back. "We have to leave . . ."

"All right." She ignored him. "If you don't want to go into the next room, we'll do it here," she said, then started to take off his robe.

Collier whipped her hands away. "We're leaving!" he tried yelling at her. "Now!"

What a loser, his id conceded. *I give up . . .*

Collier grabbed her shoulders and *shook.*

"Your name is Dominique Cusher! You're a brewmaster and a celibate Christian! Your name is NOT Penelope Gast!"

Had Dominique's eyes . . . yellowed? Hatred and disgust tightened her face and next—

flump!

—Collier was thrown to the bed. Her bare thighs fastened his hips to the mattress as securely as a metal girder, and her hand—

Collier began to choke.

Her hand squeezed his throat so hard he thought his vertebrae would separate.

"You will indulge my fancy, sir, or I will kill you—"

Her strength was beyond fathoming. When he grabbed her forearm, it remained firm as a steel post. The hand was digging into his trachea.

"Jesus Christ, you're killing me!" he gagged.

"Um-hmm." She lowered her crotch. "Unless you fuck me right now . . ."

For a split second, she released his throat and Collier

dragged in a breath just before he would've passed out. He tried to lurch up—

In an inhuman blur, she grabbed one of the pillows and was now vising it against his face with both hands.

Sightless, Collier felt his lungs start to expand.

Her accent sounded so sweet around the ultimately profane words: "You will *fuck* me, sir, and then you will void your bladder—"

Collier was convulsing.

"—or I'll smother you right now."

Collier wasn't sure if he'd passed out or not. Some reflex hooked his fist in an arc; then he felt his knuckles crack into the side of her head.

Dominique fell off the bed.

He jerked to a sitting position, wailing as he sucked in air. Black spots before his eyes began to dissipate. He saw Dominique sprawled on the floor, but—

Something unidentified seemed to cover him. The pillow she'd been smothering him with had torn open . . .

Feathers?

He brushed the unpleasant substance off his face.

What IS this stuff? He almost threw up when he realized it was human hair.

Mostly brown but with swathes of blonde and some streaks of red . . .

Next, he threw *himself* off the bed, revolted, but he moved like a madman. Dominique was out cold. He hauled on his clothes, then flopped Dominique around on the floor and redressed her. He skipped the hassle of putting her underwear on but when he paused and noticed her cross twinkling on the bedpost, he put it back around her neck.

Collier's adrenaline more than made up for his negligible physical strength. He flung Dominique over his shoulder and plodded out of the room.

Oh, Christ . . .

The stench of urine in the hall choked him like tear

gas. He took a few steps, blinking hard, and then suddenly Dominique's unconscious body felt heavy as a sack of bricks. Collier stopped a moment, to reestablish his balance . . .

Did he hear these words?

"Come inside . . ."

He looked to find himself standing immediately before the door to the next room.

Room two.

The room that was always locked.

"Come inside my secret room," came the plush accent.

Collier's eyes were riveted to the doorknob. Very slowly, it began to turn.

Something *clicked* . . .

The voice started to warble.

"Come inside, sir, and oblige a lady . . ."

The door swung open, revealing a black void. The stench quadrupled and slammed Collier in the face so hard he could've staggered backward and flipped over the rail with Dominique still on his shoulder.

He trudged away just as he thought he detected a shapely nude figure stepping out of the room.

Senseless, Collier tore off like someone wading through mud. He almost fell down the stairs but probably wouldn't have minded because it would've gotten him to the bottom all the more expediently. The stench followed him as though it meant to run him down.

Only a few yards to go! his mind yelled when the vestibule doors surfaced in the murk.

"But, sir," a squawky male voice rose. "Why did you not sign your check? You must know that cash money cannot be rendered without your signature . . ."

The scrawny man sitting at the writing table looked perturbed, wearing an odd red hat.

A gold nose flashed.

Collier actually used his head to bang open the vestibule doors. Then he banged through the next set and was scrambling out into the night.

Before the doors could close behind him, her wanton voice beckoned him one more time:

"It was a pleasure to make your acquaintance, Mr. Collier. I trust you'll be back to see me again very soon . . ."

Collier flopped Dominique into the car, then drove away from the house. In the rearview, he thought he glimpsed four figures standing between the pillars of the front porch, two of them short, and two taller.

The sound of a dog yapping faded as he sped away.

He parked in front of the restaurant. The town lay dark and silent before them.

But it seemed normal.

Dominique murmured something in her unconsciousness, then curled in the seat, asleep.

A final silent throb of lightning marked the end of the storm. Collier's adrenaline rush finally drained. He fell into a black and gratefully dreamless sleep.

CHAPTER FOURTEEN

I

Collier awoke to a wall of sun in his eyes, and an agitated rapping sound.

Ugh. What the—

A frowning man in a police uniform was knuckling the window. Collier rolled it down, shielding his eyes.

"Oh, it's you, Mr. Collier," the cop said. "I heard you were in town. I'm Sheriff Legerski. Here's your ticket."

Collier tried to shake off his grog. "Ticket for what?"

"Not even big-time TV stars can illegally park." The sheriff indicated the sign right next to Collier's lime-sherbet fender. NO PARKING 9-5.

Collier looked at the ticket. "A hundred bucks?"

"Usually it's twenty-five, but you get the celebrity rate." The sheriff guffawed. "Just kidding. But thems the breaks, you know, Mr. Collier?"

Jesus. Collier signed with a proffered pen.

"Just send your hundred in anytime you like. Check, money order . . . or, you can just put twenty-five in my hand right now, you know, if it's more convenient."

Collier gave him the cash, head aching from the sun.

"Thanks. Say, is that Ms. Cusher in there?"

"Uh, yeah."

The sheriff winked. "I won't ask." He tore up the ticket. "But I really love your show! Hope ya have a great day. Oh, and move the car, huh? And you might want to get it painted a better color, too. Something more . . . manly?"

Collier moved the car several yards to another sign that read FREE PARKING ALL DAY. Beside him, Dominique roused.

She blinked around. "What the hell?"

"Good morning."

Her hands felt around the car as if in disbelief. "What am I doing in this weird-looking car? And—what time is it?"

"Quarter after ten."

"Damn it!" She brushed a tangle of hair out of her face. "I was supposed to open at ten! How could you let me sleep so late?" A fretful look at the restaurant's front doors showed several employees grinning at them. "Damn it!"

She smirked down at her shoes. "Where are my socks?" A hand came to her bosom. "Where's my bra?" Then her eyes bugged when she briefly slipped her hand below her belt line.

She gave him a long, hard look. "Justin. Where's my pubic hair?"

Collier leaned back and sighed. "You shaved it off last night. In the bath closet. By candlelight. With a very old straight razor."

He could see her mind churning behind her eyes.

"I . . . think I . . . remember," she said. When she touched the side of her head, she glared. "I also remember you punching me in the head!"

"It wasn't like you were giving me much choice, Dominique."

"I was . . ."

"Smothering me with a pillow?"

Her open stare told him she remembered. "And we didn't . . ."

"No, we didn't have sex. Your celibacy is secure."

She was rubbing her face. "But . . . I wanted to, didn't I?"

"You didn't want to," Collier said. "Someone *else* wanted you to."

"What do mean?" Then another eye-bugging stare. "Oh my God, did I grab your—"

"Dominique, just forget about it. It's all over."

"But what *happened?*"

Collier needed a beer. "I believe you were possessed by the spirit of Penelope Gast," he finally said.

She sat back in her seat, boggled.

"Just forget it. Pretend it never happened. Just go inside now, go to work, and forget about the whole thing."

She nodded slowly, was about to get out of the car, then paused, her hand to her bosom again. "Give me my underwear."

"I can't."

"What do you mean? Where is it?"

"Your underwear's hanging on the bedpost in my room, where you left it."

"Well then drive back to the inn. Justin, I can't go change at my apartment 'cos the fumigators are still there."

Collier dully shook his head. "I'm never going in that

house again, Dominique. I'll be happy to drive you up there if *you* want to go back in that room and get your stuff, but . . . not me. Ain't happening." He eyed her. "Want me to drive you up?"

"No, on second thought—"

"It won't kill you to work one day with no undies," Collier guaranteed her. The image of her breasts swam in his head. "Trust me, a braless Dominique behind the bar will keep the place packed all day."

She got out of the car and walked to his side in a daze. "Where are you going now?"

"I have to figure out a way to get my luggage and laptop out of that room. You go to work now, but I'll be back a little later."

She leaned down to the window. "You're something, you know that? Last night you really could've—"

"But I didn't." He grinned at her. More visions of her impeccable nudity swam before him. "Believe me, it wasn't easy."

"Are you looking down my blouse, Mr. Collier?"

"Yeah."

She kissed him and laughed. "See you later," she said, then rushed embarrassed to unlock the tavern's doors.

But Collier's lifted spirits began to sink when he drove back up to the inn. The blazing daylight didn't offer as much comfort as he wished. He already knew that he could not reenter the house, daylight or not.

He jumped out of the car when he spotted Jiff emptying the ashtrays on the porch.

"Hey, Jiff! I need to talk to you—"

The younger man sat down and slouched on a front bench. "Howdy, Mr. Collier."

"Jiff, are you all right?" Collier asked when he noticed the man's bloodshot eyes and sagging posture.

"Had too much to drink last night, Mr. Collier."

Good. Then maybe you don't remember watching me in bed with your mother and sister, Collier thought.

"You ever drunk so much you're still drunk the next day?"

"All the time."

"Well, that's how I feel now."

Maybe this'll perk him up. Collier took a fifty out of his wallet. "Jiff, I need a big favor. I need you to go up to my room and get my suitcase and laptop. I have to check out now."

Jiff slumped in the seat. "Shee-it, Mr. Collier, I sure hope you ain't leavin' on account'a what happened . . ." But then the sentence collapsed.

"On account of what happened last night?" Collier said. "In . . . your mother's room?"

Jiff thumbed his eyes.

"What *did* happen, Jiff? Was that really us . . . or was it the house?"

Jiff's eyes leveled. "It was the house doin' stuff to us, I guess is how ya'd put it. Shee-it. And that's why you don't wanna go back in, huh?"

"Yeah, Jiff."

"Oh, it's okay now. It don't happen much, just . . . every now'n then: the dreams and what'cha hear sometimes'n see, or *think* ya see. And what'cha do. But Ma says it's the house goin' through some sort of cycle. Been that way since the war."

Collier didn't care.

"Ma also says it's certain folks who start the cycle, but I ain't never really figured that one."

Certain folks, Collier thought.

Again, he didn't care. "I think I'll . . . stay outside anyway."

"Okay, Mr. Collier." Jiff dragged himself up and took the fifty. "I'll be right back down with yer stuff."

"Oh, and could you tell your mother to get my bill?" Collier asked. "She already ran my card."

"Sure thing."

Collier released a long breath.

When he looked at the fat oak tree out front, he smiled. The tree looked just like any other.

A man with longish blond hair—obviously dyed—was walking up the path, carrying a small suitcase. He waved to Collier.

"Damn glad I found you, Justin. Christ, what's going on?"

Collier couldn't believe his eyes. He knew that dyed hair and phony tan anywhere. "Sammy?"

The man stepped up in a tacky Hawaiian shirt, blue jeans with starched creases, and gator-skin boots. "Man, I hate those six-hour flights. And driving here? What a pain in the ass."

What the hell is HE doing here? Collier wondered.

"And congratulations on snagging that third slot from me . . . fucker." Savannah Sammy smiled with bleached teeth; they shook hands.

"Sammy, why are you here?"

"'Cos you're here, and for what reason I couldn't pretend to guess. Prentor told me you left some nutty message on his voice mail, said you're not coming back to the show. Then he tries to call you back fifty times but says you never answered."

Shit. The storm last night . . . And Collier's phone was upstairs. *Probably fifty screaming messages on it.*

Sammy's eyes thinned. "Tell me it's bullshit, Justin. Your ratings jumped. You don't turn down a contract renewal when your show skyrockets to the third slot."

"It's no bullshit," Collier said. "I'm not going to sign the contract."

Sammy smiled. "Sure, I get it. You're holding out for more—cool. That's why I'm here, my man. Prentor sent me here to convince you to come back. I know how it works—you don't take the first offer. But I'm prepared to up that by—"

Collier shook his head, amused. "I'm not holding out, Sammy. I don't want to do the show anymore."

Sammy's tan face creased. "Another channel made an offer? We're prepared to *counter*offer."

"You're not hearing me. I'm not coming back. I'm burned out. I'm sick of being on TV . . ."

Savannah Sammy looked on the verge of grabbing Collier's throat. "Justin! You just got voted sexiest man on the Food Network! You don't walk away from that!"

"I'm walking." Collier winked. "But look at the bright side. With me gone, you're back in the third seat, right behind Emeril and what's her name."

Sammy's hair spray began to break. "You just hit the big time, brother! No one says no to that!"

"I do. I'm just going to write beer books and relax. I'm not even coming back to L.A."

"Where are you gonna go?"

"Here," Collier said. "I'm staying right here, in Gast."

One of Sammy's eyes began to twitch. "This is a Civil War tourist town in bumfuck Tennessee!"

"That's right." Collier patted him on the shoulder. "Sorry you came all this way for nothing, man. But my mind's made up . . ."

"Jesus. Prentor's not gonna believe it . . ." But then Sammy's eyes flicked to the door's glass panel. "Hey, check out this old woman with the fantastic bod. Holy *shit.*"

Mrs. Butler was coming through the doors, her breasts and wide hips highlighted in a clingy dress.

"And look at the little fireplug behind her!" Sammy added.

It was Lottie who followed her mother, in a halter and cutoff shorts barely bigger than a bikini.

"Mr. Collier, I'm so sorry you won't be stayin' any longer," Mrs. Butler lamented. "Jiff said you needed to check out right now."

"Yeah, I do. But I'm not exactly leaving town." Collier signed his credit card receipt and returned it.

Lottie grinned at him. She mouthed, *Let's screw . . .*

Some things never change, Collier thought.

But Mrs. Butler was already staring. "My goodness *gracious!*" She grabbed Collier's arm. "Am I lookin' at who I *think* I'm lookin' at?"

This'll be great! "Mrs. Butler, let me introduce you to Food Network star Savannah Sammy—"

"—of *Savannah Sammy's Sassy Smokehouse!*" the old woman shrilled with delight. Lottie's eyes snapped to Sammy's crotch.

"Pleased to meet you, ma'am." Sammy extended his hand.

The woman almost fainted. "Oh, I just LOVE your show! And, please, please, call me Helen! Are we blessed enough that you'll be staying with us?"

Sammy hesitated, his eyes pasted to Mrs. Butler's bosom. "Well . . ."

"Stay a few days, Sammy," Collier goaded. He put a hand on each of their shoulders, and urged them to enter. "It's the best bed-and-breakfast you've ever seen in your life."

Sammy's eyes couldn't settle on whose body to examine harder: Mrs. Butler or Lottie. "Yeah, I guess I could stay a few days . . ."

Collier squeezed the old woman's shoulder. "Mrs. Butler, why don't you check Sammy into my old room?"

"Oh, I'd be happy to! Come on inside, Mr. Sammy!"

Lottie grabbed Sammy's bag and followed them in.

"Later, Sammy," Collier bid.

"Yeah, yeah—we'll talk—"

No we won't, Collier thought. He chuckled under his breath. *This house is gonna LOVE him . . .*

Jiff came back out with Collier's suitcase and laptop. "Well, here's your stuff, Mr. Collier. It's been great knowin' ya."

"I'll be seeing you around, Jiff. I'm moving here."

Jiff gaped through his hangover. "You kiddin'?"

"Nope. I need a change of scenery. Bad."

Jiff paused through some confusion. "Well that's just dandy . . ."

Collier took the suitcase. "I got some things to tend to right now, but I'll be seeing you around."

"Okay, Mr. Collier." But then Jiff stopped him. "Wait a sec. Before ya leave . . ." He pulled something out of his pocket. "Didn't know if you wanted these in yer suitcase, ya know?"

He handed Collier Dominique's bra and panties. "Thanks, Jiff. I'll get them back to their rightful owner soon. Take care!"

Collier stowed his gear in the car and drove off.

Jiff just shook his head. "What the hell does he wanna move *here* for?" he muttered.

II

Jiff decided to blow off the rest of the day; the hangover had thoroughly ragged him out, and with his mother and sister fussing over that Sammy guy who'd just checked in . . .

They'll never know I'm gone.

Instead, Jiff moseyed over to the Spike, but not to turn any tricks. *Shit, I'm even too hungover for that* . . . For a hangover of this magnitude, there was only one real cure.

The long, dark bar had no customers this early, just Buster—in his vest and Frankenstein's-monster haircut—hanging up some glasses.

"Jiff. Can't believe you're in here after all those beers you pounded last night."

"Buster, I need me some hair'a the dog."

"Don't know where you put it." Buster slid him a beer. "How's business?"

"Sucks."

They both laughed at the same time.

"Heard you're cutting off old J.G. That true?"

Jiff sat slumped. "Yeah, that old whack job was gettin' too kinky even for me."

"I'll bet the poor old guy is heartbroke. He'll probably jump out his window."

"Hope not." Jiff paused. "He'd crack the street wide-open."

Both men honked laughter.

"Or maybe you're just gettin' too old yourself," Buster kept it up, "and don't want to admit it."

Jiff glared abruptly. "Hey. Jiff Butler will *never* be too old to hustle. Fellas'll be paying for my hard peckerwood till I'm ninety."

"Yeah? What are you now? Thirty-eight?"

"Thirty-*two*, bitch."

Buster wheezed. "If you're thirty-two, George Clooney's a Republican."

On the TV, Jiff spied the opening of *Savannah Sammy's Sassy Smokehouse*. "You ain't gonna believe this, Buster, but that guy just checked in, right after Justin Collier checked out. Kind'a weird, you ask me."

"Two Food Network guys in the same day, huh? That *is* weird. But the weirder part is him being in here the other day." Buster leaned over, grinning. "You turn a trick with him?"

"Naw—"

"Sexiest man on the channel they've been saying all day."

Jiff shrugged, then remembered with some shame what he'd almost done last night during the storm. *Jesus . . .*

He could only hope the house would settle down for a while now. "He's straight, believe me. Got the hots for Dominique Cusher."

"The Christian chick?"

Jiff nodded. "Straight folks are ALL fucked up, ain't they?"

"Tell me about it."

When Jiff signaled for another beer, Buster frowned. "You got money, Jiff? You're not going to stiff me like the other day."

Jiff pretended to look offended, and pulled out the fifty-dollar bill that Justin Collier had given him. "Just pull me another cold one . . . faggot."

"You got it . . . fairy."

Both men laughed.

Jiff felt better into the second beer.

"Wouldn't mind going a round with *that* one," Buster said, gesturing the screen.

Savannah Sammy was basting some ribs.

"He's older than he looks, probably had a facelift," Jiff speculated. "And his teeth are white as wall paint. Probably got hisself one'a them fancy California bleach jobs. Don't like all that fake stuff . . . unless the money's right."

Both men laughed.

Jiff looked down at the fifty he'd put on the bar. Something seemed to be under it.

Oh, them check things, he remembered. He'd pulled them out of his pocket along with the fifty.

"What's that?" Buster inquired.

Jiff showed him one. "Old paychecks from the original Gast Railroad."

"From the Civil War?"

Jiff nodded.

"Yeah, damn, look at this." Buster examined one. "This one's from 1862."

"I found 'em in Mr. Collier's room."

"Why would they be there?"

"He probably found 'em in an old bookcase or desk. These things are all over my ma's inn." He took the check back and looked at it, bored.

But the beer was going down but good. Jiff had a feeling he'd be hanging around for a while.

He was about to put the old checks back in his pocket

when he happened to notice that one of them, though signed at the bottom, hadn't been dated or filled out at all.

III

When Collier walked into Cusher's at just before noon, there was only one seat available at the bar. Employees whisked back and forth as the lunch rush commenced.

Dominique came over, still looking a bit abraded from last night.

"Not even noon yet and the bar's totally full," Collier commented.

She leaned over the bar on her elbows. "I know. It's never this full so early."

"Well, I told you so."

"Told me what?"

Collier cocked a brow. "Braless Dominique equals full bar."

"Get out of here." She lowered her voice. "Did you get my underwear?"

Collier calculated the question. *If I'm going to get involved with a girl who's celibate then I at least deserve a perk or two.* "Damn, sorry," he lied. "I forgot." He discreetly eyed the shadows of her nipples beneath the blouse. "My fault. Look, I'll buy you some new underwear."

"Thanks." She frowned and suddenly seemed perturbed. "Do you want a beer?"

"No. From now on I'll be adopting your deal. One beer a day."

"Oh, so I guess you'll be having it in L.A.?"

The comment, and her tone, befuddled him. "What?"

She sighed. "Look, Justin, I'm really lousy with good-byes . . ."

"I'm . . . not following you."

"Earlier you told me you had to go back to the inn to

get your luggage." She pointed to the front window. "And right now I can see that funny green car of yours parked right there, with your suitcase in the backseat. That means you're leaving."

"Well . . ." Collier began.

"I didn't know you were leaving this soon—I thought you were staying at least a few more days. But—damn it—it's my own fault."

"Your *fault?*"

"I always knew you'd be going back to L.A., so I had no business letting myself get attached to you. It was stupid. You just walked in here to say good-bye. I understand that. But I hate good-byes, so let's just leave it at that, and you be on your way. Good-bye."

Collier grabbed her hand. "I'm in love with you."

"Justin, don't say stuff like that—Great. You're in love with me. And now you're going back to L.A. and I'll never see you again."

"I—"

She tried to pull away. "Just go, all right? Just—"

"Would you let me talk, damn it!" he yelled.

Everyone at the bar turned their heads. The St. Pauli barmaid and the other waitresses stopped in their tracks.

Collier talked lower. "I'm not going back to L.A."

"What?"

"I'm staying here."

"For a few more days, you mean."

"No, no. Permanently. I quit the show—"

Dominique blanched. "You did *what?*"

"I turned down my contract renewal yesterday. I'm tired of being on TV. I'm fried. I'm sick of rush hour, I'm sick of shooting schedules, and I'm sick of California. My lawyer's going to send me the divorce papers. I'm going to give half of everything to my asshole wife and be done with it." He squeezed her hand. "I want to stay here, in Gast."

She was staring at him.

"I want to stay here and have a relationship with you," he said.

Now the employees were listening attentively.

"Justin, I don't know . . . You know what I'm like, you know—"

"I don't care about all that. I can live with it. What's the big deal? We'll give it a shot. I'll get an apartment in the area—or, hell, I'll move in with you. If you get sick of me, just tell me. I'll boogie. If it doesn't work out, we split. We'll just be friends. Nothing ventured, nothing gained, you know?" He gave her the eye. "So what do you say? Sound good to you?"

Dominique leaned all the way across the bar and kissed him. It was a serious, tongue-tussling kiss, and it went on long enough that he could hear some employees giggling and someone at the bar remark, "Get a room." In the most absurd fantasy, Collier imagined himself making love to her . . .

But that's never going to happen, he reminded himself when he looked down her top again and saw the cross floating between her breasts. *Unless* . . .

"And, who knows?" he said. "Maybe it *will* work out."

"Yeah," she gushed back. Perhaps it was a joke and perhaps it wasn't, when she added, "Maybe it will work out and someday we'll get married."

Collier got dizzy when she kissed him again.

Yeah, maybe someday, he thought. *Or maybe REAL SOON* . . .

EPILOGUE

"If you don't get'cher lazy, do-nothin' butt out'a bed right this minute, I'm gonna kick you out'a this house!" The ragged yell pierced Jiff's ears.

Sunlight dumped onto Jiff's face when the curtains were yanked open.

"Aw, jeez, Ma!"

"Don't jeez Ma ME! Get up! It's past noon!"

Jiff squinted into the face of his very displeased mother. *Past noon?* he thought. Then: *Aw . . . damn!*

"Your poor sister'n me have been workin' our heinies off and here you are still in bed sleepin' off another drunk!" The voice boomed. "I didn't raise no drunken lout!"

Jiff lay amid tousled sheets wearing only briefs. His head *pounded* as his memory ground backward.

I got drunk again last night, didn't I? Shit, I drank ALL DAY LONG at the Spike and then wound up closin' the joint . . .

"This place stinks like a pool hall!" his mother bellowed. "You got any excuse at all fer yourself?"

He leaned up with difficulty. "Dang, Ma, I'se sorry. But you're right, I have been drinkin' too much lately. But I only git that way . . . you know. When the house has one'a its fits."

Her finger wagged at his face. "I don't wanna hear nothin' 'bout the house or any of that ghost stuff. You best keep your yap *closed* about it. Damn it, boy, we got the pleasure'a havin' Savannah Sammy at our inn, and you WILL NOT be talkin' any of that ghost stuff to him! Ya hear!"

"Sure, Ma," Jiff groaned.

"Savannah Sammy is an important guest, even more important than Mr. Collier—"

"Come on, Ma. You're just all in a swivet 'cos you got the hots for him, just like ya had fer Mr. Collier—"

"Watch your mouth, boy!" his mother cracked even louder, "or you'll be out'a here just as sure as pigs can shit!"

Jesus . . .

"Now you GET that grass mowed and you GET those hedges trimmed and you GET those weeds pulled! And did you even pick up the ham hocks yet?"

Jiff rubbed his temples, agonized. "Ham hocks?"

"Jesus, boy, everything I SAY to you goes in one ear'n out the other! I done told ya *yesterday* to go to the butcher's and pick up twenty hocks'n start gettin' 'em smoked 'cos I'll be makin' my ham hock and wild green gumbo fer the guests this weekend! But I guess yer just too drunk to remember!"

Jiff groaned.

Mrs. Butler waved a stack of something in his face, then *thwacked* it all into his lap.

"What the hell's all that, Ma?"

"It's yer *mail,* if ya can believe it!"

Letters were scattered all over the bed. *I never get mail,* he thought.

"I don't know *what* you got in that pea brain'a yours, boy, but you better get it out and I mean in a jiffy!" Her finger wagged before his face one more time. "You ain't responsible enough to have a credit card, so what'choo doin' applyin' for 'em?"

Credit cards? Jiff scratched his head, looking at some of the mail dropped in his lap. Multiple letters from Visa,

MasterCard, American Express. "Ma, I ain't applied fer no credit cards."

"Well that's good 'cos if your lazy, drunken, do-nothin' ass ain't out of that bed in two seconds, you ain't gonna have a fuckin' JOB to PAY fer a credit card!"

Jiff knew she was serious. His mother *never* said "fuckin'."

"Two seconds, boy!" she yelled one last time and then slammed the door so loud, the walls shook and his George Clooney poster rattled.

Damn. That ain't no way to start the day. He creaked out of bed. *And what's all this credit card stuff?* Just junk mail, but why this?

A cold shower barely revived him. But he knew that he would indeed have to watch the drinking. He was about to get to work but noticed his message machine flashing. He hit the button, then regretted it because he could guess who it was.

"Jiff, my God," the voice croaked. "I'm a wasteland without you. Please, please, don't do this to me. You must come and see me—I'll pay whatever you want. I-I-I . . . love you—"

Jiff deleted the message and saw that all of the others were from him, too.

Poor fat old bastard. But . . . shit on him . . .

The phone blared, spiking Jiff's hungover brain. *Damn!* He knew it had to be Sute. *Might as well get this over with—*

He snapped up the phone. "Listen, J.G., I done told ya we'se finished. I'se sorry you're so bent out'a shape but you're gonna have to stop callin' here—"

A pause. "I'd like to speak to Mr. Jiff Butler."

Jiff frowned; it wasn't Sute. "That's me. Say, look I'se got a lot of work to do and if you're one'a these telemarketer people, I ain't inter—"

"No, sir, this is the bank. Sorry to disturb you, but about that check you deposited last night—"

Jiff strained his brain. *That last one Sute gave me.* "Damn, don't tell me that hunnert-dollar check from J.G. Sute bounced. His checks never bounce."

Another pause. "No, sir. We're just calling to confirm your most recent deposit, which you made last night from our twenty-four-hour ATM. Typically, we don't do this by phone but given the amount of the check, we just wanted to confirm."

Jiff scratched his head. "Oh, you mean that hunnert bucks . . ."

"No, sir. I'm referring to the check you deposited last night, at 1:55 A.M."

More wheels began to turn in Jiff's booze-stepped-on brain. *What's this guy talkin' about?* he thought but then—slam!—it clicked.

Holy shit! What the hell did I do?

He remembered being drunk out of his gourd at the bar, and he was fiddling with those old railroad checks he'd found in Mr. Collier's room. He'd shown them around to everyone. He also remembered that one of the checks had been signed but not filled out . . .

"Hey, Jiff," Buster had joked, "why don't you fill that check out to yourself for a million dollars?" and everybody had laughed, but the thing was . . .

Jiff had been so drunk that he'd actually done it.

"Oh, look, sir," Jiff bumbled. "About that check. See, I was drunk last night and, see, I'se only did it as a joke. I never meant—"

"Mr. Butler, I'm not sure what you mean; perhaps you've misunderstood me. The only reason I'm calling is to confirm the deposit and let you know that the check cleared."

Now it was Jiff's turn to pause. "You mean—"

"Your current balance is now $1,000,141.32."

Jiff stared into space.

"But if I may, sir, let me switch you over to our investments manager—"

There was a click, and then another man's voice came on the line.

"Hello, Mr. Butler, I'm Mr. Corfe, and since you're a valuable customer I want to make you aware of some investment possibilities that are at your disposal."

Jiff felt as though he were standing atop a mountain . . .

"Your current balance is an awful lot of money to keep in a checking account, after all."

"What, uh, what's your name again?" Jiff droned.

"Corfe. William Corfe. I'm the investments manager here at Fecory Savings and Trust, and I'd just like to offer my services in the event that you're interested. We want your money to work for you, Mr. Butler, and we can transfer as much as you want into a money-market savings account, a high-interest certificate of deposit, treasury bills, short-term CDs, whatever you want. You'd make a lot of money in interest, Mr. Butler, and it's all F.D.I.C. insured."

Jiff nearly hacked out the words. "Do I really got a million bucks in the bank?"

"One million, one hundred and forty-one dollars and thirty-two cents to be exact, Mr. Butler . . ."

And then the silence between the line began to get scratchy . . . and so did the voice . . .

"And, Jiff, about that old iron forge in your backyard? You use that for a barbecue sometimes, don't you?"

Jiff's mouth stretched open. "Well, yeah, but what's that got to do—"

"And I happen to know that your mother wants you to get it fired up so you can start smoking some ham hocks in it, isn't that right?"

"How . . . can you know . . . *that?*"

More scratching over the line. "Start thinking about some *other things* to put in that barbecue once you're done with the ham hocks, all right?"

The phone was hot against Jiff's ear.

"You won't understand it all right now, Jiff, but believe me, in time, you will." Then the crackling faded, and clarity came back to the line.

"—for example, a 4.4 percent interest rate on a ten-month CD for starters. So please feel free to come down to the bank at your convenience, Mr. Butler, and I'd be happy to discuss a solid, protected investment package with you."

"Uh, uh, yeah. Sure."

Jiff hung up.

He stared out the window for a long time, and the thing he stared at the most was the old forge.

The man on the phone was right: Jiff didn't understand it all yet, but he did have a strange feeling he'd be calling J.G. Sute back in the very near future and maybe even inviting him out to the inn.

✂

☐ **YES!**

Sign me up for the Leisure Horror Book Club and send
my FREE BOOKS! If I choose to stay in the club, I will
pay only $8.50* each month, a savings of $7.48!

NAME: _____

ADDRESS: _____

TELEPHONE: _____

EMAIL: _____

☐ I want to pay by credit card.

☐ **VISA**   ☐ **MasterCard.**   ☐ **DISCOVER**

ACCOUNT #: _____

EXPIRATION DATE: _____

SIGNATURE: _____

Mail this page along with $2.00 shipping and handling to:
Leisure Horror Book Club
PO Box 6640
Wayne, PA 19087
Or fax (must include credit card information) to:
610-995-9274
You can also sign up online at **www.dorchesterpub.com**.
*Plus $2.00 for shipping. Offer open to residents of the U.S. and Canada only.
Canadian residents please call 1-800-481-9191 for pricing information.
If under 18, a parent or guardian must sign. Terms, prices and conditions subject to
change. Subscription subject to acceptance. Dorchester Publishing reserves the right
to reject any order or cancel any subscription.